THE
HUNGRY
DARK

Also available by Jen Williams

THE HUNGRY DARK

A THRILLER

JEN WILLIAMS

CROOKED
LANE

NEW YORK

Published in the United States by Crooked Lane Books, an imprint of The Quick Brown Fox & Company LLC.

Crooked Lane Books and its logo are trademarks of The Quick Brown Fox & Company LLC.

Library of Congress Catalog-in-Publication data available upon request.

ISBN (hardcover): 978-1-63910-617-2
ISBN (ebook): 978-1-63910-618-9

Cover design by Heather VenHuizen

Printed in the United States.

www.crookedlanebooks.com

Crooked Lane Books
34 West 27th St., 10th Floor
New York, NY 10001

First Edition: February 2024

10 9 8 7 6 5 4 3 2 1

For the Penge Thelemites

PROLOGUE

AT FIRST, ROBBIE stayed by the glow of the candles, caught in their light like a fish in a bowl.

The candles were tall and thick, coated in runnels of white wax that spilled over the sconces, which were screwed into bare stone walls. They were quite unlike the ones on Robbie's last birthday cake; there had been twelve of those, blue and glittery. The light these cast seemed old, much older than the neat little electric lights at home, or the night-light by the side of his bed in the shape of a Minecraft creeper. This light belonged down here. Down in the tunnel.

He sat with his knees drawn up to his chest and his arms wrapped tightly around his legs. Beyond the candlelight, there was the wall opposite—more large gray stones, like every illustration of a castle Robbie had ever seen—and to either side there was a thick and syrupy darkness that sometimes had noises in it. Robbie sat there for hours, the cold seeping through the thin white shift he wore, turning his legs and his bottom numb. When he had first woken up in this place, he had shouted and cried and even slapped his hands against the wall, until his throat had started to hurt, and still no one had come for him. The noises got louder, though.

Eventually, he stood up shakily, a swarm of pins and needles flowing up through his feet right up to his rump. He shivered and wiped his face on his forearm.

"Is anyone there? I don't know what I'm doing here."

There was no answer, but a sudden gust of air barreled down the tunnel toward him, pushing his lank hair back from his face and playing with the candle flames. They flickered and stretched, close to being blown out, and Robbie realized that he could be stuck here in this tunnel *in the dark*.

"Help! Please!" He tiptoed toward the very edge of the circle of light and stopped there, the toes of his bare feet not quite touching the darkness. "Is anyone there? I'm . . . I'm sorry."

He didn't know what he was sorry for, but this had to be a punishment. Like the punishments in the old days that his teachers always spoke of so fondly: canings, beatings, going to bed without any dinner. Someone would come for him eventually. They couldn't just leave him down here. It wasn't allowed. Other questions nipped at his heels, but he avoided them, knowing they were questions too dangerous to look at in the dark.

Why didn't he remember how he got here? Who had dressed him in this weird white dress? Where were Jill and Stewart, his foster parents?

Eventually, hunger got him to leave the candlelight behind. His stomach had gone from a grumble to a howl, and it made it difficult to think of anything else. Besides, perhaps the punishment was also a test. Perhaps they were expecting him to figure this out himself, and once he passed the test, they'd let him out, back up into the daylight. Whatever the answer was, he was sure it wasn't going to be found here, sitting underneath these strange old candles. Taking a deep breath, he stepped beyond the circle of light, heading toward the place from which the gust of wind had come.

With each step the candlelight dwindled, darkness seeping around his feet like a dangerous riptide. Soon it felt like he was walking into a darkness so deep it was a solid thing, so he thrust out one hand and touched his fingers to the wall, scuffing his fingertips over its rough-hewn surface. Every now and then, he would call out again, mainly because he couldn't bear the silence, or the distant noises that sometimes broke it apart.

"Hello? Is anyone there? I need help."

At that moment, his stomach growled so loudly that it made him jump, and then, as he was laughing shakily at his own foolishness, the ground under his feet vanished and he dropped sickeningly, arms flailing, only to hit the stone floor a moment later.

He lay where he fell for a few minutes, crying with pain and shock. Eventually, he realized that here the darkness was not so solid, and he could see a little better. Farther up the tunnel, there was another set of candles, and their thin buttery light just about reached him. The small set of steps that he'd fallen down from was a couple feet away, and on the edge of one step was a dark dash of blood where he'd bashed his knee. Slowly, Robbie uncurled himself and got back on his feet, wiping one grimy arm across his face again.

"Bloody . . . stupid steps." He hiccuped, then his stomach growled again. He limped up the tunnel, his knees throbbing, heading toward the next set of candles, when he saw that there was something sitting on the floor beneath the candles, something shockingly red and wet and glistening. He approached cautiously, but once he got into the warm circle of light, he realized he knew what it was; it was one of the weird fruits that Jill sometimes picked up from the Turkish Food Center. She seemed to like to find things that he hadn't seen before, which was, Robbie had to admit, not exactly difficult. In his old home, they had considered bananas exotic enough. This was a pomegranate, cut in half so that the crimson jewellike seeds were spilling out. His stomach roared at the sight of it. He'd picked it up and had his fingers wedged into the partitions before it occurred to him that it was weird to find a pomegranate here, that someone had to have placed it underneath the candles, and recently too.

He held up a rough handful of juicy seeds, his fingers already stained pink, and looked out into the dark again.

"Is anyone there? Hello?"

There was a distant sigh, the wind moving down the corridor again, and then . . . nothing.

A tiny voice in his head, some half-remembered ancient instinct, was telling him that the food was dangerous, that it was a trap. *Too good to be true*, it whispered, this voice from the bad old days. *Eat this and you'll never be allowed to leave.*

But the voice was crushed beneath Robbie's persistent hunger. He sat down under the candles and ate the first handful of seeds, his mouth filling with their sweet, tart juice. He crunched the tiny, gritty pips between his teeth. As he was popping more of the seeds out of the pomegranate, he noticed that he hadn't grazed his knees after all; in fact, he hadn't broken his skin anywhere, but his white shift was smeared with blood, big wet patches of it, as though he'd rolled around in it, or fallen into a puddle.

He looked up, seeking out the steps where he'd seen the smudge of blood, and that was when he saw the shadowy shape moving in the dark, coming toward him. It reached out its hand, and Robbie screamed.

CHAPTER

1

"Is the name John important to anyone here?"

Ashley Whitelam let her gaze flicker out across the audience. It was one of the smaller nights at the working men's club, only around sixty punters or thereabouts, so it didn't take long. She saw a handful of faces brighten, eyebrows raising, hands clutching handbags. Ashley felt as though she really could read their minds: *Does she mean my John? Surely not my own John?* Thanks to her brother Aidan's quiet voice in her ear, she already knew who she was looking for.

"Now, what I get when John is coming through is a sense of tightness here." Ashley pressed one hand to her chest, her eyes half closed. She wasn't focused directly on the audience, but she could see hands rising hesitantly into the air. "This John, perhaps he had problems with his heart, or his lungs, later in life. John, who are you coming through for?"

Aidan's voice came through in her earpiece. *"Green scarf in the third row."*

Ashley let her head nod forward slightly, her long silvery-blond hair falling over her shoulders like a length of silk. She pictured in her mind how the audience saw her: a thin, frail figure, pale skin and hair, half a ghost herself. She was wearing one of the blouses her mother insisted on—cream with slightly puffy shoulders, buttoned up to the neck—with a pair of stonewashed jeans and a sober pair of white flats on her feet. Altogether, it gave the impression of someone only half of this world, a faded apparition, a soul in transit, a half-developed photograph. Only her eyes were dark, surrounded by expertly applied eyeliner and kohl pencil. Ashley insisted on the eye makeup; she wanted the punters drawn to her eyes so they could look into them and believe they were not being lied to. Her mother said she looked like God's own angel, but then, she would say that.

Ashley moved down the left side of the stage until she was facing the woman in the green scarf, whose hand hung in the air, trembling slightly.

"It's you, my love, isn't it?" she said to the woman in the third row. She was older, in her sixties, and her face was pinched around the eyes and mouth. There was sagging skin on her neck and arms, and apart from her green scarf, the rest of her outfit was black. There was a gold wedding band on her ring finger. *He's gone recently*, thought Ashley. *And it was a shock to her. Not her dad then, that wouldn't have been so surprising at her age, but her husband.* The woman was nodding, her eyes already moist.

"What's your name, my love?"

"Sandra." At first, her voice came out as a squeak, and she cleared her throat. "Sandra. John was my husband."

Ashley smiled and nodded. It was always nice when they volunteered information, although it took some of the fun out of it.

"John is here with me, Sandra. He's looking out for you from the spirit world. He says he's sorry to have left you with so much to deal with, but he knows you can handle it." Everyone always had a lot to deal with when someone passed away unexpectedly, so this was a relatively safe guess. "He had a problem with his chest, is that right?"

Sandra nodded tearfully. "His heart."

"That's right, my love, his heart. And he's sorry that he didn't go to the doctor when you told him to, okay? John says he's very sorry about that. Does that make sense to you, Sandra?" This was another safe bet: men were always ignoring advice from their wives, especially when it came to doing something they didn't want to do.

Sandra wrestled a hankie from her bag and dabbed it under her eyes. She let out a slightly strangled yes.

Aidan's voice murmured again, and Ashley resisted the temptation to touch a finger to her ear. The new earpieces were expensive and nearly impossible to spot if you wore your hair long over your ears, like she did, but they also tickled slightly whenever her brother spoke.

"*Three kids according to her Facebook page,*" said Aidan. "*Two boys, and a girl. Eldest son built like a brick shit house.*"

"John says—and he's right here with me, Sandra, standing on this stage—John says that he's proud of your boys and his special girl. Does that make sense to you, Sandra?" Men always doted on their daughters. An image of her own father wandered into Ashley's mind, and she fought against a grimace. "He was the stoic type, your John, never liked to make a fuss, but they do say still rivers run deep—he knew when to relax and have a laugh too, didn't he?" Sandra nodded into her hankie, and Ashley smiled warmly. These kinds of contradictory statements always went down well. Everyone wanted to believe that they or their loved ones were strong and resilient as well as the life of the party. "He wants you to know, Sandra, that he's doing well in the spirit world, and that he's here with . . . It's faint, much fainter, but there's another older man here who's keeping John company. I can't quite make him out . . . Who could that be, Sandra?"

"My brother?" Sandra looked a little less weepy. "My brother, Stan, he died . . . oh, eight years ago now."

"That's right, it's Stanley. John wants you to know that he has Stan with him and they're having a fine time."

"Because they didn't really get on, not when they was alive." Sandra sounded uncertain now. "John always said Stan was a flash git."

"They want you to know they've put all that behind them now," Ashley said smoothly, still smiling. "Thank you, Sandra. John and Stan are fading now, and someone else is coming forward."

In her ear, Aidan was laughing quietly. Ashley moved away up the stage again, her head bowed slightly, and an expectant hush settled over the audience. In many ways, this was her favorite bit of the show. All eyes were on her, and for a while, the silence was all hers. No one would dare to break it, in case it shattered the spell—except Aidan.

"*Next one up is a real shit show.*"

Ashley raised her head and looked toward the back of the room, a carefully cultivated faraway expression on her face.

"The spirit that is with me now is someone who left us very young, when she'd barely even started in the world." Ashley held out one of her hands at waist height, as though she were about to take the hand of a child. A murmur of something—pain, excitement—moved through the audience. "Every loss is a source of great agony for those of us left on the mortal plane, but this girl's passing was especially hard."

Several people in the audience were tearful at this point. Ashley let the moment hang suspended in the air while Aidan whispered his next packet of info.

This one was easy to find; the poor woman has a memorial website set up. The kid was Marian Brooks—the mum is Jackie. Second row from the back, hair the color of a bus, big gold cross. Can't miss her.

Ashley let her eyes wander to the back two rows. And there Jackie was. She even had a small soft toy clutched on her lap, a pale-pink bunny rabbit. *Oh, this is too easy*, thought Ashley.

"The spirit—she only knows you as Mum of course—but I'm getting a J name. Jenny? Jacqueline?" The red-haired woman jumped as though she'd been pinched. "No, Jackie. Everyone calls you Jackie." Ashley settled her gaze on the woman with the rabbit. "Isn't that right, Jackie love?"

The woman leaned forward, and one of the bar people skittered down the row with the microphone.

"Is she all right? Is my little girl in heaven?"

Ashley nodded, still smiling, but inside it felt like her heart was contracting around a long slither of ice. These were the hard ones, when the subject was a child, when the bereavement was still very fresh. When the parent was still carrying around some beloved toy, as though that kept some tiny link between them alive. It was the desperation that Ashley found hard to take. She could tell this woman anything, any tiny scrap of information, and she'd take it and hold it as close as she was holding that bunny.

"*What are you doing?*" Aidan hissed in her ear. "*You're losing them.*"

"Jackie, my love, your little girl is in the spirit world, and for her, it's all playtimes and ice cream, I promise. She's with the angels now.

You'll forgive me, but she had quite an old-fashioned name, didn't she? Was she named after someone?"

Jackie's eyebrows disappeared under her post-box red fringe. "Yes! My mother. We named her after my mum, and she died long before she was born. Marian, her name was Marian. But we . . . we called her Marie."

If she loved the old woman enough to name a child after her, Ashley thought it likely she'd be happy to know that little Marie had company in heaven.

"That's right, and Marie wants you to know that she's happy in the spirit world. She gets to spend all her sunny days with the granny she never knew. Does that make sense to you, Jackie?"

The woman squeezed the toy bunny with her fingers and nodded rapidly. There were no wedding rings on her fingers, and the extreme dye job suggested she was beginning to pick the pieces of her life back up again. She had come alone, no husband and no teary-eyed friends to hold her hand. There had been a marriage, probably, and it hadn't survived the tragedy of Marie's death. Except you never used the D word, not in this place.

"Jackie, it's been so hard on you, all of this, and Marie says—she's very insistent about this—that you will find love in your life again. Does that make sense to you? She wants you to be happy."

"*That's laying it on a bit thick, don't you think?*" Aidan's voice almost sounded bored, but Ashley knew better than that. He loved when she couldn't answer back. "*Fortune-telling is on Wednesdays.*"

And that was the moment everything went to shit. Technically, it was Aidan's job to properly vet the audience list, but usually Ashley would give it the once-over herself too. Not today though; she had been too hungover from a night propping up an anonymous hotel bar. Which meant she couldn't entirely blame him when a very familiar figure stood up in the back row.

"That's not what you told our Joe!"

David Wagner was in his late sixties, with an old-fashioned, faintly sinister haircut and broad shoulders. Despite his gray hair and the lines at the corner of his mouth, the hands with which he grabbed the back of the seat in front of him were large and strong, and Ashley

felt her stomach drop at the sight of him. Quickly, she sought out the
bar staff, who had been warned about people potentially getting out
of hand. She dropped them a quick nod, and they began making their
way toward him. In her ear, Aidan was swearing.

"Please bear with us a moment," Ashley said smoothly, smiling
warmly at the rest of the audience, who were looking a little put out.

"What about our Joe?" Wagner was shouting. He'd clearly seen
the staff approaching his aisle from either side, but that had never
stopped him before. Ashley knew from experience that Wagner would
still be shouting the odds as they dragged him through the fire exit.
"Where was his 'you will find love in your life again,' aye? My boy was
grieving, and you stuck the knife in and twisted it! You're a monster,
a vulture—all of you people are the same." Wagner's face had gone
pink, his eyes bulging slightly from their sockets. "Preying on grieving
people! You should be ashamed."

Two of the bar staff had reached Wagner by that point. Taking
his arms, they began to try to shift him back down the row of seats.
Ashley could see from their lips that they were talking to him, trying
to calm him down perhaps. She could have told them it wasn't worth
the effort. Eventually, they got him into the aisle, and at that point
he seemed to go slack, energy spooling out of him as they pulled him
toward the back of the room. Ashley wondered if his little campaign
against her was running out of steam—every time he snuck into an
audience or turned up in the queue at a trade fair, he looked a little
thinner, a little frailer.

"I'm sorry about that." She turned back to the audience, beaming.
"What we do here, connecting you with your loved ones in the spirit
world, can be very hard for people to take. It's a brave thing, facing
your grief and looking for answers." Confused and angry faces softened, and she saw people glancing at each other, small smiles on their
lips. People liked to be told they were brave and special. "Now, let's get
back to it. I've lots more spirits here waiting to come through."

2

THE GREENROOM AT the working men's club was clearly a space usually used to store things. Ashley sat by the mirror, her eyes wandering over the cardboard boxes, some labeled things like *spring fete*, others open to display various wares, like old plastic takeaway cartons or even, in one box covered in peeling Sellotape, a collection of felt cowboy hats and plastic silver pistols. From beyond the closed door, she could hear her father having a heated argument with one of the bar staff. She picked up the empty glass on the dressing table and wiped a smudge of her pale pink lipstick away with the pad of her thumb. The door opened and Aidan came in carrying a fresh glass of what she very much hoped was vodka. For a second, the sound of their dad's raised voice was much louder. "I gave you very clear instructions! I even sent you a photo of the bastard." Then, Aidan pushed the door shut with his foot.

"One double vodka for the lady," he said, plonking the cold glass down on the dressing table. Ashley picked it up and took a sip. It tasted clear and bitter, how you'd imagine the ancient ice in Antarctica to taste. "If I were you, I'd knock that back quick and get another one in. They won't be on the house for much longer the way Dad's carrying on."

"Fucking hell." Ashley took a gulp and pushed a box off the other chair in the room. Aidan sat. "It didn't make much of a difference in the end, did it? The punters all went away happy. David Wagner isn't winning anyone over with this stuff."

"Ash, he just wants to make you suffer. I don't think he cares about anyone else in that room." Aidan took a sip from his own drink: a pint of something with half an inch of foam on top. "This is what I mean about not laying it on thick. When you get too involved, you end up attracting the likes of Wagner. This is the problem with the general public; they're too unpredictable. Which is why you need to branch out. Do some jobs where you can't cause any trouble. Or *they* can't cause any trouble."

The vodka was nearly done. Ashley put the glass down and pressed her fingers to its sides, trying to absorb the cold. The alcohol was sending out warm fingers from the center of her stomach, and her head was beginning to feel heavy. Perhaps tonight she might even get a decent night's sleep.

"If I wanted a job where I didn't cause trouble, I'd hardly be in this game, would I? Have you got any fags?"

Aidan gave her a look. "You can't smoke in here, Ash. Do you think it's 1985 or something?"

"Fuck off. You should have got me two of these." She tapped her carefully manicured fingernails against the glass. On the table beside it were the two earpieces she and Aidan wore during the show. They looked like two pale little ticks, fat with lies. "If I had a shred of decency, I'd pack in this racket and go and earn an honest living. Become a politician. A bank robber. Something respectable like that."

"Yeah, Dad would love that. And you're the one who got us into this business, Ash. Remember?"

"As if this was my choice."

Aidan went quiet then, the way he did when Ashley pushed against the restraints holding them both in place. From outside, they could hear the manager of the social club getting irate.

"Here." She downed the rest of the vodka and handed him the glass. "Get me another one, quick."

* * *

They weren't staying in a hotel that night, and the drive back home was a long one, down twisty English country lanes devoid of streetlights.

Ashley sat in the back seat, her head against the cold window while Aidan and her father bickered in the front. Outside, the world was an inky blackness, flashes of trees and hedgerows looming in the headlights. If it weren't for the vodka swimming in her stomach, it could almost have been a car trip from her childhood; the smell of petrol and cigarettes, the droning warmth of the car, her brother and her dad snipping at each other. All that was missing was her mother. But of course she had been very different back then.

"You were the one doing the research, Aidan. You should be able to spot that bastard's aliases by now. Did you not even google the fucker?"

Ashley looked at her dad, lit by the glow of his overcomplicated dashboard. A decade ago, he had started to lose his hair, so he had shaved the whole lot off; he had been proudly bald since, transferring his attentions instead to his thick, dark mustache, which had its own comb and oils in the family bathroom. Like David Wagner, he was broad across the shoulders, but it went further than that; on meeting Logan Whitelam, most people assumed he had some military background. He had the sort of bearing that suggested he had spent his life shouting at subordinates. At his throat, he wore a small silver pentacle.

"You think Google solves everything," said Aidan. He was looking at something on his phone, unconcerned by their father's mood. "It's not a magic button, Dad."

Aidan was dark like their dad, but slim and wiry with it. His hair was lush and thick and slightly too long, and he was tall, a couple of inches taller than Logan.

"Anyway," Aidan continued, closing his phone screen, "this is exactly why you should listen to my idea about new types of jobs for Ash. This sort of stuff—the grievers in the social clubs and the mind body spirit fairs—it's all small change."

"That small change keeps you in cars and bloody Lacoste shirts," rumbled their father. "And don't you forget it."

"All I'm saying is, we should consider the job. I think it's a whole new revenue stream for us, if it comes off."

"Hmm."

"You are only against it because you didn't think of it," said Aidan, a little sharply. "You're never interested unless it's your idea."

Ashley leaned forward.

"What are you talking about? What idea?"

Aidan turned around in his seat to talk to her directly.

"Police consultation."

Ashley laughed. "What?"

"Offering your services to the police, preferably on high-profile cases. You know the sort. Finding lost people, locating bodies, giving them an idea of where to look for people. It used to be in the news all the time, back in the day—*psychic helps police locate missing woman,* that sort of thing."

Ashley shook her head and glanced at their dad, who still had his eyes on the road.

"Are you hearing this?"

"I am," Logan said shortly.

"It's a *good* idea," said Aidan, a shadow of the sulky teenager he had once been coloring his words.

"Aidan, you can't google where dead bodies are hidden." She laughed again, shaking her head. "If you could, the police would hardly need to pay me, would they? What am I supposed to do, pick a random location and hope for the best?"

"You know that a good . . . what, eighty percent of what you do is spin, right?" said Aidan. "It's about delivery, confidence, all that stuff. Make an intelligent guess, say the right words, get paid, and more importantly, get publicity."

"Would the police actually pay?" Logan's voice had a musing tone to it. "I doubt they have a budget for psychic services."

"No, all right, maybe they don't." Aidan turned back to address their father. "So, Ashley offers her services for free, at first. And then with the publicity it generates, we get more house calls, more punters at the clubs, longer queues at the MBS fairs. All we really need is one or two good stories to get on the internet or in the newspapers, and we'll have a sizable bump in business."

"Don't I have enough on my plate with the Red Rigg House thing?"

Her father and brother both fell silent at that. Ashley felt a prickle of heat move across the back of her neck. They didn't like when she mentioned the *house*, but they still expected her to go.

"That's next month," said Aidan, his usual laid-back tone returning. "I just think it's worth exploring as an option. I mean, I'm not talking about the Met here."

"I should bloody hope not," their father growled.

Outside, the roads and verges were taking on a familiar pattern, and Ashley let it soothe her. Somewhere out there were the lakes of Cumbria, their dark silty depths still and unmoving in the night; the Lake District contained Red Rigg House, a place she'd been terrified of since she was a child, but it also contained these silent, natural places. She found it comforting. Ashley leaned back in her seat and rested her temple against the cold glass.

*   *   *

It was the same old dream. She was in one of the narrow beds in the dormitory. The long windows let in moonlight as crisp as rice paper, etching the outlines of the beds and bedside tables with their jumble of clothes and belongings. All the other beds were empty, but there were other children in the dormitory; they stood silently in the aisles, watching her, their faces still. In the dream, Ashley always wanted to jump out of the bed and run, but the floor was completely black, and she knew that if she set one foot on it, she would fall into that suffocating dark and never return. The dark was hungry.

And then, as it always did, the dormitory began to grow hot. The crisp moonlight wavered.

I wasn't there, Ashley thought desperately. *The Heedful Ones saved me.*

The other children, their faces still in shadow, began to sink down into the darkness . . .

*   *   *

"Wake up, Ash, we're home."

Ashley sat up, the heat of the dormitory receding. They were parked outside the house, and her father was already out and marching up to the door. Aidan had turned around in his seat again and was watching her closely.

"Bad dreams?"

"Are there any other kind?"

"Here, look." Aidan reached into his pocket and brought out a small, anonymous-looking pill bottle. He rattled it and passed it to her. "I thought you could try these."

"What are they?"

"Amitriptyline. Take one before bed. Maybe try it tomorrow though, when you don't have several vodkas inside you. And don't tell Dad. Or Mum, for that matter."

Ashley turned the bottle over in her hands. The tablets were tiny and blue.

"Where'd you get them?"

"A friend." Aidan smiled at her and unclipped his seat belt. "Don't say I never do anything for you."

He got out of the car, and Ashley slipped the tablets into her pocket. Out on the gravel driveway, the air was cool, and Ashley stood for a moment, letting the cold seep under her collar and across her brow. Aidan's car was parked to one side, and he clicked the doors open with his key.

"Are you not staying tonight?"

"Here? In this madhouse?" Aidan grinned at her. "I've got my own home to get back to."

"You prick," Ashley said, without heat. Aidan rarely stayed at the house anymore, preferring to scuttle back to his flat in Ulverston after every show. For a long time, she had expended a lot of energy trying to get him to stay so that she would have one ally against their mother and father, but although he did what he could for her, ultimately he would not give up his own hard-won freedom, even for one night. She waved him off, listening to the crunch of his car wheels against the gravel, and then when he was lost to the dark, she turned and looked up at what her mother insisted on calling a "cottage." No more than ten years old, it was a new build gussied up to look like an old farmhouse, with eaves and gables and an old coal scuttle by the front door, but none of that could quite distract from the solar panels on the roof, or the double-glazed windows.

Inside, every light was on, and the smell of chocolate wafted from the large open-plan kitchen. Her father was nowhere to be seen, but her mother was by the stove, stirring something in a pan. When she saw Ashley, she laid the wooden spoon carefully on a piece of kitchen towel, and then came over to her, placing her warm hands on either side of Ashley's face.

"There you are, my angel." She swept her thumbs across the tops of Ashley's cheeks, as though chasing away invisible tears. "How was it tonight? I hope it wasn't too hard on you." Already her voice was wavering slightly, taking on that querulous tone that set Ashley's teeth on edge.

"It was fine, Mum." She made herself smile, then took her mother's hands and gently pulled them away from her face. "Nothing exciting to report."

Her mother nodded vaguely, her eyes a little wet. If Logan Whitelam was a brusque mountain of a man, Helen Whitelam was a sapling, a whip-thin shrub that looked as though it wouldn't survive a hard frost. Her hair was prematurely gray, but she had it dyed blond once a month at a hair salon in Ambleside, and under the powerful kitchen halogens it looked a brassy kind of yellow. She turned back to the hob and picked up her wooden spoon.

"I'm making you some hot chocolate. Go and sit down and I'll bring it through."

Ashley opened her mouth, wanting to tell her mother that she'd spent the night drinking vodka and the last thing she wanted was a cup of rich, foaming cocoa to dump on top of that, but she looked again at the slumped angle of her mother's shoulders and thought better of it. The living room was ablaze with lights, the huge TV on mute. Ashley went and turned off a couple of the lamps and sat on the cream leather sofa. She wanted to be gone, back into the sanctity of her own bedroom, but the thought of her mother coming into the room with her steaming hot chocolate only to find it empty struck at Ashley's heart.

There was a newspaper open on the coffee table, so she pulled it toward her. The headline read:

POLICE COME TO DEAD END IN GINGERBREAD HOUSE MURDERS

"Mum? Have you been reading the paper?"

Helen came into the room carrying a huge steaming mug. Tiny pink and white marshmallows floated on the top.

"Just a quick look. Your father said there was an advert in the back for your convention at Red Rigg House."

Ashley took the offered hot chocolate and held it on top of her knees with both hands. Her mother sat on the sofa next to her, barely making a dent. "Mum, we talked about this, didn't we? This stuff upsets you." Ashley unhooked one hand from her hot chocolate and tapped the newspaper. Her mother's mouth turned down at the corners.

"I can hardly avoid it!" Helen's watery eyes grew wide. "It's on the news, it's on Facebook, it's on the radio. Those poor children." She patted her hair with trembling fingers.

"Facebook? Mum, come on—"

"Did you know that when they did their autopsies, when they cut open those poor children, did you know—"

"*Mum.*" Ashley grabbed her mother's hand and squeezed it, forcing her to make eye contact. "Gruesome child murders, bloody hell. This kind of thing makes you unwell, remember? I thought we'd agreed you'd stay off those Facebook groups. They're full of shit."

Helen blinked rapidly. Ashley was in her early thirties but it was still a struggle for her mother to hear her use curse words.

"*Ashley.* There's no need to be *coarse.*"

"If there's adverts and things, or anything to do with our work in the newspapers, I'll show you myself." Ashley folded the newspaper over so the headline was hidden. At that moment, her father appeared at the door. He was dressed in his vest and pajama bottoms. Now that they were home, the silver pentagram was stored back in his bedside cabinet; he wouldn't wear it around the house.

"Girls," he said, his eyes flicking between them. "Don't stay up too late, Ashley, we've an early start tomorrow."

Helen leaped up, smoothing the creases of her dress. So many of her mother's movements reminded Ashley of a startled pigeon. When both her mother and father had gone off to bed, Ashley opened the newspaper again and flicked to the classified adverts in the back. Sure enough, there was a sizable color ad with her name on it, squeezed between notices about car boot sales and plumbing services. She read it with her lips pursed.

> *Come to the Annual Moon Market at Red Rigg House*
>> *October 29th to November 1st*
>> *Join us at this beautiful stately home for a festival of the psychic arts! Featuring tarot, palmistry, past life hypnosis, crystal healing, and a host of holistic treatments.*
>> *With noted psychic mediums Cleo Bickerstaff, Donald St. Clair, Alison Mantel, Desmond Morris, Merlin Jones*
>> *SPECIAL GUEST STAR Ashley Whitelam, "the Spirit Oracle," in her first visit to Red Rigg House since the events of 2004. Ashley will perform an open séance in what is sure to be an UNMISSABLE and EMOTIONAL event.*

The advert featured a small photo of Red Rigg House at the bottom, an aerial shot that showed off the sprawling gardens and the edges of the deep green forest that surrounded it, and then a photo of Ashley was transposed to one side. She recognized it as one of the new publicity photos her father had insisted on last year. She was smiling softly, her eyes full of light and her chin tilted slightly up, as though she were taking a quick peep at the denizens of heaven itself.

"Bloody hell."

Ashley folded the paper up again and took it and her hot chocolate into the kitchen. She threw the paper in the bin, and almost poured the hot chocolate down the sink before she remembered the tablets Aidan had given her. She took the bottle from her pocket and rattled a tablet out onto the palm of her hand. There was no label on the bottle, but if you couldn't trust your brother, who could you trust? And if there was a chance she could avoid any more Red Rigg nightmares . . . well, that was a chance worth taking.

She swallowed the tablet with a gulp of sugary hot chocolate and threw the rest of the drink in the sink.

Upstairs in her own bedroom, she changed into pajamas and sat on the bed. From a drawer, she took a battered hardback notebook, which was held shut with several elastic hair ties. She snapped them off and retrieved a pen from the little pile of bric-a-brac on her nightstand.

It was her ritual, her confessional. Back when she had still been young enough to complain to her parents about her nightmares, her therapist had recommended she keep a journal—he had suggested it might help to get what she was thinking and feeling out onto the page before she went to sleep. It had never stopped the nightmares, but it had become a habit. After every night, or at least every night after a gig, she would write an entry in her journal. It was a place where she could truly be honest with herself, could spill all the discomfort and guilt so that it didn't sit on her chest all night. Something about the act of scribbling a few lines was familiar and soothing. She scrawled the date and added a few notes.

Plenty of sad stories tonight, but when aren't there? A woman who lost her child, a wife who lost her husband, and—a rancid cherry on top of the cake—David Wagner turned up to cause trouble again. Dad likes to say that without sad stories, we wouldn't be able to make a living, and I suppose he's right. If they didn't come to me, they'd go to someone else—and as far as I can tell, we're all crooks.

She looked at the last line for a while, completely unaware of the frown that creased her brow. Abruptly tired, either from the vodka or the tablet she had taken, Ashley put her journal back in the drawer and snapped off the light.

3

S OME PLACES ARE just bad.

You will have experienced this yourself, but you might not have been aware of it at the time. At its most basic level, perhaps you crossed the street once because you spotted the mouth of a dark alley and didn't want to walk past it; you knew that doing so would expose yourself somehow. You might have stayed in a hotel and been unable to properly relax, experiencing several nights of terrible sleep, or the kind of nightmares that leave you morose and exhausted the next day. You may have crossed the threshold of a church and felt immediately that you should not be there. Bad places.

Sometimes there will be obvious reasons why a house or a park or a classroom feels wrong—blood spilled, bodies broken, a violation, a secret shared that should have been taken to the grave. More often though, there is no particular reason—or at least none that we can comprehend—and even places that appear entirely pleasant can leave you with the desperate urge to be elsewhere as soon as possible.

And it isn't only urban places that can be bad. The oldest ones have existed since before humankind was little more than a particularly curious ape. They predate architecture, cities, plumbing. They could even predate mammals, trees, the first animals that dragged themselves out of the oceans. For all we know, the first amino acids in the primordial soup could have felt a shiver of wrongness as they passed over a particular piece of molten rock. But we're getting away from the point.

Hundreds of thousands of years ago, when the mountains of northern Britain were already unimaginably old, there was a fell where no birds flew. The people who lived in its vicinity were frightened of it, and none of them would venture near it after sunset. They told stories about the mountain—how people would walk up it and never come back down, how the wolves howled from its summit. They whispered that it was hollow, that there was a secret way inside the mountain, and if you stumbled across it, the gods of wood, spring, and earth would forsake you.

Bad things happened on the fell. Just as most people are repelled by bad places, there are always those who are drawn to them instead. It was a place for violence and hatred, a place for oaths sworn and broken, and for terrible desires shared. Men and women fought and were killed there; the weakest elders were brought there by their grown children, in secret, to die on its exposed flanks.

During one especially vicious winter, a winter that heralded a longer period of darkness and ice, a girl child was taken to the mountain by a group of men. These men were from her own village, but as the snows came and the food dwindled, there was no longer room for a wan girl with fragile bones. She had eyes of two colors, which they believed marked her as an evil spirit, and so it was decided that she would be given in sacrifice—perhaps if she were expelled, if she were given to the mountain, this particular winter would lose some of its teeth, and more of them would come through it alive. Not even her family would speak out in her favor. Bad places have a way of streamlining these kinds of thoughts, a way of neatly knocking off the thorns and burrs of conscience so that the arrow of violence can fly true. They beat her, and she was left bleeding her last on the icy ground. Abandoned, starving, and betrayed.

Seeking shelter from the freezing wind, the girl pulled herself into a narrow crack in the side of the fell and found that at least some of the stories were true—there was a way through, a hollow place. With death's cold hands around her neck, the girl gave her heart's blood to the hollow, along with all of her rage and her hunger. And with her last breath, she whispered a curse on the people who had brought her to this place, a curse that would last as long as the hills.

"Feed the fell," she whispered. "You'll feed the fell forever to stop it eating you."

When the men and women came walking up the mountain again as the first thaws began to ease the grip of winter, they were startled to find that the blood of the girl was still there, miraculously frozen into the ice, streaks of crimson sparkling in the early spring sun like a vein of rubies.

They gave it a new name in honor of its bloody countenance and then they left, uneasy in a way they had yet to understand.

It had always been a bad place.

4

2004

"RISE AND SHINE! One more day of school, and then you're off on your adventures, aren't you?"

Deep under her duvet, Ashley curled up to make herself as small as possible. She heard her mother laugh, then a hand snaked under the cover and gave her a poke. Ashley gave a grumpy sort of snort.

"Up you get. Don't make me come in here with a wet flannel."

With deep reluctance, Ashley pushed her feet toward the edge of the bed and felt the cool morning air on her toes. It was nearly Easter weekend, but the weather had resolutely refused to brighten, deciding instead to go for the more traditional Bank Holiday options of unseasonal cold and driving squalls of icy rain.

"There you go." Her mother gave one of Ashley's toes a squeeze. "Now get the rest of you out as well. I want to hear you brushing your teeth in five minutes."

"Mum."

When her mother had left the room, Ashley slid all the way out of bed. She glanced at her brother's bed, but he was already up; likely, he was already out the door, on his way to the half an hour's worth of football training he liked to get in before school. The football posters on his side of the room were full of glum-looking men in red shirts;

the trophies on his bedside cabinet reflected the dour morning light
back at her.

Once she'd washed her face and brushed her teeth, she came back
into their bedroom, ignoring the shadowy figure standing by the curtains, and began to drag clean clothes out of her small plasterboard
chest of drawers. She chose the navy skirt that had once been her
cousin's and a pale blue shirt that was a little small on her now, but it
had dark blue buttons, which she liked. She scooped them up in her
arms, along with a pair of cream tights and her knickers, and very
quickly scampered down the hallway and into the living room. Her
mother had put the electric heater on ready so that the three orange
bars were the brightest thing there. Outside, the day was overcast, rain
lashing intermittently at the windows. Ashley went and sat in front
of the heater, already glad to be near a new heat source. Her mother
appeared at the door, dressed for her shift at the supermarket.

"Hurry up, Ash, we aren't made of money. I've already put ten
quid on the electric key this week."

Ashley nodded, the taste of toothpaste still strong in her mouth.
She felt the cold easily, and consequently she heard about the electric
key and how much it cost to keep the flat warm regularly. She peeled
off her pajamas and dressed in front of the fire. When she was done,
her mum came back into the room, briskly switched the heater off,
and handed her a bowl of cereal. Ashley took it, still crouched in front
of the fading orange bars. Her mother leaned down and pushed a few
errant strands of hair away from Ashley's forehead. Ashley leaned away
from her.

"Did you even brush this barnet, Ashley?" she said fondly. "Make
sure you do it before we leave. Are you excited about Red Rigg House?"

Ashley nodded, although she was mainly nervous. It would be her
first time away from home without her parents, save for a couple of
sleepovers with her cousins, and she was the only one from her school
who was going, so she wouldn't have any friends there, or even any
familiar faces. Four nights away from home, in a part of the country
she knew nothing about, with strangers. Thinking about it gave her
a tight feeling in the back of her throat. As if she could read some of
these feelings on her daughter's face, her mother smoothed the girl's

hair back again. Ashley's hair was so fine it was constantly escaping from her ponytail.

"Don't make that face, love. You're going to have fun," she said. "All that fresh air, all those trees. I wish *I* were going. It'll bring you out of your shell a bit, being away from home with a bunch of kids. Right? You'll make the most of it, won't you, Ash?"

Ashley's father stepped into the room. He was fully dressed, his jacket damp from the rain. Her mother straightened up, her bearing changing as she looked at her husband.

"'Ere, take those boots off on this carpet."

Logan Whitelam paid no attention to her. Instead, he went over to the cooling heater and briskly rubbed the top of Ashley's head, causing her already untidy hair to fizz and tangle. She tutted and leaned away, but she was smiling.

"You keep an eye out when you're in that big house, won't you, Ash? Make note of where they keep their valuables, let us know if there are any broken windows or missing locks." He winked at her.

"Logan . . ." Ashley's mother began in a dangerous tone of voice.

"Come on." Her father turned away from them both, as if suddenly uninterested. "If the pair of you want a lift in this morning, I'm going now."

* * *

At school, they were learning about the French Revolution. Normally, history was one of Ashley's favorite lessons—she loved hearing about these impossibly old people with their chaos and their guillotines—but the thought of Red Rigg House and, more specifically, being away from home kept circling in her mind. At break time, she was even quieter than usual, something her closest friends immediately picked up on. Hannah, usually kind but also seething with jealousy over the Red Rigg trip, nudged Ashley's beaten-up trainer with her own carefully polished black shoe.

"Are you going to do archery there?" she asked, before rushing in to answer her own question. "I bet you don't. We did it at Center Parcs last year, but my dad says you need to have a special license."

"There's a lot of different things," Ashley said uncertainly. The brochure they'd been sent by the charity was full of color pictures of children of all ages running around with grinning faces. She couldn't remember if any of them had been playing around with bows and arrows. "Rambling, rounders, table tennis." None of these particularly appealed to Ashley. "And there's arts and crafts."

"Sounds crap," said Sarah, who was rarely kind. She had a tiny electronic toy on a key chain, and she was pressing the buttons savagely as the thing made a series of frantic beeps. "It's not like a proper holiday. It's for *poor people*." Sarah spared them one withering glance. "For kids whose families can't afford to do proper things."

Ashley flushed with shame. It was true that her parents had applied for the trip through a charity called the Cumbria Arts Trust, and she knew that they had filled in a form with details about their jobs and wages—her dad had complained about it endlessly, saying they were "taking liberties." More and more she wished that they hadn't, that she could spend the Easter weekend at her nan and granddad's, as they did every year. But they would be disappointed in her if they knew that she didn't want to go.

Hannah, never able to sustain a bad mood for very long, rallied to Ashley's defense.

"That doesn't matter, does it? Everyone should be able to have holidays. And I bet it'll be fun staying in a big old house. I mean, it's basically a mansion. I bet you'll have a brilliant time, Ash."

Ashley nodded, one hand rubbing self-consciously at the slightly worn material of her skirt; the skirt that had arrived in a bin bag of clothes that her cousin had grown out of. The bell rang for the end of break, and they began to file slowly toward the big red-brick building. Ashley dawdled, letting her friends go ahead of her. Beyond the playground, there was the road, and crowded on the other side of it were garages and shops. Above them, the high-rise flats of Lewisham stood gray and ominous against clouds still heavy with promised rain. The drone of traffic, punctuated by the odd shout and car horn, was so ever-present that she barely heard it anymore. On the far side of the playground fence, a pair of figures stood, watching. The Heedful Ones, as Ashley thought of them, looked to be covered in a layer fine pale dust, and they did not move. Ashley didn't like to look at their faces, which were strange, smeared things, but she knew they were watching her. It was what they did. She saw them every day, in the bedroom she shared with her brother, by the bus stop, in her grand-dad's back garden; silent shadowy figures that watched her, that no one else could see. The Heedful Ones were her own silent companions, so familiar now that much of the time she barely noticed them.

A teacher appeared at the doors and began to call the stragglers inside. Ashley skipped away, her mind already back on the French aristocracy.

CHAPTER

5

ASHLEY STOOD AT the back of the conference room behind the rows of proud parents and watched the kids read aloud their poetry and the occasional short story. Her friend Malory was standing to one side of the stage, easily as proud as the mums and dads. She looked neat and professional, her dark hair cut into a sleek bob, her skirt and blazer elegantly tailored to her lanky form. When the children were finished, a florid man in his fifties with a gingery beard came out onto the stage and read one of his own poems in a pompous tone that immediately put Ashley on edge. And then it was over. As the kids streamed over to their parents to receive their congratulations, Ashley met Malory at the door.

"A poetry recital? I'm not sure what I've done to deserve that, Mal."

"Was it so dreadful?"

"The kids were all right. That bloke though." She nodded at the bearded man, who was talking loudly and importantly to a group of parents. "Where'd you drag him up from?"

"Cumbria is known for its poets," Malory said primly. "And I've asked you to fill this spot lots of times. It'd be so interesting for the children to learn about your work."

Ashley snorted. Most of the children and parents were leaving now, some carrying small Cumbria Arts Trust trophies under their arms.

"Only you and my dad would describe what I do as work. What am I going to teach them? How to swindle the especially gullible?"

"The Trust is about giving these children a glimpse of different paths they could take, visions of other lives. It broadens their horizons. It doesn't actually matter that much who the speakers are or what they do."

Ashley thought about her own experience with the Trust at Red Rigg House eighteen years ago. That had broadened her horizons all right.

"If you say so. Why did you really badger me to come to this, Mal?"

Malory gave her a sly look from under her eyelashes, smiling coyly. Her friend was a few years older than Ashley, just breaching her midthirties, but sometimes she seemed very young, as though growing up at Red Rigg House had frozen her in place, like some Victorian child ghost in an enchanted garden.

"I wanted to make sure that you're still coming to our Moon Market."

Ashley glanced away, uncomfortable. "I said I would, didn't I? I know my name is already on all the marketing."

"Yes, well, Ashie, seeing it written on an email is quite different to hearing it from the horse's mouth." And then, in a quieter tone of voice, she said, "I can feel you drawing away the closer it gets. I've barely heard from you in weeks."

"Sorry." Ashley forced herself to smile, slightly ashamed.

Malory took her arm and squeezed it.

"I know it's difficult, and I'm so proud of you for making this final leap. It'll be fun, I promise—the main hall is going to be packed with vendors, and we're setting up special rooms for all the different mediums. And, honestly, you'll probably barely recognize the place. A lot of it was rebuilt after the . . . well. So much of it was refurbished, I can hardly remember what the east wing used to look like."

There was a cough from behind them, and Malory's brother, Richard, gave Ashley a cold smile.

"Can I have a word with you, Mal?" he said. Richard had always been icily handsome—black hair, blue eyes, skin like cream—and he had grown his hair out since Ashley had last seen him, which had been at least three months ago. He also had the sort of thick, black, well-maintained beard that Ashley associated with a certain sort of hipster barber, and he was wearing soft black trousers and a dark gray cashmere jumper, no doubt outrageously expensive. Ashley turned her head slightly, as though something on the far side of the room had caught her attention. Malory sighed.

"Can't it wait?"

"No." Even from the corner of her eye, Ashley could see the glare he was aiming at his sister. "It really can't, sis."

"All right, give me a minute, will you?"

Malory slid her arm through Ashley's and the pair of them went outside, where fat October clouds were piling up above glowering fells. The town hall and the scattering of cottages that made up the tiny village of Green Beck looked especially ancient and wizened, like old teeth plugged into the green gums of the Lake District.

"I don't suppose," Malory said lightly, "that the pair of you will ever make up your differences?"

"I don't know," Ashley replied. 'Will your brother ever stop being a relentless dickhead?" Years ago, when Ashley's family had moved to Green Beck, she and Richard had briefly been an item; Ashley had been in her late teens, still of an age to find arrogance thrilling instead of just tiresome, and Richard had a kind of dark glamour. Or at least, he had for around six months or so.

Malory laughed and shook her head. "Pigs will fly, etcetera, etcetera. Where are you for the rest of the afternoon? If you're not busy, we could get a sandwich or something. I'm absolutely starved."

"I said I would visit Melva," Ashley said. "You could come with me if you like? You know what her place is like. Everyone is welcome."

Malory grimaced in a good-natured fashion. "Bless you, Ashie, but you know that lady gives me the creeps these days. Don't be a stranger though, okay?"

Ashley left Malory, heading deeper into the village, and got into her battered little hatchback, flicking the radio on and taking the quickest route out of Green Beck. Back inside her car, she felt some of the tension leave her shoulders; the car was her space, filled with her crap. For years, her parents had insisted that she didn't need her own transport, that they would gladly drive her any place she needed to be. But she had recognized this for the bullshit that it was—for the *leash* that it was. If there was a way that Logan Whitelam could keep his daughter—his *golden goose*, Ashley thought acidly—within his eye line at all times, he would undoubtedly do it.

Over the years, Ashley had saved money from her own share of the business and quietly squirreled it away, before meticulously researching the best secondhand cars in the area. She had spent a portion of the money on driving lessons, which her brother had driven her to each time, sworn to secrecy, and when she had passed, they had had a quiet celebration in a pub their father had never visited. When she finally drove home, her very own car, with its lilac paint job and the *L* sign in the back window, she had been both very proud and slightly afraid. Their mother had been distressed, because that was her default reaction to most things, but Logan had gone very quiet and thoughtful, looking at his daughter as though she'd revealed a secret ability he had been completely unaware of. Initially, he tried to tell her that she couldn't park it at the cottage, that the driveway was already crowded enough with their family car (emphasis on the *family*) and Aidan's own Ford Focus, but her brother had, almost gleefully, nipped that protest in the bud by claiming he had no real need to park there. It was a moment Ashley was unendingly grateful for.

Aidan had referred to the car, as boxy and as lilac as it was, as the Parma Violet, and the name had stuck. It was freedom, it was the ability to drive away from her parents and head out into the hills. And if she always had to come back to the world of spirits and working men's social clubs and tarot and tea leaves, at least she had those hours alone in her car, with the pretense that she could go wherever she wanted.

Melva Goodacre's house was on the outskirts of Green Beck, nestled at the western foot of Red Rigg Fell. Whereas the Whitelam family home was a sprawling house masquerading as a sweet country cottage, Melva's abode really did look as though it belonged in the pages of a storybook. The thatched roof slumped toward the ground like porridge pouring from an enchanted pot, and ivy and roses climbed gray slate walls. The garden smelled strongly of the basil, mint, and thyme that grew there, and Ashley was fairly sure that bats lived in the eaves. Despite the nip in the air, the front door was open. Ashley rapped her knuckles against the door and leaned into a darkened hallway.

"Are you there, Melva?"

There was a skittering of dog claws against lino and Pester, Melva's excitable Jack Russell, came pelting around the corner.

"I'm in the back room, love!"

Ashley made her way down the hall, Pester nipping joyfully at her heels. Melva's back room was also her "work" room, and it was filled with the kind of paraphernalia that Ashley had become very familiar with over the last couple of decades; the kind of paraphernalia that her father would not allow in the house, save for her mother's ceramic angels. There was a big crystal ball on the coffee table sitting atop its own puddle of purple silk; there were several sets of tarot cards next to it, and a big pewter scrying bowl painted with silver runes. The walls were hung with various paintings and etchings depicting a whole host of spiritual guides, from wolves to faeries to fat little buddhas. An incense stick on another small table was sending a patchouli-scented line of gray smoke up toward the ceiling, and very faintly Ashley could hear the sound of pan pipes leaking from the CD player. Melva herself was sitting on the comfy sofa with a newspaper spread over her knees. She was smoking one of her poisonous-smelling cigarettes and frowning at the newsprint.

"Have you got a client coming?" Ashley asked, nodding at the incense. She reached down and gave Pester a scratch on the head, which made him plonk his behind on the rug and sit still for a few moments.

"Will you look at this." Melva poked her finger at the headline. "Gingerbread house killings? They make it sound like something *cute*."

"I've come to ask you about that, actually."

Melva's head snapped up, her gray eyes sharp. "Have you now?"

Clients meeting Melva for the first time were often taken unawares.

Given the witchy cottage feeling of her home and the esoteric nature of her business, they usually expected a free spirit with a tendency toward kaftans and tie-dye. What they got was a steely-eyed woman in her early fifties, with straight gray hair pulled back into a ponytail, and broad farmer's hands. Quite often, she wore a battered pair of green wellies.

Ashley sat herself down on the armchair that usually housed clients. Pester, satisfied that Ashley wasn't smuggling any pork scratchings into the house, went to sprawl underneath the coffee table.

"What do you think about working with the police? As a kind of consultant?"

Melva sat back on the sofa. "On this case?"

"It's Aidan's idea. You know they've had a kid missing for a couple of weeks now. He told the police that I can help them locate him." Ashley paused. Aidan hadn't gone as far as to say "if he is now in the spirit world," but she imagined that's what he had meant. "Like I'm some sort of bloodhound or something."

Melva took a long drag of her cigarette before answering. "And they've gone for that, have they?"

Ashley shrugged. "I think they must be getting desperate at this point. This has been, what? Eight kids in six years. And we're not charging anything either. Aidan says the point is the free publicity it'll get us." She shifted on the armchair. It was too warm in the little parlor. "Although he doesn't seem to be bothered that I will look like a proper idiot when I inevitably don't find anything helpful."

"There's no need to play down your talents in front of me, girl. You'll have to do some research though, of course," Melva said in a musing tone. "What do you know about this horrible business?"

"What anyone knows, I suppose. That these kids keep going missing and turning up around the Lakes. Sometimes *in* the Lakes."

Melva stubbed the last of her fag out in an ashtray. "I've got a woman coming at two. She wants her tea leaves done." This was often the way with Melva; you would ask a question and eventually the answer would make it round to the front of her mind, whether you still needed to know or not. "You can sit in if you want. I'm sure she'd be thrilled to have the company of the *spirit oracle*. I might get a better tip out of it."

"I don't want to cramp your style."

"Do you know why they're calling them the Gingerbread House Murders?"

"No."

Melva brightened up, always pleased to impart a bit of unpleasant knowledge. "When they find these poor little tikes and cut them open for the autopsy, they find all this rich food in their stomachs. Like Hansel and Gretel at the witch's house. Someone treats those kids well before . . . well, before what happens to them happens."

Pester whined under the table.

"Here, look, I brought you your sherry." Ashley reached into her bag and pulled out the bottle. She didn't want to talk about the Gingerbread House Murders anymore. "Sweet and red."

"Thanks, love." Melva reached for the bottle eagerly. "A little glass of sherry and my ladies loosen up nicely."

"That's a horrible image—thanks for that." Ashley stood, preparing to leave.

"You'll not stay?"

"I have my own appointment to keep, I'm afraid. Although knowing my luck, there won't be any sherry."

Melva laughed, waving her out the door, but just as Ashley stepped into the shadowy hallway, the older woman called after her.

"I think you should do it."

Ashley leaned back in through the doorway.

"You do?"

Melva had an odd look on her face, one Ashley could not interpret. But she nodded firmly enough.

"You have to open yourself up to these new experiences, Ash. I know you see more than you let on, and I think it's the path you have to walk, for better or worse."

As she was walking through the front garden toward her car, Ashley found herself face-to-face with Melva's divination client. She was a young woman, her mousy hair shaved into an undercut on one side, a silver bar through her nose. When she saw Ashley, her eyes grew wide and she came to a sudden halt.

"You're Ashley Whitelam," she said. "You were there when—"

"I'm so sorry." Ashley smiled politely, the skin on the back of her neck crawling. She hated to be recognized when she wasn't, as her father would put it, "performing." "I'm late for something."

She brushed past the woman and headed straight for the sanctuary that was her car, but she felt the woman's eyes on her back for every single step.

6

THAT EVENING, BACK at the cottage, Ashley was in the middle of the washing up when the doorbell rang. Her mother and father were watching *EastEnders*, a program they both watched religiously; her mum because it reminded her a little of living in Lewisham, her father because he enjoyed pointing out how ridiculous it all was. Ashley dried her hands on a tea towel and made her way down the hall to the front door. She opened it to find Richard Lyndon-Smith standing there in the frigid night air. She scowled.

"I told you not to come to the house anymore. What do you want?"

He smiled at her, his hands shoved casually into his pockets, but there was an edge to it she didn't like.

"I can't catch up with an old friend?"

Ashley crossed her arms over her chest. Richard had been her first serious boyfriend, the one with which she had shared a number of firsts. Despite her deep dislike for him, seeing him again always brought back uncomfortable memories: driving to remote places with him and doing the sorts of things hormonal teenagers did; going to parties thrown by his friends, who were all older than her, where they would experiment with drugs or drink until they passed out.

"Friends is a weird fucking term for what we are." Ashley sighed and glanced behind her, in case her father had appeared in the hallway. "Let's walk down the road a bit."

The night was still and clear. Together they walked down the drive and out across the main road. Without having to discuss it, they both moved to the field opposite, which had a stile over the hedgerows and a path they were both familiar with, even in the dark. They walked until they came to the great oak tree that stood like an island in the middle of the field. In the pale glow of the moonlight, it looked bewitched, a thing from a fairy tale, with every leaf lined in silver.

"So . . ." Ashley put on Malory's voice, something she knew annoyed Richard. "To what do I owe this displeasure?"

"I've been away for a couple of months, I'm sure you've noticed." He came over to where Ashley was leaning against the tree. He stood too close, his feet planted to either side of hers. She could smell his aftershave, and it made her stomach churn. Too many memories. "You know I like to check in on you."

"Where've you been off to this time?"

Richard shrugged. "A few weeks in America, a few weeks in Canada. It's so different to this place. To Green Beck, and the house." He shrugged, then looked away. "None of these bloody dour green hills. You either get proper mountains or miles and miles of flat land." As usual, when he spoke of being somewhere else, an anger she didn't quite understand seemed to boil just under the surface. "You should come with me sometime, Ash."

"We both know that will never happen."

He smiled. "My poor, trapped little bird." He leaned forward, his hands pressed to the tree trunk on either side of her head. Ashley swallowed, the churning in her gut turning into something else. This was always the way it went, and she hated herself for it. "When will you fly away, aye, Ash?"

Just leave, she told herself. *You don't have to do this.* But when he took a step toward her, closing the gap between them, she didn't move, and when he pressed his body against hers, she didn't resist. Instead, when he kissed her neck, she let herself enjoy it. He was already hard, pressing against her with his usual urgency, and for a moment she wondered what did it for him: was it her, never quite able to resist revisiting what they had once had, or was it being out in the open, in the dark, hidden but not quite hidden enough? She slipped her hand under the waistband of his trousers, and he slid his hand between her legs.

Afterward, as they tidied themselves up, she noticed that Richard was quieter than usual, and that he was watching her closely.

"What is it?" She buttoned her shirt up with jerky movements. She always hated him even more after the act. "What are you bloody looking at?"

"Are you really going to be working with the police?"

She dropped her arms, leaving the shirt half-buttoned. "How the fuck did you hear about that?"

He shrugged, giving her his usual lopsided grin, but there was something off about it.

"Green Beck gossip," he said. "Nothing stays secret around here. Well, almost nothing. You're not really going to do it, are you?"

"Are you worried I'll lead them to your secret coke stash or something?"

Richard rubbed his hand over his beard, tugging at it slightly. His movements were tight, rigid; there was none of his usual triumph after they'd met up like this. A warm wave of dread rolled through Ashley's stomach.

"These kiddie murders . . ." He shook his head. "It's fucked up, that's all. I don't think you should get involved."

"I'm not getting involved—I'm just doing a PR stunt with the police. It's Aidan's idea, and Dad's going along with it." Ashley glanced back in the direction of the cottage. She could just make out the smudge of yellow light from a window. It occurred to her that if she shouted, her parents would never hear her—that was, of course, why she and Richard came to the field in the first place. "The whole thing is stupid, but"—she raised her hands and gave him a bitter smile—"as you well know, I have little bloody choice."

"It's drawing attention to yourself. Have you thought of that?" Richard came over to her. A few strands of black hair were stuck to his forehead with sweat. "Drawing attention to the killer. What if he doesn't want you doing that?"

Ashley looked at him. "What are you talking about?"

"Can you not just take advice from me for once without throwing it back in my face?" The anger that had been bubbling under the surface since he'd knocked on her door was emerging; in the moonlight, his eyes looked black. "But then you never could take the sensible fucking option."

"That's enough." Ashley turned away from him. "Do me a favor— next time you need to get off, go and bother one of your posh friends, all right?"

She strode away from him quickly, her neck prickling with anxiety, but he did not come after her. When she reached the edge of the field, she turned back to look for him, but despite the silvery moonlight, she couldn't see him. *He's just hiding behind the tree to freak you out*, she told herself. *Or it's just too dark. Your eyes are playing tricks.*

Feeling disgusted with herself, Ashley climbed the stile and headed back up the driveway to the cottage.

CHAPTER

7

ASHLEY PUSHED A sweet wrapper under the seat in front of her with her foot; somehow, she had not imagined the inside of an unmarked police car to be so untidy. Her father was in the seat next to her, dressed in his most imposing suit, the silver pentacle back at his throat. In the front passenger seat was DCI Kim Turner, a short woman with chin-length curly hair who had introduced herself to Ashley with a perfunctory smile that hadn't quite disguised the fact that she was clearly furious about the entire business. Driving the car was DS Eric Platt, a young Black man who had seemed bemused by the whole thing.

"Is there anywhere you would like to start, Miss Whitelam?" Turner asked pointedly. They had been driving for around twenty minutes, heading deeper into the National Park area of Cumbria. Ashley leaned forward in her seat. Over the last couple of days, she and Aidan had spent a lot of time reading up on the Gingerbread House Murders, taking in the number of victims, where their remains had been found, trying to find a pattern. It had made Ashley deeply uncomfortable, as though they were playing at being detectives, but at the same time it had fascinated her. As far as she and Aidan could tell, there appeared to be no correlation between where the children were taken from, and where their sad remains were left. The child they were specifically looking for today was Robbie Metcalfe, a twelve-year-old from Darlington who had vanished on his way home from school three weeks ago. The other seven actively being investigated by the police had been left in a variety of locations: on the banks of Troutbeck, in Esthwaite Water, just off the path up Fairfield Peak. Most of them had been found by traumatized hikers, and on one particularly unpleasant occasion, a family taking a paddle boat out for a spin. Privately, Ashley thought the police already had an excellent team of searchers in the number of tourists that swarmed the Lakes at all times of the year. If they hadn't found Robbie Metcalfe yet, she doubted she would do any better.

"Just keep heading north for now, please."

Her father reached over and squeezed her shoulder before fixing DCI Turner with a stern look. "It's best to let Ashley concentrate. She needs to become attuned to the spirit world. We will tell you when we need you to change direction."

Ashley caught DCI Turner and DS Platt exchange a glance before the car settled into silence once more.

After another fifteen minutes worth of driving around, Ashley leaned back in her seat, tipping her head against the backrest, closing her eyes. She heard her father shift in his seat, and she sensed the attention of DCI Turner settle on her once more.

"Is she all right?"

"She is communicating with the spirit world," her father said softly. "*Please* be quiet.'

With her eyes closed, Ashley went over the information they had collected over the last few days. What Melva had told her had indeed been widely reported online, and queasily hinted at in newspapers: that each of the children had been fed a strange variety of foods shortly before they died, barely giving them a chance to digest it. Richly iced sponge cakes, fatty pastries, biscuits and chocolates, pears, plums, and strawberries. Steak had even been found in the stomach of one of the young victims. The newspapers Aidan had trawled through had also reported that the cause of death for each victim had not been released by the police, but hints were dropped that it was something gruesome, something unthinkable. Websites, particularly the ones populated by amateur sleuths, were crammed with speculation about this:

stabbed, throttled, burned, dismembered. Aidan had brought out an old Ordnance Survey map, and they had marked on it all the locations where bodies had been found—the gingerbread children were scattered across the Lakes like bread crumbs.

With her eyes still closed, Ashley imagined them like dandelion seeds, floating high over the hills, skirting over towns and villages, seeking out the remote places, the high lonely places where it might take a day or two to be found. She opened her eyes.

"Here, please." She leaned forward again and put her hand on the seat in front of her. "I would like to stop here."

* * *

At the side of the road, there was a fence and a stile, marked with signs for a public footpath. Without looking at the two police officers, Ashley made her way into the grassy field beyond. At the edge, she could see a line of oak and hawthorn, and underneath her boots there was long thick grass that made each step oddly springy. It was late morning by that time, and the birds were calling from all around; she could hear blackbirds, finches, even the ghostly call of a cuckoo. It was a beautiful place.

There is nothing bad here, she thought, distracted. *How could there be?*

"Where are we?" she asked her father in a low voice. He had been keeping track of their journey on his phone.

"Near Great Worm Crag," he said, stuffing his hands in his pockets and sniffing noisily. He made her think of a horse. "East of Devoke Water."

"Can we help at all?" DS Platt was making his way over to them, taking big strides to get over the thick grasses.

"Need us to do anything?" DCI Turner was by the fence, her arms crossed over her chest.

Ashley smiled at her, squinting into the sun. "Thank you, but I'm fine. I . . ." She turned to look out across the field to the hills beyond, which rippled like enormous dunes in the ancient landscape. "I will do what I can to connect with the spirit world. I can feel something nearby, but I don't know yet if it is Robbie." Saying the kid's name gave her a tight, sick feeling in her chest. She remembered what she had said to Aidan in the green room while their father argued with the bar manager outside: *If I were a decent person, I wouldn't have a job like this.*

She took out the photograph from her pocket that DCI Turner had given her. Robbie was a stocky-looking lad with brown hair that stuck up in awkward waves. In the photograph, he was standing next to a table laden with party food—little sausage rolls, pineapple and cheese, colorful biscuits and cakes. There were a bunch of other kids in the background. Was this the children's home where he had lived before going to his foster parents?

For a time, Ashley walked slowly around the field, stopping now and then to close her eyes, as though thinking deeply. She made sure to face the police officers once or twice, so that they could observe her doing this. Eventually, when her back began to prickle with the discomfort of being watched, she stopped and shook her head. DCI Turner and DS Platt were both looking at her, a flat expression of dislike clouding Turner's features.

When Ashley went back to the car, she could see that the woman was tense, almost bubbling with the need to say something. She paused in front of the detective and prepared her mildest expression.

"Was there something you wanted to say to me, DCI Turner?"

A few feet away, she heard her father blow more air through his nose. He would have words with her later about this.

The other woman smiled tightly. "I've been told to help you, Miss Whitelam. What I think or feel about that is irrelevant."

"You don't think this is worthwhile?"

DCI Turner gave a flat, toneless laugh.

"As relevant as asking a banana for the lottery numbers."

Despite herself, Ashley smiled. "I've been called a lot of things over the years, but a banana is new, at least."

The policewoman held up one hand, palm out. Over by the car, DS Platt was studiously looking off down the road.

"You can hardly blame me for being skeptical, Miss Whitelam. While I am here with you, I am not following more . . . credible leads. DS Platt has, I know for a fact, a whole stack of tips to go through from the phone line."

Ashley dropped her eyes, ashamed. The heat that was always waiting deep in the center of her flooded outward, making her scalp prickle. Even so. *If I am a fraud, and they know I am a fraud, yet they still waste this time on me . . . what does that make them?*

"Those credible leads don't appear to be getting you anywhere, Detective Chief Inspector," Ashley said. She lifted her eyes to meet the other woman's, and was viciously pleased to see a flicker of real anger there. "Isn't it right to try anything you can to bring poor little Robbie Metcalfe home?"

Back inside the car, they drove on in a simmering silence. They stopped three more times in locations that weren't quite randomly chosen—she and Aidan had reasoned that since the dump sites seemed to have nothing in common, it made sense to look at places where nothing had been found so far—and by the late afternoon Ashley told the police officers that she was sorry they hadn't been more successful, but she had exhausted her connection to the spirit world and had to rest. Turner looked disgruntled and Platt looked relieved. Neither of them had objected.

Driving back toward Green Beck, where the officers had offered to drop them off, Ashley sat and looked out the window, watching the familiar fells grow closer. She was already thinking about the next step in this stupid plan of Aidan's. He had arranged for interviews with a couple of local papers, and she was trying to decide how failing to find anything could be spun into something mysterious and ominous. Perhaps she could tell them that she had felt Robbie's presence, but that he had been too shy to make proper contact. Did that commit her too strongly to the idea that the boy was already dead? Or, she could tell them that the landscape of the Lakes was particularly haunted, making it difficult to find one ghost among many. She liked this idea, and she was smiling to herself faintly when she happened to glance out the window as they made their way down a curling country lane.

To her left, a long stretch of ancient forest was pushing out toward the road. The earlier autumnal brightness of the day had faded and a light rain was beginning to fall, giving the trees a rich darkness that Ashley could almost smell even inside the car. Standing against the green and red shadows of the forest, bright against the tree line, were several dark figures. Initially, Ashley took them to be the usual Lakes hikers, dressed in dark waterproof coats. But as they drove on and she saw more and more of them, she realized that they weren't moving. Smudged pale faces were turning to watch the car as it passed.

The Heedful Ones.

Ashley sat up, her body rigid. Her throat felt closed with something thick and poisonous. She hadn't seen the Heedful Ones in eighteen years—had long since, in fact, assumed they had been no more than a weird mental blip from childhood, a kind of imaginary friend she had believed in too much—but there was no doubt what they were. The farther they drove along the lane, the more of them there were, their long arms hanging loosely by their sides, pale hands like dead spiders.

Ashley leaned forward in her seat, eyes glued to her window. She was vaguely aware that she wanted to be sick. *Am I losing my mind?*

Her father gave her an odd look.

"Ashley, are you all right?"

And still the Heedful Ones appeared, looming under the tree line. As she watched, their numbers grew and grew until they were a crowd—a crowd of mournful, dusty figures, bodies like shrouds, dark holes where their eyes should be.

I've never seen so many, she thought. *Never so many in the same place. Not since . . .*

The car was about to turn off the road and head back onto the highway, because of course no one else could see them. Before she even knew what she was doing, Ashley reached forward and grabbed DCI Turner by the shoulder. She grasped a handful of the woman's blazer and yanked at it, causing the woman to turn sharply in her seat.

"What are you playing at?"

"Stop! Stop the car. I have to get out."

All of them were looking at her now. Even DS Platt had taken his eyes off the road. Outside, the Heedful Ones were moving away, into the trees.

"Now then. What's the matter, Ashley?" Her father's tone was dangerous. It was the one he used when she embarrassed him in front of someone.

"For fuck's sake, I have to get out." The car had slowed, so Ashley yanked at the door handle and half jumped, half fell out onto the road. There were shouts from behind her, and she even felt her dad's hand brush across her back, but she was already off, heading for the woods across the scrappy band of grass. The last of the Heedful Ones were just vanishing into the thick line of oak and Scots pine.

"Miss Whitelam!" DS Platt sounded worried, but Ashley did not look back. Instead, she followed the pale forms of the Heedful Ones deeper into the woods, which was immediately harder than she was expecting. There was no path here. Instead, there was a strangled thicket of gorse and holly that easily came up to her knees, and in some places her waist. Ashley crashed through, gritting her teeth against the thorns and branches that scratched at her bare hands, and the water that immediately sank into her boots and jeans.

The Heedful Ones were all around her, all heading in the same direction. Her heart was beating so hard that her teeth seemed to throb. Ashley found herself going slightly uphill; she had to grab onto the gnarled trunks of black poplar trees to keep up with her ghosts. Eventually, they came to a little pocket of clear space, the ground under her boots slippery with emerald-green moss and large gray stones. And that's where he was.

Robbie Metcalfe.

The boy lay on the stones, his skin blackened and wet. The moss had found a new home in places—growing across his eyelids, his cheek. One arm was missing. Around him, the Heedful Ones crowded, watching him, and watching her, their empty eyes accusing.

Barely aware of what she was doing, Ashley began to scream.

2004

RED RIGG HOUSE was the biggest house Ashley had ever seen—to her, "house" did not seem the right word at all. This building looked more like her school, with all its windows and the way it stretched out across the gravel. Their coach had stopped at the bottom of the driveway, and the children had all piled out, spilling into the warm spring sunshine in a cacophony of exclamations and questions. Mr. Haygarth, one of the supervisors, was trying to get them to form two lines, but it was a thankless task. The children were all from inner-city schools, most of them never having left the south of England before, and the landscape around them seemed fantastical. Great, dramatic hills had been visible through the windows all the way from the train station, and behind the house itself, there was what Ashley thought had to be a mountain; an immense craggy pile of grass and rock, gorse and wood. To Ashley, it looked like a place from a fairy story—it made her think of the school for boy wizards from a series of books she had read from the library. It looked like the sort of place Chrestomanci would live.

When Mr. Haygarth and his counterpart, Miss Lyonnes, had managed to get the children inside, they were finally awed into silence. The foyer of Red Rigg House was huge and beautiful, with darkly polished wood gleaming in all directions. The tiles under their feet were green and decorated with slyly smiling moon faces. At the back of the room was a great sweeping staircase that led up to the next floor, splitting off into the east and west wings. It was at the bottom of these stairs that a small group of people were waiting to greet the children; an old man, a middle-aged woman, and a boy and a girl who looked to be in their late teens—perhaps two or three years older than Ashley herself.

"Here we are," Mr. Haygarth was saying. He was a twitchy young man in his twenties with a strawberry-blond beard and a tendency to blush intensely at a moment's notice. He was already bright pink with the stress of getting the children into the house. "Children, this is Lord Lyndon-Smith, whose house this is, and who is very kindly allowing you all to stay for the weekend. Say hello."

The children muttered and shuffled their feet. Ashley found herself looking at the two kids on the stairs; like the house itself, it seemed to her that they belonged in a book, or a film. Both of them were strikingly attractive, with the same silky black hair and creamy skin. The boy was slightly taller than the girl, who looked enough like him that they had to be siblings, and he was wearing a pair of dark gray trousers with a pale green shirt. Ashley couldn't believe a teenager would wear trousers outside of a school day. The girl was slim and beautiful, with big dark eyes and a pink stain to her lips. She was wearing a crisp white blouse under a short, dark blue velvet jacket, and she was also wearing trousers, with a narrow silver belt at her waist. The entire outfit made Ashley think of the strangely dressed little men that waved sheets of red fabric at enraged bulls.

"Welcome, you are very welcome," the old man was saying. He was short and rather egglike, with a pair of round spectacles on the end of his nose. He was beaming at the children, apparently delighted. "These are my grandchildren, Richard and Malory." He nodded to the two teens, who looked as if they would rather be anywhere else. "They will be hosting you. And this is my daughter, Biddy."

There was a ripple of laughter at this, and the middle-aged woman in the middle of the group frowned slightly. Of all of them, Ashley mistrusted this one. She had a narrow, pinched face and rigidly curled hair that made Ashley think of an old, much-hated prime minister.

When the pleasantries were over, the children were ushered out of the foyer and up the stairs. Malory Lyndon-Smith led them through the east wing, down dark-paneled corridors lined with framed paintings and small tables holding vases of fresh flowers. Eventually, they came to a large high-ceilinged room at the far end of the wing, which contained two neat rows of beds lining the walls. Long windows looked out onto the towering hill behind the house, and Ashley's shoes sunk into the soft red carpet. Everything was very clean and very neat, yet the room made her uneasy. She looked around, thinking she might spy one of the Heedful Ones, crouched in a corner or standing half-hidden by a curtain. But there was nothing. Mr. Haygarth was encouraging them to pick a bed, so Ashley wandered over to one and put her rucksack at the foot of it. Around her, the kids who had come with others from their schools or who had made new friends on the coach journey were excitedly rushing to claim bunks next to each other. Ashley watched them with a familiar pain in the back of her throat. She did not make friends easily. Most of the time it felt simpler to keep quiet and pretend that she was happier alone.

"This room used to be for convalescents."

Ashley turned, surprised to see the girl, Malory, standing beside her. Up close, the teenager was even more arresting. There was a tiny mole under her left eye, which drew more attention to the sooty thickness of her lashes.

"It was?"

Malory looked at her closely.

"Do you know what 'convalescent' means?"

"A sick person," said Ashley. "When you're ill for ages, and it takes a while to get better. I'm not an idiot just 'cause I'm from London."

Malory raised her eyebrows, impressed. People often were impressed with Ashley's vocabulary, which seemed to range far and wide and included words most fourteen-year-olds weren't familiar with. When she had been little, one of Ashley's favorite parts of school was the Word Wall and the Word Tin. There had been a stand in the corner of her classroom with hundreds of words written on thick cardboard tabs. Every day, the children would go to the wall and choose five words to take home and learn, either on their own or with attentive parents. Ashley had zoomed through the wall, getting the teacher's permission to take extra words, until eventually the teacher herself began writing out new ones, just for Ashley. It was how she had learned what "heedful" meant, and how it might apply to the strange figures she saw everywhere, their blank faces always watching.

"After the First World War, some of the soldiers that came back had shell shock, and for a while, Red Rigg House was one of the places that they came to get better. What's your name?"

It took Ashley a moment to answer. She was imagining the soldiers, still in their uniforms, lying prone in the dormitory beds. They were missing arms and legs; they were crying for their mums.

"Ashley. My name's Ashley Whitelam."

"Do you know anyone here, Ashley?"

Ashley looked up at the older girl, that tight feeling growing in her throat. She didn't mind not having friends, not really, as long as no one else noticed.

"No," she said, very quietly.

Malory smiled. "Don't worry." She reached out and took hold of a length of Ashley's pale hair, running it gently through two of her fingers. "I'll keep an eye out for you."

9

"**I**'M TELLING YOU, I don't know anything about it. How could I?"

Ashley curled her hand around the beaker of water DS Platt had given her. She was sitting at a small gray table in a small gray room. DS Platt and DCI Turner sat opposite her, a shallow pile of papers in front of them. At the top of one page, Ashley could see the name of the boy she had found in the woods. Her eyes were drawn to it. *Robbie Metcalfe*.

"Normally, when someone takes us to a body, Miss Whitelam, it's because they know plenty about it." Turner sat rigid in her chair, her shoulders so tense they were nearly up by her ears.

"Is there anything you'd like to tell us?" Platt asked softly.

"Only that this has been a pretty awful day and I'd like to go home."

"Do you really expect us to believe that you just picked a random place and that was where Robbie Metcalfe had been left?" Turner leaned forward in her seat. Underneath her freckles, she was pale. "That you had no prior knowledge whatsoever?"

Ashley shook her head, smiling slightly. Ever since she had found what was left of the boy, her heart had been beating rapidly, strong and fast enough that she could feel her pulse in her eardrums, in her gums. How long could her body keep it up?

"I'm a psychic, DCI Turner. That's the whole point of being a psychic. It's all in the job description. The ability to pluck information out of the air, to be guided by spirits to a place of truth." She thought of the Heedful Ones, their smoky bodies flocking into the tree line, and she coughed, a hint of bile at the back of her throat. *Why were they back?* "All I've done is exactly what I said I'd do. Now you're acting surprised that I did it."

DCI Turner made a strangled noise in the back of her throat and leaned back again. The detective was angry because she was frightened. Ashley had seen the attitude before on a couple of unfortunate occasions—when a reading had struck an unexpected chord. It was an effect she usually tried to avoid. When she eventually phoned Aidan to let him know just how successful his idea had been, her brother laughed, assuming she was making some sort of terrible joke. When she finally got him to understand that she had indeed found the body of Robbie Metcalfe, he was silent for almost a minute. When he spoke, his voice had a strained, frightened quality to it. Her father had been the first to reach her through the trees, crashing through the undergrowth like an enraged bear, and even he had been struck silent by the sight of the dismembered boy in the forest dirt. He had looked at her, an expression on his face she knew she would not soon forget—he had been horrified, frightened. Frightened of *her*. Since then, however, he had gone into full protection mode; when the police insisted she come back to the police station and wait, he came back with her and then drove to Ulverston to consult with their lawyer.

She glanced at her watch. It was nearly 10:00 PM.

"Perhaps you could make this easier for us to understand," Turner said eventually.

"What do you mean?"

"Explain the process to us," Platt said, his tone incredibly reasonable, as though he were asking her to fill in a form. "How did you go about finding the body?"

Ashley pressed her lips together. The Heedful Ones flickered through her mind's eye, their movements too quick, too angular.

"I . . . Robbie's spirit reached out to me," she said. She took a big gulp of water and placed the beaker carefully on the table. She did not look at the two police officers. Could she tell them instead that it had been a weird coincidence? Would they be any more likely to believe that? "I had thought that I had failed, because we'd been looking all morning and I'd felt nothing, but then, just as we passed that road . . ." Ashley cleared her throat. "I felt him there, in the dark. He wanted to be found."

"And you just happened to find that tiny space where he was hidden, amongst all those trees?"

Ashley forced herself to look up at the woman. "You asked me how I did it. And I'm telling you."

"Are you protecting someone, Miss Whitelam?" Turner's voice was quieter, as though inviting Ashley to confide in her. "Someone you're close to?"

"People will phone in anonymously sometimes," Platt added. "When a member of their family has done something wrong. Could this be your version of that?"

"A member of my family?" Ashley raised her eyebrows. "What are you talking about?"

"Your father is a man with an interesting past," said Turner, looking down at the papers in front of her.

Turner took the first page off the pile, and Ashley caught a glimpse of a very old picture of her father, from the bad old days. Her heart began to beat even faster, almost seeming to crash against her ribs. Faintly, she was aware that she was very close to being sick. *How had they found that so quickly?*

"You still live with your parents, don't you, Ashley? And you're thirty-two years old. It can be difficult to stand up to someone when you have to share a home with them. Perhaps this is your way of escaping him?"

Ashley forced herself to laugh, although it was little more than a short, ugly sound in her throat. "Oh, here it is. My dad has been harassed by the police before, and none of the charges stuck then either. I think I've had enough of this."

She stood up, a little unsteady on her feet. Reluctantly, the two police officers stood too.

"You can, of course, leave," Turner said stiffly. "But if there's anything you know, Ashley, I strongly recommend you tell us now. It'll be better for you in the long run."

"Thank you so much for the advice." Ashley snatched up her bag, her head swimming—how long had it been since she had eaten anything?—and left the small gray room.

She made her way to the doors of the police station with her head down, concentrating on not being sick, so she did not spot the crowd of people waiting outside until she was already out in the cool air. At once, a number of men and women surged forward. They were carrying microphones and TV cameras; some of them were wearing TV makeup and had expensive haircuts, and others—the ones behind the cameras—looked as though they'd just rolled out of bed.

"Ashley Whitelam, can you tell us how you found Robbie Metcalfe?"

"Has the body been officially identified?"

"Did you speak to his ghost, Ms. Whitelam?"

"Ashley! Ashley, look this way, love, if you could . . ."

Horrified, she threw herself through the crowd, using her slim frame to slide between people, her long, pale hair hanging in her face. Hands grabbed at her arm once or twice, and she wrenched herself away violently, until she reached the far side of the crowd. The press took more photos as she went, but as a group, they seemed reluctant to leave the front of the police station.

Her own car was parked down the road a little, and when it came in sight, she felt a wave of relief that made her head swim. She placed her hand on the door handle and briefly rested her forehead against the glass.

What a day. What a fucking day.

When she closed her eyes, she saw him again. A boy who'd once had a family and had gone to school and been alive. Now he was something that was a part of the forest floor, a thing that had been taken and accepted by the green place even as the close attentions of insects and other scurrying things had slowly taken him apart.

She opened her eyes, and that was when she saw the piece of paper stuck under the Parma Violet's windscreen wiper. She plucked it out and unfolded it, her hands trembling slightly.

The note said, *I love this car! And I'd love to get your side of the story, if you have time to speak to me. Please get in touch.* There was an email address underneath—freddiem@murderonthemindpod.com—and a mobile phone number.

Frowning, Ashley put the note in her pocket and got into the car.

10

A T HOME, ALL the lights in the house were still on, and as soon as Ashley let herself in, her mother appeared, fussing around her like a moth around a lamp.

"Ashley? Ashley, what happened? Are you all right?"

As usual, when faced with her mother's shrill panic, Ashley felt herself draw away from it, her own raw emotions carefully packed away and hidden. She forced herself to smile, even though all she wanted was to go to bed and cry in the privacy of her own room.

"Mum, I'm fine." Realizing that this was a painfully obvious lie, she added, "I mean, it's been a horrible day. But I'm all right."

"Are you hungry? I can warm you up some dinner."

Ashley let herself be drawn into the kitchen, then watched helplessly as her mother shoveled a portion of shepherd's pie onto a plate and then into the microwave.

"Where's Dad?"

Her mother seemed to shiver, and she ran her hands up and down the sleeves of her jumper.

"The phone kept ringing. People from newspapers, TV, all of it. I stopped picking it up in the end."

"What?" Ashley thought of the crowd of reporters outside the police station. She was lucky they weren't camped outside the house, she realized. "Fuck me, what a mess."

"My angel, *please* don't speak that way."

"Sorry. Where is Dad? Is he back?"

The microwave dinged, and her mother placed the steaming plate of lamb mince and mashed potato in front of where she sat at the breakfast nook. Ashley picked up a fork and then looked at the food, her stomach churning.

"Your father." Her mother's voice was flat. "Yes, he came back. All of a . . . all of a tither. You know him." She rubbed her fingers compulsively on a tea towel, her mouth thin with distaste.

I know him, Ashley thought. *What will this be to him? An awkward scandal? No. Free publicity more like.*

"He went back out again though. I didn't ask him where."

Helen Whitelam had learned many years ago not to ask her husband where he went at night.

"It's all over the news, you know, that the little lad has been found." Her mother was twisting the tea towel in her hands now, wringing it back and forth like the neck of a chicken. "And I thought, thank God, thank God my angel was there to bring him home."

Ashley thought of how the moss had been growing merrily across his cheek. She put the fork down and pushed the plate away.

"Mum, I don't think I can eat this. I'm sorry. I'm just going to go to bed."

At that moment, the door slammed, and they heard the familiar sound of Ashley's father stomping down the hall. He got to the kitchen and stood for a moment, glaring at them. His eyes looked watery.

"I'm not sure I know what to say to you, girl," he said eventually. "How did you do it?"

"Dad, I . . ."

"Because if someone's giving you tip-offs, you'll have to tell me. I've spoken to our solicitor, and if we share this information with the police up front, it might clear up some of the mess you've made."

"Tip-offs? No one is giving me tip-offs!"

"Then what?" He took a step toward her, his hands curled into fists by his sides. Ashley couldn't tell if he was angry with her or frightened of her.

"I . . ." Ashley shifted in her chair. "I saw something."

"Saw what?" He scowled. "You can't have seen the poor lad from the road."

"No, I mean, I saw . . ." How could she possibly explain this? "I saw shapes, figures. Shadows. Crowded around the trees."

For a long moment, no one said anything at all. Ashley listened to the hum of the fridge. Heat was prickling across her back.

"You're seeing the angels again," her mother said brightly into the silence.

"No." Logan took another sharp step toward Ashley, almost as though he meant to strike her. His face had turned red. "Not this bloody nonsense again. I'm not having it. I will not have it."

"My mother used to see the angels too," Helen said softly, just as though Logan hadn't spoken. "Did I ever tell you that, Ashley? When I was little, she talked about them all the time."

"Yes, and your fruitcake mother ended up in the looney bin," Logan snapped. He pointed at Ashley with one thick finger. "We had all this nonsense when she was a kid! I won't have you telling these lies again, Ashley."

Despite herself, Ashley laughed. "You could have fooled me, given that's how we make a bloody living!" She stood up from the table, the chair screeching over the kitchen tiles. "I'm telling you the truth, Dad. The Heedful Ones, they're back. They showed me where the kid was."

"Angels," Ashley's mother added quietly. "They're *angels*. That's what my mum called them."

"You will shut up about your bloody mother." Logan turned his furious gaze on Ashley again. Sweat had beaded on his shining scalp. "You've had a difficult day, Ash, so I'm going to let this slide. Go to bed, get some sleep. In the morning I expect to hear some bloody sense out of you. Right?"

Ashley froze, swallowed hard, then nodded. This was always the way it had been with them. It had been a mistake to mention the Heedful Ones at all. Her mother looked at her with wide, bloodshot eyes, the tea towel still twisted around her pink fingers. Under the bright kitchen lights, she looked like a lurid mannequin.

Up in her own bedroom, Ashley closed the door and then locked it—the lock on her door was another hard-won concession, one that she was only supposed to use during the day and never at nighttime. She went and opened the window and stood by it, letting the cool air from outside move against her skin until she had goose bumps. Then, she took her phone out of her pocket. She had several missed calls from Aidan, so she called him back.

"Bloody hell, Ash. Are you all right?"

Ash laughed softly. Speaking to Aidan was easier. "I've had better days. Who would have thought your plan would be quite so successful? The police certainly weren't expecting it, I can tell you that much."

"Shit. I am sorry, Ash."

"What are you apologising for? You could hardly have known I'd actually find him." *You couldn't have known*, Ash repeated to herself. She thought of DCI Turner asking if she was protecting anyone, and she shook her head. "Dad's having kittens, as you can imagine."

"*How* did you do it? I've been thinking about it all day, and I can't get my head round it." Aidan gave a hoarse bark of laughter. "I mean, fuck. You really are the prodigy of the family."

"I don't know." Ashley thought of trying to tell Aidan about the Heedful Ones, but the idea of him dismissing her the way their father had was too much. He had not believed her when they were kids, and he wouldn't believe her now. "I had a . . . hunch."

"A *hunch*?" This time Aidan laughed properly. "I never thought you'd actually find the kid. Or anything useful. I thought we'd generate some publicity, get some more punters in, try a few more police jobs, go from there. You've managed to skip that stage and propel us straight into the big time."

Ashley frowned. "What do you mean?"

"Ah." Aidan sighed. "He didn't tell you? Dad's on the case. He's been arranging interviews with newspapers, TV people, you name it. You're in for a busy week."

"Fuck." Heat prickled across her back. "I don't want to do any of that. What is there to say? I found the poor little sod, and I'm probably scarred for life because of it." She made a strangled noise that was something like a laugh, but she felt close to crying. "I certainly don't want to relive the whole bloody thing over and over."

"Ash, come on, you'll have to speak to someone about it. I know it's awful, but"—his voice became very quiet—"it couldn't have worked out better, could it? Your name and face all over the news, you'll be booked in advance for years. Red Rigg House will be at capacity."

"A little boy *died*, Aidan." Ashley pressed her lips together.

"Yeah, and now his parents have a body to bury, thanks to you." Aidan sighed. "I am sorry, Ash, but I feel like this is something you can't avoid. People will want to know how you did it. So you'll have to come up with a good story."

"It was luck," she replied. "Just luck. Good or bad, depending on how you look at it."

She wished her brother good night, put on her pajamas, and crawled into bed. She took one of the small blue tablets Aidan had given her to help her sleep, and then she got out her MacBook and the slip of paper that had been under her windscreen wiper. The *Murder on the Mind* podcast had a swish-looking website, and it had feeds on Apple Music and Spotify, but so what? Anyone could make a podcast look professional these days. With a bit of poking about, she found that it had over 30,000 regular listeners, and that made her pause. Previous episodes covered a variety of old and new true crime cases. There was an episode on the mysterious deaths of three Girl Scouts in America in the 1980s that had recently been solved through DNA analysis, and an episode on the disappearance of a young man who had been seen walking into a busy bar on CCTV, only for him to never reappear. On the About section of the website, there was a brief biography of the person behind the podcast. Freddie Miller was an audio engineer from Maine with a degree in criminal psychology. From the photo, he was in his early thirties, handsome in that clean-cut and firm-jawed way Americans often were, slightly undercut by an infectiously goofy grin and a big pair of wire-framed glasses. To Ashley, he looked as though he ate apple pie every day and drank a glass of milk with dinner. It was difficult to imagine him chasing her for salacious details about the body she'd found. She looked again at his handwritten note. *I love this car!*

"What would Dad do if I went over his head?" It was an interesting thought. If Aidan and her father insisted that she had to talk to someone, perhaps it was only fair that she should get to choose who that someone was. She ran her finger across the trackpad and opened up Gmail.

11

2004

I T WAS A busy first day for Ashley at Red Rigg House. They had a
choice of activities: croquet or archery on the lawn, tennis or badminton on the tennis courts, or watercolor painting by the pond that
sat just under the thick trees at the bottom of Red Rigg Fell. Ashley—
never a particularly sporty child—chose to do painting, which turned
out to be the least popular activity. Only five of the ten easels were taken
up when she got there, and they had a wide range of paints, papers, and
brushes to choose from. At first, she felt stricken with choice. At school,
there was just the one large jar filled with stiff brushes that hadn't had
the poster paint washed out of their bristles properly and five or six big
squeezy bottles—the blue and black down to their last inch of paint.
Here, each child was given either a box of acrylic paints or a dainty set
of watercolors, each little pat of color freshly unwrapped. They were all
given pencils, erasers, and big sheets of white paper too.

"Now tape your canvas to your easel with the masking tape." Lord
Lyndon-Smith's daughter, Biddy, was leading the class. She was wearing an apron splashed with paint. "I want to see what you make of our
pond. Don't be afraid to experiment!"

Ashley picked out her pencils and sketched out the pond,
then filled it in with green watercolor paint. She added trees, long

light-green reeds, and then, as an afterthought, a quick wash of blue for the sky. The last part was the mountain, and it was only when she picked up her pencil again to sketch out its outline—looming as it did over the woods—that she realized she didn't want to look at it. Something about it made her chest feel oddly tight, as though there was a clenched fist behind her ribs.

"It's just a big stupid hill," she told herself.

She made herself look. The huge green mass of rock and grass loomed behind the woods, jagged against the blue sky. Aidan had once shown her a dog's tooth he had found over at the dump, and Red Rigg Fell made her think of that; the top edge was uneven, with one large curving spike and then a number of smaller ones. The surface of the mountain was scrawled with what looked like scars, and she wondered what could be big enough and mean enough to wound a mountain. Reluctantly, she filled up her brush with black paint and placed it on the far left, meaning to trace the erratic outline of the mountain across her page, but she found all she could do was press it there against the paper. Runnels of inky paint seeped down her canvas, blurring and infecting the nice clean greens she had.

"Stupid hill," she said again. One of the children sitting near her, a boy with carroty red hair, frowned at her.

Ashley put the brush back in her jar of water and took a stick of black charcoal from the packet they had given her. Then, with deliberate black lines, she began to draw figures down by the pond, dark figures with smudged faces. This was much more interesting to her than any old mountain. She lived with these figures every day of her life. They waited on street corners, or clustered in the bin room in their block of flats. It was strange to see them out here in this green place, far away from the concrete and buildings she associated with them. She became quite lost in the project, and when Biddy Lyndon-Smith appeared at her shoulder, it made Ashley jump violently enough that she knocked over her jar of water.

"What *on earth* are those supposed to be?"

Ashley froze. The woman was making a face of deep disgust, as though she had trod in a fresh dog's turd.

"Well? Answer me, child. You've made a good start there, with the pond and the trees, and then you've just ruined it with these mucky marks."

Around them, Ashley could hear the other children sniggering. Her throat went dry.

"She's just expressing herself, Mum. Isn't that the whole purpose of art, or whatever?" Malory was there, her beautiful face smiling faintly.

Ashley felt a wash of relief.

"Oh really, Malory." Biddy rolled her eyes. "I might have known *you* would like it." The older woman reached over and snatched the wet paper off of Ashley's easel. There was a soft ripping noise as the tape tried to hold it in place. "You'll just have to start again, girl, and try and paint what you can actually *see* this time."

Much to her own horror, Ashley felt her eyes fill with hot tears. It wasn't so much the loss of her painting—even she knew it hadn't been very good—but the fact that she *had* been painting what she saw. She'd made the same stupid mistake she always made, eventually. She'd let the truth of the Heedful Ones out, just a little. She'd let it out into the light. And it had made her look stupid in front of the other kids. And Malory.

"*Mum.* Hey." Malory crouched down and put an arm around Ashley's shoulders. She gave her a light squeeze. "Do you want to go for a walk, Ashie? Come on. The woods are much more interesting than this stupid old pond."

Ashley nodded and stood. She wanted to get away from Biddy, from the other kids—she could feel them all looking at her, hiding smiles behind their hands.

"Malory, the child has come here for an art class," Biddy said, frowning. "Leave her be."

"They come here to have some fun," Malory said. She took Ashley's arm and smiled, but not before the younger child saw the poisonous look she shot her mother. "Come on, Ashie," she said. "I want to show you my favorite tree."

* * *

"Do these woods belong to you then?"

Malory looked amused by the question. The trees were thick on all sides and full of the new green life of spring. Underfoot, the ground was dark and wet, and the straggling branches of bushes clung to Ashley's jumper as though they wanted her to stay with them. She was glad to be there. There was a fresh scent in her nose that she had never smelled in London, and there were magpies chattering overhead.

"This bit of the woods? No. Beyond the pond belongs to the national park, although you wouldn't think that to hear my mother talk about it. Where do you live, Ashley?"

"In Lewisham. It's in London? It's nothing like this place."

"No," agreed Malory. "I bet stuff actually happens in Lewisham."

Ashley looked at the older girl's face, trying to read her mood. "You don't like it here?"

Malory smiled again, although there was a fragile look to it that made Ashley feel uneasy. Her mother had a similar smile when Ashley asked where her father was that evening.

"I suppose it seems daft to you that I might not like it. Living in such a big house, with all this space." She reached into a pocket and pulled out a packet of cigarettes. Ashley did her best to conceal her shock, but she couldn't quite stop her eyebrows raising as the older girl put a cigarette to her lips and lit it with a heart-shaped silver lighter. Malory took a long drag, the end of it glowing hot and yellow, then blew smoke through her nose in a kind of sigh. She offered the packet to Ashley. "You want one?"

Ashley blinked rapidly. This wasn't something she'd expected to be dealing with at all.

"I've never . . . I mean, I don't . . ."

"Give it a go." Malory shook the packet at her. "You're only a couple of years off being able to buy them yourself anyway. Here you can try them out safely." Malory grinned and held her arms out to either side. "I am your responsible adult!"

"Okay." Ashley took a cigarette, and Malory lit it. On her first breath, her lungs seemed to fill with hot, arid smog. She coughed until her eyes were running. Malory gave her a cheerful pat on the back.

"How'd you like it?"

"*Eugh.*" Ashley rubbed a hand over her eyes. The taste in her mouth was undeniably disgusting, but her head was swimming in a way that felt new and exciting. "Do you get used to it?"

Malory beamed. "You do, unfortunately."

They walked for a while, traipsing along a tiny muddy path while Malory made short work of her cigarette and Ashley did her best to take brief tugs from her own without coughing. She got halfway through it before she had to admit defeat.

"That's okay, just chuck it," said Malory. "You did well. I was sick as a dog when I had my first one. I thought Richard was going to have an aneurysm, he laughed so much. The prick."

Ashley looked at the shortened cigarette in her hand before chucking it in a muddy puddle. She was thinking about how her dad smoked all his roll-ups down to the nub, and how her mum was always complaining about the price of her weekly packet of Silk Cut.

"So, you're rich," Ashley said, aware she was being blunt but unsure how else to say it. "That must be nice."

Malory laughed, and Ashley smiled. Malory's laugh was a big, bright thing. It was the moment that Ashley began to love her, just a little.

"Red Rigg isn't always a nice place to be," she said. "And Green Beck, the village down the road, it's not all fudge and afternoon tea. Sometimes it's a lot harder than you think, growing up here."

There was a rustling of leaves nearby, as though something large had crashed through a bush, but Malory didn't seem to notice. Ashley looked around, but the place looked green and identical to her. She wouldn't have been able to find her way out on her own, she realized.

"The big hill," she said slowly. "Behind these woods. I tried to paint it, but . . . there's something about it."

"Technically it's a mountain," said Malory. "Red Rigg Fell." She looked at Ashley out of the corners of her eyes. "What stopped you painting it?"

Ashley shrugged. "I don't know. It just gives me the creeps. Like it's an evil place. I know that doesn't make sense."

Malory gave her a sharp, delighted grin.

"I've always thought that too. Here we are, look." She pointed to a tree ahead of them that seemed to stand on its own, slightly set apart from the other trees. The trunk was warped and twisted, almost forming a spiral before low branches spread out their gnarled limbs. The leaves had serrated edges, and there was a deep hollow filled with old forest litter in the base of the trunk. Malory stubbed her own cigarette out in the mud and patted the thickly ridged bark as though the tree were an old friend. "It's a red mulberry tree. It's not native to these woods, so once upon a time someone came all the way out here and planted it. Doesn't it look like a witchy tree to you? Like a witch might live inside it?"

Ashley agreed that it did. Malory retrieved some paper and charcoal from her bag, and she showed Ashley how to make rubbings of the bark, filling their sheets with smudgy gray whorls and loops, like a giant's fingerprints. And then she showed Ashley how to make animals and monsters from the rubbings; adding a pair of eyes or ears, a set of claws and teeth. It was, Ashley thought, a lot more fun than Biddy's lesson.

"Do you live with your mum and dad, Ashie?" asked Malory. They both sat on the wide roots of the tree, sketchbooks in their laps.

Ashley hesitated before she answered. It was in her nature to want to give accurate responses, and truthfully her dad wasn't around all that much. There were weeks when he wasn't there at all.

"Yeah," she said eventually. "Most of the time."

"And are they nice to you?" When Ashley looked up in surprise, she saw that Malory was looking at her intently. "It's all right to tell me if they aren't, you know. You should always tell someone older than you if someone, even someone you love very much, is being horrible to you."

"Oh. No, they're okay, I guess." It was true that her mum and dad doted on Aidan, who they firmly believed was going to be their big football star one day, and she often wished that she received the same attention and enthusiasm. And even at fourteen, Ashley knew it was easier to ignore the bookish, shy child who preferred her own company. But that didn't feel like the sort of thing that Malory was asking about. "They argue a lot, and I wish they wouldn't do that so much, but they don't take too much notice of me."

Malory looked oddly disappointed in this response, and Ashley was trying to think of something else to tell her—some morsel of misery to complete this rich girl's picture of her—when the crashing noise came again. Ashley looked up, thinking that she had seen something in the space between the trees. Not a Heedful One, but a real, solid figure. She stood up, feeling uneasy, but there was nothing there.

"Yes, you're right," said Malory, standing up too. "It's probably time to head back in for lunch. It'll be sandwiches and crisps and pop, but you'll get something hot at supper, I promise. Look . . ." She took a packet of Polos out of her pocket and passed it to Ashley. "Eat a couple of these, will you? If my mother smells cigarettes on your breath, we'll both be for the high jump."

They began to walk back, crunching through fallen leaves on the muddy path. Ashley felt oddly proud; she hadn't made friends with anyone on the coach, but she had been interesting enough for Malory to want to spend time with her. That felt much more important. It felt special. At that moment, she happened to glance off to their right and she saw a man watching them, half-hidden by a row of younger, shorter trees. He wasn't wearing a shirt or trousers, and he had mud smeared across his chest and thighs. His hands were black with dirt, and his untidy hair was plastered to his cheeks with sweat. The look he gave them both was wild, and it was this last part that made Ashley afraid. She gave a little hop of surprise and grasped Malory's arm.

"What is it?"

Malory looked up, and Ashley was sure the older girl must have seen the man—his skin was shockingly white against the green, where it wasn't covered in dirt—but all she did was frown slightly and turn away. She squeezed Ashley's arm.

"Come on," she said. "We don't want to be late."

12

THE NEXT MORNING, Ashley made a point of getting up especially early. She showered, dressed, then headed downstairs to the kitchen. Her mother was still in her dressing gown, and she visibly startled to see Ashley already fully dressed.

"What are you doing up at this time?" she said, her eyes widening. "Is something wrong? Do you feel all right? I imagine you had nightmares all night, with what you saw yesterday."

Ashley took a piece of toast from her mother's plate and swept some black currant jam over it quickly. Helen Whitelam was very insistent on three meals a day, although she herself barely pecked at food.

"I'm fine, Mum, just got a lot on today."

"Indeed you have." Her father loomed in from the living room. He was dressed too, a charcoal gray waistcoat over a crisp white shirt. "We've interviews this morning, Ash, and the Bluebird Inn has called about having you back for an impromptu 'evening with,' can you believe it? When they were such snooty bastards about the event last time."

"I don't want to do interviews, Dad." Ashley took a few bites of toast and chewed rapidly. "I don't want to do any of that."

"What? This is a prime piece of publicity, Ash. You will not be wasting it. Do I make myself clear?"

"Publicity?" Ashley put the slice of toast down on the counter, her fingers trembling slightly. "I found a *dead kid*, Dad."

"Ashley!" her mother said sharply.

"Have you forgotten that part?" Ashley could feel her cheeks getting hot. Her father was scowling, the fingers of one hand picking at the strap of his expensive watch. "I actually walked into the woods, and I saw . . . I saw . . ." All at once, the color seemed to be draining out of the day. She leaned against the sideboard and took a deep breath, even as her mother fluttered around her anxiously. "I've been questioned by the police, Dad, because they think I have something to do with a dead kid. Don't you think I deserve a . . . a sick day or something?"

"You are in the business of the dead, Ashley," her father said evenly. "It's the business we've all been in since you—"

Ashley cut him off with a strangled laugh. "Unfuckingbelievable. I'm going out to get some fresh air." Now that she felt like she could move without falling down, Ashley strode past her parents to the hallway and snatched her car keys off the telephone table by the front door. Her father was following, making her think of an angry old bear roused from sleep.

"Your first interview is at ten," he said, his voice raised. "I will expect you back here at nine thirty so we can go over what you're going to say. Nine thirty *sharp*."

"Wouldn't miss it," Ashley muttered, before slamming the front door behind her.

*   *   *

Ashley drove out into a gray, damp morning, the clouds hanging heavy over the glowering hills. She passed near the road where she had found Robbie Metcalfe, noting the bright yellow police tape across the turning, and the men and women standing around in uniforms, drinking from flasks of coffee. There were no Heedful Ones to be seen there now. She turned her face away and kept her eyes on the road ahead.

She reached Birkrigg Common just as the day was starting to grow lighter, and in the small parking area, she spotted Freddie Miller immediately. Firstly, his was the only other car there, and secondly, there was just something so obviously American about him. He leaned against the bonnet of his car with his arms crossed over his chest and a wry smile on his face. He was tall, wide at the shoulders and narrow at the hips, and his curly brown hair was a little long on top; the boisterous Cumbrian wind pushed it and pulled it in all directions. Despite the drabness of the day, he was wearing a short-sleeved shirt, and Ashley could see well-defined muscles on his forearms and biceps. When she got out of the car, his face broke into that "aw shucks" grin she had noted from his website.

"Miss Whitelam?"

"It's me." Next to him she felt incredibly shrimpy and underfed, as if she'd been raised in the dark like a mushroom. "Freddie, right?"

"Thanks for meeting me," he said, before extending his hand.

Half amused and half charmed, Ashley shook it, noting that his hand was warm and dry.

"You must have had a pretty awful day yesterday."

"I did actually, yeah." She gestured to the grass beyond the parking area. It was already possible to see the standing stones. "Do you want to go and look at the stones? You may as well, while you're here."

"Sure, that would be neat."

They walked out over the grass, the bright strip of Morecambe Bay glittering in the distance. The stone circle was a small one, and Ashley felt a strange sense of defensiveness building in her chest as they neared them. Surely he would be expecting Stonehenge. He came from the land of Disney World, after all.

When they reached the stones, he stopped and looked at them in a considering way. He nodded. "They do have their own atmosphere, don't they?" he said. "I looked them up, and I'm sure you already know this, Miss Whitelam, but they could be as old as 1700 BC. Isn't that incredible? And here they are, just sitting out here."

"In the middle of nowhere." Ashley smiled. She was pleased that he had gone to the trouble to look them up. "Please, call me Ash. And thanks for coming out here. I know it's a bit . . . unorthodox."

Freddie shrugged. "I've done interviews in weirder places, I promise. Although I don't think the sound quality will be especially great." The wind chose that moment to pick up again, bringing with it the cries of a herd of nearby sheep.

"Ah. Well, actually, I'd rather you didn't record me this time." Ashley pushed her hair out of her face. She'd been in such a rush to get out of the house she hadn't tied it back, and now she was regretting it. "Can we just, I don't know . . . talk for a bit first? I'm not sure about any of this."

Freddie had his phone out in his hand, but he put it back inside his jacket.

"Of course, Ash. Whatever makes you feel comfortable."

Ashley nodded. She couldn't decide if she found his politeness annoying or endearing. "Tell me about the podcast. And why you wanted to talk to me."

"Well, for a start, I wanted to do more than interview you." He seemed to realize what he'd said a fraction too late, and as one hand went to straighten his glasses, she noted a faint pink blush to his cheeks. "What I mean is, I would like you to work directly with me on this series of the podcast."

Ashley blinked. "You want me to what?"

He grinned again, his face lighting up. "Ash, when I work on a case—I know what that sounds like. I don't mean to make out like I'm a detective or anything like that—when I work on a story like this, I like to find a deeper way into it. A unique angle. Right? It gives *Murder on the Mind* a selling point that other podcasts don't have. For a previous series, for example, I did some in-depth episodes on the Zodiac Killer. Have you heard of him?"

"Yeah." Ashley shifted from foot to foot. She could smell rain in the air. "I saw that creepy film, anyway."

"Right. So anyway, I found this group of code nerds in San Francisco—people who enjoy solving puzzles and ciphers and such. That was the thing about the Zodiac, he sent these weird puzzles to newspapers for people to solve. So, I took them all through the case myself, and I asked them what they thought about it, what sort of person they thought the Zodiac Killer was. I got them to look at the ciphers and see what they could get out of it. They had a good time." He smiled lopsidedly. "It gave the podcast extra color.

"Another time I did a ten-episode stretch on all the people that had gone missing on the Appalachian Trail. I ended up walking a portion of the trail myself, with this incredible older lady who had walked it five times. She knew everything there was to know about it. Yeah, she was a real character."

"So you think I'm a real character too?"

He nodded, pushing his curly hair back from his forehead. The wind came in a big rush across the grass, and with it came a spatter of cold autumn rain.

"I think you're perfect. For the podcast." The rain came again, harder this time, the wind pushing them both so insistently that Ashley stumbled, and they both laughed. "Do you want to go and sit in the car for a minute?"

"Yeah, it's getting a bit hairy, isn't it? We can sit in my car."

Inside the Parma Violet, Freddie looked almost comically large, his hair brushing the ceiling and his knees bent. He looked around the interior with real pleasure though.

"I sure do love this car."

"So, you think I'm perfect for *Murder on the Mind*?"

He nodded, becoming serious again. "Thanks to what happened yesterday, you're connected to the Gingerbread House Murders."

"Hmm. Not the most reassuring thing I've ever heard."

"I know, and I'm sorry you had to experience that." He looked at her then, incredibly earnest, and she felt something tighten in her chest. Earnestness was not something she was very familiar with. "Really, genuinely sorry. As glad as I am that Robbie Metcalfe's family have a body to bury, I'm sorry that you've experienced something none of us should."

"Yes. Well. Thank you." She shifted in her seat.

"So you found the missing child. But it's more than that. You live here, in Cumbria. You make your living from communing with the dead. Am I right?"

"We call them spirits." With them both in the small car, the windows had misted up, erasing the wet green world outside.

"Talking to spirits, right."

"Do you believe in it?" she asked quietly. "Do you believe in what I do?" She found she wasn't sure if she wanted him to say yes or no.

"I'm open-minded," he said easily enough, which Ashley noticed wasn't really an answer. "I've spoken to people with . . . unusual talents before, for this podcast, and I can definitely say you have a better claim than most of them. And there was the incident at Red Rigg House in 2004."

Ashley looked at him sharply, and he winced. "I'm sorry, it's part of my work to do this kind of research. Your life has been linked to tragedy before, is my point."

"You could say that."

"And I think you might be a deeply intuitive person. Intuition is a fascinating phenomenon. I've seen it over and over when I've been making the podcast—someone will just get a feeling about something, a tiny detail that sticks in their head and won't leave them alone, and sometimes that's all that's needed to break the case. If you'll agree to come on the show, we'll talk more about how you actually found Robbie Metcalfe, but I think it's got to be some breed of intuition." He took a slow breath. "If I'm talking a load of garbage, tell me now and it's no harm no foul."

Ashley sat for a moment, looking out over the steering wheel at the blank fog of the screen. Could the Heedful Ones be thought of as intuition? They certainly seemed to know things she didn't.

"So what are you asking me? Really?"

"Look into this case with me, for the podcast." He turned in his seat to face her. That faint blush across the tops of his cheeks was back. His eyes, she noticed, were green, like sea glass. "You're already involved. What I'm suggesting is that we work together. We'll look at the other missing kids, what happened to them and where they were found, and as we go, you will tell me what you're thinking and feeling about it all. That's it."

"I'm not a detective either," she said. "I might not have anything useful to add at all."

"I don't believe that," he said quickly. "But either way, it gives me the extra angle I'm looking for. What do you say?"

* * *

Ashley spent the rest of that day in a tiny pub she knew of called the White Stag, eating sandwiches and drinking cold drinks. Her phone rang several times, at one point so insistently that she turned it off.

When she got home, the house was quiet, no sign of either her mum or dad, but there was a big wicker basket on the kitchen table, covered in clear plastic and topped with a large red bow like a bouquet of flowers. Inside it, she could see a large selection of sweets—kid's sweets, like Curly Wurlys, refresher chews, bags of brightly colored sherbet and big swirly lollipops. There was a card on the basket, a message printed on it in a cheerful typeface.

For Ashley Whitelam. Eat up!

"Jesus. What a weird thing to send."

She pulled the cellophane off and dug around in the sweets. At the very bottom, there was something large and flat wrapped in tissue paper. Feeling scared but unsure why, Ashley tore the paper off and dropped it on the floor. Inside, there was a large gingerbread man, with eyes and a smiling mouth in bright red icing.

13

H I, EVERYONE, AND welcome to the *Murder on the Mind* podcast. Longtime listeners will know that I like to do what I call
interludes in between the main meat of the episodes. These are little
vignettes, if you will, that provide context and color for the stories
we're investigating, and let me tell you, the pieces we have for the
Gingerbread House Murders are some doozies. I don't want to sound
like some terrible tourist here, but England's history is *impressive*. And
weird. So let me tell you a little about Red Rigg Fell, the mountain
that sits just behind the house where Ashley Whitelam, my guest for
this series, had her disturbing experience in 2004.

There are the ruins of a small, ancient copper mine on the northern
side of the fell. The people of the Lakes are fond of the area's history,
and there are many places here designed to teach you about it—visitor's
centers, guided walks—but you won't have heard of this mine. It doesn't
appear on any maps, and the societies that preserve the history of mining in Cumbria . . . well, if they do know about it, they have decided to
pretend it doesn't exist. But if you go and look in the right place you can
find traces of it: holes in the ground, something that looks like it could
have been the foundation of a tower. The traces of human work on this
land are scratches on glass—faint, but impossible to remove.

The mine was opened in the late 1500s. A man called Sackloc
came from Germany to supervise it, and miners lived with their

families in cottages they built themselves, scattered around the hem of the fell. One of the families was the Milligans: John Milligan and his wife, Mary, and their two sons, David and Wesley. Wesley was too small and scrawny to go down the mine just yet—he would have to at least gain his twelfth year, his mother thought, before he could do that. But David went with his father, every day, to the beginnings of that excavation. Picture it: dark and cold and wet, the weight of a mountain hanging over your head.

Before gunpowder, before dynamite, mining was done by hand, a slow and backbreaking process, yet Sackloc was glad to have the project. It wasn't coal mining, which was considered much more dangerous because of the bad air that could wait for the unwary, trapped deep in the ground. No, the great difficulty with the copper mine was the water, the wet; with the River Keckle so close, and Green Beck not so far, the risk with the copper mine was always collapse, or drowning.

Young David Milligan hated the mine. He knew it the moment he first stepped on that craggy hill and saw the beginnings of the tunnel. He hated the shape of the fell, how it loomed against the sky like some great lousy animal, not asleep but waiting, and when his father first took him into the coffin level—that was what they called those first access tunnels—David felt as though someone had indeed walked over his grave.

Now David was a good boy, eager to help his father and his family. He did not want to shirk his duty, and was even less keen to admit that the place scared him, but when they returned from their work on that very first day, he told his mother and father that he did not want to go back. *"Let me do anything else,"* he told them. *"Let me go to any other mine, but not that evil place."* His mother struck him and called him every name under the sun, but his father, who had some idea of how terrifying the places of the underground could be, told his wife to leave the boy alone. He told David that he understood his fear, but that he'd get used to it. *"Soon,"* he said to David, *"being underground will be as normal to you as strolling down the lanes to church."*

David was quiet. He didn't think his father understood at all. Not really.

But he was a good boy, so he went back with his father the next day
to continue the work. Inside the hill, he was always a little frightened,
with the rock seeming to weigh down on his head, and somehow the
wet ground always looked to be moving just out of the corner of his
eye, but he did his best not to think on it too deeply. They worked
for months, scratching deep into the rocky flesh of the hill, burrowing like ticks, and the deeper they got, the harder the going. Other
men—men of forty and fifty years—also began to distrust the mine.
They reported strange noises, deep in the tunnels: knocking, where
there was no man to knock, and sometimes a deep kind of slithering, as
though something large was moving very slowly deep inside, dragging
itself across the stone. The men who had come up from Green Beck
village to work in the mine began to mutter that the place had a dark
history, but Sackloc, being a sturdy German Lutheran, would hear no
such superstition.

And one season there came a long period of rain. Nothing strange
about that, you should understand, not up here in the north of
England, but it went on and on. It was dangerous to work in the mine
when the weather was so heavy, so work stopped for a good long while.
Days and weeks passed, with the rain a great gray curtain, breaking
the banks of the River Keckle and Green Beck, blurring the edges
of Blindscale Tarn, sending fingers of smoky damp into every creak-
ing cottage at the foot of that mountain. Eventually it stopped, and
Sackloc, by now desperate to resume work, ordered the men back in.
Much too soon, as it turned out.

When the roof of the mine caved in, John Milligan was at its
mouth and young David Milligan—who had turned fifteen years old
two weeks before—was deep inside, along with ten other men. There
was a rumble, John would tell his distraught wife later, and a kind of
cough, as though the hill itself convulsed. Then, a wall of strange-
smelling air came out of the access tunnel, before a terrible crash of
falling rocks and timber.

John Milligan was one of the first back inside, desperate to find his
boy, but what he found was a wall of broken stone, still shifting and
unsafe. From behind this wall, it was possible to hear the shouts and

cries of the trapped men. John was sure he could hear David too, calling out in fear and horror, and he thought of how his son had begged not to go back inside the mine, how he had asked to do anything else.

Alongside the other men, John set to frantic work, pulling down the fallen stones, digging and scraping and clearing to reach the other side. They knew they didn't have long, because the air in the trapped space would turn bad quickly, but they also thought that the fall wasn't too deep; after all, they could hear the men's voices, in some cases so clearly they could make out single words. They worked all day and into the night, burrowing through the wreckage while listening to the cries of the trapped men, but the rock fall didn't end.

Some of the men, those who didn't have family behind the rocks, climbed out of the mine, filthy wet and ragged, to rest, but John kept going. As he did, he called to David, and he thought he heard David answer. With each rock removed, he thought, *This will be the one; here I shall see my son's face again*, and yet . . . The men worked for three days solid, clearing the rocks until they were sure they must be in the section where the men were trapped, but they never found them. The voices remained, growing quieter and stranger, until many of the miners began to say that they didn't think they ever heard the voices at all—that it had simply been the knocking and the sliding that the hill was known for. And in any case, the men could not still be alive. It was a fool's errand.

John Milligan never did give up. He insisted that he could still hear David, somewhere deep in the tunnels, and he continued his fruitless search until Sackloc himself closed the mine. The rich vein of copper they had been following had seemingly stopped, and despite all of his German common sense, he had also started to fear the place. Milligan's wife tried to get John to put his hopes in their youngest son, Wesley. David, she told him, could not still be alive, so deep underground, lost for months. And he would say, *"I can hear him, Mary. He's calling me from under the mountain."*

For five years after the cave-in, John Milligan wandered the red mountain, following the sound of his dead child. And one day, he never came back.

14

2004

THEY HAD A hot dinner that night, sitting at a pair of long tables in a great hall filled with the echoes of their excited chatter. Ashley sat between a girl whose name she didn't know and a boy who she had heard the other kids call Chris. Both of them took little notice of Ashley, instead chatting excitedly with their neighbors or the children across the table. They were full of talk about the activities they had done that day—the fishing, the archery, the tennis—and deep in her gut, Ashley felt a faint squirming of uncertainty, even jealousy. While she had been off walking in the woods with Malory, the other kids had bonded over piercing worms on hooks, or chasing tennis balls they had whacked over the high fences. She had felt special while she was with Malory, as though she'd been singled out, but now she felt even more isolated. The older girl was sitting at a separate table with her grandfather and her brother. Ashley had to lean back in her chair slightly to get a look at her.

"Are you gonna eat those or what?"

Ashley turned back to see Chris looking at her frankly, a fork jabbing in the direction of her plate. She had chicken nuggets and chips with beans, a longed-for feast at home, but the tension in her stomach meant she had barely touched them. Instinctively, she leaned over her plate and picked up her own knife and fork. She had an older brother, so she knew how to guard her food.

"Yeah, I am actually."

Chris gave her a disgruntled look and turned back to the boy on his left.

When the plates had been cleared, bowls of ice cream were brought out, and the noise in the hall grew even louder. Ashley snuck another glimpse at Malory and saw that the older girl was leaning forward over her own bowl of ice cream, her long dark hair framing her face. She looked sad. Belatedly, Ashley saw that her brother, Richard, wasn't in his seat; she looked around and spotted him at the other table, walking down the row with his hands behind his back. He was pausing now and then to talk to the children, and each time he did, a little pocket of quiet surrounded him.

The windows that looked out over the lawn were filled with early evening light, but there were still shadowy places in the hall. Ashley saw a Heedful One detach itself from the dark, its flickery, stilted movements especially strange amongst the color and noise of the other kids. She put her head down and concentrated on her ice cream, savoring the sweet vanilla and chocolate sauce.

At least there's this, she thought, swirling more sauce through the pale yellow ice cream. *At home, we hardly ever get ice cream, and never chocolate sauce, unless we had money for the ice-cream van.* Even so, as the chatter around her continued, she felt her cheeks grow warm with shame. *Why can't I just make friends, like I'm normal?*

"Enjoying the food, are we?" The voice cut through the general hubbub, and Ashley glanced up to see Richard, now at their end of the table. He looked tall and handsome and somehow sharp; his hair was brushed back from his forehead and the angle of his jaw against his throat was stark. He was smiling faintly, as though amused by something, but the look in his eyes was cold and hard. The kids nearest him were quiet, as though he were a teacher that had caught them talking. Richard moved closer to speak to them more directly, and Ashley couldn't catch what he said, but she saw one boy lower his head and another frown slightly. After a moment, Richard proceeded up the table, until he stood just behind and to the left of Ashley. He was a smudge of color in the corner of her eye, but his voice was clear and loud.

"That's it, eat up." Ashley felt his knuckles brush the back of her shirt as he curled his hand around the top of her chair. "All that free food," he said in a slightly lower voice. "You must love it." He leaned down until his head was at the same level as theirs, and his tone seemed to grow friendly even as his words dripped with scorn. "Get your chow, you little scroungers, eh?"

Ashley turned her head to glare at him, regretting it even as she did it, and he grinned at her and slung an arm around her shoulders. Shockingly, he was as hot as a stove, his fingers where he rested them on her arm hot enough to burn. Ashley felt herself instinctively trying to pull away from him, but there was nowhere to go.

"Oh, it's *you*," he said conspiratorially. "Ashley, isn't it? You don't look so special to me." He put his lips against her ear, and she felt his breath, hot as a furnace against her skin. "Do you think you're special, Ashley?"

Someone from across the hall called his name—his grandfather, perhaps—and he straightened up and stalked off. Ashley turned to watch him go, her throat tight with trepidation. The Heedful One that had been moving slowly around the hall peeled off and followed him out of the great room.

*   *   *

That night, Ashley lay in her narrow bed in the long dormitory room, listening to the other kids' whispers and giggles gradually die down as the lights were turned out. It was late, but she felt wide awake. The pillow under her head was too big and smelled wrong, and the quilt was stiff and scratchy. All she could think of was their cozy flat, so warm and so familiar. Normally, in bed she would have been listening to the sounds of Aidan's snores, the click and thump of her dad returning home from wherever he had been that evening, or the faint sound of her mother's voice as she talked to one of Ashley's aunties on the telephone. She missed them all acutely, so much so it was almost a physical pain in her chest—a hollow, scooped-out feeling just behind her breastbone. She wanted to go home. She wanted to go home *so much*.

As the other children gradually fell asleep, all she could hear was the wind wailing down off the fell behind the house, and the tick of some big clock somewhere.

Just close your eyes, she told herself. *Close your eyes and go to sleep.*

She found that she couldn't, though. To close her eyes would be to give up her vigilance, and the big dormitory was so long and wide, so much bigger than their entire flat. It had so much room for things to hide in.

You're being daft. There's nothing to be afraid of here.

And then, just as she really was starting to drift off to sleep, a thin yellow beam of light shot soundlessly across the room, splashing against the far wall. The door on the other side of the room had opened, just a crack. There was someone standing there, watching.

Ashley pulled the covers up to her neck. The door opened a little wider. It was possible to see a slim figure there, and in the brief wink of yellow light before he pulled the door shut behind him, Ashley recognized Richard's sharply angled face, although all trace of his previous smugness had vanished. As she watched, he came silently into the room and walked past a few of the beds, pausing at the foot of each one as though he'd forgotten something. Then, he bent over one of the beds in the row opposite Ashley's bed. When he came up again, he was carrying something in his arms. *Someone,* Ashley corrected herself.

Richard lifted the bundle in his arms closer to his face, although if he said anything, Ashley couldn't hear it.

He left the dormitory, shutting the door once more behind him.

15

WHEN ASHLEY WENT downstairs in the morning, her father sat waiting for her at the kitchen table, leaning forward over his folded arms. He looked as immovable as a granite gargoyle.

"Where the bloody hell have you been?"

Ashley paused in the doorway, not wanting to come any closer.

"I went out to clear my head. I needed some time by myself."

"I had Aidan out there looking for you, checking all your usual haunts. Where did you go?"

Ashley smiled bitterly, her heart beating faster.

"If I have a few last secret places that you and Aidan don't know about, why on earth would I share them?"

"Ashley, I had four interviews lined up yesterday. Four!" His big shovel-shaped hands clenched on top of the table, his knuckles turning white. "I had to cancel every bastard one of them."

"I told you." Ashley took a step into the room, feeling light, as though she were made of straw. If he reached for her, she thought she might just fly away. She wondered where her mother was. There was no sign of the big bouquet of sweets from the night before. "I told you, I didn't want to do any of that shit."

Logan Whitelam bared his teeth at her in a dry, humorless grin. "You made me look like an idiot, Ash. And you're chucking away perfectly good publicity! I won't have this behavior from you." He took a long deep breath, pushing away from the table, as though he were preparing to forgive her. "I've rebooked the interviews. Luckily, most of them were keen enough that they put aside the fact we messed them about. The first one is in an hour. Your mum is getting the living room ready to receive them."

"What? They're coming here?" Ashley backed out of the room again. "You gave them our address?"

Logan revealed his dry grin again, the one that meant he was getting one over on her. "What is it they say? If Muhammed won't come to the mountain . . ."

"For fuck's sake, Dad." Ashley turned and headed for the hallway, but the space on the sideboard where she usually left her car keys was empty. She stood stock-still for a second, a terrible dropping sensation in her stomach. *I'm an idiot. Why did I ever leave those keys where he could get to them? It was my freedom, and I just left them there for him to take.*

"If you're looking for your car keys," Logan called from the kitchen, "you can have them back when the interviews are done."

Despite everything, Ashley went to the front door and put her hand against the cold, frosted glass. She could still leave, she told herself, just put her coat and shoes on and head out—it would serve him right, if she made herself vanish for a second day. But the reality was, they lived in the middle of bloody nowhere. It was a good hour's walk to Green Beck, and that was the closest place with cafés, shops, and pubs; the closest place that she could hide out for the day. Besides, Aidan knew all those places, and so did her father. She wouldn't even reach Green Beck before one of them arrived, offering a lift back in their own car. Malory would come and pick her up, if Ashley called her and asked, but the thought of inviting dear Malory—sophisticated, genteel Malory—into the midst of what was likely to be an ugly family drama made her feel even worse. Freddie Miller, she supposed, might come for her too, but she had known him all of five minutes. What if her ugly relationship with her parents ended up being a splash of exciting "color" for his podcast?

Stiffly, Ashley walked into the living room. Her mother was in there, plumping pillows and fussing over the good armchair. The smell of polish was strong.

"Mum, please leave it." Ashley could feel all her energy to resist draining out of her and sinking into the floor. It wasn't worth the fight. "You don't have to do all this."

"Don't be daft," Helen Whitelam said, cheerfully enough. "We have to look our best, don't we? How are you feeling today?"

"I've been better," Ashley replied. "And now I suppose I get to relive all the horrors of finding that little boy. For the *publicity*."

Helen winced, but she came over to Ashley and took hold of her hands. When she spoke, it was in a whisper. "You have a gift, my angel. The same one my mum had. It's not an easy path you have to walk—God knows my mother suffered for it."

Ashley eyed her mum warily. Her grandmother had died when she was still quite small, and she only had a few memories of the old woman.

"What do you mean?"

Her mother squeezed her hands. "The . . . home, where she stayed. Things are better now, I'm sure, but back then, those places were brutal. And your nan, she was a delicate soul. You've always reminded me of her, you know. Your hair, your eyes."

Ashley blinked. She had, she knew, unusual eyes—one blue, one brown. Had she known that her nan had mismatched eyes too? She couldn't remember.

"What did she *see*, Mum? What made them put her in that home, or whatever you want to call it?"

But Logan coughed somewhere in the hall, and her mother startled, as she often did. She dropped Ashley's hands and moved away, plucking up a cushion and giving it a shake.

Helen had moved the good armchair in front of the big wooden cabinet in the living room, and had arranged all of her angel paraphernalia on the cabinet's shelves and alcoves. Cherubs with big blue eyes stood with the trumpets of heaven pressed to their lips; a tall sexless figure made of fine gray porcelain bowed its head under a halo of gold. There were no less than five framed embroideries claiming things like *The wings of angels are hope and faith* and *When in my heart I feel a tug, maybe it's an angel hug.* There were tiny wooden prayer boxes too, and on the shelf just above the top of the armchair, there was a glass frame containing a single white feather. Around about the time that Ashley's mother began losing her mind, she had found the feather on the concrete steps outside the block of flats where they used to live. She maintained it belonged to the angel that "gave Ashley her insights." Ashley glared at it dully. The gulf between the angels her mother insisted clamored around them at all times and the Heedful Ones was vast.

Ashley's mother stopped fussing with the armchair and turned to her daughter. She took a lock of her daughter's fine, pale hair and ran it gently through her fingers.

"You've less than an hour to get ready, love," she said. "Get in the shower, and I'll lay some clothes out on the bed for you."

* * *

Ashley sat in the good armchair, her back straight and her hands in her lap. She was wearing the baby-blue cashmere jumper her mother had picked out for her, and her freshly washed and dried hair lay softly against her cheek. She had arranged her face in the neutral expression she often used when communing with spirits on stage. The reporter leaned forward, her tanned face glistening with earnestness.

"Did Robbie Metcalfe speak to you directly, Miss Whitelam?"

Ashley let herself smile sadly. She was finding it difficult not to look at the camera, which was smaller and sleeker than she had been expecting. Her father stood in the doorway of the living room, as though he expected her to try and make a run for it, and was willing to take her down with a rugby tackle. Aidan was there too, out of shot on the sofa, watching everything with his quick, dark eyes. Her mother had gone upstairs to her bedroom. Having lots of people in the house tended to make her anxious.

"It's not quite as straightforward as that," said Ashley. "And not very easy to explain, I'm afraid. When I do my work on a stage or with clients, I am almost always working with the loved ones of the spirits themselves. The presence of a husband or wife, mother or father, left behind on the material realm will draw the spirits to them. Most of the time, they want to make contact, you see. But with poor Robbie Metcalfe, it was a much sadder situation." Ashley paused and swallowed. Her throat felt dry. "His spirit had come untethered from those who loved him, because he left us in such a violent and despicable way. So when I went out looking for him with the police, with DCI Kim Turner . . ." Ashley felt a small amount of pleasure at naming Turner—*If I have to go through this, I don't see why she shouldn't be humiliated too*—"I was casting a wide net, trying to find a lost, unconnected spirit."

The reporter nodded. Her eyes were a little glassy, as though on some level she couldn't believe the conversation she was having. *You're not the only one,* thought Ashley.

"And you did indeed find him, in your, uh, net. Can you describe to us what that was like?"

An image of the body flashed in her mind, black mold creeping across a slack face, one arm little more than a ragged stump. Ashley looked down at her hands, her hair falling forward to cover her face a little.

"It was a privilege to find him and help bring him back to his loved ones. His spirit is at peace now." For an awful, terrible moment Ashley thought she might laugh. Peace? Peace was a joke in the face of the horror that had been visited upon Robbie Metcalfe.

"So far, the police haven't named any suspects in the Gingerbread House Murders," continued the reporter. "Will you continue to help them with their investigations? Can you use your talents to help track down the killer?"

Ashley looked up and caught her father looking back at her, unblinking.

"Obviously I will do everything I can to assist the police, but I am simply one of many tools they will use to catch the person who hurt Robbie so badly. I have every faith in them."

* * *

When the last reporter had gone, Ashley's father closed the door on them with a grin.

"There, wasn't so bad, was it? That was a nice touch, throwing in a good word for the police at the end, useless bastards that they are. You're a natural at this stuff, Ash."

Ashley stood up, a little unsteady on her feet. Aidan came over to her and took her arm, trying to look her in the eyes, but all Ashley could think of was how she had sat there so neatly and so sweetly, her hands in her lap, talking about Robbie Metcalfe as though the whole thing hadn't been a publicity exercise to sell more tickets to the Moon Market.

"Ash, are you all right?" asked Aidan.

"Of course she's all right. She did brilliantly," said their father. "I knew she'd ace it if we could just get her to sit still for five minutes."

Ashley shook her brother off. She left the room and ran up the stairs, taking the steps two at a time before crashing into the bathroom. She dropped to her knees in front of the toilet and then noisily threw up. After a few minutes, when the sickness had passed, she realized that someone was watching from the doorway. Wiping her mouth on a towel, Ashley turned to see her mother there, as frail and as uncertain as a ghost herself.

"I told you not to eat all those sweets," she whispered.

"What are you talking about, Mum?"

"That big basket of sweets you brought home." She frowned. "What a silly thing for you to bring home. I threw the rest of them away, tipped the whole lot in the bin."

Despite herself, Ashley felt a flicker of anger in her chest. Standing up, she leaned against the sink.

"Why would you do that? They were mine. Someone sent them to me. You can't just throw my stuff away." *And you can't keep me prisoner here either.*

Helen Whitelam wrinkled her nose. "Don't be ridiculous. You're not a child." She moved back into the hallway. "Take that jumper off and give it to me to clean. You've gotten it dirty."

Ashley yanked the jumper off in a series of brisk movements, and in doing so realized that they were alone. Aidan and her father were both still downstairs; she could hear their voices, low and muffled, no doubt discussing her performance with the reporters.

"Mum." She balled up the jumper and passed it over. "Can you tell me about Nanna Maisie? About why she was in that home?"

Her mother took the jumper and folded it neatly with fingers that trembled slightly. "You know your dad doesn't like me talking about it."

"She was your *mum*," Ashley replied, some of the anger returning to her voice. "Talk about her all you like. What was wrong with her?"

"She saw things. Things other people couldn't see." Her mother glanced behind her, in case her husband had teleported silently up the stairs. She lowered her voice to the barest whisper. "When we were little, it was just one of her funny ways. She would tell us our guardian angels were watching over us, things like that. But as she got older, she seemed to become frightened of these things she could see. She would tell strangers in the street about it, warning them. My dad was embarrassed. She kept showing him up to the neighbors. And then one day, she went missing. We eventually found her at Euston Station, trying to get on a train with no ticket. She said the shadows wanted her to go north."

A terrible creeping heat had enveloped Ashley even as she stood in her shirt in the chilly hallway. *The shadows.*

"And what happened?"

Her mother shrugged. "My father got her help. That's all. You saw the home she lived in. I know you did. We took you to visit her."

Ashley did remember, through the cloudy lens of early childhood. She remembered a place that smelled always like sickness, an old lady with strong bony fingers who seemed to look at her too intently. Was that a vision of Ashley's future? Locked up and medicated?

They both heard Logan's heavy tread on the staircase, and in silent agreement they left each other on the landing. Exhausted, Ashley went back into her own room. She took out the bottle of tablets her brother had given her, shook two of them out into her hand, and swallowed them with a tepid gulp of water from the glass on her nightstand. The journal was where she had left it, tucked under some paperback books in her drawer, but by the time she had wrestled it out and found a pen, the tablets had begun to make her feel drowsy. She put it back in the drawer, promising herself she would add a few notes tomorrow. After that, she drew the curtains and crawled into bed.

CHAPTER

16

I N THE MORNING, Ashley got up before it was light out, taking care to lock her bedroom door behind her. She could hear her father moving around downstairs; he had always been an early riser. In fact, he hardly seemed to sleep at all. She cornered him in the kitchen, where he was smoking a cigarette out the back door. The look he gave her was speculative. Wary.

"What do you want?"

"My car keys." Ashley took a deep breath. "I've got things I need to do today."

Her father shifted in the doorway, his bulk briefly blocking out the brittle early morning light. He narrowed his eyes at her.

"Do you now?"

"Dad, I'm thirty-two years old." Even as she said it, a wave of humiliation moved through her. She didn't feel thirty-two; she felt like a sulky eight-year-old. "I can do as I please."

"Not while you live under my roof, you can't."

Ashley opened her mouth, ready to point out that she would happily live under her own roof, given half a chance, but Logan Whitelam talked over her.

"But you did well yesterday, Ash. We're proud of you." He reached into his pocket and pulled out her car keys. He weighed them in his hand for a moment before throwing them to her. "What are you up to today?"

"I'm going to meet Malory for breakfast at her office. Then, I have a few in-person appointments." *Which*, she thought to herself, *is technically true. I will be meeting Freddie Miller in person.*

"Hmm." Her father took another long drag on his cigarette before carefully blowing the smoke out the open door. Most of it wafted back in with the cold breeze. "Never understood your liking for that toff. A lot of airs and graces, that one." This was an old argument of theirs, and that morning, Ashley found it easier not to rise to the bait. "Anyway. Keep your phone on, will you? I might need you for more interviews later."

"Fine."

Ashley left him in the kitchen, clutching her keys in her right hand, vowing not to let them out of her sight again.

*   *   *

"I saw you on the local news last night," said Malory.

Ashley winced. She had seen the footage online that morning. In the interview, she had looked wan and washed out, her pale skin and hair seeming to fade into each other, like she was an old tea towel slung over her mother's plush dove-gray armchair. Even worse, the camera had framed her perfectly with the cabinet in the background so that all of her mother's angel shit was in the shot; seeing the little cherubs with their feathered wings made her flesh crawl. There was something obscene about them, made worse by the realities of Robbie Metcalfe's fate. She was glad to be away from the place. Malory's office in Green Beck was a kind of oasis, a place she could escape to for a glimpse of the normal world. That morning, they were drinking bad coffee and sharing croissants.

"What a shit show," Ashley replied in a low voice. Around them, Malory's small team of charity workers were answering phones, sending emails, and talking quietly. From where she sat, she could see several posters for the Moon Market. "Dad just couldn't resist. I had to remind him to give me back my car keys too, the bastard."

"Are you going to do any more? Interviews, I mean?"

"Not if I can bloody help it." Ashley paused, remembering Freddie Miller. "There is one guy I might speak to. He's American."

Malory glanced up from her computer screen, startled.

"American TV is interested in the murders?"

"No." Ashley snorted. "Well, I dunno—they could be. What do I know? This guy, he does a podcast. You know, one of those true crime things everyone is mental about these days."

"Oh." Malory leaned back in her chair. Her dark hair was as thick and lustrous as the day Ash had first seen her, standing at the bottom of the stairs at Red Rigg House. If anything, she'd only become more beautiful. "Are you sure that's a good idea? These things can get very popular. You could find yourself under even more scrutiny."

"I don't know. He seemed genuine enough." Ashley realized that she didn't really want to tell Malory that much about Freddie, and to her private shame, she suspected that was because she wanted to keep him to herself. She knew all too well what happened when she introduced handsome male acquaintances to Malory. The few boyfriends she'd had seemed to lose interest when rich, attractive Malory Lyndon-Smith appeared in their line of sight. "I'll see what happens, I suppose." She cast around for another subject. "How are the preparations going for the Moon Market?"

"I'm so glad you asked." Malory picked up her coffee cup and smiled at Ashley over the top of it. "I mean, I really am glad. I've been so worried that we've forced you into this, Ashie."

Ashley shrugged. "It's about time I got over it, I guess."

"Well, it's going to be great. All the vendors are booked in. We've got a special catering team at the house this week checking that our kitchens have everything they need. And as part of the charity's outreach program, we've selected a child from a low-income background to come and shadow me."

"You have?" Ashley forced herself to smile even as her stomach seemed to seethe with snakes. "What are they going to do at the Market? Surely kids will find all this occult stuff ridiculous. These days it's all Snapchat and TikTok."

"Not with our shitty Wi-Fi it won't be," Malory said dryly before reaching over to squeeze Ashley's arm. "I can see that look on your face, and I know what it means, Ashie. Please don't tie yourself in knots over this. It *won't* be like before. There is no chance of it being like before. Okay?"

"I know it's important to you," Ashley said quietly.

"The Market?"

"This stuff." Ashley gestured at the cramped office space. "You don't have to do any of this, but you do."

Malory tucked a loose bit of dark hair behind her ear and shrugged one shoulder. "You say that, but . . . I don't want to sound like an insufferable twat, Ashie, but I *do* have to do this stuff. The world I was born into, all the money and the land and the house, it's a ridiculous privilege. I *have* to give something back, or I just couldn't live with it. These kids, they deserve something better, even if it doesn't last."

Ashley leaned back in her chair, nodding seriously. "Saint Malory, it has a ring to it."

"Oh fuck off." Malory laughed. "I should be thanking your father, actually."

"Er. Why?"

"Because since you did those interviews, attendance at the Moon Market has shot up. We've sold all the rooms for those people staying the whole weekend, and day tickets have nearly sold out too. Face it, Ashley Whitelam"—Malory fluttered her eyelashes at her—"you're a star!"

17

ASHLEY DROVE TO Bowness-on-Windermere, where she met Freddie in a car park by the lake. From there, he insisted they take the ferry across to the other side. There were plenty of people around on the more populated side of the lake, but when they alighted at the Ferry House, numbers had dwindled significantly, and as they began to walk north up the side of the lake, they quickly found themselves alone.

"This place is beautiful." Freddie had one of those backpacks hikers were fond of, with all the pockets and strings. He was wearing short sleeves again despite the autumnal chill in the air. Ashley was wearing a pair of leggings, a pair of trainers, and a black parka that swamped her. She looked out to their right, where the lake stretched on and on, still and sky-saturated as a few big clouds moved overhead. There were birds calling, and every now and then she caught the raspy quack of a duck. The place smelled good; it smelled green. On their other side, Scar Wood stretched up, a riot of green, gold, and orange.

"It is," she said, meaning it. "You can't go far in the Lakes without falling over something beautiful, but this place is special." As soon as she said it, she felt embarrassed. "What are we doing here, Freddie?" she added quickly.

"I want to find a quiet spot and record a little intro," he said. "An outline of the murders to date."

"There's plenty of quiet spots." Ashley gestured around them. Somewhere nearby, there was the outraged rattle of a magpie. "Take your pick."

Freddie grinned at her. "Let's walk a bit farther. I want to absorb the atmosphere."

For a time, that's exactly what they did. They walked, following the green route suggested on Freddie's OS map app, and here and there they came across other walkers: lots of older couples with dogs, a few families with bored-looking teenagers, and one school group, the children all wearing bright orange vests. Freddie enthusiastically greeted every one of them, smiling in his easy way, talking in his effortlessly loud voice. Ashley kept quiet, happy to let him be the friendly one, but when they passed the school group, she found herself walking on while Freddie stopped to chat with the teachers. Seeing the little kids with their baseball caps and their scabby knees made her think of Robbie Metcalfe. It made her think how it could have been any of these children, their bodies left to be claimed by nature in a nondescript wood. But that probably wasn't true—these kids wore expensive-looking clothes, and they had a whole group of adults looking after them, watching their every move. Robbie had been a foster kid, bounced from home to home. Who had been looking out for him, exactly?

"Are you all right?"

The school party had passed, and Freddie was looking at her with a concerned expression. Sunlight winked off of his glasses.

"I'm fine." She smiled to prove it was so. "How much farther do you want to walk before you do this recording?"

"Not much farther," he said. "I've brought us some sandwiches too."

"You're so prepared. I'm impressed."

"Hey. I was an Eagle Scout." He tipped her a lazy salute. "We don't mess around."

They walked on. The path eventually moved up, away from the lake, taking them deeper into the wooded area known as The Heald. It grew very quiet, and Ashley found herself wondering what it had been like a hundred years ago, three hundred years ago, or longer. If she looked out into the trees, it was possible to imagine they had slipped through time, the ancient landscape carrying them away. *What am I doing here? What am I doing with this bloke I barely know?*

"Here we are." Freddie had been looking at the map on his phone, but now he looked up, confirming they were in the right place. "This is a good spot to record the introduction, I think. What do you say?"

The path had brought them back down to the level of the lake again. There were yachts moored up on the far side, and a stiff breeze was rippling the surface of the water. Behind them, the woods were still and silent. There was no one else around.

Freddie put his bag down on an old wooden bench that faced the water.

"What do you need me to do?"

"Whatever you feel like." When he saw the expression on her face, he chuckled. "Don't worry, I just want you—and your intuition—here for the beginning of our journey."

"I think that's the most American thing you've said so far."

He laughed again and shook his head. He took out his phone, winked at her, and pressed the screen. Ashley heard the chime that meant the phone was recording.

"Ah. Okay." He cleared his throat. "Hello and welcome, listeners, to the newest series of *Murder on the Mind*. I'm your host and guide on this darkest of paths, Freddie Miller, and this season I am inviting you to explore, with me, one of the most beautiful places in the world—one that happens to hide a terribly dark story. As I speak to you now, I am standing on the shores of Lake Windermere, England's largest lake, in the county of Cumbria. It's at the heart of one of England's National Parks, the Lake District. And, guys, it truly is a beautiful place." He glanced at Ashley and smiled, slightly bashfully, before continuing. "It's a land of jagged hills and wide shimmering lakes, a land of mists and farms, old pubs and hidden streams. The poet William Wordsworth lived here and was inspired to write reams of poetry. The artist and dreamer John Ruskin built a home here. It's a place that inspires the, uh, the creativity in all of us." He paused. "What do you think so far?"

"Laying it on a bit thick," Ashley said. "You should work for the Cumbrian tourist board."

He nodded. "Yeah, maybe. It's important to give the listeners a sense of place." He cleared his throat again, and his voice switched back into podcast mode; his tone was smooth, calm, and serious. "The place where I'm standing right now is so peaceful. I can see boats, birds wheeling overhead. It smells *great*. You could hardly imagine a more tranquil place. Yet this is also the scene of incredible violence and incredible loss. Over the last six years, eight children between the ages of nine and twelve have lost their lives in the most abhorrent ways, their bodies mutilated and left in beauty spots across the Lake District. When they were recovered, most were found to have eaten a variety of foods before they were killed: cake, cookies, burgers and fries, candy—as if they had been to a party before they were heartlessly murdered." Freddie paused.

Ashley stuck her hands deep into the pockets of her parka. Music started playing from one of the boats on the lake, and then stopped.

"What is it?"

"I try not to script the intros," he said, "because I want it to sound natural, but sometimes I lead myself into these little circles." He shook his head, annoyed with himself, and then repeated the last line. "As if they had been to a children's party before they were brutally murdered. Like Hansel and Gretel in the old fairy tale, they were treated to a diet of sugary treats before the witch came for them. This is why the British press have dubbed the killings the Gingerbread House Murders, and standing here on the edge of a wood, it feels strangely appropriate. This is a fairy tale place, and everything here is tinged with the ancient, with the mythic." He frowned. "Not sure about that last bit."

"Keep going," Ashley said.

"Okay. In this series of *Murder on the Mind*, we are going to take a deep dive into the Gingerbread House Murders. I'm going to introduce you to the victims, the mysterious circumstances surrounding their disappearance and their horrific deaths, and I'm going to take you to the places where these terrible things occurred. For the GBH murders—"

"You can't call it that," Ashley put in.

"What?"

"GBH." She smiled lopsidedly. "It stands for grievous bodily harm over here. Might get confusing."

"Oh! Right." He ran a hand through his curly hair, making it even more untidy. "You just saved me from a lot of snide emails, I reckon. For the GH murders," he continued. "I also have a special guest coming on this dark journey with me." He grinned at Ashley. "The renowned psychic Ashley Whitelam has agreed to be a long-term guest on this season of the *Murder on the Mind* podcast. Ashley is already inextricably linked to the case, having recently discovered the remains of missing schoolboy Robert Metcalfe at a location only a few miles from where I currently stand."

Ashley felt her smile grow stiff. The last thing she wanted was to be inextricably linked to the Gingerbread House Murders.

"And there's a place even closer that has seen the dark events of the GH murders." Freddie picked up his backpack and slung it one-handed over his shoulder, his phone still in his other hand, and then he headed up the path and into the tree line.

"Hey, wait! Where are you going?"

Ashley followed after him, casting a glance back over her shoulder at the lake. Freddie was talking into his phone again, his voice still perfectly smooth despite the uphill walk.

"On August 8, 2018, ten-year-old Katherine Sturges went missing during her walk home from school. She lived in Manchester, in a high-rise block of flats, yet on August 22, she was found in the far north."

The walk was getting harder. There were more trees, and a deep coat of dead leaves underfoot. Gorse and blackberry bushes tugged at Ashley's parka, and she cursed herself for not wearing proper walking boots. The path they had left, and even the lake itself, was lost beyond the cover of the trees.

"Where are we going?" She found she was no longer worried about interrupting his recording. "Do *you* know where we're going? We've gone off the walking trail."

"Found by one of the many men and women employed to keep the forest of The Heald in shape, Katherine Sturges lay in the leaf litter beneath a great old oak. She was found, here, just yards from where I'm standing."

Freddie stopped, and Ashley nearly crashed into the back of him. A large oak tree rose before them, its leaves a fiery mixture of yellow and gold, a collection of sad tributes at the roots. Bouquets of flowers, mostly wilted and some rotted away entirely, lay next to stuffed toys, pink-and-purple fur turning green with rot. There were a few candles too, some of them wedged into the ground where someone had swept away the leaves. They were long since extinguished.

"Fuck," said Ashley, then winced, glancing at Freddie's phone. Freddie nodded solemnly.

"Her left leg missing below the knee, discarded like trash. A child lost in the woods. If this is a fairy tale, then there is a monster here, somewhere. And at *Murder on the Mind*, we intend to find it." He turned back to Ashley. "Do you feel anything here, Ashley? Do you sense the, uh, spirit of Katherine Sturges?" He held the phone out in her direction.

"I . . . Fuck. Can you turn that thing off?"

"What is it?"

"Ah." She turned away from the sight of the floral tributes, the ruined teddy bears. It hurt to look at them. "This was a pretty rotten trick. You could have warned me."

"I wanted to get your pure reaction to it," said Freddie in an infuriatingly reasonable tone of voice. "Didn't you know one of the victims was found up here? You must have seen it in the news, right?"

Ashley shook her head. "I guess I did, but . . ." She stopped. Beyond the oak, tall and thin by a patch of Scots pine, there was a dark shape. A Heedful One, moving down the hill, its face thankfully obscured. Beyond it, another one, half-formed. A flood of heat moved up through her body. She pawed at the zipper of her parka, her head down. "Fuck."

"What is it?" Freddie sounded alarmed as she wrenched her coat off. "Are you okay?"

"A little kid died here, of course I'm not all right. I just feel like I need to sit down."

The first Heedful One was coming toward them now, moving jerkily through the trees toward the oak. Its arms were coming up, the things that served as its hands stretching out, brushing Ashley's arm.

Then, for the barest second, Ashley saw her: a child lying in the leaf litter, the white shift dress she was wearing stained green and black with putrefaction. Ashley stumbled backward, the edges of her vision growing dark.

"Ashley? Hey!"

The strength went out of her legs, and then someone had his arms around her, someone strong. She had a moment to think that Freddie smelled good, like soap and expensive aftershave, and then all the light winked out of the day.

18

2004

IT WAS ANOTHER full day of activities at Red Rigg House. Tennis, football, archery, rambling, croquet—there were so many choices that Ashley felt overwhelmed. She chose to do pottery, which took place in a big airy space toward the back of the house, where patio doors looked out toward the forest and the mountain that loomed over it. A lady from a nearby art college had been brought in specially to teach them, and for a few hours, Ashley was perfectly happy. She learned how to use long gray sausages of clay to make pots and cups, which was called coiling, and she learned how to paint what they'd made with muddy-looking stuff called "slip," which would, the lady promised them, look colorful when the pots were fired. There was even a chaotic hour where they were shown how to "throw on the wheel," which mainly resulted in a lot of mess and misshapen clay blobs. At the end of the session, the lady told them that if they wanted the pots they had made, they could fill in a form, and once the pots were fired, they could be posted to their homes. Ashley was handed the form and was eager to fill it out, until she saw that it would cost around ten pounds for what she had made to be finished and sent home. She glanced at the rows of names on the forms, and then passed it to the kid next to her without signing it.

After that, they were given sandwiches and lemonade on the lawn, sitting on large tartan blankets spread across the grass. Ashley tentatively sat at the corner of one, near some girls she vaguely recognized from dinner, but they gave her one brusque look and carried on with their own conversations. Stung but determined not to show it, Ashley turned away slightly and concentrated on her sandwich as though it were the most interesting thing in the world. It was a bright and sunny day.

"Hey, Ashie, do you want to come and meet a friend of mine?"

Ashley looked up to see Malory standing over her. The sun shone from behind, turning the older girl's black hair into a halo of reddish brown.

"Okay." Ashley downed the rest of her lemonade and stood. She could feel the other girls on the picnic blanket looking up at her, and she felt a surge of strange pride. *She* was the only one Malory deemed interesting enough to talk to. "I've finished my sandwich."

The two of them walked across the lawn, toward the east wing of the house. Beyond the gardens was a series of smaller brick buildings, yellowed and old-looking to Ashley's eye. There was a van parked outside one of them, its back doors open. Standing near it wearing a bloody apron was a tall, stocky woman, her graying hair tied back in a ponytail. At the sight of her, Ashley felt a shiver of unease. This couldn't be who Malory was taking her to meet, was it? In Ashley's world, adults were not potential friends—not bad, necessarily, but certainly separate. However, Malory was smiling and waving, and the woman with the bloody apron raised her hand to them.

"Ashie, this is Melva Goodacre. She supplies us with meat from her farm. And"—Malory leaned down to get closer to Ashley's ear—"she's a *witch*."

"Less of that now, you," said Melva, although she was smiling as she wiped her hands on her apron. The ends of her fingernails were semicircles of dark red. "There was a time when throwing the word 'witch' around could get me burned at the stake."

"Are you though?" asked Ashley. She found she couldn't stop looking at the blood smeared across the apron. "A witch?"

Melva grinned. "Some may say that, I suppose. Come on, do you want to see something interesting they won't show you on your little school tour?"

Malory squeezed Ashley's hand. "I'm sure Ashie would love that."

"All right then." Melva took her apron off and threw it in the back of her van. Then, she went to one of the low stone buildings and used an outside tap to wash her hands. The door of the building was open slightly, and inside, Ashley glimpsed raw red bodies hanging from the ceiling.

"That's for your dinner later," Melva said, winking. "There's always a hungry mouth to feed. Come on, let's go up to the fell."

The three of them walked together through the grounds of the house. They passed through an herb garden, which had a small section behind a fence dedicated to poisons—Melva pointed out hemlock, foxgloves, and opium poppies—and into the forest that clustered at the foot of the fell. As they walked, Melva kept up cheerful commentary about the trees and the birds, the flowers and plants that they passed, touching on the history of Green Beck and the house itself, while Malory occasionally added comments of her own—how she'd once found a jackdaw chick in the woods and looked after it until it was able to fly, how she and her brother had buried a time capsule somewhere in the trees several years ago and had since lost the map that told them where it was. Ashley listened to them both, nervous but happy.

Eventually, the trees thinned a little and the mountain began to sneak in at the edges of their vision, gray and green and black. Here, they followed a small path until they came to an untidy pile of rocks. A tiny creek sprang from them, clear water running quietly over smooth pebbles.

"Ah, now, here we are." Melva knelt by the water and dipped her wide shovel-shaped fingers into it. "This is a sacred spring, dedicated to the goddess Andraste."

"See," said Malory, elbowing Ashley lightly in the side. "Told you she was a witch."

Melva chuckled, but she didn't deny it. "It's said that if you drink from this spring, you'll live to be a hundred years old, and all your wishes come true. Andraste was a goddess of secret places and secret rites. She keeps an eye out for the wild world and for the innocent and blameless." The old woman looked wistful now, her eyes bright, as though she might cry. And then she seemed to pull herself together. "Hardly anyone knows about it now, so it's a special secret we're sharing with you."

Ashley nodded, uncertain what to say or do. For a few moments, it was quiet between the three of them.

"Do you . . . do you want me to drink from it?" She hoped not. Ashley had a city child's suspicions of the natural world and was quite certain the water couldn't be clean.

Melva laughed. "Oh no. Lord, can you imagine if we encouraged the children to drink the spring water, eat the mushrooms, just generally live off the land? Red Rigg House would be sued within an inch of its life the moment one of you gets a tummy ache. No, love, you don't have to drink the water, but here, take some with you as a blessing."

The older woman dipped her hand back into the water and, with wet fingers, drew a shape on Ashley's forehead. The water was shockingly cold. A few drops ran down Ashley's nose and cheeks.

"What did you draw?" Ashley reached up with one hand, as if to touch her own forehead, then thought better of it.

"A secret sigil," Melva said, grinning. "A sign so that the spirits will know you are Andraste's own, blessed and kept safe by her. It's protection."

Malory, who had been very quiet up until that point, squeezed Ashley's shoulder.

"Melva showed me this spring a few years ago."

After that, the three of them began to make their way back to the tree line. Red Rigg House was in the distance, almost invisible save for the flashes of color peeking through the canopy. Ashley stood on a rock, caught for a moment between the house and the mountain behind her, a strange sense of new energy flowing through her.

I am blessed by the stream, she thought, still not sure what that meant. *I am protected.*

And then she hopped down and followed the others into the wood.

19

"I FEEL JUST AWFUL."

Ashley took another sip from the bottle of water Freddie had given her. They were sitting on the bench overlooking the lake again. Physically she was feeling much better, but she did not want to look back up at where the trees loomed over them.

"It happens more than you think." She smiled at him. "Low blood sugar or something. I used to pass out so much when I was a kid, there was a pillow at school with my name on it."

Freddie did not look convinced. The green eyes behind his wire-rimmed glasses looked stricken with worry.

"I pushed you too hard," he said. "All that walking, and then surprising you with something unpleasant. Jeez. I'm such a tool."

"Like I said, a warning would have been nice." She looked at him, with his earnest expression of guilt. It was difficult to believe he would deliberately try to freak her out. "Did you really carry me back down the hill?" Ashley grinned. "My hero."

"What was I supposed to do, roll you down it?" He saw the look on her face and laughed, shaking his head. "I've got a candy bar in my bag. I suggest you eat it before we attempt to go anywhere."

"It's a deal." Ashley picked a dead leaf out of her hair while Freddie rummaged through his backpack. It was a Snickers, and from the first bite, she felt significantly better. A pair of walkers passed them on the path with a dog at their heels. Freddie waved hello while Ashley concentrated on her chocolate bar. When the other walkers were gone, they sat together in silence for a few minutes.

"Do you mind if I ask you something?" Freddie said eventually.

"Are you recording me?"

"No."

"Then sure." Ashley stuffed the empty wrapper into the pocket of her coat.

"When we were up there, by the oak tree, did you . . . feel anything?"

Ashley looked out over the lake. The temperature had dropped a little. It looked like it was going to rain soon.

"You mean, did I have any special psychic insights?"

"Did you?"

She thought of that brief flash she'd had of the girl lying on the ground, so cold and alone. And she thought of the Heedful One that had skittered its way down the hill toward them. When she was a kid, she saw them all the time. They had been as unremarkable to her as any stranger on the street, as familiar as bus stops. And then, after 2004, after the incident at Red Rigg House, they vanished from her life. Until now. Back then, she had never been able to predict their behavior. Most of the time, they didn't seem to know she existed. Most of the time. When they did notice her, it usually meant something bad was about to happen. How could she explain the Heedful Ones to Freddie? The simple answer was she couldn't. She thought of how her family reacted when she tried to talk about them when she was a kid—there had been laughter at first, then anger when they realized she was serious. There was no way to explain them to anyone. Not without making her look like a lunatic.

"Perhaps," she said eventually. "The place certainly felt wrong to me. A residue of something bad, sunk into the roots of that tree. I don't know."

Freddie nodded seriously. "There are a lot of rumors about this case flying about online, you know. A lot of people are convinced that it's been going on for much longer than the last six years."

"They are?"

"The last eight victims are just the ones the police have linked. I've looked at missing persons cases from the north of England going back the last forty years, and there were clusters of disappearances in the late '90s, across the 2000s, the late '70s and early '80s. From there, records start to get difficult to track down. Kids who disappeared in the first half of the twentieth century mostly got reported as runaways, but I can't help feeling like that's the perfect place to hide something terrible." He looked at her. "I know, heavy, right? I should stop going on about it."

Ashley touched his arm. "I'm fine, honestly. This is interesting. But if children have been going missing for decades, surely it can't be the one murderer behind it all?"

"You're probably right. But something about it niggles at the back of my mind. Jack Crispin in 2017, Katherine Sturges in 2018. Eva Nowak in 2019, and then in 2020, you have two in the same year—Harry Cornell in the spring, Jessie Williams in the winter."

"Not even COVID slowed them down."

"Another two in 2021—Sara Foster and Thomas Allen—and then this year, Robbie Metcalfe. Jack and Eva's bodies were never located. And I think there's another one to come this year, maybe another two, because it's escalating."

Ashley frowned. "My brother told me there had been eight in six years, but hearing their names . . ."

"And I've found similar clusters in previous decades. Slow at first, and then two or three kids were disappearing each year. And then it stops for a while." He paused. "You see, Ashley, this is what happens when you make your living out of investigating true crime," he said, shaking his head. "You start to see conspiracies everywhere. Even if it's all bunkum, it does make for great background color for the podcast."

"But tons of kids must go missing every year," Ashley said. "How do you even know that Jack and Eva were victims of the same murderer?"

"That's an interesting question, isn't it?" Freddie gave her a lopsided smile. "There's something about the way these kids disappeared that links them—something that the police know and haven't divulged. I would love to find out."

"Okay. What's our next step?"

"I have a list of people to talk to, and a few more I need to try and track down. How'd you feel about coming with me?"

Ashley looked back at the lake. Her initial instinct was to hold Freddie at a distance. She was so used to that: hiding her real feelings, her real self, giving a performance onstage and never really connecting with anyone. But was that really living?

"I'd be glad to." Ashley nodded slowly. An adventure that had nothing to do with her family; an adventure that her father couldn't control or manage. "I really would."

20

THAT NIGHT WAS a working night for Ashley. She drove to the venue herself, a surprisingly spacious room above a pub in Ambleside, and met her father and Aidan in the bar downstairs. The place was packed with punters, and Ashley caught a discernible murmur as she pushed through the crowd. Aidan was already at the bar ordering drinks, while her father could be seen in a corner, talking to a couple of men in suits that looked out of place in a pub that was clearly more used to locals and hikers.

"Where you been all day?" Aidan passed her a vodka soda, which she took gratefully. "I've barely had a chance to prep you. Did you get my emails?"

"Sure. I read through it all this afternoon." She sipped at her drink. "Is there no greenroom in this place?"

"Just the bogs. I'll be out in the car. Here"—he passed her the small nondescript box that contained her earpiece—"stick it in before we go up, okay?"

"Who's Dad talking to?"

"More journalists, of course. Some of them have bought tickets."

Ashley swore. "Taking places from proper punters so they can what? Ask me more stupid questions?"

"You think this place is usually this packed?" Aidan rubbed at a greasy mark on his own glass. "This is your five minutes of fame, Ash. I hope you're enjoying it."

* * *

Ashley found the toilets and, locking herself into one of the cubicles, she positioned her earpiece. There was an odd, oily static noise, and then she heard her brother clearing his throat.

"You hear me okay, Ash?"

"All good."

From there it was a short set of wooden stairs to the function room. The audience was already seated—a smaller place than the last one—but here every single chair was taken. Ashley made her way to the narrow stage at the front, and there was a ripple of applause. She looked out across her audience and smiled, clasping her hands in front of her chest.

"Thank you all for coming on this journey with me tonight. Before we begin, just a little housekeeping. Stepping into the spirit realm can be an intense experience, and you may be confronted with unexpected truths, or exposed to emotions and even trauma that had previously been hidden from you. If, at any point, this evening becomes too much for you, the exit is at the rear of the room. Please do not think it will offend me if you need to leave. Your spiritual health is of the utmost importance."

There was a murmur of nervous laughter.

Ashley smiled her softest smile. All of this patter was as familiar and as well-worn as a pair of old slippers. "I do ask that you keep an open mind. I ask that for this evening, you leave your concept of the material world at the door and trust that this is a journey you have been preparing for all your lives." She let her tone become more serious, and she looked not at the audience, but over the tops of their heads. "We step now into the spirit realm, that place that exists side by side with ours. We push through the veil that separates them, and we ask that if any spirits wish to make contact, they do so now."

Ashley let her chin drop down to her chest, her white-blond hair falling to either side of her face. She closed her eyes and imagined herself as the audience saw her; a thin, pale shape on a bare wooden stage, fragile and uncertain. Silence spooled out across the room as the fidgeting and coughing stopped.

"Come to me now, spirits of the next world."

For a brief second, her mind was filled with the image of Robbie Metcalfe's body lying in the spongy leaf litter. Her heart skittered in her chest, and she cleared her throat. She went to speak again and found that she couldn't. A sickly heat prickled across her skin.

"Ash?" Aidan in her ear. *"Are you okay?"*

She forced herself to open her eyes just as the audience was starting to shift in their seats.

"Here we go. I have someone here with me. An older woman." Ashley walked down one end of the stage, one hand reaching out as though she could read the audience through her fingers. "She suffered with her feet during her life, that's what she's telling me." Again there was that nervous giggle from the audience. Ashley spotted the suits her dad had been speaking to—they were down at the front, watching her intently. "She says that she had many medical problems, but it was her feet she complained about. Bunions. Ingrown toenail, even. She passed recently, and she's the sort to worry about her family. She doesn't feel like she can rest before she knows that they're doing well. Does that mean anything to anyone here?"

Three hands went up. Ashley glanced at all three of them and recognized one from the pictures Aidan had sent that afternoon. A man in his fifties, lank hair pushed greasily across a bald spot. He was wearing a beige parka fastidiously zipped up to his collar.

"You, sir. Is this lady your mother?"

He put his hand down and nodded tightly.

"Her name began with D . . . Diana . . . no. A soft-sounding name, a name she was proud of. *Daphne.*"

"That's her. Is she all right? Where she is now? Does she still suffer with her feet?" It was as though, having identified the spirit, his reticence had vanished. "I'd hate to think she was still dealing with that pain. Is she with her sister, Marge? They were ever so close. I like to think of them together, now that they're both in the same place."

Ashley smiled and held up a hand. "There is no pain or discomfort in the spirit world, my friend." Another image flashed across her mind: little Katherine Sturges, lying cold and exposed on the roots of an oak tree. In the face of that, all of her words felt even more hollow than they usually did. To her horror, a hot rush of vomit lapped at the back of her throat. She swallowed hurriedly. "Your mother is touched by how much you worry about her, and how much you worried about her while she was alive, but she wants you to know that you don't have to do that anymore. You must go on with your life."

The man was nodding, an uncertain look on his face.

"Daphne is retreating now. She's moving away." Ashley walked to the other end of the stage. As she passed him, one of the men in suits leaned forward and raised his hand. She ignored him, but he started speaking.

"Ashley Whitelam—can you tell us any more about how you found the body of Robbie Metcalfe? I understand you've been talking to the police?"

Ashley looked down at her feet for a second. Aidan was cursing in her ear.

"Are you a loved one of Robbie Metcalfe, sir?"

The man smiled ruefully. "Just an interested party, Miss Whitelam."

"This evening is for those people who want to make contact with those they've lost." Ashley opened her arms to indicate the rest of the audience. "This time is for them. If you want to ask me questions about my work with the police, it will have to wait until after the show."

"*Show* is an interesting way of describing it," said the man, sitting up straighter in his chair. "And you're a difficult person to get hold of—we were supposed to have an interview with you some days ago, but it seemed you had vanished yourself."

"Those interviews were rescheduled," Ashley said quickly.

"And really," the man continued, "I think everyone here would probably be interested in hearing more about it. Right?" He looked over his shoulder, and to her horror, she saw the rest of the audience nodding, glancing at each other. They were looking at her in a different way now—not as the mysterious psychic who could lead them to personal truths, but as a sordid source of gossip. One or two of them muttered their agreement.

"I . . . this is really not the place."

Aidan whispered urgently in her ear. *"Tell them you can't discuss it publicly because it might disrupt the police investigation."*

And then her father's much louder voice began speaking over Aidan's; it took all of Ashley's self-control not to wince.

"Never mind that, tell them about it. This is the stuff that's going to get your name in every paper, Ash. This is what will bring in the money! Forget these sad, old weirdos, they can wait."

It was at this point that Ashley spotted Freddie. He was sitting toward the back, somewhat noticeable now that she looked; his broad shoulders and correct posture stuck out a mile. Catching her eye, he smiled and raised his hand in a brief wave. Ashley felt the blood rushing to her face.

Jesus, is everyone here? Will David Wagner stand up in a second and declare me a murderer too?

"I . . ." Ashley paused, then cleared her throat.

The audience was riveted to her, their eyes wide with the need to hear about this tragedy that didn't directly affect them, and she could almost understand it. They had all experienced sadness in their lives—that's why they were here, after all—but this was a sadness that was safe, because it belonged to someone else. It wouldn't cause them pain to look directly at it.

"Robbie's story is not mine to tell, because he is not here with me now. This was a child who died in terrible circumstances, and I don't believe it would be right to use his death as part of my show." Ashley stopped. She didn't like to use the word "death" on these evenings, as it tended to scare people. Her father was shouting in her ear. "Not to mention, of course, that Robbie's murder is part of an ongoing investigation by the Cumbrian Police, and I could be making things difficult by talking about it here."

"You can't tell us anything at all?" asked the suit. There was a tone to his voice that she didn't like. She raised her hand and wiped a thin sheen of sweat from her forehead. "Why were you drawn to that location? Did Robbie's *ghost* speak to you?"

"Sometimes . . ." Ashley licked her lips. Out of nowhere, she felt painfully thirsty. "Sometimes, finding spirits is like hearing music from very far away. Usually, when I am communing with the spirit realm, I am in one place. I am here, in front of you all." She raised her hands and smiled, hoping to get the audience back on her side. "I am not looking for one particular spirit, I am letting them come to me. But with Robbie . . . His music drew me to him. Discordant and broken, maybe, but he wanted to be found, and so I found him."

There was an appreciative murmur from the audience at that. Ashley made a mental note to use music as an analogy more often. The suit, however, was not satisfied.

"Will you be working with the police again on this case?" he asked. And then, "Are they going to call you in every time someone goes missing? How do you think your success rate would fare if it was a regular job?"

"Oh, fuck this guy," muttered Aidan.

"I really do think that is a tangent we don't need to explore tonight," said Ashley, as smoothly as she was able. "If you want to discuss it further, I suggest you talk to my father, who I believe you have already met. He'll be more than happy to set up an official interview."

The suit frowned slightly, but he did sit back in his seat. Ashley took a deep breath and turned her attention to the audience again.

"Now. There are several spirits impatient to make contact here. First of all, there is an older man here with me, and what I'm getting here is a sense of . . ." She looked out across the audience again, searching for the mark, but what she saw were several dark shadows—shapes that shifted and convulsed, taking up seats in the small room. Heedful Ones, sitting next to the men and women who had come to see her. She had thought the room was at capacity, but she was wrong. *They* were here. They were watching. "I'm getting a sense . . . his name begins with . . ."

The Heedful Ones in the audience—at least five of them, she realized—slowly began to stand. Their shadowy bodies rose up, the pale nubs of their faces somehow expectant. Ashley swallowed, feeling her throat catch. Both her father and her brother were talking rapidly, asking if she was all right.

"No." Ashley took a step backward on the stage. The audience's murmurs grew louder. "Don't come near me. Why did you come back? Leave me alone!"

The Heedful Ones began to move forward slowly, their inky bodies passing through the people sitting uneasily in their seats. Ashley

took a few more steps backward, stumbling slightly. She could hear
people in the audience talking now, asking what was going on, if this
was part of the show. She was aware of other things too—her brother
shouting in her ear, Freddie rising up from where he was sitting, a look
of concern on his face—but she couldn't tear her attention away from
the approaching figures, their ragged arms reaching out for her.

"Stop it. Stop it!"

She realized a little too late that her father's voice was no longer
coming through the earpiece, and that was because he was marching
up the aisle, a furious look on his face. He was dressed in all black, the
silver pentacle at his throat. She saw people reacting to his presence—
they were relieved. *Here is someone who knows what's going on,* they
were thinking.

"Ladies and gentlemen." Logan Whitelam's deep gravelly voice
boomed around the function room; he had never needed a microphone. "I'm afraid that the events of the last few days have taken their
toll on my daughter. I would ask for your kind cooperation at this
time."

The Heedful Ones were still coming. They had reached the edge
of the stage; they were reaching out for her. Ashley bumped into the
back wall and instinctively folded over, curling in on herself. Heat
moved through her in a wave, her eyes stinging. She could smell smoke
and something else, something sweet. Her father was still speaking.

"If you speak to the landlord, or to me directly, I will be very glad
to offer you a discounted ticket for a future event with the spirit oracle,
as a goodwill gesture."

A shadow fell over her, and Ashley shrank further, trying to vanish
into the wall, but then there was a warm hand on her shoulder and a
quiet voice speaking into her ear.

"Ashley? It's all right. I'll get you out of here. Can you walk?"

It was Freddie. She nodded and, with his help, stood up. The
Heedful Ones were gone, vanished back to wherever it was they came
from, but the audience was in disarray. Some stood to claim their
cheap tickets from her dad. Others were taking pictures and even,
God help her, video.

What a fucking mess.

Freddie had his arm around her shoulder, and in a very business-like manner, he walked her off the stage and toward the door at the back of the room. A few people tried to intercept him—including the suit who had caused all the trouble in the first place—but he moved them aside with his large American shoulders. Very quickly they went down the stairs and out into the larger bar area below. The place was much emptier than it had been. Ashley saw a couple of drinkers glance up at her with interest.

At that moment, the pub door flew open and Aidan came in, his face pinched with worry. When he saw Ashley with Freddie, he stopped as though he'd been slapped.

"Who is this, Ash?"

Still not letting go of her shoulders, Freddie reached out his free hand toward her brother. "I'm Freddie Miller. Good to meet you. I'm making a podcast series, and your sister has kindly agreed to appear in it."

Aidan looked at the hand for a few seconds before cautiously grasping it. Freddie shook it vigorously.

"Er. Okay." Aidan looked at Ashley. "What the fuck is going on, Ash?"

"I'm fine. Look. Can you just give me a minute? And you'd better go up there and retrieve Dad. God knows what he's promised those bastard journalists by this point." No longer caring who saw, she pulled the piece out of her ear and passed it to her brother. "I'm just going to go and get some fresh air."

Aidan looked for a second as though he wanted to argue with her, but after one more uncertain glance at Freddie, he went to the far door and disappeared up the stairs.

"Now." Freddie let his grip on her shoulders loosen. "Can I get you a drink? Something with a lot of sugar in it maybe? I almost don't want to say this, but you look as if you've seen a ghost."

Ashley gave a hollow laugh. "A double vodka soda, please. And bring it outside."

CHAPTER

21

IT WAS A clear night, with a thick belt of stars visible overhead. Ashley found herself looking up at it repeatedly. Growing up in London, she hadn't realized it was even possible to see that many stars, and she never grew tired of seeing them.

"So, what happened? Do you want to talk about it?"

They were sitting on the low bars of a climbing frame. This particular pub had a children's play area to one side of the pub garden; another drastic difference from living in the city. Ashley had drunk most of the vodka soda, and a pleasant, distant fuzz was descending over her senses.

"You weren't recording the show, were you? Recording devices are strictly prohibited, you know."

"I wasn't," Freddie said evenly. "I just wanted to get an idea of how your work . . . works."

"Ha. Work. That's an interesting word for it." She swirled the melting ice cubes at the bottom of her glass. It was cold out under the stars, and she could feel her fingers growing numb. She relished it.

"I take it that's not what usually happens?"

"Not really, no. I just . . ." She sighed. "What my dad said was mostly right, actually. It's been a very weird and disruptive week, and if I'm honest, I probably wasn't up to doing a show tonight. It's my own fault."

"If you'll forgive me for saying so, your father doesn't look like the sort of person it's easy to say no to."

Ashley sniggered. "You don't know the half of it. But listen"—she patted his arm, the muscles pleasingly firm under his shirt—"you've got to stop rescuing me from stuff. It makes me look bad."

"Then you need to stop passing out around me. I'm starting to get a complex."

The back door of the pub opened and then shut again, a brief flash of yellow light scattering across the children's play area. They both grew quiet. Ashley fully expected her father to come storming up the path, but instead she saw a small, bent figure coming toward them hesitantly. It was an older woman, she realized, one she recognized from the audience.

"Miss Whitelam?"

"Yeah, hi." Ashley straightened up a little. "Sorry about the show. It's not usually so chaotic. If you speak to my father, he'll tell you when I'm next available."

"I wondered actually if I could speak to you away from the others." The woman shuffled forward a little, and the soft light from the pub windows fell across her face. Ashley found herself examining her the way she would if she had picked her from the audience; she was in her forties but much of her hair was gray already; her cheeks were a little sunken and there were dark circles under her eyes; she wore a wedding band on her left hand and her coat had a little dust across the shoulders, as though it had been languishing in a wardrobe for a long time and had been called into service for tonight. *And she's here, hoping to communicate with the dead person,* thought Ashley. *Recently bereaved, and it wasn't an anticipated death.*

"Sure. How can I help you?"

The woman glanced away. One hand smoothed down the lapel of her coat, as if on some level she knew it was dusty and needed to be cleaned.

"My name is Elspeth Sutton, Miss Whitelam. I saw your interview on the news, about how you found that poor Robbie Metcalfe. How you found his . . ." Her voice broke a little. "How you found his remains."

Ashley felt her heart skip a beat. "Did you know Robbie?"

"No, I . . . Early this year, in April, actually, my daughter, her name is Eleanor, she's only twelve . . ."

"Take a breath," Freddie added. "It's all right."

Elspeth glanced at him and nodded. "My Eleanor. She didn't come home one day, and whoever it was that got Robbie Metcalfe, I think they got her too. But the police, they won't listen. They keep telling me it's not related, but God help me, I know in my heart that it is." She lunged forward and took hold of Ashley's wrist, squeezing it hard. Her fingers were hot and dry. "I want you to find her, Miss Whitelam. Find her for me, please."

* * *

When they got home that night, Ashley made straight for the stairs, hoping to make it to her room without answering any questions, but her father got there first, positioning his bulk so she'd have to shove past him. Her mother fluttered around both of them, clearly eager to know what had happened at the evening's event.

"Dad, let me go to bed, all right? I'm bloody knackered."

"Off to bed like you didn't just show us all up?" He laughed and crossed his arms over his barrel chest. "You've got some bloody front, I'll give you that."

Ashley felt her hands curl into fists. "We'll talk about it. But in the morning. Please, Dad. My head is pounding and I need to sleep. You won't get anything sensible out of me until then anyway."

"You were acting like you were seeing things," her father said sharply. "Are you starting this nonsense again?"

Her mother came over to her, a stricken expression on her gaunt face. She pushed a strand of Ashley's hair behind her ear. "What is it, sweetheart?" She looked searchingly at Ashley's face, as if the answers were written there, and then turned to her husband. "Look at her, Logan. The angels have worn her ragged this evening. Let the girl sleep."

Normally this would have infuriated Ashley—the cloying protectiveness, the use of the word "girl"—but she saw how it made her father uncross his arms and sigh.

"Fine," he said. "But we will talk about this in the morning."

22

2004

MALORY'S BEDROOM WAS a revelation to Ashley. For a start, it was easily bigger than their entire living room and kitchen at home, so large that there was room for a double bed—Ashley had never heard of a kid sleeping in a double bed. A smart cherry-wood desk sat under the windows, and there was a small table and chairs, even a two-seater sofa and armchair. The walls were a tasteful shade of pale lilac, while much of the furniture was cream or white. There were a few posters, much neater than the ones of football players Aidan had on his wall; there was one of the elves from the Lord of the Rings movies, which Ashley had loved, and one of the vampires with the white hair from Buffy, which she was less keen on—she would rather die than admit it to Aidan, but sometimes she found Buffy a little scary. Dinner was over, and most of the children had been shuffled along to the "games room," which contained a number of ratty board games and a big television, but Malory appeared just as Ashley had been dawdling down the corridor behind the main crowd.

"Your bedroom is so cool." Ashley paused by the desk. It was scattered with tubes of half-used paint and long, thin paintbrushes. Paintings and sketches—Malory's own work, she assumed—were pinned to the walls. The view from the window showed the forest and Red

Rigg Fell rising above it, doused now in the uncertain tangerine light of dusk. "I have to share mine with my brother."

Malory threw herself on the bed and sprawled there for a moment, looking up at the ceiling.

"Oh God, you poor thing," she said, with feeling. "I can't think of anything worse than sharing a bedroom with my brother. The pervy little bastard that he is."

Ashley laughed. Being with Malory made her feel grown-up.

"Is he really bad?"

Malory rolled toward the edge of the bed and planted her stockinged feet on the floor. She grinned at Ashley through the curtains of her dark hair.

"You don't know the half of it. I cannot stand him. Here, come and sit on the bed with me. I have some stuff I want to show you."

Feeling shy again, Ashley went over and perched on the edge of the bed with Malory. The older girl winked, and then leaned down and reached under the bed. She pulled out a large old-fashioned suitcase covered in a paisley print. Malory hauled it up onto the bed between them and opened it by turning a neat silver switch on the top.

"I hate throwing away good clothes, even though I've grown out of them, and I don't have a little sister to pass them on to . . ." Malory began pulling garments out of the suitcase and piling them next to Ashley on the bed. There were clothes of all colors in there, made of shimmering, expensive materials—Ashley saw the shine of satin and silk, even the twinkle of sequins and thick brocade. "Mother says I should just dump it all at the charity shop in Green Beck, and she's probably right, but I can't bring myself to do it. I think I've been saving them for you, Ashie, without knowing it. A lot of this stuff will fit you, I believe."

Ashley was dumbstruck. Hesitantly, she reached out and touched the pile of fabrics, her fingers tracing the embroidery, the thick weight of wool and velvet under her hand. The idea that these things could belong to her gave her a strange feeling in the pit of her stomach. She knew what she was supposed to say, though.

"That's nice of you, Malory, but I can't take these things. They're yours!"

"Nonsense. All they're doing at the moment is sitting in this suitcase under my bed. I'd much rather they went with you. Oh, here, you must try this on!"

The older girl had pulled out a simple white dress from the suitcase and was holding it up, pinching the shoulders between her thumb and forefinger. It was a summery-looking dress, with a lightly embroidered bodice and a skirt made from many layers of a gauzy material. It made Ashley think of ballerinas and princesses from stories.

"I really can't," she said again. She was thinking now of what would happen if she took these clothes home with her. Her mother would be mortified. She would wrinkle her nose and snap about how they "didn't need anyone's charity" and she would ask, "Does this girl think we are paupers?" She might even—and this was much worse—assume that Ashley had stolen the things. To cap it all, her father would assume the same thing and be pleased about it. "It's not fair to the other kids, is it?" she added in a small voice.

Malory laughed. "Balls to the other kids! Here, try it on. I want to see if it fits."

She passed her the white dress. In Ashley's hands, the material felt heavy and soft and cool, completely unlike any of her other clothes. When she paused, her cheeks growing flushed, Malory nodded to a long mirror in the corner of the room.

"There, use that. I won't look."

Feeling nervous and strange, Ashley went to the mirror and took off her thin blue sweatshirt, and then her T-shirt, so she was only wearing her bra and jeans. It took her a moment to figure out which way up the dress was. She pulled it on over her head, the heavy silk dropping down over her chest and stomach like a cool breeze. The jeans she was wearing crumpled up the gauzy skirt, so she unzipped the fly and stepped out of them. It was only then she realized that despite the sunny day, Malory's room was chilly. Gooseflesh stood up on the backs of her arms.

"There! It fits you perfectly. I must insist that you take it," said Malory, who had gotten up from the bed at some point and now stood behind Ashley in the mirror. "It would be a crime for you not to have it."

Ashley looked at herself in the mirror. The dress certainly did fit, but she wasn't sure it suited her at all. With her pale skin and fair hair, the white dress made her look washed out somehow. Only her blue and brown eyes seemed real.

"I can really have it?"

"Of course. Oh, you could wear it to the big farewell dinner on Monday!"

"Thank you. That's really kind. But I don't want to be the only one wearing a dress." She thought of the other kids, who were all from schools or cities similar to hers. She doubted that any of them had fancy dresses in their bags ready for dinner. "I don't think they expect us to put nice clothes on."

"Hmm. Well, okay, you could be right about that." Malory put one hand on Ashley's shoulder. "I forget that not everyone dresses for dinner."

At that moment, the bedroom door flew open violently enough that the door handle smacked into the wall. Ashley jumped, but Malory just sighed.

"Richard, you know perfectly well that Mother made it a house rule that we knock on each other's doors."

"And you know perfectly well how much I listen to anything Mother says." Richard slid through the open door, his hands thrust into his trouser pockets. At the sight of Ashley standing next to the mirror, an oily smile crept up one side of his face. "So this is your little project, is it? I have to give it to you, you couldn't have picked a more pathetic specimen."

Standing there in her borrowed dress, Ashley felt horribly exposed. Richard's sharply handsome face and his finely tailored clothes looked like a threat.

"Oh, fuck off, will you, *Dick*," Malory replied, her voice dripping with manufactured boredom. "I haven't got the patience."

"And don't I get a say in anything that goes on around here?" To Ashley's horror, he joined them at the mirror, pushing his sister out of the way so that he stood behind Ashley. He leaned down so that his chin rested on her shoulder, and his eyes met hers in the mirror. One hand rested on her bare arm, his long fingers burning against her skin.

There was a long, uncomfortable silence, one where Ashley was too petrified to say anything, and then he snorted.

"I don't know, Mal, she doesn't look like anything special to me."

Ashley felt her cheeks burn. She looked down at her feet.

"I think we've had enough of the pleasure of your company, brother dearest." Malory took hold of his arm and started to drag him toward the door; they were both laughing, Ashley realized. "Go back to that sordid cave you call your bedroom, unless you want me to tell Mother about your own disgusting—"

There was a flurry of shouts from the corridor outside. Malory dropped her brother's arm, and they both went to the open door. Curious, Ashley followed them, her feet sinking into the thick pile of the carpet.

"THIS IS THE DEVIL'S HOUSE!"

The shouts were nearer now, accompanied by the sound of running feet and a crash as someone collided with something. Ashley poked her head into the gap left by the Lyndon-Smith siblings just in time to see a dirty disheveled man pass by the doorway. He was wearing only a pair of grimy, mud-encrusted jeans, and his bare chest was streaked with filth. He glanced at them as he passed, and just for a second, Ashley caught his eye; he was crying, she realized with a stab of shock. Crying and shouting as he ran.

"Bloody hell." Malory took a step back, putting one arm out as if to shield Ashley, then two more men ran up the hallway in pursuit of the strange intruder. These were dressed in neat shirts and jackets— the barely seen servants that attended to Red Rigg House. The dirty man was past them and gone around the corner; they heard another crash as he collided with something out of sight. There was the unmistakable sound of something expensive smashing into pieces.

"What's going on?" shouted Richard.

One of the pursuers skidded to a halt. His face was flushed. "Some kind of homeless person has broken into the house, sir," he said. His colleague disappeared around the corner in pursuit. "We'll have him out shortly."

Richard laughed as though he were genuinely delighted.

"Well, off you go then, Paul—you don't want to let him get away, do you?"

The man nodded awkwardly and then sped off.

Malory put her arm around Ashley's shoulders and squeezed her. "Wow, I'm sorry about that, Ashie. How weird. I promise we don't normally have lunatics running around the house. Are you okay?"

Ashley nodded, although she didn't feel okay. The wild crying man had been familiar—it was the man she had seen in the woods days before. What did he want?

23

The next morning, the light coming in through Ashley's bedroom window was dreary and strained; a thick layer of dark clouds stretched across the sky while the odd squall of rain dashed against the glass. It was difficult to get out of bed, which she suspected was the fault of Aidan's little blue tablets. Her first instinct was to delve down under the duvet and sleep until the afternoon, but instead she slipped out of bed as quietly as she could, pausing to look at her journal, which she had left open on her bedside table.

> *Another shit show. Am I having a bad run at the moment or what? Bloody journalists causing havoc. Dad is over the moon about the "free publicity," but if we have this much scrutiny every time we put on a show, it'll go tits up sooner or later. No psychic needs someone looking too closely at their methods.*

Ashley grimaced and put the journal away in her drawer. She crept into the bathroom, and when she was dressed, locked her bedroom and tiptoed down the stairs. The whole house was quiet aside from the hum of the fridge and the ticking of the clock in the hallway. She fingered the car keys in her pocket with some triumph; all she had to do was get out of the front door and she'd be free. Her father's griping could wait until the evening.

When she opened the front door, though, a cold feeling of dread filled her throat. The Parma Violet was not there. She jogged down the path and onto the gravel, wondering if she had left it parked round the corner of their drive perhaps, hidden by bushes, but she already knew the truth. It wasn't behind the bushes. It wasn't anywhere to be seen. When she turned back to go inside the house, her father was there, leaning against the doorframe with a big grin on his face. One of his skills left over from the bad old days was an ability to move very quietly when he needed to.

"Going somewhere, Ash?"

"Where's my fucking car?" To her horror, she already felt close to crying. Her one fragile piece of freedom had been taken from her, and all at once, it was like she was being suffocated. She took out her keys and shook them at him. "What did you do with it?"

He laughed.

"You know I don't need keys to get into a car, Ash. Now, come on inside and we can talk about what happened last night. I'm very interested to hear your explanation."

For a second, she teetered on the brink of running down their drive to the main road. It would serve him right if his daughter got splashed all over the tarmac. But in the end, she walked, stiff-legged, into the house. Her mother was standing in the kitchen in her pink silk dressing gown, pouring hot water into their green-and-yellow-striped teapot that had come with them from the flat in London. Looking at it hurt Ashley's heart. The old flat might have been tiny and damp, but she had had so much more freedom then, even as a child.

"Did you sleep well, dear?" Her mum smiled at her in her vacant way. "I thought I heard you in the night, calling out."

"No, Mum. I slept fine."

"So, what about it?" Her father, who stood by the door, said, "What was up with you yesterday? Absolute bloody pandemonium, Helen. She started talking to something that wasn't there, and then she started behaving like bloody Shelley Duvall in *The Shining*, all wide-eyed and terrified. It's fine, Ash, if you want to change things up a bit. I get it. Maybe the show is starting to get boring for you after all these years and you want to add a bit of drama. But you *have* to discuss it with us first. I need to know what you've got planned. As it is, I've ended up giving out a load of cheap tickets for your next performance, which'll eat into our margins."

"Wow, Dad, I'm so sorry about your margins." She bit her lip. Despite everything, they were her parents, and she wanted to confide in them. Perhaps then they could help her. "Has it occurred to you that what happened to me—finding that little boy—has messed me up?"

Her father snorted. "You want therapy again? Is that what you're saying? Because that went so well last time. I *know* you're tougher than that, Ashley."

She closed her eyes. This was useless.

"I won't have any nonsense," her father was saying. "This is a delicate time for the business, with the potential for us to make a lot of cash. Right? The last thing I need is you going off the rails."

Ashley's phone buzzed briefly inside her jeans pocket. She took it out and saw a message from Aidan:

ARE YOU ALL RIGHT, SIS?

"Who's that?'"

"It's just Aidan. You know, the one who is actually concerned about my well-being." Her mother made some stricken noises about that, but the text had given Ashley an idea. Rather than texting Aidan back, she opened a new chat and sent a message to Freddie instead.

CAN YOU COME AND PICK ME UP? MY CAR IS OUT OF ACTION. JUST PULL UP AND KEEP THE ENGINE RUNNING AND I'LL COME OUT. BEEP FOR ME.

She added her address and pressed send before looking up to meet her father's eyes.

"I just told him you're keeping me prisoner."

"Very funny," said Logan. "Your brother won't take any notice. He's always been the sensible one. Now what were you playing at last night?"

Ashley put her phone back into her pocket and shoved past him into the hallway. From there, she went into the living room and sat on the far side of the room. After a moment, her father followed her in, tailed by her mum, who was murmuring with her eyes downcast.

"It's the angels, Logan, you know how they exhaust her. They take so much. She is a vessel of their grace."

"Helen, why don't you make yourself useful? Elsewhere."

Her mother skittered back toward the door, her hands fluttering up to her mouth.

"I'll start pouring the teas."

When she was gone, Logan settled himself in the armchair nearest the television, his thick arms on top of the armrests. Inside her pocket, Ashley felt her phone vibrate again.

"While your mother's out of the room, we can talk sensibly, can't we, love?" He smiled encouragingly at her, but Ashley was familiar with her dad's smiles. They had more in common with the flash of tooth an antelope sees just before the tiger bites than any expression of happiness. "What was that all about, aye?"

Ashley took a long, slow breath. There was no room for the truth in this household. "I don't know. I thought I should capitalize on all the publicity. Give people something more interesting for their money. It just occurred to me in the moment, you know? I saw this video of an American medium on YouTube, this woman with huge hair. She fell onto her knees in the middle of the act and started talking in tongues. It went down a storm."

Her father shook his head, but he did look slightly mollified. "Well. I never thought you had it in you, Ash. But you have to be careful with that showy stuff. British people, they don't go in for that spouting gibberish or possession or whatever. Puts them off their tea. That's why you have to talk about it with me first."

"Yeah, I guess." As casually as possible, Ashley stood and moved to the coffee table where there was a bowl of fruit. She picked out a banana and began to peel it. Her father watched her from his chair. "I'm sorry. I was just caught up in the moment." She thought of the Heedful Ones rising from their seats and took a bite of the banana to distract herself. "What do you think though? I expect it got us a few more lines in the local rag. Maybe even not so local ones."

"Well." Her father leaned forward, his broad hands hanging between his knees. "Maybe you're right. We can work in some smaller moments, perhaps. We've always said we don't want to scare people, but a little scare could make the night memorable. The best way would be to introduce these things slower, in small amounts. You could, I don't know, get a faraway look in your eye in the middle of a reading. Perhaps something startles you that the audience can't see." He shifted in his chair, warming to the subject. "I would like to be there, to begin with, so I can observe the reactions of the audience. We don't want to put them off with your histrionics. What if . . ."

A car horn beeped outside, three times in quick succession. Ashley jumped, already on her feet, and ran out the living room door.

"ASHLEY!"

In a handful of seconds, she was down the hallway and out the front door. She could hear her father running after her, but he wasn't fast enough. When she crashed out onto the gravel drive, she saw Freddie's shiny red car, his window down and his face creased with puzzlement. Ashley grinned at the sight and ran toward the car even as her father started bellowing. Impulsively, she threw the half-eaten banana behind her and yanked the back door of the car open before throwing herself across the seats.

"GO!" She yelled as she reached over and slammed the door shut. To her enormous gratitude, Freddie didn't need telling twice. With a deafening crunch of gravel, he spun the car almost in a doughnut, and then they were facing the drive down the main road. Ashley whipped around, eager to see the look on her father's face. He had gone beet red, and the slimy remains of a banana skin were slapped across the top of one boot.

"Who the fuck is that?" he bellowed.

But it was too late. Freddie's car sped down the drive onto the road, and Ashley whooped with delight from the back seat.

"All right." Freddie laughed nervously. "Um. What is going on, exactly?"

"You helped me escape!" Ashley leaned forward through the front seats and kissed Freddie on the cheek. "Sorry." She sat back and laughed again. "Sorry, but that was hilarious. He's going to be furious."

"Uh. Am I going to wake up in the morning with a horse's head in my bed, or whatever the British equivalent is?"

"Nah, it'll be me he's annoyed with."

"Yeah, I'll be honest, that worries me too."

Ashley took a breath. There would be consequences for this particular piece of disobedience, but that was for later.

"Pull up over here so I can get in the front seat, will you?" Ashley grinned, feeling mildly dizzy. "My knight in shining armor."

CHAPTER

24

WELCOME BACK TO *Murder on the Mind*, with your host, Freddie
Miller. In today's interlude, I'm taking you back to the nine-
teenth century, 1852 to be exact. Queen Victoria was on the throne,
Charles Dickens had started his serialization of *Bleak House*, and a
young romantic poet by the name of Samuel Bickerstaff moved from
the bustling city of Liverpool to a small cottage on the outskirts of
Green Beck. He had it in mind that he would walk the same hills and
mountains that William Wordsworth himself had walked, and be so
inspired that he would finally be able to write the great works that had
so far eluded him.

An Oxford scholar adopted Bickerstaff as a project a few years
back, including him in a short book titled *The Shadow of Wordsworth*; I highly recommend it, if you can track down a copy. This
is why Bickerstaff's letters, and particularly those written to his
lover, Patrick McClory, are a matter of public record. McClory
was at that time on his Grand Tour; Samuel intended to spend
two months in Cumberland, as it was known then, and then join
Patrick in his final destination of Rome. I'll read now from a few
of these letters.

* * *

March 13th

Dearest Pat,

You were right, of course, that the cottage itself is as basic as a rude shepherd's hut, but despite this, I love it (which you will not be much surprised to hear). At night, the wind bellows down off of the mountains like a beast, and I cower around my meager fire like a peasant in the days of King Harry; you would laugh to see it so, I'm sure. Yet, in the mornings, the wild wind has scrubbed the sky clear again, and the sheep cluster together, black and white, while noisy jackdaws chatter. Dear Wordsworth saw the shivering connection between Man and Nature in this beautiful, wild place, and I think I begin to glimpse it too.

* * *

April 4th

. . . the weather here is delightfully unpredictable, Pat. I walk about in all weathers, but I must confess that there are times when it blows up so black and stormy that I fear I will be blown into a lake if I am not careful in my wanderings. My notebooks are filled daily with gushing observation—I have yet to weave a skein of poetry from this bountiful matter, yet I feel soon that I will be moved to do so. My evenings I spend drinking ale in the only tavern in Green Beck, or in my cozy abode reading back through my notes. I have been saving "the red mountain" for my bravest day, for it looms over us tiny creatures at all times, and there is something magnificently unknowable about it. My bravest day must come soon.

* * *

June 29th

Today I followed a sheep trail up alongside the River Keckle, which I then followed into the lower reaches of Red Rigg Fell.

There were more sheep here and lambs with their thick legs and large heads, but none of them ventured onto the rocky sides of the mountain itself. I sat on a low rock nearby, and, Pat, my words came and flowed as never before—just to look upon the fell is to be filled with a cascade of thoughts, images, dreams, and phrases. I could scarcely write fast enough to keep up with my muse, and this evening I find that my fingers are stiff and cramped. No matter. I am eager to return tomorrow and see what else this wild landscape has to tell me.

* * *

June 30th

I slept late this morning, borne to consciousness on a tide of dark dreams of great ill-feeling. Nevertheless, I was eager to be out, pursuing my art; even the violent storm that blew in around three o'clock in the afternoon could not chase me inside. I made my way to the same rock that had served me so well the previous day, and with no sheep in sight, I set to work again, scribbling away with the graphite pencil you so kindly gifted me for this very purpose. Eventually, the weather pushed me so that I had to move, and I took my first steps onto the flanks of the mountain that had so teased the corners of my imagination all week.

* * *

July 3rd

I returned to the mountain again today. It draws me back like a tide. I think that I could spend my whole life in examination of its crags and gorse, its tarns and scree. There is a silence up there, Pat, which I feel I have never experienced elsewhere. It is a waiting silence. Does that worry you? It worries me at times, but my notes continue unabated.

* * *

August 30ᵗʰ

On my explorations of the mountain today, I was not alone. I glimpsed a figure briefly, held in black against the light of the setting sun, yet when I hurried forward to see who I shared the mountain with, I could find no trace. Is that not curious? The southernmost flank, where I stood today, is a landscape of boulder and gorse and pine, so it seems likely I simply lost the man in the befuddlement of sunset. I stayed until dark, listening.

*   *   *

October 1ˢᵗ

The mountain has caught me in a dream. I went to it at sunrise this morning and return now in the deepest inky night, but I could not tell you where I have roamed and what I have seen. I am cold to my bones. I sit here now by the fire and I think of you, darling Pat, with the good strong Italian sunlight on your skin, and deep within me a worm begins to creep. Do you miss me, Pat? Do you think of me at all? Or do you keep the company of other men? Forgive me.

*   *   *

October 5ᵗʰ

I found my way to the summit of the mountain, Pat. The view was uncanny; I could see so far I almost thought I could see you. Is that not strange? But it was not you that I saw, it was a distant world of antiquity, a place where gods still trod their cloven hoofs across grass as green as Eden's fair garden. That world reaches out to us in wild places like these. Beneath me, deep in the bloody bedrock of this cursed place, I felt something old move and shift. I think that there is no poetry in me, after all, Pat.

*   *   *

Samuel Bickerstaff was seen again after this final letter to Patrick McClory; he was spotted by the people of the village of Green Beck, wandering the roads. They all reported that the young man looked like he was sickening for something. One day, he came to the church and left most of his belongings with them, insisting that they be given to the poor and needy. After that, all record of Samuel Bicker-staff ends. The vicar of the parish did as he was asked and gave away Samuel's good coats and vests to those who needed them, but he kept the man's notebooks, which is why I have in my possession fragments of the writings Bickerstaff did while sitting gazing at Red Rigg Fell, or walking in its high places. Below is a small sample—every page was the same: *It hungers and we must feed it. It hungers and we must feed it. It hungers and we must feed it. It hungers and we must feed it. It hungers and we must feed it. It hungers and we must feed it. It hungers . . .*

CHAPTER

25

As they drove out of the Lake District, the weather began to brighten. The thick layer of dark clouds washed away to reveal the vast skies that were Ashley's favorite part of living in northern England. They stopped at a service station halfway and ate coffee and doughnuts in the car, then they drove on to Newcastle, arriving earlier than they had expected, thanks to Ashley's sudden escape from the cottage. From there, Freddie put Elspeth Sutton's address into the satnav, and around forty minutes later, they arrived in the car park beneath a cluster of high-rise flats.

"This is the place."

As Ashley stepped out into the shadow of the tower block, she felt something cold pass through her. The area was run-down, the bin area by the front door unlocked and overflowing with rubbish. There was graffiti streaked across the dark gray breeze-blocks. Off to one side of the pavement, someone had left three shopping trolleys filled with bags of something she couldn't identify.

Freddie was fiddling with his phone. "I just want to record a quick piece before we go up."

"Here?" Ashley looked around uncertainly. It was on the tip of her tongue to tell him that getting his phone out was a quick way to get mugged, but the thought caused a bubble of guilt to well up like gas deep inside her. *We used to live in a place just like this,* she thought. *How would I have felt if people had assumed those things about us?* But then, she realized grimly, *They would have been right.*

"It will only take a moment." Freddie cleared his throat, then began speaking in his podcast voice. "It's a cold, bright day in Newcastle. I'm standing at the bottom of a block of flats in the Midgley Estate with renowned psychic medium Ashley Whitelam."

The wind picked up, blowing around some empty crisp packets and an old Subway wrapper. Ashley frowned.

"We are here following what could be our first break in the case. Elspeth Sutton approached Ashley and myself at the end of one of Ashley's psychic shows. She asked for our help. Elspeth's daughter, Eleanor, has been missing since April, with no real leads and the suggestion from the police that she might have simply run away. But her mother believes that Eleanor's story may be darker. She believes her daughter's story could be linked to the Gingerbread House Murders."

From across the road, Ashley watched a gathering of teenagers emerge from a corner shop. Their sharp eyes seemed to alight on them, and she heard a smattering of laughter. Hating herself slightly for it, she took hold of Freddie's arm.

"Come on. That's enough. Let's get inside."

They called up via the intercom, and after a slightly surprised pause from Mrs. Sutton—they were over half an hour early—she buzzed them in through the heavy metal door. Sutton lived on the ninth floor, and they took the lift up. It was a cramped space, the shiny mirrored wall blurred with a chaotic web of scratches, the floor dirty and slightly sticky. Freddie, standing up straight with his hands in his jacket pockets, looked very out of place.

Elspeth Sutton's flat was on a floor with eight other flats. Ashley knocked on the door, her eye drawn to the spy hole, and Mrs. Sutton opened it almost immediately. She led them down a narrow, neatly decorated hallway into a cozy living room and kitchenette area. One side of the room had big windows and a small balcony looking out at the other high-rise flats. A tabby cat, sitting with her legs tucked into the loaf position, got up, stretched, then ran out of the room.

"Please sit down. I'll put the kettle on."

Ashley sat on the edge of the dark green sofa, her hands clasped in her lap. Freddie, she noticed, looked completely relaxed; he was looking around the room with open interest, as if trying to take in every detail. She wondered how many interviews he'd done in similar places. She pictured him in a mobile home in a trailer park; in one of those exciting apartments in New York, asking his questions and recording it all on his phone.

Mrs. Sutton brought in the teacups already filled. There was a little pot of sugar on the table with a spoon. Ashley gave herself two spoonfuls.

"Thank you for coming," Mrs. Sutton said, her voice very soft. "I know it's a long way to come."

Freddie smiled. "'Not at all, Mrs. Sutton. We're glad to do it. You know, where I'm from, it's a two-hour drive to the mall, and we think nothing of it."

Sutton twitched a little and nodded.

"Would you mind telling us a little about your daughter? What sort of person is she? Oh . . ." He took his phone out of his pocket and placed it on the coffee table between them. "And is it all right if I record this? For my podcast?"

Mrs Sutton didn't look at all convinced by that, but she had clearly decided that it was worth the risk. She nodded again. There was a soft chime as Freddie set his phone to record audio.

"Would you tell us a little about your daughter, Mrs. Sutton? What happened to Eleanor?"

"She's twelve, in year eight at her school. She's quiet, a good girl." Mrs Sutton's hand trembled as she reached for her cup. "Never any trouble."

"What's she like at school?" asked Ashley. The guilt she had felt down by the front door had only increased, and for some reason she felt she had to justify her presence. "Is she popular with the other kids?" Out of the corner of her eye, she saw Freddie glance at her appreciatively.

Mrs. Sutton didn't reply immediately. She took a sip of her tea. "Not popular as such, no. She's always been quite shy, Ellie, but she had a little group of friends in the first year of secondary. But you know what kids are like as they get older. They get different interests, drift apart. I . . . I had a meeting with her form tutor at the beginning of the year, because they were concerned that she was isolated at school." She stopped then, the thin line of her lips creasing as she tried not to cry.

"I'm sorry," Ashley said. The tight feeling of guilt in her chest blossomed into something sharper, something worse. Eleanor felt painfully familiar.

"Is Ellie's father around?" asked Freddie.

Mrs. Sutton winced. "He lives down south now. Doesn't have much to do with us. The police, when I told them Ellie was gone, asked if she'd gone to stay with her dad, but that's just daft. She doesn't really know him! Why would she go there? In any case, she never turned up."

"What happened the day Ellie disappeared?" asked Freddie. "Was it an unusual day? Anything weird or strange happen?"

She shook her head. From somewhere outside and below, a police siren began to warble.

"It was a Saturday. She went to a little club on Saturdays, at the library. I was so glad when she started going to that, because I thought it would help her make friends." Once again, her voice began to break. She cleared her throat and continued. "She went there for midday. The library said later that she arrived, and they did their little activities."

"Which were?"

Mrs. Sutton shrugged. "It's a class about the arts, so they do something different every week, I think. Sometimes they're learning about a particular artist, or sculpture, poetry, things like that. It's not like school; it's less formal. Ellie loves music and art; she's always been like that. So she was there. We know she was there because the other children saw her, the librarian saw her, and then she left as usual to come home, and she didn't. She just didn't come home. Nearly six months ago." Mrs Sutton pressed one shaky hand to her lips for a moment before continuing. "The police don't have any leads. One of them asked if I thought she might have run away from home. She's at the age when some kids do that, that's what they said. But Ellie was not like that!" To Ashley's shock, the woman turned directly to her, her eyes wild. "Do you see? She was quiet, she liked to be at home! She wouldn't have just run away. She got homesick when she was at a sleepover for just one night, for goodness' sake."

"Mrs. Sutton, can I ask you . . . I know this is a difficult thing to think about"—Freddie leaned forward, his face set and serious—"but why do you think Ellie's disappearance is linked to the same person who took Robbie Metcalfe? When we met you outside of Ashley's show, you seemed very sure that it was."

The older woman looked down at her hands in her lap. A single tear escaped the corner of her eye, and she rubbed it away impatiently with the pad of her thumb.

"I have a feeling, oh God, a terrible feeling. When it's your own flesh and blood, you have this, I don't know, this sixth sense about things." She looked up at Ashley again, her eyes too bright. "*You* will know what I mean. For you, I imagine, the feelings will be a lot stronger because you have a deep connection to it. I don't know. But every time I've seen something in the news about the Gingerbread House Murders, I feel a little more lost, a bit more certain." She took a watery breath. "And Jack Crispin and Harry Cornell, they were both from Newcastle. Whoever he is who's taking these kids, he's been here. He's been close. I said that to the police, but they don't think Eleanor is connected."

Freddie tipped his head to one side. "Did the police give you any idea why they didn't think it was related to these other disappearances?"

Mrs. Sutton sighed. "No. They barely told me anything. But they did ask me if I had received anything strange in the post, which I thought was odd. If anything unusual had been posted through our door."

Freddie glanced at Ashley, and she thought she knew what he was thinking: Was this how the police connected the murders?

"I said no," Mrs Sutton continued. "But you see, our postman doesn't come up in the lifts—there's a place on the ground floor where we each have a postal locker, and he posts things there, or he's supposed to. But I told them! Those lockers are broken into all the time! Letters and parcels are always going astray."

"And they didn't say what they thought you might have received?" asked Ashley.

"No, no. Like I said, they barely said anything to me. The last update they gave me, they said they were still looking. They were following up *leads*." She fished a wad of tissue from a pocket and pressed it to the corner of her eye fiercely. "Sorry. But they won't help me. *You* have to help me, Ashley, if I can call you that. *Please.* Help me find Ellie like you found Robbie Metcalfe. I have to know, one way or another."

The room seemed to grow several degrees warmer. Ashley felt a hot trickle of sweat move down between her shoulder blades, and all at once she felt disgusted—disgusted with herself and her cruel, despicable profession; disgusted with a world that took daughters away from their mums; disgusted that she was sitting here drinking this grieving mother's tea and offering her false hope. How could she ever explain that what happened with Robbie Metcalfe was inexplicable? That she had no hope of repeating it?

"Mrs. Sutton, we are not the police," said Freddie. "And by that, I mean that we will not dismiss your feelings or suspicions, and that we do not have all the resources of law enforcement. But we will do everything we can."

Ashley felt a flicker of annoyance. Delivered in his podcast voice, Freddie's promises sounded glib, convincing for the sake of entertainment only. But she could see that Mrs. Sutton hadn't heard a word of it anyway. She was looking only at Ashley. Her eyes were a faded blue and they sparkled with unshed tears.

"Will you do it?" she asked in a thick voice. "Will you look for Ellie?"

Ashley nodded. What else could she do? Filled with disgust for herself, she was desperate to get out of the room.

"Could I see Eleanor's bedroom?" Ashley stood. "It would really help me to get a sense of her."

Mrs. Sutton looked relieved. "Yes, please do that. Anything you need. Her room is the second on the right."

Freddie rose from where he sat, and Ashley touched his shoulder, shaking her head.

"No, I don't need you with me, Freddie. It'll only disrupt things. Please stay here and keep Mrs. Sutton company."

*   *   *

Eleanor Sutton's bedroom was exactly what Ashley was expecting, and it was all the more painful for that. It was small and boxy, with a narrow single bed with a pink-and-white-striped duvet. There was a little dressing table that looked like it might collapse if you looked too hard at it, the paint peeling off around the frame of the mirror, which had stickers of heartthrobs she didn't recognize cluttering the edges. There was a wardrobe and a set of drawers, both of which looked cheap but cared for, and on top of the latter, there was a range of raggedly looking soft toys. Ellie was old enough to be experimenting with makeup, given a few No.7 lipsticks and Rimmel eye shadows on the dressing table, but also not quite old enough to let go of the threadbare teddies and bunny rabbits she had treasured as a little girl.

"Ah, bloody hell," murmured Ashley. "What a sad mess."

She went to the small bookshelf under the window—there was no dust to be seen anywhere; her mother was clearly keeping the place pristine—and when she turned back toward the door, her heart leaped into her throat. A Heedful One stood in the far corner, a tall scarecrow figure made of shadows. Its head was down, thankfully hiding its unfinished face, and its arms hung loose by its sides.

"Fuck me."

Ashley took a slow breath, her pulse thundering rapidly at her wrists and temples. Why had the Heedful Ones come back? Why did they show her where Robbie Metcalfe was if it wasn't to mess up her life? What caused them to act as they did? And what were their motives? This one was behaving in the way with which she was most familiar: it simply hung in its space, watchful yet unmoving. A witness to Ashley's shame.

"Leave me alone," she said in a low voice. "Why can't you just go away?"

The shadowy figure did not react. It simply stayed where it was, its unnaturally long arms moving slightly, as though in some secret breeze. After a moment or so, there was a soft knock on the door, and Ashley jumped for a second time. It was Freddie, his voice oddly respectful.

"Ashley, are you okay in there? Just checking in."

"Yeah." Ashley cleared her throat and made her voice louder. Her eyes never left the Heedful One. "Yeah, I'm good. I'm ready to leave this place."

CHAPTER

26

"SHIT. I'VE GOT about a hundred missed calls on this thing."
They sat in a Pret A Manger on Northumberland Street,
eating a lunch of sandwiches that were too cold and cups of dubious
coffee. Freddie had bought a large chocolate chip cookie too and was
carefully splitting it in half while Ashley checked her phone.

"You turned it off?"

"I hardly wanted my phone ringing while we talked to Mrs. Sutton,
did I? Oh look, most of them are from Dad anyway, so they can safely
be ignored. And then he clearly called Aidan to badger him about it,
because after that I have several missed calls from Aidan, as well as
texts, and then *he* clearly phoned Malory to see if she knew what I was
up to, because I have calls from her too. It's like bloody Spanish Inqui-
sition dominoes. There's an unrecognized number on here too."

"What do you want to do?'"

"I should reply to one of them at least so they know I'm not dead.
Then, I don't know. But judging from your face, I think you have an
idea."

He grinned in an alarmingly appealing way and passed her half of
the cookie. "See, you *are* psychic. Eat that before you call them—the
sugar will help."

* * *

Ashley stepped outside to make the phone call. It was a busy day out there, with people rushing back and forth on their daily business that likely didn't include murders or impossible tasks to find dead bodies. The light had that overly desperate brightness of autumn afternoons, when the evening was bearing down faster and faster.

"Ash?"

"Hi, Aidan. I'm sure Dad has been annoying the living piss out of you today, so apologies for that."

Her brother laughed quietly. "Where are you? They're doing their nut. Dad has been telling everyone you were abducted, and Mum is threatening to call the police and report you missing."

Ashley sighed deeply and leaned against the wall. Aidan sounded quiet and small down the phone, as though he were in Australia or on the moon rather than a couple hour's drive away. "I should have known there was no chance of a sensible response from them. And as if *Dad* would go to the police. What did you tell them?"

"I told them that you'd met this American guy and you were probably having a fling."

"Fuck you."

"Well, aren't you?"

"We're investigating the Gingerbread House Murders." As soon as she said it out loud, she felt ridiculous, but it was true. That's what they were doing, wasn't it? "I don't have any appointments in the book for today, so I can do what I want, right? Dad took my car away from me, Aidan. I can't . . . I can't live like this forever. I have to have my own life." She took a breath. Years of unsaid things felt like they were boiling under the surface. "Dad treats me like the golden goose, like I'm a thing that produces money for him on demand and I can't be let out of his sight. Mum treats me like a doll made of glass. Which is actually worse. I can't do it anymore.'"

It was Aidan's turn to sigh. "Where are you, Ash? Let me at least tell them that you're safe."

"I am safe," Ashley said firmly. "I'll text you when I'm on my way back. And that will have to do."

After she hung up on Aidan, she called Malory, who answered halfway through the first ring.

"Did you do a runner on them, Ashie? You absolute minx."

"Hi, Malory. I'm in Newcastle, would you believe?"

She gave her friend a brief outline of where she was and what she was doing, and listening to Malory's exclamations and unfettered critique of her parents gradually made her feel better. When she brought up Freddie, she had to field a barrage of questions, but she made sure not to mention the name of the podcast so Malory couldn't go looking him up.

"Keep your secrets then, wizard," said Malory in the airy voice she used when quoting *The Lord of the Rings*. "But look after yourself. And keep me updated."

* * *

Back inside Pret, Freddie had finished his coffee and sandwich, and he had his laptop out on the table. When Ashley sat down, he closed it again.

"How did it go?"

"I live to fight another day." Ashley put her phone back on silent and tucked it in her pocket. "What's the plan?"

"Mrs. Sutton quite rightly mentioned that two of the victims were also from Newcastle. Now, Jack Crispin's family I have never been able to locate, but Harry Cornell's father has a work address. Since we're here already, what do you say to the idea of making our way over there? I reckon we've a couple of hours before he finishes work for the day, and I really want to know what the police were expecting to find in Mrs. Sutton's mailbox."

Ashley took another bite of the cookie and chewed. Bothering the parents of a murdered child did not seem like a great or worthy way to spend the rest of the day, but her alternative was a long drive back home, where she would be greeted by her mother's hysteria and her father's continued ire. She swallowed.

"Fuck it. Let's do it."

CHAPTER

27

2004

IN THE EVENINGS, the children were given mugs of hot chocolate before bed, served in the great drawing room, a large but cozy room featuring big armchairs and sofas covered in cushions. There was a fireplace, empty save for a tall porcelain dog sitting where the fire would be in the winter. Ashley sat in one of the armchairs, sipping her hot chocolate and feeling oddly content. The bag of clothes Malory had given her had been taken to the dorm room and placed under her bed, and knowing that she had such a gift made the awkwardness of spending time with the other children less painful. She was special, after all, despite what Richard had said. Even the strangeness of the dirty man in the corridor had not, in the end, been enough to dampen the day for her. The lamps were low, and the tall windows were filled with the dark blue skies of twilight.

And then, she began to see the Heedful Ones.

They flickered into existence like silent blasts of soot, one after the other. Two at first, then three, then five. In her seat, Ashley drew back a little, uncertain what to make of this. She had rarely seen more than two Heedful Ones at a time, yet here they were, crowding into the drawing room like guests at a party. Nine, ten, twelve. Ashley drew her legs up onto the armchair; she wanted to make herself as small as possible.

"Ashley? Get your feet off of that chair, please." Mr. Haygarth appeared in front of her, his eyebrows raised. "This is someone else's home, remember? You're not to treat it like a slum."

"But, Mr. Haygarth . . ." Ashley couldn't move. To put her feet down on the floor was to expose herself. "No." She had no reasonable explanation for him, after all. Mr. Haygarth shook his head slightly.

"Really, Ashley, I expected better of you. Feet off. Now."

Gritting her teeth, Ashley put her feet back on the thick rug, and at that moment, a Heedful One moved noiselessly toward her, passing right through the body of Mr. Haygarth. For the barest second, while he was contained with the shifting, smoky black, the teacher had looked different. Changed in some huge, fundamental way that was difficult to look at. Then the Heedful One was gone, moving off behind the fireplace.

"There you are." Mr. Haygarth smiled, some warmth coming back into his face. "I'm sure your mum doesn't like you getting your feet all over the furniture, does she?"

Ashley shook her head, looking down at her knees until she heard Mr. Haygarth sigh and walk away. But when she brought her head back up, the Heedful Ones had only increased—there were so many of them now that the room was filled with their slender, sooty bodies. They were moving faster than they normally did, as though they were agitated in some way.

"What do you want?" Ashley asked under her breath. "What are you all doing here?"

"Look at this weirdo! She talks to herself."

Ashley recognized the boy from the communal dinners; he had big eyes and thick eyelashes, in that way boys sometimes do, and permanently flushed cheeks. He made her think of one of the words from her word tin she had never had to use: *cherub*.

"You having a nice little chat with yourself, are you, weirdo?" The boy had two other boys with him and a girl. They had all finished their hot chocolate.

All of Ashley's contentment drained away into the floor. The children had begun to notice her again, and the Heedful Ones were swarming.

"Leave me alone," said Ashley, her voice little more than a whisper. She didn't know if she was talking to the cherub boy or the teeming shadows. *"Leave me alone."*

The boy laughed, apparently delighted with her demand. One of the Heedful Ones came and stood behind him and *inside* him. The shape of the boy, with his blond hair and his pink cheeks, was lost. Instead, he became a dark thing of sticks and smoke, his human shape little more than a sketchy impression, a bag of animated bones. She saw the teeth in his skull, cracked and blackened.

Ashley's mug of hot chocolate slipped in her hands, a slop of the brown liquid splashing over her jumper. One of the other kids laughed. As if the sound had attracted it, another Heedful One slipped across, covering the child in its darkness and revealing something skeletal within; Ashley could see tiny flecks of burning orange in that darkness too, rising up on some unseen wind.

The other children were still speaking, but she wasn't listening anymore. As she looked around the room, the other kids were smothered by the forms of the Heedful Ones, revealing to her some dark secret she didn't understand. She had never seen them do this before. Had never even guessed that they could.

"Right!" Somewhere in the fog of the drawing room, Mr. Haygarth had clapped his hands together once. His raised voice was a beacon of ordinariness. "Time to make your way up to the dorm, kids. We've got another busy day tomorrow!"

The Heedful Ones followed them up to the dormitory.

Ashley moved along in the crowd, feeling about as alone as she had ever felt, even in the midst of a large gang of children. She couldn't tell anyone about what she was seeing—she knew that without question—so she just had to suffer it and hope it would be over soon. As she crept into her pajamas, she snuck looks at the other children. Almost all of them were now shadowed by a Heedful One. The shifting patches of darkness hung over each like a shroud, slightly out of step with their movements but clinging on as though attached by some unseen cord. Mr. Haygarth still had his shadow too. And where the flesh-and-blood person met the insubstantial form of the Heedful One, some dreadful truth was revealed: black, smoking bones; glistening body cavities; steaming fluid—all seen in flickering glimpses.

Ashley got into bed and burrowed down under the scratchy covers, the top blanket pulled right up to her chin. The larger strip lights on the ceiling had been turned off, and the room was lit only by the small table lamps that sat on each bedside table. One by one, these were turned off too, patches of safe yellow light surrendering to the dark. Ashley watched them go, frozen with fright even as the giggling and the chatter of the other children rose slightly in pitch; bedtime always saw a peak of excitement.

"That's enough now," Mr Haygarth called good-naturedly. From her vantage point, Ashley could see the top half of his torso. His head was a charcoal skull. "Time to settle down. Lights off, please. Myself and Miss Lyonnes are just down the corridor if you need anything, but do try to sleep. Good night!"

The few lights clicked off, and there was a flurry of giggles again. The night sky from the tall arched windows seemed much closer, a splash of stars like cream across blue velvet.

"It's harder to see them in the dark," Ashley whispered to herself. "I can pretend they're not there. And they're not, not really, anyway. No one else can see them."

"Uh, can you shut up, please?" The voice came from the girl in the bed next to hers. "Why did I have to get stuck next to the weirdo that talks to herself?" There was a ripple of laughter from the larger room. Ashley pulled the covers up to her nose.

After that, the whispers and the laughter gradually stopped. Ashley lay very still, her arms and legs rigid, and kept her eyes on the windows. She had never been afraid of the Heedful Ones before, but then she had never seen them do this before, had never seen them swarm or cover people with their shadows. She didn't like what their shadows revealed. A busy silence filled the long dorm room, punctuated with the odd squeak of a mattress as someone turned over in bed, the fluting snores of someone near the door, the occasional cough.

And then, just as Ashley's eyelids were getting heavy, the blue starscape caught in the window frames was broken by a tall, dark shape. One of the Heedful Ones was at the bottom of her bed. Its face, such as it was, was hidden in shadow, but it was looking at her.

Ashley moaned. Was this what the Heedful Ones had always been waiting to do? Her whole life, they had been an odd but innocuous presence. It was as alarming as the old family dog that turns on the baby and as treacherous as the swing that breaks at the peak of its trajectory. The shape moved along the bed toward her, passing through the frame and the mattress and the duvet as though they were made of mist. Ashley shrank back, but there was nowhere for her to go.

The first thing she felt as it passed into her was a dreadful heat, a crisp crackle of hot air that instantly dried out her mouth and stung her eyes, and there was a roar of sound that pressed against her eardrums. Looking out from within the Heedful One, it was as though the whole dorm room had been covered in a fine, black gauze. The other Heedful Ones had vanished, but she could see the other children—they weren't in bed any longer but rather crowding around the door, trying to get out. The door itself was shut fast, and the ceiling was on fire.

"What's happening?"

Ashley sat up in bed, choking in the smoke and heat. As she watched, pieces of fire fell from the ceiling onto the floor and the beds. The old feather-filled duvets and scratchy blankets lit up like they'd been waiting to do it all their lives. Very quickly, much of the room was ablaze. Ashley sat where she was, unable to move beyond the Heedful One that held her in place. Some of the children had given up battering down the door and had moved to the windows instead; one of the larger boys picked up a suitcase and hurled it at the glass, but it bounced off. The ceiling was now too bright to look at. The rain of flames was starting to alight on the children too; a piece of fiery debris landed directly on top of one girl's head, giving her a flaming cap, and her screams became a shriek of agony.

"No, no, no." Ashley felt her eyes well up with tears, but it was too hot in the dorm room to cry. Some of the children had started to hide under their beds; she saw a boy slide down the far wall, overcome with smoke. Other children were trying to break the windows, but none succeeded. One boy, his pajama top on fire, ran into the corner of the room and curled up there, as though trying to hide from the flames that were burning him alive. The choking stench of the smoke changed slightly, becoming the hot, sweet smell of burning flesh. Ashley bent over in her bed, her head on her knees, but somehow she could still see it all, and more: she saw the room become a roaring inferno, and she saw the children screaming, their flesh burned away. At one point, three of the windows simply exploded, but by then it was far too late for any of the children trapped inside the dorm.

And then, in a blink, it was all gone. Ashley sat in her bed, in a clear, unburned room. Around her were a few children, their faces pale and their eyes wide. Mr. Haygarth was there too, and he had one hand on Ashley's shoulder, shaking her lightly. He looked both alarmed and slightly exasperated.

"Ashley, wake up. Wake up! You're having a nightmare."

It was at that point that Ashley realized she was screaming.

28

Harry Cornell's father, Ben Cornell, worked at the large branch of B&Q, not that far from the River Tyne itself, although any sense of the river was lost under the rumble of ever-present traffic. By the time they'd driven there and parked, the light was already seeping out of the day, and even though it was only four o'clock, it felt much later. Ashley paused just before the automatic doors, her hands in her pockets.

"Nervous?"

She gave Freddie a lopsided smile. "It's not very British, you know. Confronting someone at their place of work. Perhaps we should write him a letter first."

"I already did," said Freddie. "Or at least I wrote emails. Ben Cornell never replied. Anyway, we're not confronting him, Ashley. We're just here to ask some questions. Ben Cornell is a victim in all this."

They passed under the bright orange signage and into the bulk of the shop. The place was cavernous, with high ceilings, square lights, and a squeaky gray floor. Near the entrance were several rows of tills, which Freddie made a beeline for. The first one he came to was manned by a young woman in her early twenties with a bored expression and thick false eyelashes that made Ashley think of the bristly attachment for her mother's vacuum cleaner. She brightened up considerably when Freddie appeared.

"Excuse me, Miss," he said, turning the full wattage of his smile on her. "You don't happen to know if Ben Cornell is here today?"

"Yeah, he's in," she said, sitting up a little straighter in her booth. "He'll be over by the garden stuff if he's not on a break."

"Thank you kindly, Miss. Have a great day!"

Following the big signs that hung over the aisles, they made their way toward the gardening area. Freddie was wearing a checkered lumberjack shirt, and Ashley wondered if the other people in the B&Q—couples mostly, pushing trolleys and snapping at each other—assumed that she and Freddie were together. It was an amusing thought, and she allowed herself to imagine that they were looking for entirely mundane things, like tiles for the second bathroom they had planned, or a new shed that they would playfully argue over the use of. She was just picturing his mini office, which would double as a sound studio, when Freddie stopped and nodded.

"There he is," he said in a low voice.

Ben Cornell was a short wiry man with a blunt, stubbly face. He was wearing the B&Q uniform, but it was baggy on him. As they watched, he moved large bags of compost from the trolley onto a larger display. There was a blank expression on his face that made Ashley uneasy. It was impossible to guess what he was thinking.

Stop it, Ashley told herself. *You're being ridiculous.*

"Excuse me, sir? Mr Cornell?"

The short man straightened up and looked at them warily.

"Yes? Can I help you?"

Freddie's face was solemn. "I wondered if I could ask you a few questions."

"There's a customer query desk just back down that aisle," said Cornell. He had dark gray bags under his eyes. Underneath the usual discomfort of asking a stranger for something they were unlikely to want to give, Ashley felt a deeper dread unfurl in her chest. *We shouldn't be speaking to him.*

"It's about your son, Harry," Freddie continued.

Cornell's eyes flashed. "Are you the police then?"

"No, Mr Cornell. I am a freelance journalist. I wondered if . . ."

"You come to my place of work now, do you?" The anger in the shorter man's voice was rising. He rubbed his hands together, brushing off dirt, and shook his head. "Unbelievable. You people are fucking unbelievable."

"We're sorry to bother you." Ashley was speaking before she even knew what she was going to say. "We're trying to find out a bit more about what happened, and . . ."

For the first time, his attention turned fully to Ashley, and as his face changed, she realized they had made a huge mistake.

"You!" The banks of fury went from embers to a volcano in seconds. People along the aisle were turning to look. "I saw you on the bloody news! The worst of the lot, preying on grieving parents to line your own pockets. I ought to smash your bloody face in."

Freddie was between the two of them quickly, his hands up. "Please, Mr. Cornell, there's no need to be like that."

"No need?" The man was shouting now. Ashley heard someone calling for security, and a wave of warmth crept up her body from her toes to the top of her head. *Get out, get out, before it all goes wrong.* "No need? She's the one on TV parading herself around on the backs of dead children!"

"Fucking hell," muttered Ashley.

"What did you say?" snapped Cornell. He leaned forward and around Freddie, as though trying to grab her. "What did you say to me, girl?"

Freddie took the man's arm and pushed him back. "That's enough."

The punch was so quick that Ashley had barely registered it before Freddie was reeling back, both hands clutching his face. There was a shriek from the people watching, and then a nervous laugh. Quickly, she stepped in front of Freddie; the heat was prickling at her scalp, and her heart was thundering.

"Get out of it," she snapped, her voice pinched with anger. "Control yourself, you idiot."

Mr. Cornell deflated a little, unsure of himself. A large man in a dark blue security guard uniform was jogging down the aisle toward them.

"What's going on here then?"

Ashley ignored them both and turned to Freddie. His glasses were hanging from his face and there was a ragged cut to one side of his left eye where the lens had broken awkwardly, and blood was running down his cheek. Hesitantly, she pushed his hair back from his temple to get a better look. By this time, Cornell was having a pitched argument with the security guard.

"You can't go around lamping customers, Ben. I'll have to call the police."

"They're harassing me in my place of work!"

Freddie straightened up, one hand over his bleeding eye.

"Please, there's no need for that. I'm sorry to have disturbed you, Mr. Cornell. We'll be leaving now."

The security guard looked at them skeptically, and Ashley found she couldn't blame him. There was a growing mutter coming from the small crowd that surrounded them.

"Are you sure, Freddie?" Ashley's heart was only just beginning to slow down. "You'll probably need a stitch or two."

He shook his head, smiling slightly. "I won't report this, Mr. Cornell, if you don't. I think we can at least both agree that the police aren't needed."

The short man looked like he might argue, but Freddie lowered his hand to reveal that his face was now streaked with blood, and Cornell looked away.

"Fine," he muttered. "Just get out of my sight."

*   *   *

Five hours at A&E later, Freddie walked out with four stitches and an incongruously cheerful expression on his face. Ashley, who had been sitting in a cramped waiting room, stood up and winced.

"You look a mess. So what are you so cheerful about?"

"Your National Health Service is incredible."

"We just had to wait several hours to be seen."

"But, I didn't have to pay for any of it! Can you believe that?" Without his glasses, he looked younger, more vulnerable, and Ashley felt an uncomfortable tremor of affection for him. In truth, sitting in the waiting room for hours had been a strange kind of endurance test all of its own; the Heedful Ones were thick on the ground here, lurking around corners or following patients down the halls like they were tethered on a leash. She was keen to leave the place.

"Okay, yeah, fair enough. It is pretty incredible. It's amazing to me you can call yourselves a civilized country without proper health care, you know."

She meant it as a mild kind of joke, but Freddie nodded seriously. Outside, it was cold and gloomy. They stood on the steps for a moment, doused in blue light from an approaching ambulance. It seemed like a hundred years since she had fled her house and jumped into Freddie's car.

"Do you have any spare glasses?" she asked.

Freddie sighed. "I do. In my room at the B and B in Green Beck."

"Ah. I assume you need them for driving?"

"My eyes are absolute garbage without them, yep."

The back of the ambulance opened and a large man with a sling on his arm practically fell out of it, shouting something unintelligible. Two paramedics helped him back onto his feet again.

"I could drive us back," said Ashley, carefully. "I'm a bit nervous about driving cars that aren't the Parma Violet, so it'll probably take longer than two hours. And I could drop you off in Green Beck, then return the car to you in the morning. Assuming I'm allowed to ever leave the house again. We'll get back pretty late."

"We could do that," Freddie agreed. "But?"

She turned to him, feeling as though the wild weather had infected her blood. "Fuck it," she said. "Let's go to a hotel and head back in the morning."

29

"HAVE YOU EVER even stayed in a hotel before, Ashie?"

Ashley laughed. She was lying on a double bed with white sheets and too many oversized pillows, her phone pressed to her cheek. She felt tired, but also much too awake.

"Obviously I have, Malory. I spend half my time traveling about with my ridiculous job, don't I?"

"I meant without your brother or your father." Ashley could hear the smile in her friend's voice, and it was equal parts amusing and annoying. "I imagine you and Aidan sharing a twin room while your father prowls the corridors outside."

"Oh piss off." Ashley thought of their old council flat in London, and the tiny room she'd shared with her brother. "Listen. I just wanted to let someone know where I was tonight. Just in case."

"In case this podcaster turns out to be an axe murderer?"

"Yes, exactly. So if I turn up in pieces, you'll know why." Unbidden, an image of Robbie Metcalfe's mutilated body flashed across her mind, and nothing seemed particularly amusing at all. She said goodbye to Malory and sat for a moment on her bed, peering around at the hotel room. It was deeply plain and functional, in the way that hotel rooms were, and small—at such short notice, they hadn't had a huge amount of choice—but it still seemed to her that there were too many places to hide: the curtains that fell right to the floor and hid the cavernous windows, the dusty space under the bed, the wardrobe.

Stop being ridiculous.

Once the thought was in there though, it was impossible to dislodge, and a few minutes later she was standing outside Freddie's room, knocking on his door. He opened it, blinking slightly—she wondered how strong his glasses prescription was—and then he grinned.

"I'm starving." She held up the room service menu. "Shall we order something in? My treat."

* * *

Neither room had the luxury of a mini bar, but it turned out they could order whatever they liked over the phone. Very quickly they had two bottles of excruciatingly cheap wine, a platter of doorstop sandwiches and, for afters, a tub of rapidly melting Ben & Jerry's Phish Food. They sat on the bed together with the platter between them and began working their way through the sandwiches. In his socks, his shirt undone to reveal a plain white vest underneath, Freddie looked almost boyish. She imagined that this was how he had looked at college, sitting up late in the library studying for his criminology degree.

"So," he said. "How do you feel it went today?"

For a few minutes, they both roared with laughter, caught in that infectious hilarity that often follows a stressful day. They were also both one glass of wine in already.

"Oh, you know," she said eventually, wiping moisture away from the corner of her eye with her index finger. "As well as can be expected, I reckon. You only got punched in the face *once*. This is practically a record for a night out in Newcastle."

"Okay, so it didn't go exactly according to plan, but it's all excellent material for *Murder on the Mind*."

"You recorded it?"

"Some of it. I doubt I'll get permission from Ben Cornell to use what I got, but I might use snippets for trailers and so on." He shifted on the bed, making it dip and rise slightly, and reached for the wine bottle before topping up their glasses. "What did you think about

Eleanor Sutton? Do you think you'll be able to find Ellie the same way you found Robbie?"

Ashley looked at him over the top of her glass.

"What?" he asked.

She shook her head, then took a big gulp of wine. "Do *you* think I can?"

Freddie shrugged. "Like I said when we started all this, my mind is completely open. It's the key to a good true crime podcast, in my opinion. You have to be open to all of the possible clues, suspects, and outcomes. Did you feel anything in Eleanor Sutton's room?"

"I felt sad." Ashley picked at the crust of a half-eaten sandwich. "And angry, I suppose. Which is what anyone would feel."

Freddie nodded.

Eventually, Ashley continued. "It felt familiar. That's what I thought. Tiny, cramped bedroom in a shitty block of flats. I've been there before. Not in any mystical sense, but in an I-literally-lived-in-a-place-like-this sense."

"You certainly don't live in a place like that now," said Freddie, his tone neutral. "Big house in the middle of the remote countryside. I'm assuming everything changed for your family in 2004?"

"It certainly changed, that's true."

"Can I ask you about it? About what happened at Red Rigg House?"

Ashley shrugged and picked up her glass of wine from where she'd rested it on the floor. She drained half the glass and shrugged again for good measure. "What is there to say about it? You're a . . . What did you say to Ben Cornell? A freelance journalist. I reckon you'll have looked up all of that before you contacted me. There was plenty about it in every newspaper—my dad made sure of that, and that's one of the reasons we now live in that ridiculous house."

"That's fair," said Freddie. "Jeez, this wine is . . . is it supposed to taste like this? I'm more of a beer man, really."

Ashley laughed. "Why did you order wine then?"

"Because that's what you wanted."

"You don't have to be such a gentleman all the time, you know. You'll make British men look bad." The words hung between them for a moment, and Ashley felt herself grow a degree warmer—not in the crushing, panicky way it usually happened, but in a sweet, exhilarating way. To distract herself, she picked up the platter and put it on the TV unit, then sat back on the bed. "All right, so do you think Eleanor Sutton is related to the Gingerbread House killings? What do you think the police were after when they asked if she'd received anything strange in the post?"

Freddie moved his long limbs around until he was sitting cross-legged on the bed. "Firstly, yes, I do think Eleanor might be another victim, sadly, but I also don't have any firm reasons for that hypothesis—aside from the fact it seems extremely unlikely that she ran away from home. I believe somebody got her. Secondly, serial killers, or at least organized ones, have been known to stalk the families of their victims beforehand—the Golden State Killer likely phoned the houses in the weeks before he attacked the occupants, and he probably watched the house during that time too. Both BTK and the Zodiac sent letters."

"BTK?"

"It stood for Bind Torture Kill." Seeing Ashley's expression, he smiled lopsidedly. "Shit. Yeah. I forget sometimes that other people don't spend their working lives reading about this stuff. Sorry."

Ashley shook her head, half smiling herself. "There are some really fucked-up people out there. So a letter then?"

"Maybe. But whatever it is, the police clearly haven't been able to trace it back to the killer. So, perhaps it's not handwritten; perhaps there's no DNA or fingerprints. Perhaps it's something else entirely." He paused.

"What?"

"It won't make you feel better."

"*What?*"

"If it was received after the child went missing, it could have been . . . well, one of the things we know is that all the victims were mutilated."

"Shit. You're right. That doesn't make me feel better." She thought of her small dark room again, the big gap beneath the bed, the blank stretch of curtains within grabbable distance of where she'd lay her head. "This is going to sound completely fucking unhinged, or even like a terrible come on, but . . . would it be all right if I didn't go back to my own room tonight?"

She saw a flash of something pass over his face—pleasure, or more likely surprise—and then he nodded.

"It's not a problem. Listen, we've already shared hours in a hospital corridor, one act of random violence, a getaway, and two bottles of shitty wine. And that's just today. I feel like I've known you for years."

Ashley let go of the breath she'd been holding.

In the end, they got the spare pillows from the wardrobe and used them to prop themselves up in the bed. Freddie gave Ashley one of the big T-shirts he had left in his car—it easily came down to her knees. They put the TV on, found a channel that was playing a long run of cheesy old horror movies, and ate the partially melted ice cream between them. Eventually, Freddie nodded off in front of *Theatre of Blood*, and oddly reassured by that, Ashley crawled under the duvet herself and fell swiftly into a dreamless sleep.

* * *

The next morning, Ashley woke with an intense feeling of disorientation; the room was wrong, the bed was wrong, even the light coming in through the windows was wrong. When she turned over and felt the warm space in the bed next to her, the events of the previous night came flooding back. She turned over so that her face was pressed into the pillow.

"Oh God," she mumbled. She was filled with the sense of having exposed too much of herself, not physically but emotionally. *Why did I ask to stay? Too scared to sleep in my own hotel room. Maybe my dad is right to treat me like a five-year-old.* When she slid out of bed, she noticed the sticky wine glasses on the TV unit next to the remains of their sandwiches, like sentinels watching over her bad decisions. The taps were running, and when she crept up to the open bathroom door, she saw Freddie in a pair of Batman boxer shorts and his white vest, shaving in front of the mirror. He caught her eye in the reflection and raised his eyebrows.

"I hope I didn't snore. I've been told that I do."

Ashley smiled and looked away. The sight of his tanned legs was too much.

"I was dead to the world," she said, trying to rest her eyes anywhere but on his boxers. "I'm gonna go back to my room and have a shower, okay? I'm sorry for being such a weenie last night."

"Hey. Anytime."

* * *

Ashley scampered down the hallway with her shoes in one hand, hoping she wouldn't bump into any hotel staff. Once she was back in her room, she stepped straight into the small bathroom and had a shower. It wasn't until she emerged, a towel wrapped around her dripping hair, that she noticed the bed covers were all tangled, as though someone had been thrashing about in them. But it was daylight, and the paranoias and fears of the darker hours felt far away. Assuming that she had made more of a mess before she went to Freddie's room than she realized, Ashley grabbed a corner of the duvet and yanked it, trying to straighten it out. On the white sheet there was a long wet smear of red. Blood. It had to be blood.

Ashley dropped the quilt and stepped away, heart hammering.

CHAPTER

30

ONCE SHE HAD dropped Freddie back at his B and B in Green
Beck, Ashley drove his unfamiliar car back home in a kind
of daze. After she found the bloodstain on the bedsheet, she had
dressed, gone downstairs to the reception area, and had a heated
discussion with the receptionist—a pretty young man with a tat-
too on the back of his left hand who clearly thought she was off her
rocker—but by the time she had convinced a member of manage-
ment to come up to the room, the bloodstain had vanished and the
bed was made.

Nothing to see. She hadn't even thought to take a picture of it on
her phone before she went downstairs to report it.

When she met Freddie in the foyer, she decided not to mention
it. She was tired, stretched too thin. Now, back home at the cottage,
she was still weary and not quite paying attention; it took her a few
minutes to realize that the Parma Violet was back. Her stupid little
lilac car was parked in its usual spot in the driveway as though nothing had happened.

Hopping out of Freddie's car, she dashed over to the Parma Violet,
unable to resist pressing her hands to its cold windows.

"There you are, sweetie. Don't leave me again, all right?"

When she got to the front door of the cottage, her phone rang,
and it was only as she was pushing her way into the kitchen that she

realized Aidan's voice was coming from inside the house. She hung up on him and walked into the living room, where Aidan was standing over DCI Turner and DC Platt, who were parked on her mother's best sofa.

"There she is." Aidan's easy smile couldn't hide anything from his sister; he was clearly rattled. "I told you she would turn up eventually, didn't I?"

Ashley stood stock-still in the doorway, half-tempted to run back out again.

"What are they doing here? Where's Mum and Dad?"

"Your parents are out doing the"—DC Platt looked at the notebook on his knee—"the weekly shop. We were wondering if we could ask you some questions, Miss Whitelam."

"It's a really bad time, actually." Ashley stepped to one side of the doorway, making space for them to pass. "So if you wouldn't mind?"

DCI Turner stood up but made no move to leave. "It does sound like you're busy at the moment. You were involved in an altercation in a B&Q in Newcastle yesterday, isn't that right?"

"She did what?" asked Aidan.

Ashley pushed a hand through her hair and sighed. "How could you even know about that?"

Turner grinned, a little too sharply in Ashley's opinion.

"Mr. Miller might have decided not to press charges, but several members of the public called emergency services. And even more took video and uploaded it to social media. One of them recognized you from the television, Miss Whitelam."

There were a few seconds where no one said anything. In Ashley's head, several things seemed to collide at once: the bloodstain, the icy patch of woods where she had found Robbie Metcalfe, Eleanor Sutton's stricken face.

"Shit." She came into the room and sat down. "Why do you want to talk to me? I'm sure you have hundreds of more important things to do."

"Just eliminating a few possibilities," said Turner. "Can you tell me how you knew where to find Robbie Metcalfe's body?"

Ashley laughed, although she felt sick. "This line of questioning rings a bell. Don't you remember?" She tapped the side of her head. "I'm a psychic. That's how."

"And where were you yesterday evening, after the incident at the B&Q?"

"Hold on." Aidan, who still hadn't sat down, raised both his hands. "I think my father would rather we had our legal representation here for this."

Ashley leaned forward, speaking over him. "I'll tell you where I was if you go back and have another look at Eleanor Sutton's case."

"What?" DCI Turner looked genuinely startled. "I . . . How do you know about that?"

"Never mind how I know. She has been missing since April and you've not done anything." Something else struck Ashley. "How about, I will tell you where I was if you tell me what it is the families of the victims received in the post? What is it that's linking these cases together for you?"

"Miss Whitelam," DC Platt's voice was the calmest in the room, "you can surely see how this looks to us? You approach us about helping with the case. You lead us straight to Robbie Metcalfe's remains. You are involved in an incident with another victim's parent. Everywhere we go in this case, there you are."

"Fine. I spent most of yesterday evening in A&E, it's the one on Queen Victoria road, waiting for my friend Freddie Miller to get his eye stitched up. I then spent the night in a Premier Inn." From the corner of her eye, Ashley saw her brother give her a judgmental look. "This morning, I drove back, dropping Freddie off in Green Beck. Besides Freddie, there will be plenty of witnesses at the hotel who saw me there. I complained to the receptionist about a, uh, housekeeping matter."

"You can be sure we will check each of these claims," said Turner. "We have also looked into your father's criminal history."

Aidan laughed. "Oh, come on. Enough of this." He got his phone out of his pocket. "I'm calling our solicitor."

"Charges for burglary, grievous bodily harm, and being in possession of stolen goods. It's enough, Miss Whitelam, for us to keep a close eye on you and your family. Just bear that in mind."

* * *

When they left, Ashley accompanied them to the door while her brother spoke on the phone in the kitchen. DCI Turner marched off down the driveway—they had apparently parked down the road to avoid tipping Ashley off to their presence—but DC Platt stood for a moment on the threshold, looking pensive.

"You're wasting time here," said Ashley, her arms crossed over her chest. "Your boss knows that, right?"

Platt gave her a grim half smile. "I'm afraid you've annoyed her. DCI Turner is an exceptional detective, and when someone gets under her skin, it usually means she's on the right track."

Ashley, surprised by this sudden bit of honesty, stepped a little closer. She lowered her voice. "It's not the right track though, is it? Even with my dad's dodgy history. And his track record has been clean since we moved to this place, by the way. People are relying on you to find a murderer, and you're harassing Mystic Meg here."

Platt's half smile faded away. "Listen. The thing the parents have received through the post. I happen to know that Eva Nowak's mother took photos of it before it was taken into evidence, and I strongly suspect she has copies. If you want to know what was in the post, you should speak to her."

Ashley blinked. "Why are you helping me?"

"Officially, I haven't." Platt turned and walked off down their gravel driveway.

"What was that all about?"

Ashley jumped. Aidan had appeared silently at her shoulder.

"Christ, Aidan. You nearly gave me a heart attack." She took a deep breath. "And it's nothing. He's just warning me off."

"Because you're doing a podcast with this yank. I looked him up." They stepped back into the house together. More than anything, Ashley wanted a pint of coffee and twelve hours of sleep, but she could see that her brother wasn't going to drop it. "You're lucky Dad hasn't realized yet."

"And you're going to tell him, are you?"

"Maybe I should, Ash! We've spent years building your reputation as a reliable, trustworthy medium. How do you think this is going to look? Swanning off to harass the parents of dead children?"

"Reliable, trustworthy medium? That's quite a contradiction in itself." Ashley laughed, but inside she could feel her temperature rising. She hated arguing with Aidan. "And I'm sorry you've all spent *so long* working on my reputation. That must have been *so hard* for you all. Never mind that it was my work and my fucking trauma that bought this house, this life. God. That's exactly what I am to you, isn't it? The golden bloody goose."

For a second, Aidan looked as though he'd been slapped. Then, his face changed; his eyes took on a darker, crueler aspect. The smile that flickered across his lips was sharp and unhappy.

"Better to be that than the also-ran, Ash. Or have you forgotten that I only ever exist in your shadow?"

They looked at each other. For a long, elastic moment, the only sound was the ticking of the clock in the hall. *We're saying all the things aloud that we shouldn't,* Ashley thought miserably. *Neither of us can take those words back.*

"Leave me alone, Aidan." To her own horror, her voice was thick with tears, and she felt like she was a sulky five-year-old again, distraught over her brother's teasing. "I never asked for any of this, and you know it."

He turned away from her, shaking his head.

"You have it better than a lot of people, Ash. Maybe you should try keeping that in mind while you torpedo the family business."

* * *

She had a second shower to try and calm down a bit, and after that she phoned Freddie. It hurt how much it reassured her to hear his voice.

"Listen, the bloody police have been here, and I've got some new information," she said. "I'll bring the car back to you in a little while and tell you all about it."

"You have? That's great." Despite his words, Freddie sounded distracted, even uncertain.

"What is it?"

"I've . . . I've had a contact too, Ash. And it's going to be great for
the podcast. For the whole case, maybe."

"And?"

"You're really not going to like it, I'm afraid."

CHAPTER

31

2004

"DRINK THAT AND sit still for a minute. You'll feel better."

Ashley had been taken—screaming—out of the dormitory and into a small office nearby. Mr. Haygarth and Miss Lyonnes were both there, along with Biddy Lyndon-Smith, who had made the cup of sweet milky tea being pressed into Ashley's shaking hands. She sat on a big leather swivel chair.

"It's just a bad nightmare, love," Miss Lyonnes was saying. She pushed some strands of pale blond hair off Ashley's sticky forehead. "We all have them every now and then, don't we? It's natural to have some nerves when you're away from home."

Ashley took a sip of the tea. She did not feel better. The images of the burning dorm seemed to press in on every side. She could still hear echoes of the other children screaming.

"They'd only been in bed for ten minutes," Mr. Haygarth said. Miss Lyonnes gave him a sharp look. "It'll take a while to settle the rest of them again."

The heat of the burning dormitory was still with Ashley too, and the hot cup of tea was making it worse. Ashley shuddered in the chair, trying not to be sick.

"I want to talk to my mum." Her throat still felt parched with the heat and the smoke, and her voice came out as a tiny whisper. "Please."

"Ashley, it's just a bad dream," said Miss Lyonnes. "You don't want to worry your mum, do you? You'll feel better soon, and then before you know it, you'll be back playing croquet or badminton or . . . It's the fishing trip tomorrow, isn't it, Jonathan?"

"It is."

"There, see, that's something to look forward to."

"I want to talk to my mum." Ashley hiccuped. A few more tears tracked down her blotchy face. "Can't I phone her or something?"

"Let the child talk to her mother," said Biddy, straightening up. "It's barely ten o'clock. I dare say people on the estate stay up later than that, don't you? Do you have her number?"

Mr. Haygarth retrieved a folder from the desk and flicked to a certain page. Biddy passed him a cordless phone from the desk, and he punched in the numbers. As if from very far away, Ashley heard him talking on the phone, his voice a murmur of soothing words. Not long after, they were passing the handset to her. She clasped it to her head and heard her mother's voice.

"Ashley, honey. You're not showing us up, are you?"

"Mum." Tears began streaming down her face again, each one burning hot. "Mum. Mum, the house is going to burn down. The house is going to burn down tonight, and we're all going to die."

The adults standing around her made a variety of noises. Mr. Haygarth stepped forward as though to take the phone from her, but she folded up, holding on to the receiver for dear life.

"What? What did you say, Ash?"

"I saw it, Mum, the whole place was on fire. I saw all the people b-burning."

"Now then, Ash. Your teacher said you had a nightmare, that's all. You need to be a big girl for once, okay?"

"Mum, please, can I come home?" Ashley squeezed the words out, desperate. "Please, can Dad come and get me? I don't want to be here." They would have to come and get her if she asked. They couldn't just leave her there. That's not how parents worked. "Please, can I come home, please?"

"Ashley." Her mother's voice was taking on the steely tone that she dreaded. "Of course you can't come home! You're miles and miles away, halfway up the bloody country. You're just being silly and showing us up. Go back to bed now—you'll feel better in the morning. I don't want to hear any more about this nonsense."

"Mum, please." Ashley took a big shaky breath. *"Mum, please I don't want to burn. I don't want to—"*

The phone was yanked from her grasp, but Ashley barely noticed. The terrible heat had returned, and with it the images of flesh melting from bone and the screaming of the children.

"Christ, she's off again."

Dimly, Ashley could hear Miss Lyonnes on the phone, talking to Ashley's mother. Biddy was talking to Mr. Haygarth.

"Here, look, give her a slug of this in her tea."

Haygarth snorted. "That's more than my job's worth, Mrs. Lyndon-Smith. No, absolutely not."

The older woman tutted at him. Underneath the burning and the screaming, Ashley heard the gentle glug of something being poured into a mug. After a moment, the tea was pushed back into her lax hands.

"If anyone ever asks, you can tell them I did it," Biddy was saying. "It's exactly what I would do for any guest of mine who's had a shock. It's just enough to help her sleep." And then, in a louder, closer voice, she said, "There you are, Ashley. Drink up. I promise it'll make you feel better."

Having lost all hope since her mother's voice had been taken away, Ashley did as she was told. The tea tasted strange, a flavor that made her think of her dad for reasons she didn't understand. She felt it burn its way down her throat and pool in her belly like lava.

"At least she's stopped screaming now," said Mr. Haygarth. The three adults stood around Ashley, making sure she drank every last bit of the sharp-tasting tea, and when it was done, she felt very heavy and loose, like a big pile of wet clothes. When Miss Lyonnes put her arm around her shoulders to help her up, she didn't fight it. Everything seemed to be happening from very far away.

"There you go, sweetheart," Miss. Lyonnes said. "Back off to bed with you."

32

ASHLEY AGREED TO meet Freddie in the car park of Green Beck's rather grand Norman church. When he appeared, hunched over slightly against the rain, he was wearing his pair of spare glasses. The strip of adhesive over his stitches looked very white against his tan skin. Ashley got out of the car and handed him the keys.

"Hi, roomie."

Ashley laughed. "How's your bonce?"

"*Bonce*, wow. Uh, it's pretty sore, but I'll live. Come on, let's get in the car before I rust."

Once they were inside, Ashley back in the passenger seat, she tapped her fingers pointedly on the dashboard.

"So. Who is this contact I'm not going to like?"

Freddie winced. He took his glasses off and wiped away the raindrops beading on them with the corner of his shirt.

"No, you first. What did you find out from the police?"

Ashley sat back, pleased to be able to contribute in a concrete way. "DC Platt told me that Eva Nowak's mother took photos of whatever it was she was sent after Eva had gone missing. He wouldn't tell me what it was, but he did say it was very likely she still had copies of the photos. So we should go and ask her. Don't you think?"

Freddie was nodding slowly. "I don't have an address for Mrs. Nowak, but it's been a year or so since I looked for it. Perhaps I'll have better luck if I try again now." He paused, then smiled. "Well done. I knew asking you to be on the podcast was a good idea."

She beamed at him, ridiculously pleased with herself for a few seconds. And then she saw his smile flicker and fade.

"What is it?"

"I had an email from a patient at Ashworth Hospital. I don't know if you know Ashworth . . ."

"I know it." All of her good feelings had fled. Instead, a wave of warmth moved through her blood. She almost thought she could taste whiskey on her tongue, mixed with sweet milky tea. "A high-security psychiatric hospital. Near Liverpool. Am I right?"

"That's the one. This patient has been at the hospital for years, and he says he's made significant progress, with therapy and with drugs. He wants to talk to me about the Gingerbread House Murders." Freddie stopped and bit his lip. "By that, I mean he wants to talk to *us* about the murders. He believes he knows something about who's behind it."

Ashley swallowed. "It's Dean Underwood, isn't it?"

"Yeah. I'm sorry, Ashley."

"Fuck."

* * *

Freddie drove her back home and dropped her at the end of the driveway. It was a quieter, tenser drive than Ashley had been expecting, but they agreed to talk again in the evening, when Ashley had finished the house visits that were booked in for that day. The cottage was quiet. Aidan's car was gone, and her parents weren't home yet, so Ashley went through the kitchen and out the back door, down the rugged stone path into their slightly sunken garden. The rain had stopped, but it was still bracingly, wonderfully cold. Ashley walked right down to the bottom where a trio of Scots pine trees crowded around an iron-and-wood bench. Rainwater dripped down through the branches onto her head and down the back of her neck. After a few moments, she began to shake a little. Eventually, it passed.

Dean Underwood. She couldn't remember the last time she'd even heard the name before Freddie's reluctant confession. People tended not to say it in front of her, and they certainly never said it in front of her mother, who was guaranteed to have a full-fledged breakdown if she heard it. She remembered his face at different times: smeared with dirt and glimpsed briefly in dappled tree light; washed and shaved and somehow still wild, standing in the dock of the court.

Somewhere close by, a blackbird was warbling his song, a liquid sound that seemed to talk about earlier, brighter days. When she and her family had moved to Green Beck, years ago, she had spent much of that first summer with Malory and Melva. Never in or even close to Red Rigg House, but in any number of secret places that Melva alone seemed to know: secret springs, paths, wooded places filled with bright purple foxgloves and vibrant buttercups. On these walks, Melva would tell them secret things about gods and goddesses that once filled Britain like honey in a pot—lost now, scraped clean by a new world.

Sitting at the bottom of their garden, which was so overgrown that it wasn't possible to see the house, Ashley remembered Melva's stories about the "fair folk"—impossibly beautiful and strange people who lived in a world that existed cheek to cheek with the normal human world. The faeries crossed over sometimes, she had said, in places where the veil between worlds was thin, and there were many thin places in Cumbria.

Not long after, Ashley started her ill-advised relationship with Richard, and for a time, both Mallory and Melva seemed to drift away from her a little—or perhaps, as often happened when girls had their first serious boyfriend, she had drifted away from them. But when she was older and making a living as a medium, Melva shared more stories with her about spirits of the land spoiling milk, stealing away pretty girls and boys, and moving from one world to another. And as part of her act, Ashley was always telling the audience that she could see through the veil. Did that mean that the fair folk could see her too? Here, in the dripping wet and cold of the overgrown garden, it was easy to believe that they could.

* * *

Ashley's first two clients of the day were regulars: Mr. James Olyphant, a reclusive man in his eighties who lived in a tiny cottage that looked more like a warehouse stacked with cardboard boxes and piles of news-papers; and Freya McIntyre, an artist living on the edges of Ambleside who insisted on making nettle tea for Ashley, despite how it smelled. Ashley read the cards for them almost on autopilot, her mind on Dean Underwood and Freddie. She sat and chatted with Mr. Olyphant, who she suspected only had her over for the company, and she delivered messages from Miss McIntyre's muse, who had been quiet of late. The third appointment was an unusual one; she was to meet Melva at Bowness-on-Windermere where they would be the entertainment for a hen party. When Melva had brought the idea to her the previous year, Ashley had laughed, sure that she must be joking, but it had turned out to be a reasonably steady earner—brides these days were keen to find unique things to do with their hens, rather than the more tradi-tional bar and nightclub crawl.

"I hope your loins are girded, pet."

Despite her gloomy mood, Ashley had to grin at Melva. The old woman took a great deal of pleasure from the generally raucous hen party gigs, and she often brought her own hip flask of rum to the proceedings.

They stood together at the door of a lavish holiday home. Ashley could hear thumping music and a great deal of laughter coming from inside.

"Will they be drinking already?"

"No judgment here," Melva said. "The sun's over the yardarm and other such bollocks."

The door opened, and they were ushered into the open-plan liv-ing room by Daisy, the maid of honor. Ten women were sitting on the sofas and chairs, and the low coffee table in the center of the room was covered in a forest of dirty glasses. One of the women, a tanned blonde in her midtwenties with glittery false nails, had a bright pink sash across her chest and a plastic tiara moored in the midst of her up-do. This would be the bride-to-be.

Their entrance was met with a roar of approval, and the coffee table was cleared in short order so that Melva could get out her crystal ball and other mystical equipment. Ashley took possession of the long wooden dining table—which had been the perch for a colorful array of handbags—and began laying out her tarot cards on a large piece of black silk. Melva was wearing a purple shawl for the occasion, embroidered with silver moons and stars, and the women flocked around her, demanding that their palms be read. Ashley watched her work for a while, happy for the older woman to take the lead. The phrases "tall, handsome stranger" and "consummated before the first hunter's moon" began to float up from the chatter, producing a great deal of hilarity.

"I saw you on the TV, didn't I?" One of the women had peeled off from the pack. She wore more black than was usual at a hen party, and she had thick-framed glasses and a mop of dark curly hair.

"I'm afraid that's likely. Would you like to know your future?" Ashley touched one finger to the deck of cards. The woman nodded and sat down. On the other side of the room, Melva had moved on to her crystal ball and was "peering through the mists of antiquity."

"What's your name? It will help me pinpoint your fate."

"Fleur." The woman fidgeted as Ashley shuffled the cards. "Can I ask you something?"

"That's what I'm here for."

"I watch a lot of true crime documentaries, you see. Can't get enough of them. Freya tells me it's morbid, but I just find it fascinating, don't you? I wanted to know what it's like. Speaking to the dead."

Ashley paused. She had dealt the first three cards of a seven-card formation. There was a hot prickly feeling on the back of her neck, and she wished she had access to Melva's hip flask.

"Because, I mean, if what you did was real"—Fleur laughed in a tinkly way—"well, you'd be able to solve all the crimes, wouldn't you? Just tune in to the dead people frequency, or whatever, and ask them who killed them. Job done."

Ashley dealt the rest of the cards, keeping her face very still.

"It's a little more complicated than that."

"Oh, I'm sure it is." Fleur had a cocktail with her, and she took a noisy sip. Ashley wondered if the group had been drinking all day. "I saw that interview with you on the telly, where you were sitting in front of all those statues of angels. Wow. Is that what you think? That angels give you the information? Or, I mean, that's probably what you tell people, when actually you trawl people's Facebook pages for info."

Ashley rested her fingertips on the first card. There was a thick wad of anger blocking her throat, all the worse because, yes, she had indeed looked up the Facebook accounts of each of the women there—it was part and parcel of what she did. Being caught out in a situation like this was especially unpleasant. This was a hen party gig; it was supposed to be silly. And safe. For once she wished her father was there with them so he could loom over people and put them off their cocktails.

"If that's the case, Fleur . . ." Ashley met the woman's faintly glassy eyes. "How did I find the body of Robbie Metcalfe? You might not realize this, but murderers don't generally post the whereabouts of their victims' remains on Facebook."

Fleur's mouth turned down at the corners. "Oh please. The police had already found him, and they gave you the information so you could drum up some publicity for the case."

Ashley laughed. "Is that what you actually think?"

"It's obvious."

There was a dip in the noise around the coffee table. Ashley was aware that they were both raising their voices, but she also felt disinclined to calm down.

"Do you not think that recovering the body of a twelve-year-old child—the mutilated body of a twelve-year-old child—would create enough publicity by itself? Or perhaps you think the police did it to help publicize me? Honestly, the shit people will convince themselves to believe."

Fleur stood up, scraping her chair across the flagstone floor. The tops of her cheeks were very pink. "It's not my fault you're a fraud. Taking money from vulnerable people."

Ashley gestured at the rest of the room. "Oh, yes, the vulnerable monied middle classes, how ever do I live with myself?"

"Fleur, darling, what's going on?" The bride-to-be had stood up. "Are you all right?"

Melva's eyebrows were raised, her large farmer's hands still clasped over the crystal ball.

"No, wait, don't go. I haven't read your fortune yet." Ashley flipped over the cards rapidly, one after the other. The Three of Cups, the Empress, the Tower, the Five of Swords, the Ten of Swords, the Page of Pentacles, and the Queen of Wands. "Here we are. Fleur, you are a self-important loner with a string of failed relationships that ultimately flounder because desperation makes you too clingy with every new partner. You watch true crime documentaries because you believe that you yourself could never get into a dangerous situation—you think yourself much too clever for that, and seeing other people with lives worse than yours gives you a, frankly, worrying degree of satisfaction. Ultimately, you will only grow more and more set in your ways, unable to let anyone else in. You will die alone at the age of eighty-three after falling down the stairs in a multistory car park."

There was a sudden silence. Everyone had stopped to listen to Ashley's reading. Fleur herself stood by the back of her chair, her whole body rigid. There was a strangled laugh from one of the other women, followed by a ripple of giggles, and Ashley knew that her summary of Fleur had been close to the mark indeed.

"I think I'm done here." Ashley stood and swiped her cards back into the deck with one practiced movement. "Melva, I'll be in my car when you're done."

* * *

Melva and Ashley sat in the car together. The older woman had brought out a white paper bag of lemon sherbets and was crunching her way through them, one after the other.

"It seems to me," she said eventually, "that finding that poor little bugger in the woods has unsettled you, Ashley. Which isn't surprising, is it? You never hear about it in the news, but I bet all those dog walkers that come across bodies in parks or whatever, I bet it takes them years to get over. They probably have nightmares about it. And you have more reason than most to have nightmares."

Ashley snorted. "Everywhere I go, I'm surrounded by the dead." They were parked in a small layby outside of Green Beck. It hadn't seemed prudent to remain parked outside the hen do holiday home. "Sorry, that sounded very melodramatic, didn't it?"

"Oh, I don't know." Melva shrugged. "Just sounded accurate to me."

"Great."

"*Tsk.* What I mean to say, Ashley, is that finding Robbie has given you a bad scare, and I'm not so sure that making a . . . What did you call it?"

"A podcast."

"Yeah, I'm not so sure that making a podcast about it is the best idea for you. You'll make yourself ill."

While they sat in the car, the dark all around them, Ashley had told Melva about Freddie and *Murder on the Mind.* Melva was about the only person Ashley felt she *could* speak to about it in any detail; her father would think it was a waste of time, her mother would find it distasteful, and Aidan still wasn't talking to her after their spat. Even Malory felt like a poor option—she would sweep in and take it over somehow.

"You're dredging it all up for yourself. Fancy even entertaining the notion of going to speak to Dean Underwood!"

"What if it did me some good? I'm already going to Red Rigg House soon. Perhaps speaking to Underwood would be some sort of closure for me. People are always talking about closure."

"Pft. Better off keeping your head down. I reckon the Moon Market is more than enough for your plate right now, don't you think?"

"Maybe. I don't know." For a second, Ashley felt a fresh flare of anger for her brother. If she hadn't listened to him, she would never have gone for that drive with the police, and she wouldn't be caught in this web of pain and grief. The Gingerbread House Murders would be just another grim item on the news, and nothing to do with her. Swiftly on the heels of that, she felt a deep pang of guilt. If she hadn't found him, Robbie Metcalfe could have been lost forever, a small skeleton in the woods, hidden beneath inches of undergrowth and dirt, his bones scattered by curious animals.

"Let the Yank figure it out." Melva put her bag of sweets down to reach across and squeeze Ashley's hand. "Tell him you need to step away from these things, for your own health. It's for the best."

Ashley smiled and nodded, knowing full well that she would do no such thing.

"That's a girl. You know you can always tell me anything, don't you? Now you better drive me back. Pester will be wanting his second dinner, the greedy little sod."

33

"AIDAN TELLS ME you have agreed to do a podcast. Not just a one-off either, but a series."

It was the weekly family dinner. Aidan was not present, which was unusual for him—he usually took any opportunity to get a home-cooked dinner and his laundry done by someone else—but Ashley thought she knew why. There was the argument they'd had, and the fact that he'd clearly grassed her up to Logan. The sneaky little bastard.

"It's good for business," Ashley said firmly. She had already spoken on the phone to Freddie, agreeing to go and visit Magda Nowak's house in the morning, and was prepared to stand her ground. But to her surprise, her father simply nodded in a thoughtful way.

"Yes," he said. "I've looked up the listening figures for this podcast, and I have to say I was amazed. These true crime documentaries are making quite an impact."

Ashley's mother shifted in her chair, glancing at the angels on the mantelpiece. "I don't like it," she said in a quiet voice. "Why are people so *obsessed* with blood and gore?"

Logan didn't even glance at her; his cool gray eyes were focused on his daughter.

"Yeah, well, that's why I'm doing it, isn't it? I do know what I'm talking about sometimes." Ashley chased some potato around her plate with her fork. "Freddie wants me there to add color to the recording, and I get free advertising. It'll bring more people to us."

"We'll see," said Logan. "As long as it doesn't interfere with your preparations for the Moon Market. You've a lot to do. We all have a lot to do."

Ashley clamped down on her usual annoyance at being spoken to like a child. This was a fragile truce with her father, and she didn't want to endanger it.

"Sure." She thought briefly of her blowup at the hen do that day, and wondered if that would end up getting back to her father too. "Everything's fine. I can handle it."

* * *

That night, Ashley had a series of dark and chaotic dreams, images of places and people seeming to pass through her dreaming mind faster than she could register them. There was a constant sense of movement, as though something could reach up from underneath her feet through that uneasy landscape and wrap its cold fingers around her ankle if she didn't keep moving. When she woke up, the room was still dark and everything felt too close, suffocating almost. She moved weakly under the duvet, somehow not quite able to push the covers off. She had taken three of the tablets Aidan had given her, and that had clearly been a mistake.

"Uff. Get off."

She managed to push the top of the duvet back—how was it so heavy?—and that was when she saw the dark shape of a Heedful One standing at the foot of her bed. Ashley went very still, a rabbit caught in headlights. The thing came forward. It was holding something in its stick arms.

"No. No, no, no."

The small, sad skeletonized body of Robbie Metcalfe was cradled in the Heedful One's arms. Thick green moss had grown inside his empty eye sockets, spilling out like emerald fur; orange lichen had colonized his teeth and the joints of his fingers. She knew it was him because his left arm was missing, brutally shortened just above where the elbow joint should have been. The Heedful One crept forward. She imagined it saying, *"Here, look at my child, see the pieces of him."* She imagined it coming forward until the shadow of it flooded through her as it had in Red Rigg House, and she would be given another terrible vision of the future. Then, Robbie's body sat up, his blistered skull turning to look at her.

When Ashley woke—for real, this time—the tendrils of the dream seemed to hold her in place. There was someone in her room still, she thought, some shadowy shape moving around. She tried to sit up, but the duvet was too heavy; she couldn't move. She watched the figure come closer, standing over her bedside table. Against her will, a great wave of tiredness moved through her and she slipped back under, into the darkness of true sleep.

34

"HAVE YOU THOUGHT any more about coming with me to see Dean Underwood?"

Ashley squeezed the steering wheel. She was glad she was driving because it gave her an excuse not to look at Freddie while he said this. It was early the next morning, and they were driving to Penrith, where Magda Nowak lived with her four other children. The day felt fully autumnal, filled with that strange golden light that only appears in the mornings and early evenings of autumn days. The sky overhead was peerless and blue, and the spectacular hills and mountains of northern Cumbria tore pieces from it with their jagged teeth.

"You're definitely going, whether I do or not?"

There was a beat of silence. The Parma Violet was not a quiet car, and Ashley was glad for its rumbling in that moment.

"I have to explore every avenue, Ashley." He cleared his throat. She wanted to look at him, to try and gauge his mood, but she was worried about what she would see there. "The likelihood is that he will spout a load of garbage and none of it will be useful. But I can't just assume that."

"He tried the insanity defense, and it didn't work," she said, her eyes still on the road. "But you can't tell me he was sane. The stuff that he said in court . . ."

"He's since been diagnosed as a paranoid schizophrenic, and he's medicated. Do I really think he holds the key to the Gingerbread

House Murders? No. Do I think it's very likely that he's heard about your involvement and wants to use it as an excuse to have contact with you? Yes."

They had come to a junction, all lights red. Ashley sat staring ahead, biting her lower lip.

"Hey." Freddie put his hand on her hand. "Can you look at me a sec?"

Reluctantly, she looked at him.

"I won't lie, I want you to come with me. But I also will not let anything harm you, all right? I won't put you in any danger. Ever. I enjoy your company too much for that. If you don't want to come with me, it's fine. I won't pressure you to do anything."

A car beeped behind them, and Ashley realized the lights had turned green. She cleared her throat and accelerated away from the lights. She could still feel the faint press of Freddie's fingers on her hand, the warmth of it.

"Let me think about it," she said, when she was sure her voice would sound normal. "I need to get used to the idea. Just let me think. And I enjoy your company too."

*   *   *

Magda Nowak lived in a run-down semidetached house with a variety of rusting cars in the front garden. She was expecting them, and was even at the door before they were both out of the car. Standing in the darkened doorway with a toddler in her arms, she was a short, slight woman with thick dark hair and circles under her eyes. From within the house came the sound of children shouting and shrieking.

"Mrs. Nowak?"

"You are the podcast people, yes? Come in, I have tea."

The hallway was cluttered with toolboxes and car parts. As they stepped inside, Ashley briefly caught sight of a child of undetermined gender on the stairs, but as quick as a bird, they were off out of sight again. There was a brief thunder of small footsteps overhead.

They settled eventually in the kitchen, at a table that appeared to be the only place in the house free of car parts. As she filled their mugs from a teapot, Magda Nowak picked up another lump of oily metal and moved it elsewhere.

"My husband, his business is cars. You would think cars, that would be outside the house, but not so much, as it turns out."

"Thank you for agreeing to speak to us, Mrs. Nowak," said Freddie.

"Call me Magda. The police, they were here every day at one point, but now I barely hear anything, from week to week. Eva has been gone three years." She sat down at the table with them, her face stern. "So I think, why not speak to you? My niece listens to these podcast things, and she tells me that sometimes they can change a case, or help solve them."

"That can sometimes happen, but I feel like I should tell you it's not very common," Freddie said carefully. "We do have a good chance of getting more people to think about Eva, though, and perhaps someone will remember seeing her. Getting more publicity around the case is always, I believe, a good thing. Would we be able to record this conversation?"

Magda nodded, and there was a faint chime as Freddie set his phone to record. It was chilly in the kitchen. Steam rose from their fresh cups of tea.

"What happened to Eva?" Ashley cleared her throat and started again. "I mean, what happened the day she disappeared?"

"It was a school day. She went missing from school." Magda reached into her bag, which sat next to the table leg, and pulled out a large photograph of a girl in school uniform. She had dark curly hair, which was partly held in place with a yellow hair clip in the shape of a pineapple. "It was her first year of high school, and she loved it. Loves it." Magda blinked rapidly and passed the photo to Freddie. "She is such a sunny soul, excited to do everything. She had signed up for every after-school club going—learning musical instruments, editing the school newspaper, football club. It got so that I had to get her to sit down and choose just a few, because she would need two of her to get to everything." She smiled tightly. "And some of the clubs, of course, they cost money. Eva has four brothers and sisters. They can't always have everything they want."

Freddie passed Ashley the photograph. She knew it was the power of suggestion at work, but Eva did indeed look like the sort of kid who wanted to be into everything—a kid who made friends easily. *The opposite of me when I was a kid.*

"Was she at one of these clubs when she disappeared?"

"No. It was in the middle of a school day. It was lunchtime. I remember the day for obvious reasons, but also I remember because she was excited they had a visitor at the school that afternoon. A writer or poet, something like that. But then at lunchtime, she went off somewhere by herself, and she never came back. Just gone. Poof!" Magda made a gesture with her hand as though chasing away a moth, and Ashley noticed that her fingers were trembling.

"The school doesn't know where she went?" asked Freddie.

"She was caught on the CC television going up to the big field. And that is where the camera coverage ends. She was not seen on the road that runs alongside that field. There was a hole in the fence though, that had been there for some months. The children knew about it and would use it to go to the café up the road. They would buy doughnuts."

"Did the school know about the hole?" Ashley asked. There was a tight, sick feeling in her stomach.

Magda let out a long, ragged sigh. "At first, they said they did not know. But it had been there for months! Eventually, the police found a memo for the groundskeeper to deal with it. He just hadn't gotten around to it."

"You must be very angry with the school," said Ashley quietly. "I know I would be."

For the first time, Magda's severe expression wavered, and it was like catching a reflection in a pond before something disturbs the surface—for an instant, Ashley saw a broken woman, her face lined with impossible grief. "You think that they are safe at school, don't you? Two of her siblings go to the same school, and I would move them if I could, but it would mean so much travel, new uniforms, the disruption. We can't afford it."

"I'm so sorry," said Ashley. She realized that she liked Magda, with her chaotic house and her stern face. Her pain was invisible yet present in every movement and every word, and it felt painfully unfair. "You must be going spare."

"My husband . . . What can we do? We have four other children, they all need our attention, our help. The youngest is four years old— she doesn't remember Eva now. She just knows her from pictures."

"If you don't mind, could you tell us what happened after Eva vanished at lunchtime?" asked Freddie. Ashley glanced at him; he looked too big for the small, crowded kitchen: his jaw too square, his shoulders too broad. It added a surreal note to the day, and she wondered how Magda felt about it.

"The school were late to raise the alarm, because the event with the poet in the afternoon meant that they didn't take register immediately. Another thing they have since said will never happen again. When they did, the police were called. At first, the police had all these awful questions—did Eva have troubles at school or with friends? Was she sad? Did we have any arguments? They asked if she might have run away! She was eleven! At night, when she slept, she would still have a night-light on."

"But they changed their minds about that," said Freddie. It wasn't quite a question.

Magda nodded. "Yes, this is what you mentioned on the phone. The police took it away. I only saw it for a few minutes, but . . ." She stood and went over to the kitchen unit. One of the cubby holes was stuffed with papers and letters; she pulled a small stack of glossy photos from it, larger than the school portrait. "I took photos with my phone, and then I had a place in town print them out, make them bigger. I imagine the police officers did the same." She put the photos on the table, in front of Ashley and Freddie. "We got a box in the post the morning after Eva disappeared. This is what was inside it."

At first, Ashley couldn't make head or tail of the images. To her, it looked like a random pile of sticks, thin and splintered, with dark brown bark and flashes of pale inner wood. There was string too, the sort of sturdy twine a butcher would use around a joint of pork or beef. She frowned and pulled one of the photos closer to her—the bundle of sticks and twigs sat inside a very normal cardboard box.

"Oak, holly, and hawthorn branches," said Magda in a matter-of-fact tone. "I could not tell from looking, but the police told us this. It was only when the thing was out of the box that I could see what it was. A child for a child."

Ashley looked up, startled by the phrase. Magda picked out one of the photos and laid it on top of the others. In it, the bundle of sticks had been laid against something white—a tablecloth, maybe—and its shape became horribly clear. It looked, very roughly, like a baby. A baby made of sticks.

Freddie was staring at the photo. "Was it delivered by your usual postal service?"

"Yes."

"And what did the police say about it?"

Magda shrugged. "Very little. They said that they could not be sure it was definitely linked to Eva's disappearance, but who would send such a thing otherwise?"

At that moment, a girl of around nine or ten—wearing pajamas—poked her head around the door. For a wild second, Ashley thought that Eva herself had just decided to come home; the little girl looked so much like her older sister, it was like a punch to the gut.

"Mum, can I have some soup or something?"

Magda waved her over. "This is Julia. She is off sick from school today." The girl came over to the table and stood next to her mum, looking up at Ashley and Freddie through her dark eyelashes. "It used to be that I told them, you must go to school every day, you can't stay home just because you feel under the weather." She shook her head, and Ashley thought of her own mother. "Now I do not worry so much. What is one day of school?" She put her arm around the girl and squeezed her fondly, burying her face in the child's hair before letting her go. "I will bring you some in a minute, Julia. Go back to bed."

When the girl had gone, Ashley drew one of the pictures to her. It was the one that most clearly resembled a baby.

"Would you mind if I took a photo of this, Magda? I have a friend I would like to ask about it."

Magda shrugged. "You can take it. I have more copies."

They stayed for another fifteen minutes or so, drinking the rest of the tea and asking more questions, although there seemed little more to say. Eva Nowak had vanished one day in the middle of a school week, in the middle of a school day, and hadn't been seen since. The next day, Eva's family had received a strange package, which the police had taken away with them. Since then, there had been very little. No concrete sightings, no more strange packages, no significant updates from the police, and, although none of them mentioned it around that kitchen table, no body either. Mrs. Nowak was left in an agonizing limbo.

Back in the car, Ashley took the photograph from her bag and looked at it again. There was something familiar about it, she was sure; some tiny detail that seemed to prick at the back of her mind.

"So this is the thing that is tying all the cases together," she said aloud. "All of the official victims received something like this in the post."

"It seems that way." Freddie was pensive. They had pulled over to the side of the road in the middle of nowhere. The shadows of clouds skirted rapidly across the green flanks of the hills. The wind was picking up. "Does it look like a child to you?"

"Yes." Again, there was that faint prickling in the very back of her mind. What was it? "Have you seen anything like this in any of the other cases you've read about?"

Freddie didn't answer immediately. He looked out the window and drummed his fingers on the dashboard. "It makes me think of Matthew Hoffman. He killed three people and hid their bodies inside a hollow tree. And his house, when they raided it, was stuffed with bin bags full of old leaves. But it's not the same, not really." He shook his head, frustrated. "He was obsessed with trees. He loved them. Trees were the point. But this"—he glanced at the photo in Ashley's lap—"I don't think the material is the point. I think the shape is the point. Don't you?"

"A child for a child, she said." Freddie's face looked uncharacteristically grim. "Are you all right?"

"Oh, I'm fine." He gave her a brittle smile. "That was just hard, you know? She was keeping it together amazingly well, but you could still feel how much pain she was in. I've done a lot of interviews with people who have suffered terrible things, and I guess you never know which ones will get under your skin."

"Magda is very brave."

"Yeah."

Ashley looked at the photo again. The discolored twine was wrapped around the neck, while the flexible twigs were bent into a rough loop that formed the head. The arms and legs were simple bunches, but the twine cinched them so that they seemed to have elbows and wrists. Here and there, the long spikes of the hawthorn sprouted, making the thing look dangerous, even evil. She frowned.

"Freddie, I will come with you to see Dean Underwood."

He looked at her, startled. "You will? What made your mind up?"

Ashley smiled slightly, then shrugged. "If Magda can suffer like that and still be brave, I reckon I can go and speak to Underwood. It's a small thing, really. And I'll hold on to this for a while." She held up the photograph. "There's someone I want to show it to."

35

2004

A SHLEY WAS TAKEN back into the dormitory at Red Rigg House, and despite everything, she slept.

It was a long time before anyone knew exactly where the fire started. For much of the household, it was in full swing when they awoke, with a large portion of the east wing an inferno. The stairs and the hallway leading to the dormitory were ablaze when Mr. Haygarth—whose room was a few doors down from the dorm— awoke to a crashing noise. He made it out of the room and banged his fists against Miss Lyonnes's door, waking her up and saving her life. She fled downstairs, her dressing gown over her head to stop her hair from catching alight, while Jonathan Haygarth moved down the hallway toward the dormitory. He had almost reached the door when a portion of the ceiling fell down, trapping him and killing him just feet from where a lot of frightened children were beginning to wake up. The debris from the ceiling prevented them from opening the door themselves.

Later, the police and fire investigators concluded that the children had tried to break the windows and failed. Most of them were over-come with smoke inhalation, and several did indeed burn to death, although this information was kept strictly within the investigation itself. Details, such as the strange contorted positions of the children's bodies as the heat caused muscles to contract and shrink, were not revealed to the families. It was thought that they had suffered enough.

Fire engines arrived within fifteen minutes of the blaze becoming visible from windows, and they fought for over an hour to bring it under control.

In the uneasy light of dawn, covered in a skein of smoke and soot, the staff of the house and the police officers present began to take account of what had happened, and crucially, began calling parents. As far as they knew, every child that had come to Red Rigg House for the Easter weekend had perished. The work of recovering bodies and identifying them was expected to take days, if not weeks.

When Helen Whitelam picked up the phone, very early on that Easter Sunday, she was half asleep, not awake enough yet to feel the panic that can sometimes come with an unexpected phone call at an unsociable hour. She listened to the voice on the other end, which sounded very far away and remarkably calm, and a great wave of terror picked her up and knocked her down. Logan Whitelam, who had been woken up by the sound of her screaming, came into their narrow hallway to find his wife curled up in the corner by the door. The phone receiver was on the floor, so he picked it up.

These were the facts as given to him on that morning:

There had been a terrible fire at Red Rigg House, where his daughter had been staying for the weekend. The police and fire investigators were still sorting through the debris, but they asked that all parents of the children travel to Cumbria as soon as possible. Logan had asked if his daughter was safe, and the person on the other end of the phone simply repeated that they should come as soon as they could, and that the Lyndon-Smith family would pay for their transport if needed. And that, in Logan's opinion, was as good as telling him his daughter was dead.

When he went to Helen and tried to pick her up off the floor, she had grabbed him by the neck, her eyes wild.

"She knew! She wanted to come home, and *we left her there to die.*"

* * *

Three days later, Ashley Whitelam walked out of the woods at the foot of Red Rigg Fell. She was covered head to foot in dirt and soot, and seemed near catatonic. She had no memory of the fire, and no memory of where she had spent the last three days. By that time, however, Helen Whitelam's fragile sanity had already been shattered, and she never returned to being the ballsy, no-nonsense woman that Ashley had grown up with.

36

WHEN ASHLEY ARRIVED at Melva's cottage later that evening, she found herself parking the Parma Violet behind a huge obnoxious Land Rover that she recognized. Frowning slightly, she let herself in through the front door and paused in the darkened hall, listening to raised voices coming from the kitchen. She couldn't make out the words, but the tone of the discussion was clear: two angry people rapidly losing patience with each other. With half a mind to just leave and come back in the morning, Ashley took two steps back down the hallway, only for Pester to come trotting out of the living room, barking in raucous greeting. The voices in the kitchen grew quiet, and then the door opened, splashing Ashley with light.

"What are you doing here?"

It was Richard Lyndon-Smith. His brows were drawn down at the sight of her, the tops of his cheeks flushed with color.

"I'm visiting my friend, *Dick*. Surely even you can work that out?" Ashley looked behind him into the kitchen and saw Melva standing by the stove. Her eyes looked very bright, as though she might have recently been crying, and her face was red. "What's been going on here?"

Pester barked into the silence that followed, then trotted into the kitchen, his claws making light tapping sounds on the linoleum.

"It's all fine, love," Melva said, her voice thick. "Come through and I'll put the kettle on."

Richard swept a hand over his head, smoothing some strands of hair away from his forehead, and pushed past Ashley in the hall. He made more contact than was necessary, one hand touching her arm as if to steady her. As usual, when Richard was around, Ashley had to combat the urge to kick him in the shins.

"Looking forward to seeing you at the House next week," he said, his voice pitched low, just for her. "It'll be just like old times, won't it?"

Ashley glared at his back until he was safely out of the house, then stormed into the kitchen.

"What the hell was that all about?"

Melva sniffed. "Never you mind. I've known that boy since he was filling his nappies. Always has to be the big man. *Tsk*." She picked up the old-fashioned stove kettle and filled it at the sink before turning on one of the stove rings. "I never did understand why you were so keen on him when you were a teenager. Handsome, yes, but cruel. I never thought you'd go for that sort."

Ashley sighed. "Oh yes, my single piece of teenage rebellion. I blame my hormones for that one. Are you all right, though, Melva? Whatever was going on there, it sounded . . . intense."

Melva waved a hand at her dismissively before going to the cupboard and retrieving a couple of mismatched mugs. She popped a tea bag in each while Pester wove his way around her ankles, living up to his name.

"It was nothing. Now, what are you doing here? Not that I don't enjoy seeing you. I've been worried since . . . well, there's one group of ladies who won't be recommending us to their friends."

Ashley winced. "I wanted to ask you something. It's about the Gingerbread House Murders."

"Oh?" Melva still had her back to her as she sugared the cups. "I thought you were gonna knock all that on the head."

The kettle began to whistle.

"I've got something to show you." Ashley sat down at the kitchen table and rummaged through her bag until she found the photograph of the child of sticks. She took it out and laid it on the table. "I wondered if you knew what this is. Something about it rings a very faint bell with me and . . . don't take this the wrong way, but when I saw it, I thought of you."

Melva poured the water and brought both cups over to the table. She picked up the photograph and held it up to the light, frowning. An odd stillness seemed to settle over her features.

"What is it? You know, don't you?"

"Where did you find such a thing?"

Ashley leaned back on her chair. It seemed wrong, somehow, to share this discovery with someone else, but who was Melva going to tell?

"We think they've been sent to the families of the children. We got that picture from Magda Nowak—it arrived the day after her kid vanished."

"That would make sense." Melva sighed. She put the photograph back down on the table, her fingertips resting lightly on it. "It's a strange bloody thing to see in this day and age, I'm sure, but it looks like a changeling charm."

"A changeling." A distant memory suddenly seemed closer at hand, of her sitting in this kitchen with Malory when they were both young, listening to Melva as she spun them endless stories of blessed springs, ancient gods, brownies and boggarts, and the "fair folk." "I knew it reminded me of something. What does it mean?"

"I'm not sure I can tell you that." Melva was using a teaspoon to squish the tea bags against the sides of the cups. "The old story was that sometimes a faerie would take a shine to a child and steal it away. They would leave a changeling in its place, a sickly faerie child that would eventually waste away and die, or turn into something like that—a log or a bundle of sticks. Some people believed that having a child made of sticks already in the home would keep the fae from taking their children."

"But don't you see? That does make a twisted kind of sense. Whoever is taking the children is leaving the parents with this replacement."

"Aye. One more cruelty on top of an already unforgivable act." Melva sounded angry, and it made Ashley oddly uneasy. She had hardly ever seen the old woman lose her temper, and tonight she had apparently witnessed it twice. "And what for?"

There was a jug of milk on the table. With a practiced hand, she removed the tea bags and set them on a little saucer before pouring milk into the cups. Ashley took hers and wrapped her fingers around it. She craved heat, which was unusual for her.

"I wonder if the police can tell where the branches were taken from," said Ashley. "That feels like the sort of thing they should be able to trace these days, doesn't it? They could be able to pin down the area the changeling doll was made. But then if they could do that, they would have done it years ago."

"If the person who made it had any sense, they would have used trees far away from where they lived." Melva took a sip of her tea. She seemed calmer than she had, but Ashley noticed she didn't take her eyes off the photograph. "*If* they have any sense, which doesn't seem very bloody likely to me, given the murdering and what have you."

"I'll ask Freddie about it. He might know the kinds of things the police will have done."

"Freddie is your young man with the podcast?" When Ashley nodded, Melva thinned her lips. "I still don't think any of this is a good idea, Ash, my love. It's . . . it's churning up a lot of stuff that's better left undisturbed."

"I'm trying to help stop a child murderer, Melva!"

"Don't take on so—that's not what I meant and you know it. I simply mean that putting yourself in the middle of all this could end up doing you harm. Bring back old nightmares, stir up old history, it could hurt you. It's already hurting you."

Ashley put her mug down. "What? What's happened?"

Melva sighed heavily, and then reached for one of the newspapers piled on the end of the table. She unfolded it and passed it to Ashley. It was *The Mirror*. On the front page, there were three photos: one of herself, clearly clipped from the TV interview she had given, one of Robbie Metcalfe, slightly out of focus, and a very recent one of David Wagner, looking stern and gray-faced. The headline read:

MEDIUM IN GINGERBREAD HOUSE MURDERS DROVE BOY TO SUICIDE

"Oh for *fuck's* sake."

37

I T WAS FULLY dark by the time Ashley left Melva's cottage. She stood at the bottom of the path—the cottage sat in the dip at the eastern edge of Red Rigg Fell, and the mountain made its presence felt via an uncanny portion of void in an otherwise star-strewn sky. The night was still and quiet, and there were no lights to be seen other than the moon and the soft orange lamp at Melva's living room window.

Fucking David Wagner. Old feelings of guilt and shame swarmed at the thought of him, his son, and on a deeper level, the entire nature of her career. Close to crying and annoyed with herself for it, Ashley turned toward her car, only to see a darker shadow in front of it. For a second, she thought it was a Heedful One, but then it moved and she saw a slither of a face caught in the amber light from the window. This was a real flesh-and-blood person, waiting for her in the dark.

"Richard? Is that you?"

The figure moved and was lost in the larger dark beyond the road, although Ashley heard the soft tread of footsteps across the tarmac.

"Wait! Who are you?"

She dashed into the dark after the shape, but very quickly realized she had lost track of it. Angry, she crashed into the field opposite Melva's cottage, long wet grass clinging to her jeans, soaking them. There was a rustle of small animals moving away from her and the call of an owl overhead. It was all too much: the murders, her father, the petty argument with Aidan, and now her name dragged through the mud because David Wagner could never move on and forgive her. A great wave of heat moved through her, causing sweat to prickle across her back and under her arms. She bent over at the waist, her hands on her knees.

"Oh fuck. Fuck all of it."

She took several slow breaths, trying to calm her racing heart, when a hand covered her mouth, yanking her whole body back to be crushed against someone. Another arm came around to hold her where she was. Ashley immediately began to thrash, to scream against the hand, but whoever it was, they were fearsomely strong. The big meaty hand pressed harder against her mouth, mashing her lips against her teeth.

"You get the message, don't you?" Ashley didn't recognize the voice, but then it sounded off somehow, as though someone were deliberately disguising it. *"Leave well enough alone."*

Then, the pressure was gone and the person behind her shoved her hard. Ashley pitched forward, waving her arms to stop herself from falling into the long grass. She failed. When she picked herself up from the cold, wet ground, she caught a brief glimpse of the figure running down the road before they were lost to the dark.

38

W HEN FREDDIE OPENED the door, he looked surprised and then horrified in short order. Ashley laughed, then winced, touching a finger to her bleeding lip.

"It probably looks worse than it is."

"What happened?"

He ushered her in, a look of concern on his face that Ashley found quite delightful. The B and B room was the largest available, with a double bed, an ensuite, and its own living area with a TV and sofa. There was a mirror just beyond the door; in it, Ashley could see her split lip was still oozing a little blood.

"Shit. Do you have a tissue?"

Freddie went to the bathroom and came back with a wad of tissue. Ashley gratefully pressed it to her sore mouth.

"I know Mrs. Templeton of old," she said, her voice slightly muffled. "So she let me in to see you. I've no doubt she'll have her biggest glass to the ceiling though to listen to what we're up to."

"Sit down." Freddie guided her to the sofa. "Did someone hurt you?"

Ashley recounted the events of the last couple of hours, including the information Melva had given her about the changeling. Ashley watched his face grow more animated as she told him about the person that had assaulted her in the dark, and by the time she was finished, he was frowning deeply.

"You have to tell the police."

"Tell them what? That someone I couldn't see or identify grabbed me and ran away? I don't think I'm their favorite person at the moment anyway."

"That's hardly the point."

"It's not even the worst part of today." Ashley sighed and pulled the folded newspaper out of her bag before passing it to Freddie. "You may as well see it now before you see it all over the internet."

Again, she watched his face as he read the article. When he was finished, he put the newspaper down on the sofa.

"So?" Ashley tried to make her tone as light as possible, but to her, the desperation in it was crystal clear. "Do you hate me yet?"

He looked at her for a long moment. Belatedly, she realized his curly hair was wet, and the skin around his throat looked damp. She realized she must have caught him just after having a shower—there was a faint soapy scent to the room as well.

"Why don't you tell me what happened in your own words?"

*　*　*

In the end, he brought a bottle of wine over and poured them a glass each while Ashley shifted on the sofa, kicking off her shoes and folding her legs underneath her. The cut on her lip was a steady throb, but a few sips of wine seemed to calm it.

"David Wagner's son, Joseph, was in his early twenties when I first started to see him. He had been at university in Manchester, doing a medical degree that I very quickly realized was more his father's dream than his. He came to see me at a show once, and then emailed asking for private sessions. I remember it quite clearly because I was surprised—people like him, who have a grounding in science, are not usually the sort of people eager to have multiple sessions with a medium. But he was keen, impressed with what he had seen in the show. And he was desperately unhappy."

Ashley frowned. It was strange to think about Joseph when she spent so much of her time trying not to think about him at all.

"That's the thing that Mr. Wagner refuses to acknowledge. That Joseph was unhappy long before I ever spoke to him. He was dragging himself through the second year of a medical degree he didn't want, and he was finding it difficult to make lasting friends—this was what I learned in my early sessions with him."

"You sound more like a therapist," said Freddie. He was sipping on his wine thoughtfully. Ashley smiled, then winced at the sharp pain in her lip.

"That's pretty much what we are, most of the time. It's ninety percent psychology—looking for clues, listening to the way people speak." She shrugged. "He was a kind soul, Joseph. One of those people who takes everything to heart. He was studying to be a doctor because he thought it would make his father happy, but I think he knew he wasn't suited for it—he had too much empathy for a profession where you have to deal out bad news.

"In my way, I encouraged him to make the choices he wanted. I told him . . ." She paused. The guilt seemed to gain weight with every word. "I told him that the spirit of his grandmother was making contact. He'd been close to her, had spent a lot of time at his grandparents' house when he was small. I told him his gran was eager for him to explore his own interests, to get out into the world and spend less time trying to make other people happy. I mean, I thought I wasn't being particularly subtle, but . . . Anyway. He ditched the degree, much to his father's disappointment, and went off to be a writer. At the time, I thought, okay. He's got a lot of empathy, he's sensitive, maybe even a little self-obsessed—perfect for a career in writing, right? While he was doing all this, I saw him maybe once a month. He joined a writing group and met a girl called Phoebe, who he fell head over heels for." She smiled. "For almost a year or so, it seemed like he was really happy. He had his girlfriend, he had the book he was writing, and I was glad. He told me to tell his grandmother thank you—he had found his vocation. The book had come leaping out of him, he said." She stopped and sighed again.

"So what happened?"

"After his good year, he had a bad one. He discovered that Phoebe was sleeping with someone else—specifically, one of the very few friends he'd managed to cling to through university. Joseph had been convinced she was his soulmate, the love of his life, and he took it really badly. He finished the book, but his writing group tore it to shreds, and it got rejected by every literary agent under the sun. He got sad. Really sad. Started sleeping all day. He was fired from the part-time job he had. He pleaded with Phoebe to come to her senses, pleaded with her so much, in fact, that she reported him to the police. One night, he turned up at her parents' house, no shoes on, and said he wouldn't leave until she saw him, so they called the police on him. He was arrested after he tried to force his way into the house."

"Ah, jeez," said Freddie.

Ashley shrugged one shoulder. "He made things worse for himself. Anyway. He came back to me in pieces. He wanted to know what his grandmother thought he should do next." She gave a hollow laugh. "His life was falling apart, and he expected the spirits to save him. I . . . perhaps I lost my patience slightly. I told him that *his grandmother* said he needed to get some proper help. Go to therapy. Take a break from the career and relationship miseries and focus on himself for a while."

"What did he say to that?"

"He was shocked. He said that his grandmother would barely know what therapy was, and asked why she would tell him that." Ashley laughed again, shaking her head. "I believe I told him that in the spirit world, we learn all sorts of things we would never have known in life. You know, the usual tripe."

Freddie looked at her over the rim of his glass.

"He pushed it further. Poor Joseph. He started to rant at me, saying that I'd been feeding him nonsense the whole time, that I'd destroyed his medical career on a whim. That the ruin of his life was my fault." Ashley touched a finger to the split in her lip. Talking about Joseph Wagner felt very much like probing an old festering wound. "So I told him that, on the contrary, everything he'd done was his own decision, and his refusal to be responsible was all part of the problem. He left in a fury, and I didn't hear from him again, but of course I heard the details later. Joseph went home, drank a load of vodka, then took a load of pills. He could have lived through that, as it turned out, but he had an undiagnosed heart condition and . . ." She lifted one hand and then dropped it again. "His father ended up breaking into his flat when he hadn't heard from him in a fortnight. He found the body."

"Jesus."

"Yeah. So." Ashley raised her glass and drained the last inch of red wine. "David Wagner, somewhat understandably, hates me and blames me for Joseph's death. I've met with him myself a couple of times, trying to, I don't know, apologize or make peace—or at least get him to understand that Joseph's problems were more complicated than taking advice from a dodgy psychic. But it has never worked." She nodded to the newspaper where it was neatly folded on the coffee table. "As you can probably tell." She let out a shaky sigh. She had hoped that telling someone about Joseph would make her feel better, but mainly it seemed to summon all the old feelings back, as vividly as ever: guilt, frustration, sorrow.

"Is that how you would describe yourself then? A dodgy psychic?"

"Aren't all psychics inherently dodgy?" She knew she shouldn't be talking so openly about this stuff—it was only her livelihood, after all—but the wine was easing the tension from her shoulders, and it felt good to be honest for once. After all, she didn't get many opportunities. "Snake oil salesmen. Con artists. Thieves. Vultures. Parasites." She raised a finger at him. "Not how I describe myself, mind you. But I have been called every one of those things."

"Ashley, you found Robbie Metcalfe. And I have no earthly way to explain how you did that." There were a few footsteps in the hall outside the door, and Ashley wondered if Mrs. Templeton had decided to come flush her out. But they kept on moving down the hall instead. "I think you spend a lot of time discrediting yourself before others can do it."

"Now who's the therapist?" She reached over and topped up her wine glass. "It's true there are some things that are unexplainable." She thought of the Heedful Ones, back in her life for reasons she couldn't fathom. "I can tell you that for sure." She shifted on the sofa so she was looking at him directly. "But now that I've spilled all that dirty laundry, I need to know what you think about it." She pressed her lips together. In the car on the way over, she had known she would have to talk to Freddie about David Wagner, but she hadn't expected this: a terrible fear that he would respect her less. Dislike her, even.

"It sounds to me as though Joseph's problems would have been there regardless of how much he talked to you," said Freddie. He pushed a hand back through his damp hair, sending his curls into corkscrews. "I imagine," he said carefully, "that your line of work attracts vulnerable people."

Ashley nodded and looked down at her hands. There was an unsettling sinking feeling behind her breastbone, there and gone. Regardless of how kind or understanding Freddie was, the truth about her line of work would always be there, like a rotten apple at the bottom of the barrel. She thought about telling him *It's the only thing I know how to do,"* or *"My family rely on me,"* but in the end, she didn't. She said, "Without vulnerable people, I guess I'd have no job at all. But I think all of us are vulnerable, to some degree."

"Speaking of inexplicable things." Freddie shifted on the sofa, stretching out one arm along the back. If Ashley let her head fall back, she could lean it against his hand. She held herself very still. "I'm fascinated by this changeling business. When we saw Mrs. Nowak's photograph, I had assumed that the killer had left the objects as a kind of taunt or mockery of the parents. But is it possible it's actually an attempt to . . . say sorry? To replace what's been taken somehow? That suggests a very different sort of killer. Someone who is reluctant, or feels some level of remorse or shame, maybe. Which, in turn, suggests it's possible that the killer knows the victims."

"Really? But they're all so . . ." Ashley shrugged. "Unconnected. And far apart too."

For some time, Freddie didn't answer. He was resting his wineglass on his knee, and Ashley found herself admiring his hands, with their long, mobile fingers and big, broad thumbs. He had hands that belonged on a Michelangelo statue. *Now you're being ridiculous,* she thought to herself, but she felt overly aware of the double bed on the far side of the room.

"I'm just spitballing," he said eventually. "I know you don't want to go to the police about what happened outside your friend's house. But do you think we should tell them about the changeling aspect?"

Ashley frowned. She couldn't see the pragmatic DCI Turner thinking much about folklore and old wives' tales.

"They've known about the stick dollies for years at this point. Surely they've figured it out? All they'd need to do is have a poke about on Google."

"Hopefully, you're right about that," said Freddie, "but I might just drop them a line about it anyway. If nothing else, being seen as helpful will get us in their good books."

"Have you found that in your previous cases it helps to have the police on your side?" She realized she didn't particularly want to keep in touch with DCI Turner, or even DC Platt, who had put them on the path to speaking to Mrs. Nowak in the first place. She thought about how they'd brought up her father's past, all those slippery little insinuations. "I mean, it was my intention to help them. And I did. And then they hauled me in for questioning."

"I suppose they weren't expecting you to lead them straight to a body," said Freddie, his tone dry. "But yes, I've found it varies from case to case. If there's a strong suggestion that members of law enforcement have been lax, in my experience, the last thing they seem to want is a member of the public asking questions. And sometimes they just think I'm overstepping the mark." He brightened up slightly. "At least in the UK I've less chance of getting shot for asking questions."

"Ha."

A small silence pooled between them then. It occurred to Ashley, too late, that she probably shouldn't have had a second glass of wine if she was driving back. Perhaps she could get a cup of coffee from Mrs. Templeton before she left.

"I wish you'd report what happened to the police," Freddie said again, his tone back to being serious. "I feel awful about it. I told you that I wouldn't let anything bad happen to you, and I've already failed in that promise."

Ashley laughed and shook her head. She half felt like she should be insulted by this patronizing statement, but something about his wholesome insistence was oddly charming.

"Give over. Listen. When are we going to see Dean Underwood?"

He raised his eyebrows, surprised. "You're quite sure you want to?"

"I am. And now that I've decided that I'm doing it. I'm anxious to get it over with."

"Great. The next visiting day, as I understand it, is the day after tomorrow. How do you feel about that?"

Ashley agreed, and soon after that, began to excuse herself. Freddie seemed disappointed, which she tried not to read too much into, and when he walked her to the door, they both paused.

"Hey. Thank you."

"What for?" Ashley pulled her bag up onto her shoulder. "Disrupting your evening?"

He grinned. "For agreeing to work on this with me. It's already been far more interesting with your presence."

"You're very welcome, I'm sure." She went up on her tiptoes and kissed him on the cheek, lingering a little longer this time. When she pulled away, his green eyes had darkened somewhat, and he was looking at her in a way that made her stomach turn over.

"Do you want to stay?" he said, his voice low.

Ashley opened her mouth, not quite sure what she was going to say, when there came a loud knocking on the door, inches away from their faces. They both jumped.

"Are you all right in there?" came Mrs. Templeton's voice, disapproval dripping from every vowel. "It's getting rather late!"

For a few seconds, the pair clung to each other in helpless, silent laughter until Ashley brought her voice under control.

"I was just leaving, Mrs. T!"

39

THE NEXT MORNING, Ashley had been expecting further ructions from her father over her absence from the house—or at least that a complaint from the hen party might have made it back to him—but instead he was focused on the David Wagner story in *The Mirror*. As she picked at her own breakfast, she watched him go from phone call to phone call, his brow furrowed as he hashed out with their solicitor the best way of finally suing Wagner, and she felt an odd wave of affection for him. He tried to protect her in his own way. When she passed him to put her plate in the sink, she gave him a quick, loud kiss on the top of his bald head, and he glanced up at her in amusement before returning to his conversation. The doorbell rang, and Ashley heard her mother's soft footsteps down the hall.

"He's finally come out into the open with this bullshit, Edward," her father was saying. "Surely this is the time we nail the bastard. Whatever he got paid for that *Mirror* article, I want double. He started this war, Eddie. My son and I tell you what—"

"Ashley!" her mother called from the front door. "Parcel for you."

It was a large cardboard box, surprisingly heavy and weirdly cold. Ashley hefted it into the kitchen and put it down on the table before fetching a pair of scissors from the drawer. Her mother appeared at her shoulder.

"Did you order something, sweetie?"

"Not that I remember."

She opened the parcel and found a layer of soft, mud-colored insulation wool inside—underneath that, several blue ice packs. Ashley pulled them out and put them on the table. Her father gave her an impatient look, then stood up, taking his conversation into the other room. A smell both familiar and unsettling was rising from the box. Ashley felt her stomach turn over.

Beneath the ice packs and the wool were several vacuum-packed parcels of meat, pink and yellow and glistening. Ashley pulled out cold packages of bacon, sausages, lamb chops, and pork chops. There were chicken thighs, legs, and breasts, and steaks too, with russet tendrils of blood creeping through the transparent packaging. There were even things that Ashley couldn't remember eating since she was a kid and they lived in the council flat: kidneys, liver, tripe, and lambs' hearts, purple and rippled with fat. It was like someone had packaged up an entire butcher's shop and sent it to her. Halfway through the unpacking, she found a small pink card. Printed on it was a message: *Eat up, Ashley!* The card was wet, curling under her touch.

Her mother was clucking over it all, picking up things and putting them down again.

"I wish you had told me you were getting so much in, Ashley," she was saying. "I'll have to clear out the big freezer in the garage for this lot. What were you thinking?"

"I . . ." Ashley's hands were numb from delving through the chilled meat, and the smell—the sweet, unctuous scent of raw flesh—was growing by the minute. *Eat up, Ashley.* Where had she heard that before?

Pulling away more sausages and a whole rolled side of beef, Ashley spotted something strange at the very bottom of the box. At first, she took it to be a whole chicken, its legs trussed up with white string, but as she pulled it out, she saw that it had four fleshy boneless limbs, and . . . a face.

There was a cry from behind her. Her mother was at the sink, retching up her breakfast all over the dirty plates. Ashley blinked at the cold slippery thing in her hands, several thoughts colliding at once.

It's a baby. A dead baby.

No, it's not. Look at it properly, you idiot.

It was meant to look like a baby, she was sure of that, but it was several different pieces of meat, bound and sewn and crushed into the sealed plastic packet. The trunk was indeed a chicken carcass, while the arms and legs were formed from thick pieces of rolled pork, folded into elbows and knees. The head—it was hard to look at the head— was a whole joint, the fat cut and sliced to hint at hollow eyes, a slit of a mouth. Perhaps worst of all were the hands and feet—not made of meat at all, but with a yellowish kind of wax.

A thing meant to look like a child but sent to me.

Ashley ran back to the front door and flung it open, but the delivery van—if there had been one—was long gone. Furious, she stormed back into the kitchen and grabbed her mother by the shoulders.

"Who delivered it? Did you see who it was?"

Helen Whitelam's eyes were very wide and wet. She blinked at Ashley, not comprehending.

"Mum! This is important. Did you see who delivered the meat?"

"What's going on in here?" Her father appeared at the doorway, his phone hanging loose in his hand, forgotten. "Why does the kitchen smell of sick?"

Ashley let go of her mother. She felt like she might be sick too.

"Dad, call the police."

* * *

When the police left, taking the whole box of meat with them and the Frankenstein's monster of a meat baby in a separate evidence bag, DCI Turner hung back, lingering with Ashley in the hallway. There were dark circles under her eyes.

"We've taken a statement from your mother, and we'll be in touch."

Ashley found she couldn't look away from the police van where the box of meat was loaded.

"Will you . . ." She cleared her throat. She was thinking about Freddie's original theory of what the parents of the missing children could be receiving in the post. "Will you test the meat?"

"Test it?"

"To make sure it's . . . animal."

DCI Turner gave her a hard look. "This is likely just a prank, Miss Whitelam. I don't know if you've noticed, but you've been all over the news lately, and I'm afraid that I can tell you, after years of watching this sort of thing happen, that bad news attracts people with a tenuous grip on reality. You of all people should know that."

"You're talking about Dean Underwood." When Turner didn't correct her, she continued. "Listen. I know that the parents of those who disappeared were sent a kind of . . . doll in the post. Couldn't this be related to that?"

"How do you know about that?" Turner shook her head, tersely dismissing her own query. "The podcaster, of course. And have you had any children go missing lately, Miss Whitelam?"

"This is hardly a fucking joke."

Turner sighed and looked away. Ashley got the impression that she'd managed to shame the woman, and she felt a bitter flare of satisfaction.

"It seems to me that if you felt yourself under suspicion, Miss Whitelam, that one way to avoid that would be to make it so you might also seem to be a victim."

"Are you saying I sent this parcel of meat nightmares to *myself*?" She shook her head. "It feels more like a warning than a prank. Like someone is trying to scare me."

Turner smiled tightly. "We'll be in touch if we have further questions for you or your parents, Miss Whitelam."

* * *

Back indoors, her mother was in the living room, sitting on the sofa with her head down. She had a glass of warm whiskey in her hands. Ashley could smell its spicy scent the moment she walked in.

"How are you feeling, Mum?"

The older woman looked up. Her eyes were red and watery, and Ashley felt a familiar stab of impatience.

"It was quite a shock. Your father made me a drink. He's gone to speak to Edward about all this in person, about David Wagner. Oh God, when you pulled *that thing* out of the box, I thought . . . it looked just like . . ."

"Try not to dwell on it, Mum. Drink the whiskey—it'll make you feel better." With a familiar tug of guilt in her stomach, Ashley realized she already wanted to be gone. Whenever her mother was in this strange watery mood, it always made her feel trapped; it was like the sadness was catching. "I have to go out and see Malory."

Helen Whitelam looked up sharply. "You can't! You can't leave me here alone! Not after what just happened."

And there it was. Her father might be more direct about trying to keep Ashley where he could see her—control her—but her mother's form of coercion was in many ways much worse. *You can't leave me here. I am vulnerable, I am sad, I am broken.*

"I'm sorry, Mum." She turned back to the door, desperate now to get out as soon as she could before her mother convinced her to stay. "I have things to do. I'll be back later though, I promise."

Not if I can help it, she thought, feeling sick and wicked. *If I had any choice, I'd never come back.*

Her mother said nothing at all, which Ashley recognized as another subtle instrument from her guilt toolbox, but when she reached the front door, a soft hand touched her shoulder, making her jump.

"Christ. What is it, Mum?"

"There are some things I think you should have."

"What? What things? What are you talking about?"

"Please. It won't take a minute."

Ashley followed her mother upstairs, then watched as she began pulling boxes out from under the big double bed in the master bedroom. There was tons of storage space in the cottage, spacious fitted wardrobes and a pleasantly airy attic, but some habits die hard, and Ashley's mother still filled the space under every bed with boxes, suitcases, and bags.

"I really don't have time for this, Mum."

Her mother wasn't listening. "Here it is." She stood up, a small old-fashioned suitcase in her arms. It was powder blue, scuffed at the corners, and had a silver fastening on the top. "I used to lock this up, just in case, but your father never goes under the bed for anything, so I think it's safe."

Ashley raised her eyebrows, now intrigued rather than impatient.

"You're hiding it from him? What is it?"

Her mother laid the suitcase on the bed and sat next to it. She fiddled with the fastening and it popped open, but for the moment, she just rested her hands on it, her head down as though steadying herself for something.

"These things were my mother's," she said eventually. "I've been thinking about what you said the other day, about how I should be allowed to talk about her. Logan doesn't like it when I do. None of my family did."

Ashley blinked. As far as she knew, there was nothing belonging to Grandma Maisie in the house; there never had been. But apparently her mother had been hiding a secret stash.

"You've got stuff of Nan's that Dad doesn't know about?"

Her mother shot her a sly look, in its way even more shocking than the meat parcel.

"Of course not," she said. "He'd go spare. But I think you should see these things. You remind me of her. I think she looks after you, from wherever she is now."

She pushed the open suitcase toward Ashley. Inside, there was a mixture of things, and to begin with, they were disappointingly normal. A few old beige cardigans, a tin of buttons, a small ceramic dog, and a handful of fat Catherine Cookson paperbacks.

"When she died, the home asked if we wanted her things. Your father told them no, but I went up there, in secret, and collected some bits and pieces." Helen Whitelam tucked a lock of hair behind her ear. "Just keepsakes, really. She didn't have a lot, in the end."

Ashley stared at her mother in astonishment; to think of her acting against her father's instructions was remarkable. And yet, she remembered, Maisie had died in 1999, years before the incident at Red Rigg House had made her mother into this timid little mouse. Once, she had been quite formidable.

"She was a . . . troubled woman," her mother continued. "But she saw more than most people. Just like you, she had a connection to the angels."

Ashley took some things out of the suitcase, handling them carefully, as though they were artifacts in a museum. Under the cardigans, there was an old blue leather purse, as soft and warm as skin, and her grandmother's birth certificate: Maisie Agatha Harker, born in 1927. And there was a thick notebook of some kind, the cover bound in tough purple cloth. It was held shut with several elastic bands. Someone had doodled a heart in black ink on the corner.

"Thanks, Mum." Ashley felt awkward. This on top of the box of meat—it was clearly a day for surprises. Troubling ones.

"Well." Her mother stood up, wiping her hands on her skirt. "These things are yours now, so do with them as you like. Don't let your dad see it though, will you?"

Ashley took the suitcase into her own room and put in her wardrobe. The notebook she put in her handbag, meaning to have a look at it while she was out and about. As she got to the front door though, her mother was there again, a more familiar distracted expression on her face.

"I'm going out for a while, Mum. Will you be okay on your own?"

Her mother shook her head slightly, dismissing the question. "Listen to them, won't you, Ashley? They are trying to help you."

"Who?"

Her mother took hold of her arm and squeezed it. Her hands were hot and dry.

"The angels, darling."

CHAPTER

40

Malory was at Green Beck's church hall again. When Ashley arrived, stepping past boxes of dried pasta and tins of beans, her friend was at the center of a crowd of people, as she often was. Since Biddy Lyndon-Smith had passed away, the people of Green Beck seemed to think of Malory as a kind of figurehead for the entire village. As Ashley pushed her way through, she saw a variety of people she had known for years, all with their own problems and concerns; Jerry Boswick, one of the many farmers from the area; Fiona McCartney, the librarian from the tiny one-room library; Mrs. Bonnier, who ran the post office. Ashley even recognized the florid bearded poet who had given a reading at the arts trust awards day. There was a lot of chatter and laughter.

"Thank you all for coming," Malory was saying, in her "now you must all disperse" voice. "And don't forget, the Moon Market is next week. If you have a friend, tell them about it, put signs in your windows, you know the drill. Speaking of which"—Malory made eye contact with Ashley and smiled—"there's my guest of honor."

When the rest of the crowd had wandered off, Ashley was surprised to see two people still with Malory. One was Melva, who looked unusually stern, and another was a girl of about fourteen; she had a lot of brown curly hair and wore a pair of wire-rimmed glasses and a sweatshirt with a school crest on it.

"Penny, this is my friend Ashley, who I was talking about," Malory was saying. "She has a very interesting job and will be one of the big attractions at the market."

"Hello." Ashley smiled at the girl, who nodded seriously. Ashley had wanted to have a private word with her friend, but it seemed she was in full mentor mode. "Hi, Melva. I seem to be bumping into everyone today."

"Aye, well, I've said my piece," said Melva, not quite meeting Ashley's eye. She turned to Malory, giving her a look Ashley didn't understand. "Make of it what you will, young lady. I've got to get back home. I've a client over before lunch."

Malory didn't appear concerned by Melva's attitude. She waved her off, then put a hand on Penny's shoulder. "Penny here is one of the kids from the foundation who will be here over the next couple of weeks. She wants to find out about running a business, so she's shadowing me for the week. Work experience. Honestly, Ashie, she's so smart, I think I could give her a job right now and she'd show everyone up."

Penny blushed faintly and looked down at her feet.

"Well, good luck, Penny. There's no one better to learn from than Malory." Ashley remembered sitting in Malory's bedroom as a kid, the same age as Penny, watching her go through a suitcase full of clothes. She felt an odd pang in her chest, somewhere between nostalgia and jealousy. "Listen, Mal, can I have a quick word?"

Penny was sent off to start itemizing the donations for the harvest festival while Ashley and Malory moved over toward the curtains that hung to either side of the small stage, where Ashley quickly caught Malory up on the events of the morning. Her friend looked bemused.

"Will they bring it back, all that meat? Will they keep it in a freezer? Seems like a waste otherwise."

"Mal! I'm not going to eat the bloody meat, am I? It was sent by some sort of lunatic. Even if it turns out to be . . . kosher, for want of a better word, it wouldn't feel right."

Malory shook her head. "Ashie, it'll just be some prank. If I were you, I wouldn't worry about it."

"You didn't see the baby." Ashley thought of the cold wet plastic under her fingertips and shuddered. "The creepiest thing I've ever seen, I . . ." Horribly, inevitably, the images of Robbie Metcalfe's body and the warped bag of meat collided. Heat prickled down her back and under her arms. "Listen. That isn't what I wanted to talk about anyway. What was Melva doing here?"

Malory shrugged. "Nothing important. You know what she's like. Gets some gossip and has to pass it on immediately or it's burning a hole in her pocket."

"She didn't look like she was in much of a gossiping mood to me." Ashley frowned. "When I went to see her yesterday, Richard was there. I think they were having a barney."

"A barney?"

"A *row*, Malory, come on. Melva looked really upset, and even Richard looked serious. Do you know what it was about?"

A chorus of voices rose, sweet and delicate, from the church next door, then stopped again. There would be some sort of practice going on. Malory sniffed and pushed a lock of her hair behind her ear.

"How on earth would I know that? Richard doesn't tell me anything much, and when he does, he's usually lying, Ashie. Perhaps he sold her some substandard weed and she wanted her money back, I don't know."

Richard traveled all over, and his status as the village's minor drug dealer had been unchallenged for years; his clients included Aidan, a handful of the local teenagers, and Melva, who claimed weed was the only thing that eased her arthritis.

"Have you spoken to him lately? How did he seem to you?" She thought about telling Malory how someone had grabbed her in the dark outside Melva's cottage, then decided against it. Ashley was normally fond of her friend's relentless optimism, but sometimes it meant that serious discussion of anything unpleasant was continually batted away, like a paper boat caught in a strong current. "He was even less charming than usual when I saw him, and I think he made Melva cry. I don't think I've ever seen Melva upset before, let alone crying."

Malory shrugged. "I'm not my brother's keeper, Ashie. If you really want to know, he plans to be at the Moon Market next week. You can ask him there."

Next week. How was the market so soon?

"I wanted to talk to you about that too, actually." Ashley took a deep breath. "I want to bring a guest to the market. Is that all right? Do I get a plus-one as your guest of honor or whatever?"

Malory raised her eyebrows. "Ashie, darling, if it means you definitely turn up to the house, you can bring as many guests as you like. You can bring a whole bloody circus. Who is it?"

"A friend. Remember I mentioned that true crime podcast?"

"Oh, the American podcaster! I've heard he's quite dishy. Of course you can bring him."

"Where did you hear that?" To her own horror, Ashley could feel her cheeks flushing pink. She thought of the moment in his B and B room the night before when he'd asked her to stay.

"Like I said, gossip." Malory winked at her, then laughed. "You can't keep secrets from me, Ashie. Not in Green Beck."

For a second, it was on the tip of her tongue to tell Malory about the planned visit to see Dean Underwood—she would have been horrified, and she knew she owed it to her friend to keep her informed—but something about Malory's tinkling laugh made her hold it back at the last minute. Instead, she smiled, then nodded toward the girl by the cardboard boxes.

"Go and play with your new protégé."

* * *

That afternoon, Ashley drove herself to a small pub called The Bear and Ragged Staff and sat in the saloon bar with a glass of iced tonic. She had chosen this place because it was remarkably well lit for a country pub, with big freestanding lamps in all the corners, and she wanted to have a good look at her grandmother's notebook.

There might well be nothing of interest in here at all, she told herself as she turned it over and over in her hands. Outside, the sun was setting, casting the last of its syrupy light against the large plate-glass windows. *She wasn't well. Even Mum said so. This could be pages and pages of ravings. Or recipes for casserole.*

Once she had the elastic bands off, the notebook fell open, a slight musty smell rising from it. Inside, a few of the pages were loose, and they were all covered in a beautiful copperplate handwriting in faded blue ink—so faded in some places that it was difficult to read. Ashley ran her fingers across the thin paper.

Helen has the measles, so the whole household is a mess. The doctor gave us a lotion to put on the spots, but it hardly seems to do anything. The poor love is scratching so much we've had to give her mittens, and she's complaining about an earache now too. An ear infection on top of measles? It seems possible with this family.

Ashley smiled. So it was a diary. The date at the top said January 1962, when her mother would still have been a toddler, and her uncle James and Auntie Amy had been in primary school. She flicked forward, noting that there was roughly a page for each day—her grandmother had managed at least a few lines every day—in some places, her elegant handwriting was squashed into the margins to fit everything in. Maisie had recorded all sorts of things: her husband's greenhouse projects, Uncle Jim's burgeoning interest in football and athletics, Auntie Amy's broken wrist, the result of falling out of a tree in the field behind their house. It was fascinating in a way, revealing an everyday history that was intimate and charming. Ashley had been reading for around twenty minutes, her soda forgotten, when a single sentence brought her up sharp.

They're watching me again.

It came at the bottom of a passage about a new cooker they were thinking of buying. No other context, just that chilling, matter-of-fact statement.

Watching her, thought Ashley. *That's what the Heedful Ones do.*

After that, it was as though a gate had opened. There were more and more mentions of the mysterious figures Maisie saw, growing in number until it was a flood of strangeness, drowning out the more prosaic things she had recorded.

Most of the time, they stand around doing nothing. It's easy to mistake them for shadows. Or at least it would be, if I couldn't

see their faces—pale, smudged, like chalk on a rainy pavement.
They are a strange kind of angel.

I saw three alone today, two at the supermarket. They were
drifting back and forth, but they didn't leave me alone for long.

Alf caught me looking. He said, "What's that you're staring
at, Maisie?" and God help me, I couldn't think what to tell him.
The shadow person wanted me to tell him the truth, I could feel
it. What else do they want from me?

Ashley paused, her heart thudding in her chest. Were her grandmother's shadow people the same as her Heedful Ones? She thought
they had to be, but what did it mean? She looked around at the rest of
the pub, filling up as the day wore on. She felt guilty but also elated.
I'm not alone. She read on.

I'm beginning to think I know who they are. I think they are
tied to me somehow. I want to tell Alf about it, get his opinion,
but I already know what he'll say. I'll be back up at the doctor's
and on those god-awful tablets again, the ones that make me feel
numb all over.

At some point, Ashley knew Maisie had stopped keeping the
Heedful Ones to herself, and she had ended up in a home for people
with severe mental health issues. Alf himself had signed her away. *So*
I'm not alone, thought Ashley bitterly. *What good does it do me? Maisie's*
long dead, and she's still classed as the family lunatic.

In the final third of the diary, the shadow people were all that
Maisie wrote about. She described them looming in the corners of
rooms or swarming at the bottom of the garden; at night, she saw
them at the end of the bed, dead eyes watching her sleep. There was no
fear from Maisie, only curiosity bending into frustration.

I tried to talk to the one that waits at our front gate again today,
but I'm not at all sure that they can hear me, or that they are even
capable of speaking. Reg from across the road was washing his car,
and I'm fairly certain he saw me, the nosy git. From the shadow,

there was nothing obvious, but I swear it looked at me intently.
There is something they want me to know.

Ashley put the diary down and went to the bar. This time, she ordered a vodka with her soda and drank it back quickly, desperate for the cold burn in the back of her throat and the pit of her stomach. *The Heedful Ones wanted to tell my nan something. Did she ever find out what it was?* The messages they had had for Ashley so far had not been reassuring ones: leave Red Rigg House, they had tried to tell her, before it all burns down. And they had shown her where Robbie Metcalfe was. But why?

And then, toward the back of the diary, Ashley found a page written in black felt tip, her grandmother's elegant handwriting scruffy and jagged, as though her hand had been shaking.

I asked them again, what did they want, and I even reached out for the shadow, desperate to understand it. Normally they move away, shifty as cats they are, but this shadow stayed and let my hand move through it—and it all makes sense now. I know who they are. I'm amazed I didn't know. They are us. They are us back through history, stretching back so far I can't even understand it, not really. It's this whole long bloodline like you wouldn't believe, marching back through time. I have to tell Alf. I have to.

Ashley leaned back in her chair, already craving the cold burn of vodka again. *They are us.* What did that mean?

After that, there were a few blank pages, the first in the diary, and when Ashley reached the next entry, it was brief—a single line.

The shadows are the ghosts of my ancestors, stretching back to some unimaginable time.

*   *   *

That night, when she got home, she saw a fresh pile of newspapers on the telephone table in the foyer; it seemed that every rag going had picked up the David Wagner story, and her father was collecting a copy of each, no doubt planning to sue every one of them. Frowning, she went up to her room, unlocked her bedroom door, and got her journal out of the drawer. For the first time in a long while, she sat and wrote in it for a good hour, pouring into it all the strangeness of the past few days and all her pain over Wagner's persecution. On those pages, she allowed herself to write what she truly thought about David Wagner, how his anger was continuing to disrupt her life when the reality was he was as much to blame for Joseph's death; if he'd supported his son instead of abandoning him when he wouldn't pursue a medical career, so much might have been different.

David Wagner is a fool, she wrote, *and I'm sick of the sight of him.*

When she'd worn herself out, she felt exhausted and hot with a kind of sick guilt. She went to the window and opened it a crack. Cold air moved against her flushed skin like the hand of some hungry ghost. Out in the dark somewhere, she heard a magpie chatter.

41

2006

Following the trial of Dean Underwood, the story of the Red Rigg House fire and its one miraculous survivor was all over every tabloid newspaper in the UK—all thanks to Logan Whitelam. While her mother retreated further and further into herself, not quite able to accept that her daughter had returned from the dead, Ashley was pushed further and further out into the world. Her memories of the year 2005 were not so much about processing trauma as monetizing it. There were interviews in newspapers, accompanied by photos of Ashley looking pale and solemn by the school gates, or in her tiny shared bedroom. There were even television appearances, little snippets on the news, and then appearances on "light entertainment" shows where men and women with shiny, unmoving hairstyles asked her and her parents lots of questions—about her time at Red Rigg, about her vision and the famous phone call to her mother, about any other psychic talents she might have. Aidan was often left at home on these outings—he wasn't a part of the story, Logan would point out, and having an older brother made Ashley seem too normal. He wanted her to be eerie, unsettling, a mystery people would want to solve.

The family made a lot of money during this period. When the phone calls from TV producers began to wane, Logan decided he was moving the whole family to Green Beck. Years later, Ashley would look back on this decision and marvel at it, but the reality was that her mother was no longer in her right mind and in no fit state to argue with Logan, and she and Aidan naturally had no say. When Aidan tried—when he pointed out that his school was in Lewisham and his football clubs all in London—Logan brushed him aside like he was nothing, pointing out that they had the money now to live wherever they pleased, and nothing about Lewisham pleased anyone.

Privately, Ashley believed there were other, quieter reasons for the move. Technically, she knew nothing about her father's nighttime business, but it wasn't hard to pick up on small details and a change of atmosphere in their tiny flat. Unmarked cardboard boxes came and went, men appeared at all hours of the night, with serious gray faces. A heavy ornamental brass from the living room had been moved to one side of the front door, as though someone thought they might need access to a blunt instrument at short notice. London had become curiously untenable to her father.

When they moved to Green Beck in the spring of 2006, other reasons suddenly became more apparent too. Around a fortnight after bringing all their belongings up from London in a van, newspapers and television crews descended once more upon Ashley and her family. This time, the story was about Ashley's return to the area where she had nearly died, about her family bravely facing what had happened to them. They interviewed her in the garden of the cottage, or out on the wild landscape of Cumbria itself, or on the village lanes of Green Beck. At this time, Red Rigg House was still undergoing reconstruction, and Ashley point-blank refused to go anywhere near it, but when the articles appeared in the newspapers she saw it again: photos of the great house, one side of it a blackened skeleton encased in scaffolding. By this time, Ashley was sixteen, a teenager who was still small for her age, and her mother began dressing her in white, letting her pale hair grow long. It made for a good picture. The first request for a private reading came in: people believed she

had a connection to the dead. Ashley finished her compulsory years
of school and never went back.

* * *

When they had been there about a month, Ashley opened the door to
find Malory Lyndon-Smith on her doorstep. She hadn't seen Malory
since the day of the fire, and for a hazy second, it was like she was
back there, sitting in Malory's bedroom with a lacy white dress in her
hands. The older girl looked much as she had then, only with a slight
gauntness to her cheeks that made her look attractively haunted. She
beamed at Ashley and held up a newspaper.

"Ashie! I'm so thrilled to see you! I can't believe you came back to
the arse end of nowhere."

Ashley blinked and stepped out onto the doorstep. After a moment,
she smiled.

"Hi, Malory."

The newspaper headline was one of the recent ones. They had taken
her up to the foothills of Red Rigg and photographed her with the mountain looming in the background. The photo picked up her mismatched
eyes, and her hair—nearly white in the spring light—was pulled to one
side by the wind. She looked like a ghost. The headline beneath read:

RED RIGG FIRE SURVIVOR SAYS SHE STILL HAS NO
MEMORY OF MISSING THREE DAYS

To her surprise, Malory put her arms around her and squeezed
her, crumpling the newspaper into her side. After a moment, Ashley
hugged her back, and when they broke apart Malory's eyes were very
bright, as though she was seconds away from crying.

"It's so good to *see* you. I couldn't believe it when Richard said
your whole family had moved to Green Beck, but then he showed me
all the newspapers. We'll be able to see each other all the time. Isn't
that wonderful? Do you want to come for a drive?'

For the first time, Ashley noticed a sleek-looking car parked in
their driveway. It was a dark, almost oily blue. It looked brand new.

"You can drive?"

"Ashie, darling, you can't get anywhere in this place without a bloody car. Can't you drive? You must be old enough."

"Dad won't let me." Ashley let herself be pulled across the gravel toward the car. "He says I can just get lifts with him."

"Balls to that. I will teach you."

*   *   *

They drove out into the brightening day, Malory talking a mile a minute about everything: the restoration of the house; Ashley's newfound celebrity; the things to do around Green Beck—and the lack of them; her brother Richard's comings and goings. At first, Ashley had a hard knot of dread in the pit of her stomach, convinced that Malory was driving them to Red Rigg House. But as the chatter washed over her, it became clear that Malory had no particular destination in mind. She was just driving for the sake of driving.

Eventually, they came to a quiet spot dotted with picnic tables. They parked the car and got out, walking across grass still wet with dew. Below them was a great sweep of dark forest, the trees moving in a gentle rush in time with the wind. There was no one else around, so they sat on the tables, their boots resting on the benches. Malory pulled a silver flask from her jacket and took a long drink from it before passing it to Ashley.

"What is it?"

"Mum's whiskey. She's got loads of old bottles in the drawing room. She never notices when I nick some."

Ashley paused with the bottle an inch away from her mouth. The last time she had tasted Biddy Lyndon-Smith's whiskey, it had been just before . . .

"Come on, drink up." Malory grinned at her. "I brought it special."

Ashley took a sip and swallowed it quickly even as her throat tried to close up against it. The alcohol burned all the way down to her stomach. "Has it been hard for you?" she asked quietly. "Since it . . . you know, since it happened?"

Malory grimaced. "It's been hell. We're lucky that only half the building burned down, of course, but it feels like a bomb went off in the middle of our lives. All our plans have been put on hold. Journalists on the doorstep every few days." She gave Ashley a sardonic look. "We're not as popular with the press as you are, Ashie. They seem convinced the fire was our fault in some way."

"But the trial . . ."

"The press don't care about the truth. Speaking of which." Malory picked up the newspaper she'd brought with her from the car, unfolding it to reveal it's headline again. "Is it really true you don't remember what happened that night? Where you went? You can tell me."

"I really don't know." The words came automatically, familiar from the endless rounds of interviews, but as she looked down at the photograph of her dwarfed by Red Rigg Fell, she wondered. "I remember being put back to bed by Miss Lyonnes and your mother. And then I'm in the woods somehow. I was so cold. And hungry."

Despite the warm sunshine on her shoulders, she shivered. Sometimes, when she was lying in her bed at night, on the verge of drifting off to sleep, she would think about that odd, blank time, and it was as though a memory danced just out of sight. She had the sense of a small hand in hers, the fingers painfully thin, and a feeling of being pulled into the dark. Had there been someone there with her that night? Not a Heedful One, but a real person who led her away from the fire before it happened? But who? There was no one it could have been.

"No," she said eventually. "I guess I'll probably never know what happened."

"There must have been a guardian angel looking out for you."

Ashley swallowed. Her mother had started talking about angels since she'd come back from Red Rigg, and it made her deeply uneasy. Whatever the Heedful Ones had been, they couldn't have been angels. Next to her, Malory took another gulp of whiskey.

"I thought . . ." Ashley took a deep breath. "I didn't think you'd want to see me. Doesn't it bring it all back for you? That night?"

"Of course not, Ashie. It all worked out for the best." She slung an arm around the younger girl's shoulders and squeezed her again. Ashley could smell the sharp scent of whiskey on her breath. "You're here now, and I'll look after you."

42

I

T WAS OVER two hours to drive to Liverpool, but it was a bright
day, the sky scrubbed blue and fresh, a handful of white contrails
appearing as they made their way out of Cumbria. Ashley had woken
up that morning full of foreboding about that day's interview, and the
purple diary peeking out of her bag hadn't helped her mood. Once she
was in the car with Freddie, she at least felt like she had some backup.
Today's mission might be unwise, but she wasn't attempting it alone.
Freddie was driving, his phone in the well between them recording
his words.

". . . making Dean Underwood one of the most infamous crimi-
nals in the north of England. He might be only tangentially connected to the Gingerbread House Murders, but I could hardly turn
down the offer to talk to him. Already, this series has taken me in
directions I could never have predicted. The discovery of Robbie
Metcalfe's remains happening while I was in England, a handful of
miles from the location. A violent altercation with the father of one of
the children—an incident I wish I could have prevented. The delightful company of noted psychic Ashley Whitelam."

He stopped and gave her a quick grin.

"That's probably not the right tone, is it? Ahem. And the company of noted psychic Ashley Whitelam, who has provided a unique
perspective on the case. What will we hear from Dean Underwood

himself? Will it also cast a new light on the Gingerbread House Murders, or will we be listening to the ravings of a mentally ill man? How will Ashley herself react to the man who was the cause of so much misery in her early life?"

He stopped again. "Do you mind me bringing this up?"

Ashley looked out the window. The hills of Cumbria had flattened, sinking back under the earth. "No," she said eventually. "Now that we're on the way to Ashworth, I'm pretty curious myself to see what the old weirdo has to say. I can't hide from it forever."

Freddie nodded and pressed a button to stop the recording, then turned the radio on low. The slow beats of something weird on BBC Radio 6 seeped out into the car.

"For what it's worth, I think you're very brave, Ash. You're directly confronting a childhood trauma and letting other people in on that moment. That's quite a thing."

Brave. She thought of Magda, sitting in her house that was so full of children yet so empty too. Ashley thought of herself, night after night, listening to her brother give her information on people who were trying to confront their own trauma while her family made money out of it.

"There are plenty of people braver than me," she said.

* * *

The weather held as they came into Liverpool, and by the time they arrived at Ashworth Hospital, the car was almost too warm. For a few moments, Ashley and Freddie sat in the parked car while the radio spoke in a low voice about a potentially record-breaking storm that was apparently arriving in the north of England in a few days. Storms seemed impossible when the sun was turning every damp surface and puddle into shimmering gold.

"Ready to do this?" asked Freddie.

Ashley shrugged. "As I'll ever be."

They got out of the car and went into the reception area. After a quick chat with the receptionist to sign them in and check their identities, they were taken to a bright window-filled room with chairs and tables and a small counter selling hot drinks and prepackaged sandwiches. In the corner of the room, a Heedful One waited, its dark shape flickering and lapping at the wall. Ashley eyed it warily.

"Have we come to the right place?"

Freddie raised his eyebrows at her. "Yeah, it's a lot nicer than I was expecting."

They found a table and sat. A few minutes later, a short wiry figure appeared at the door, his gray hair falling untidily to his shoulders. Despite his hair and beard, he was dressed well—dark jeans, a shirt under a navy jumper, soft loafers. He came into the room slowly, as though waiting for something to jump out at him from one of the tables. He was accompanied by a middle-aged woman in a blazer, her glasses perched on top of her head. When she saw them, she came over, bringing Dean Underwood with her. She eyed Ashley and Freddie suspiciously, as though she thought them the dangerous ones.

"Here you go, Dean," she said, still looking at them. "Come and get me if you need anything, all right?"

And then, without a word to them, she left the room, and Dean Underwood sat down at their table.

"Mr. Underwood," said Freddie, his voice smooth and professional. "How are you?"

Ashley swallowed hard. Could this really be Underwood, the man who had haunted her nightmares for years after the trial? He looked so small and so frail.

"Thank you for agreeing to speak with me." Underwood spoke in a soft rasp, as though his voice were sore and it pained him to form words. "I . . ." He glanced up from under his eyelashes, his dark eyes on Ashley. "I've wanted to speak to you for years, Ashley. I mean, Miss Whitelam."

Ashley blinked. On the drive over, she had spent a long time imagining what she would say to him at this moment, yet when it came time to actually speak, she felt like her lips had been sealed shut. She put her hands on the table and didn't reply.

Freddie didn't let the silence grow. "Eighteen years ago, Mr. Underwood—"

"Call me Dean, please."

There was a fraction of a pause before Freddie continued. "Eighteen years ago, Dean, you broke into Red Rigg House and set several fires there late on the evening of the tenth of April. At your trial, you claimed that you were unaware that a group of children from across the country were staying in the house that night, in the dormitory directly above the places where you set your fires."

"I didn't know," Underwood said quickly. "I would never have done it if I'd known kids was there. You're saying 'claimed' like I made it up, but it's true. I never meant to hurt those kids."

Freddie was unperturbed. "Thirty-nine children and one teacher died in the fire that night. Of the children that had been staying at Red Rigg House for the weekend, only Ashley here survived. You, Dean, were later picked up by the police in the woods backing onto the property, suffering from some smoke inhalation and mild burns."

"I didn't know they was there," said Underwood again. A muscle in his jaw flickered under his skin. "Would never have done it otherwise."

"You *did* know we were there." The words were out before Ashley realized she intended to speak. "I saw you in the woods! And I know that you saw us too, me and Malory both. How could you have missed that there were forty kids running around the estate?"

Dean Underwood lowered his head.

"You said that in the trial, Miss Whitelam, but I don't remember it. I wasn't in the best state of mind at the time. I had been drinking for days. Drugs too."

He stopped talking. From somewhere behind them, a man was buying a sandwich from the counter and asking for a coffee.

"Perhaps we could approach this from another angle," said Freddie, his voice calm and smooth again. Ashley felt a sharp stab of unreality; if she closed her eyes and listened to Freddie speak, she could be at home, watching the news on an American TV station perhaps. "Dean, what has your time here at Ashworth been like? It's a hospital with an interesting reputation."

"It's had its troubles," said Dean. He glanced over his shoulder at the door, as if expecting the woman with the glasses to be waiting for him. "But the last six years or so have been better for me. I've been improving, the doctors say. So because of my good behavior and that, I've been able to spend time outside."

"I'm sorry, you've been able to do *what*?" Ashley leaned forward in her seat. The Heedful One shifted, moving slowly down the wall away from her. "They've let you out?"

"Conditional day release," Underwood said, a petulant tone to his voice for the first time. "I can leave Ashworth and go to Liverpool, and at night I come back and sleep in the secure unit. It's all aboveboard! What happened was eighteen years ago, and with drugs and therapy, I've made a lot of progress." The way he said it made Ashley think he was repeating what other people had told him, more than once. "Eventually, they hope that I will be able to live independently, with a parole officer checking on me week to week."

"This is fucking madness."

The man with the sandwich glanced over at them sharply as he made his way to his own table.

Ashley lowered her voice. "You mean to tell me you've been out and about all this time, allowed to go wherever you like?"

"I am ill," Underwood said, petulant again. "I need treatment, not punishment."

"Fuck me," said Ashley.

"All right." Freddie leaned forward a little, putting his bulk between them. "I feel like we need to get back on track here. Dean, perhaps you could tell us why you wanted to speak to us today."

Dean Underwood cleared his throat and looked away. Ashley took the opportunity to study his face—this face that had haunted her dreams for years, the face that sometimes still caused her mother to wake up screaming in the night. During the long and agonizing trial following the fire at Red Rigg House, Ashley and her family had sat no more than ten feet away from the man who had set fires in a building where forty children slept, and Ashley had found it difficult to look away from him. He had been forty-nine years old then and had looked at least ten years older; now that he was in his late sixties, he looked thin and somehow wasted, a collection of rags that had been put through the washing machine too often. His good clean clothes only seemed to emphasize his frailty and weakness. *There's no need to be afraid of him now,* she told herself. *As small and slight as I am, I think even I could throw him across this room.*

And then another smaller, more deeply hidden voice replied: *And what has he been up to for the last six years? They haven't been watching him closely enough.*

"When I was little, I had an older brother named Neil."

Ashley glanced at Freddie—what was this tangent now? But Freddie just shook his head: *Hear him out.*

"We lived in a village on the western side of Red Rigg House. You wouldn't know it; it's gone now. The buildings that were left were turned into holiday homes for rich people, but we were happy enough there. This was in the late fifties, early sixties, you understand. Me and Neil, we used to roam all over the lakes—hiking up hills, to other villages and towns. We'd go fishing. It was quieter then. Neither of us had much taste for school, so we stopped going. People didn't care about it so much then, you see, but maybe because of that neither of us had many friends, so we was each other's best friend." He stopped, swallowing hard, then continued. "Neil was three years old than me, and he was my best friend."

"What happened to your brother, Dean?" prompted Freddie.

"He started playing there, by the house." Underwood's mouth turned down at the corners. "On the lands. They had lots of rabbits there, in the lands around the woods, and Neil liked to trap them. He was always clever with his hands like that. He used to make the traps himself and bring home the meat for dinner. Lord Lyndon-Smith, he didn't seem to mind, not as far as we could tell. We never got chased off. But I started to dislike the place, all the same. I hated it after a while."

"Why?" asked Freddie.

Here Underwood shifted in his chair, rolling his shoulders as if he had a cramp. A strange kind of energy seemed to sink into him. From across the room, Ashley noted that the Heedful One had begun to creep toward them; something about their conversation was attracting it.

"I don't know, not really. I wish I could tell you."

Ashley had the distinct sense he was lying or holding something back. *Don't try and kid a kidder, pal,* she thought.

"I had nightmares sometimes about the hill. About the fell." He shifted again, and when he looked up, he was looking directly at Ashley. A creeping kind of heat began to crawl across her neck, under her arms. "Did you ever have nightmares about it, Miss Whitelam? I did. I had so many, and I would wake up screaming. My dad would give me a slap and tell me to stop being such a silly sod." He paused. "That wasn't the right way to handle it. I know that now, because of my doctors."

"What were the dreams about, Dean?" asked Freddie.

"I was on the fell at night. It was cold, and I was afraid of the ground under my feet, as though I was treading on something I shouldn't. Or I would look down and see the house at the bottom with all its lights lit up at the windows, like it was watching me. Sometimes . . ." He stopped and pushed his fingers through his thinning hair. "Sometimes I could hear Neil calling me in these dreams, and he was frightened, really terrified, and that was the worst of all because he was my big brother, you see? He wasn't scared of nothing."

"What has this got to do with anything?" said Ashley.

"I'm getting to it," said Underwood. "I was too scared to go to Red Rigg House anymore. That's what I told Neil, that I didn't want to go no more, and he was angry with me, really angry. We went about exploring like we always did, but sometimes Neil would leave me behind, or get up early to go without me, and I knew that he was going to Red Rigg. I was scared for him, but I couldn't have made him do anything he didn't want to do." He took a big, watery breath. "And then, in the summer, 1965 this was, one day he didn't come back. And he always came home for his tea, whatever else was going on. So we knew it was bad."

"1965?" asked Freddie.

Ashley knew he was thinking of the Gingerbread House Murders, but surely a disappearance over fifty years ago was outside the realm of those crimes.

"The police weren't interested," Underwood continued. "Said my brother was of an age to run away—he was thirteen, he didn't care for school. He'd probably gone to Manchester they said, or even got a train south. He'd be in some big city somewhere."

Ashley was reminded uncomfortably of Eleanor Sutton. *So many missing kids.*

"I knew where he'd be though. He had gone to Red Rigg House without me that day, so I went myself. I walked all over the grounds, shouting for him, looking for Neil, even though the mountain was looming over me and I was stiff with fear the whole time. I don't know how to describe it. Like I was doing the looking, but something else was doing the hunting."

He stopped talking. He rubbed his face with one gnarled hand. "Do you think I could have a cup of tea?" he asked, looking at Freddie. "I don't do a lot of talking these days, and this is wearing me out."

Freddie jumped up. "Certainly. I'll be right back." He paused the recording.

While Freddie went over to the tea counter, Ashley found herself sitting in an uncomfortable silence with Underwood. He was fidgeting still, and beyond his right shoulder, she could see the Heedful One, like a restless shadow.

"You don't look so different, you know," he said eventually, his voice little more than a whisper. "From when I saw you in court, all those years ago. Such a pretty little girl."

She glared at him. Heat prickled across her skin. Freddie was still at the counter, chatting lightly as the woman there filled three cups with hot water.

"I know you saw me," she hissed back. "In the woods."

He glanced at Freddie's phone, as if to check that it wasn't recording.

"Perhaps I did," he said softly. "How could I miss two pretty girls in the trees? But how was I to know there was so many of you, aye?"

"You're a liar," Ashley said hotly. "We've no reason to trust anything you say."

"But you know I'm right," he said. "About the house. I can see it in your eyes."

"I've got no idea what you're on about."

He leaned forward over the table. "You have nightmares about it. About Red Rigg."

"Of course I bloody do! I nearly died there because you tried to burn it down."

Underwood shook his head, frustrated. "When I saw you in the woods with that other girl, you were telling her that you didn't like the mountain. It gave you the creeps, because you knew it was evil. I *need* to hear you say it. I need to know I'm not the only one that thought it."

"You're out of your mind. Do you want me to tell you that Red Rigg is evil so you feel justified in murdering thirty-nine kids? Do me a fucking favor."

"No." Underwood rubbed a hand over his sunken cheek. "*No.* I was right about that place, and you know it."

Ashley opened her mouth to ask what he was raving about, but Freddie reappeared at that moment with three steaming mugs of tea. He put them down on the table, then dropped a little cascade of sugar packets between them all. Once he was back in his seat, he started recording again.

"I've read about the 1965 disappearance of your brother, Dean," said Freddie. He had his notebook out on the table, and he turned a page, looking for some scribbled note. He seemed unaware of the tension between Ashley and Underwood. "But he wasn't found on the Red Rigg Estate."

"No, but that doesn't mean it wasn't involved!" Underwood's dark eyes glittered dangerously. "They moved the body, that's all. Easy as anything, moving a body."

"You found the body of your brother, didn't you, Dean?"

Underwood's mouth worked as though he were chewing something bitter. He quickly took a sip of his tea. The frantic energy had returned to him, making his fingers tremble. The Heedful One that had been hanging behind him moved forward, rushing over Underwood, catching him in its shadowy net. It was as though Underwood himself had become part of the Heedful One; in the bright and cheery room, he sat in a pool of darkness. Ashley leaned back in her chair, alarmed.

"Yeah, I found him," Underwood was saying.

"What had happened to him?"

"Bad things," whispered Underwood. "He'd been torn to pieces."

The Heedful One that had covered Underwood surged forward. Although Ashley instinctively moved her chair back, it caught her anyway. The café-like room seemed to fade away while another scene took its place. All of a sudden, she was cold and small; her feet were sore and her legs ached. She felt a cold breeze that tasted like the end of summer on her tongue. She was tired and knew that she would have to get back before their mum noticed that she was missing too. She was following a hedge, crossing the walkways and heading home, empty-handed.

And then she saw the mess in the grass.

It was Neil, but he was so broken, it was hard for her to understand what she was looking at. His stomach was open, as though he were an overly ripe peach that had dropped from a height, and his eyes were gone—later, she knew, they would say that Neil's eyes had been eaten by crows and other carrion birds, but she didn't believe that for a second—and his face looked blindly up at the sky. Big parts of his legs were gone. His clothes were a deep, sodden crimson, and his skin was as white as snow. There were beetles in his guts.

Then the images drained away, and Ashley was sitting back in the small café, her tea still hot under her fingers. Freddie, she realized, was staring at her while Dean Underwood continued to talk. The Heedful One was gone.

". . . There were others, not that anyone talks about them, and I'm telling you, it's something in that house. Someone. The place itself is *evil*. When I was looking for my brother, Lord Lyndon-Smith came out and told me to leave, his eyes all cold. Years we had been going there, hunting rabbits and playing in their woods, not a dicky bird from them, and then out of nowhere he wants me off his property. Because he knew too."

"Is that why you burned Red Rigg House down?" asked Freddie, his tone neutral. "Because you believed the house was . . . haunted?"

Underwood hissed through his teeth. "You're mocking me, but I'm right."

Freddie moved his head in a noncommittal gesture. "Do you believe that your brother's death is connected to the children that are being murdered now, Mr Underwood? Neil died over half a century ago. How likely is it that the same person that's snatching children in 2022 is responsible for what happened in 1965?"

"*Person* has got nothing to do with it," hissed Underwood. "What I saw wasn't the work of anything human." He pointed a finger at Ashley, jabbing viciously. "And *she* knows it too."

Ashley shivered. The Heedful Ones weren't human, but if what her grandmother had believed was correct, they had been once. So why did they show her Underwood's brother, torn to pieces? Why did they lead her to Robbie Metcalfe? And why did they save her from the fire at Red Rigg House, all those years ago? It all came back to the house. To the mountain.

"I've had enough of this." Ashley stood up. Dean Underwood looked up at her, wincing as though she had hurt him somehow. It only made her angrier. "Carry on if you want, Freddie. I'm going to wait outside."

*   *   *

Freddie joined her less than fifteen minutes later. She stood by his car, smoking one of her emergency cigarettes. The wind was picking up, throwing dead leaves against her ankles.

"I didn't know you smoked."

She took one long drag, letting the nicotine hit make her slightly woozy, and then she dropped it onto the concrete and extinguished it in one practiced movement with her shoe.

"Hey. I could have wanted a drag on that myself," Freddie said mildly, and she smiled despite herself.

"You? I've never met a more obvious nonsmoker. What else did he say? Anything of use?"

Freddie came and stood next to her, leaning against the car too. His arm brushed hers, and she let herself lean into it, just a little.

"Not really." He sighed. "More ravings about how there's an evil presence at Red Rigg House. He talked about his life after Neil died, and that was pretty sad, to be honest with you. His parents were torn apart by it, and his dad died of a heart attack a couple of years later. Dean ran away from home and lived on the streets in Manchester for a while, got into drugs in a big way as well as petty theft. He said that there are whole years of his life that he's lost track of. And then, in the early 2000s, he found a shelter that helped him get sober for a while, and that was when he really returned to thinking that someone at Red Rigg was responsible for his brother's death. He became fixated on it. Obsessed. He came up with this plan that he could burn the whole house down and end it, and around about the same time, he fell off the wagon." Freddie looked out across the car park, frowning. "The rest you know. Some of what he said was interesting, though. A child disappearing and turning up dead—not dissimilar to the Gingerbread House Murders."

"You can't think it's the same murderer," she said. "It was so long ago. How old do we think our killer is?"

Freddie shrugged. "I said it was interesting, not that it made sense."

"You're missing the point." Ashley turned to look at him, pushing the vision of Neil Underwood from her mind. "Dean Underwood has been allowed to come and go from this apparently useless place for the last six years. The same period of time that the Gingerbread House Murders have been happening. And he has killed before."

"Very different MO," said Freddie. "Going from arson to kidnapping, feeding, and dismemberment?"

"He did know the kids were there, Freddie. They were out there playing tennis in the courts while he was creeping through the woods. He could hardly have missed us." She licked her lips; smoking always made her mouth dry. "It would make sense, wouldn't it? In a twisted kind of way. A boy finds the body of the brother he idolized, violently butchered and left in the middle of nowhere. Something like that, it breaks you. So, by the time he's older, he's convinced himself that someone at Red Rigg House is responsible. He fully loses it and tries to burn the whole place down. And it just so happens that now that he's been given free rein, children are turning up butchered again."

"I admit, it does make a twisted kind of sense."

"Listen. I am going to stay at Red Rigg House in a couple of days. Come with me. You'll get a look at the place Dean Underwood claims is evil, and I'll get a bit of moral support. What do you say?"

He grinned. "It's a date."

* * *

After dinner that night, Ashley went to the bottom of their garden again, walking down to the hidden bench with darkness pressing on her from all sides. She had DCI Turner's card in one hand, and her phone in the other. Freddie had not been especially taken with her theory that Dean Underwood could be behind the gingerbread house murders, but all night the thought had tugged at her, a dog worrying at a rag: he was damaged enough, he had history with the area, he even had a weird fixation with Ashley herself. Of course he had come back out of the woodwork when she was all over the news. It was probably him who had sent the parcel of meat. There was no telling what he could do.

The wind picked up, scattering pine needles over her shoulders, stinging against the bare skin of her hands. She picked up the phone and dialed Turner's number.

CHAPTER

43

WELCOME BACK TO *Murder on the Mind*, with your host, Freddie Miller, and today we have a small story about Red Rigg House itself. In 1915, the house became a convalescent home for soldiers injured in the Great War, although it was not, it should be said, a particularly successful one.

At the beginning of that terrible conflict, the powers that be confidently predicted that England was well prepared for the casualties of such a war. Very quickly, it became clear that would not be the case, with slaughter across the theater of war happening on a scale they'd never previously experienced. A number of great country houses were requisitioned, and despite its somewhat remote location, Red Rigg House was one of those called into action, with both the great halls cleared out to make way for beds and surgical equipment. Agatha Lyndon-Smith, then the matriarch of the house, took it upon herself to organize the comings and goings of that place—the doctors, the nurses, the supplies, the logistics. She drafted her two daughters as nurses. As a family, they became celebrated in the area for their dedication to helping these injured men make full recoveries.

And yet, despite all of their hard work and enthusiasm, it was not a successful venture. Those were dark years for the house. Because of the difficulty of transporting the soldiers so far north, most of those who arrived at Red Rigg House were not the most gravely injured;

the men that arrived at the house suffered from shell shock, shrapnel injuries, or the odd clean amputation. But despite all that, the death rate was high.

On her morning rounds, conducted as the first rinse of dawn light was showing through the windows, Agatha would often come upon men who had died in the night—their hearts stopped in their chests, their eyes open and dry. Similarly, soldiers with wounds caught infections easily, despite Agatha's strict disinfectant routines, and many died of fevers, raving into the night that they could see shadows moving on the walls, that they could smell smoke. At first, those who were able to move around were given full access to the grounds, until they started to turn up missing. Sometimes they would be found wandering the woods at the foot of Red Rigg Fell. Sometimes they were not found at all. And those that were brought back seemed broken in new ways: their anxieties and fears had evolved into full-on delusions, a terror of the night or the outside world.

It became a kind of dark joke to those in the know. *"Watch out,"* they would say to each other, *"if your injuries are too light, you might get sent to Red Rigg. Better to have an arm or a leg blown off."*

The house closed as a convalescent hospital in 1917.

CHAPTER

44

ASHLEY STEPPED OUT of the car and let herself look up at Red
Rigg House. It wasn't quite the first time she'd seen it in eighteen
years—the house was visible from certain roads around Green Beck,
and more than once she had even driven to the bottom of the driveway
to pick up Malory for a party—but this was the first time she'd stood
in its shadow since Dean Underwood had tried to burn it down. She
let her eyes travel over it, taking it in. *Look at it,* she thought. *Take it
in. It's just a normal house, after all.*

Except that of course it wasn't. Red Rigg House sprawled and
loomed at the same time, a vast edifice of red brick and black lead,
glittering with windows that caught the strange yellowish light of the
day and ate it up. Reluctantly, she turned her gaze to the east wing
and was surprised to find that it didn't look all that different from how
she remembered, despite the fact that a good portion of it had burned
down. She remembered how Malory had told her that she wouldn't recognize it, which made her frown—perhaps the interior was strikingly
different. The outside of the east wing was a mirror to the west, except
that the bricks were darker in color, not as weathered, and the ivy that
clung picturesquely around the windows of the west wing was absent.

"Are you all right?"

Aidan appeared at her side, carrying her suitcase. He took her
hand with his free one and squeezed it.

"Sure. It's just a house, right?"

"Ashley's stronger than you think." Her father strode up the path, crunching gravel under his big boots. "Come on, that's enough faffing and introspection. Let's get inside and get you set up."

The big doors of the main entrance were propped open, and Malory's team was streaming in and out, carrying boxes and tables. A man on a ladder was fixing a banner over the door that read: "Moon Market 2022: Red Rigg Welcomes You." Ashley's father moved through them all like a swan through a crowd of ducks, gently pushing them aside with his sheer presence, and then he was gone into the dark beyond.

To stall going in a little longer, Ashley turned to her brother. "How's Mum doing?" One of her stipulations for attending this year's Moon Market was that her mother wasn't left alone—Ashley might have decided to face her fear of Red Rigg House, but her mother had made no such promise, and the thought of the child she had nearly lost going back to the place where she had narrowly escaped death . . . She was at home now, in bed, under the influence of a mild sedative. Before she had left that morning, Ashley had kissed her papery cheek. Her mother had turned over in bed away from her.

"As well as can be expected," said Aidan quietly. "Dad said he's going back as soon as we're sorted and you have everything you need, but . . ."

"He can't stay," Ashley said, feeling her stomach grow tight. "She needs someone to be there to talk her down, and I need you here for the shows."

"I know! I know. Don't worry. I'll drag him out and squeeze him back into the car myself if I have to. He doesn't have a room booked, so he can't be here overnight anyway. I checked with Malory."

"Good. Thank you." She made herself look him in the eye. "Listen, Aidan, about before . . ."

"It's all forgotten."

"I'm sorry. I hate arguing with you, you big twat." That surprised a laugh out of him, and Ashley felt her spirits lift a little. "Are you sure we're okay?"

"Absolutely." He smiled at her in a knowing way. "Now. Is that enough procrastination? Can we go inside now?"

"Fine." Ashley took a deep breath and one more look behind her, as though if she kept the outside world in mind, Red Rigg House couldn't claim her. She wished the weather was better; the strained yellow storm light made everything look unreal. "Let's do it."

She expected, when she passed over the threshold, to drop down in a dead faint like a heroine in an old black-and-white movie, or at least to feel like someone had walked over her grave. But there was nothing. Dozens of people were milling around inside the grand foyer; someone at a desk in the far corner was checking in guests who had arrived early; more men and women were putting up the last of the signs and information boards; and Malory herself lingered by the stairs, talking to the girl, Penny, that Ashley had met the other day. Glad to see someone she knew, Ashley left Aidan to check them in and made her way to Malory, who looked pleased to see her.

"Oh, thank God, Ashie. Not that I don't have faith in you, but I was half expecting you to bottle it at the last minute."

"Charming." Ashley grinned. Being in the great echoing foyer with Malory reminded her of being a kid, and not all the memories were bad. "Aidan is checking us in right now. Can I get a look at the space we're using for the shows?"

"Of course you can! Come on, Penny, let's show the 'spirit oracle' where she's going to be weaving her magic for the next few days."

The three of them went up the great stairs together and turned right onto the west wing—to Ashley's quiet relief—and walked down a wide hallway hung with old oil paintings. At the end of the hall was the ballroom, an impressively grand room with a high ceiling and tall, arched windows. There was a stage set up at the far end, with rows of chairs facing it.

"This'll be your main room," Ashley was saying. "Your three big shows will happen in here, and then we have you set up in the main hall with the biggest booth for the one-to-ones."

Ashley looked around. It was a pleasant, bright space filled with light.

"With the way the weather's going, it'll be dark by the time you do your first show," said Malory, as though she knew what her friend was thinking, "but there's good lighting up here, don't you worry. And we've set up lights in the garden too, which should look very pretty through the windows."

"That's great," said Ashley. It felt surreal to be back. Even the smell of the place was the same. "What's the internet connection like in here? We will need a decent setup, uh, for the Bluetooth . . ." She stopped, looking at Penny, who was standing with her hands clasped behind her back, watching them both attentively.

"Oh, don't worry about Penny." Malory put her arm around the girl's slim shoulders and gave her a squeeze. "She's not going to be sharing any trade secrets, are you?"

The girl smiled and blushed.

"Ah. Yeah. Well," Ashley tried to keep a neutral expression. It was unfair of Malory to ask her to take this child into her confidence, but her friend's mood was so buoyant she didn't want to make a fuss about it. "There's a small room nearby?"

"Yes! Here, look at this, it's perfect." Malory strode over to the back wall at the corner of the stage and pressed her hand to a part of the wall, which was covered in a Mackintosh-inspired wallpaper. To Ashley's surprise and Penny's delight, a section of the wall swung away, wainscotting and all. "A hidden door! Isn't it great? There are loads of these all over the house, God knows why."

The room was a large broom closet that had clearly been tidied up for the occasion. There was a small table in there with a chair, and a lamp.

"We've checked, and anyone speaking in there can't be heard from outside. There's no sign of the light under the door either. It's the perfect little hidey hole for your brother."

Ashley glanced at Penny again, but if the girl caught the significance of what she was hearing, she wasn't letting it show on her face.

She's just a kid, Ashley told herself. *She's not bloody David Wagner or the* Daily Mirror, *trying to catch you out.*

"Thanks, Malory, that's perfect. The acoustics in here seem good too. About the . . ."

"Ash?" Her father leaned in through the door, his bald head catching the light from the windows. "I'm off now to keep an eye on your mother." He didn't sound happy about it. Ashley left Penny and Malory by the hidden room and went to her father.

"Thanks, Dad. Tell her there's nothing to worry about, won't you?" Ashley wasn't entirely sure that was true, but she did know it was what she had to say. "I'll feel better if you're there with her." She thought of the creepy parcel of meat with its unnerving message: *Eat up, Ashley!*

"Indeed." Logan Whitelam pressed his lips together. "I've sub-scribed to some crafting channel for the weekend, so that should take her mind off things. Here." He scooped her into his arms and held her tightly for a long moment. Ashley, cocooned in his arms, felt an alarming surge of emotion. She didn't want him to go at all; she wanted him to stay. As much as he trapped her, controlled and belittled her, she did always feel safe when her dad was around. How could he leave her there, in the very house where she had nearly died? "Think of me, won't you," he said to the top of her head, "while you're here having fun and I'm at home learning about quilting and bloody lino printing."

She laughed into his chest, and he let her go.

"I will, Dad."

When he left, she quickly wiped at the corners of her eyes. Now that he was gone, she felt bereft.

Malory slipped an arm around Ashley's elbow. "He's right, Ashie. We're going to have so much fun. It feels like I've been waiting for this weekend forever!"

CHAPTER

45

FREDDIE ARRIVED A couple of hours later. Ashley, lingering by one of the windows, spotted him standing on the gravel drive, speaking into his phone as he looked up at the house. She waved at him, then realized that the last of the setting sun would be in his eyes and he wouldn't be able to see her. She had been helping Malory and Penny put up some more bunting in the main hall, where various vendors and psychics were setting up their tables for the following day, so she left them to it.

"There you are."

He turned at the sound of her voice, pausing the recording as he did so. A big gush of wind barreled up the driveway, scattering some of the tiny stones, and they both laughed.

"I sent you a couple of texts to say I was on my way. Didn't you get them?"

"Oh!" Ashley checked her phone, but there was nothing—and the space where the signal strength symbol should be simply read "No service." "Oh shit. Sorry. It looks like my phone is basically a brick for the time being."

"Not a problem." He had a long duffel bag slung over one shoulder. "Let's get inside before the weather gets worse."

They made it through the door just as a squall of rain began to batter the windows. Ashley showed him to reception, and then they went upstairs together. His room was in the same corridor as hers, but four doors down; it was decorated like any mildly upmarket hotel room: crisp blue paint on the walls accompanied by a pair of tasteful paintings, a large bed with more pillows than necessary, and a thick rug on the floor. He slung his duffel bag on the floor by the wardrobe, then threw himself on the bed, bouncing so violently he nearly went straight back off it again. Ashley snorted.

"You're almost too tall even for that bed."

"It's way bigger than the one at the B and B." Freddie spread his limbs out and sighed loudly. "I may actually get some sleep."

Something about the strangeness of the room and the wildness of the weather outside—the rain was lashing against the windows, the wind moaning around the chimneys—made her bold. She went and hopped onto the bed too, bouncing up and down to test the springs. Freddie propped himself up on one elbow.

"So," he said, his green eyes looking up at her with what she suspected was a flicker of mischief, "what's the plan for this weekend?"

What is he talking about, exactly? Ashley smiled at him coolly, her heart thudding a little too loudly in her chest. She thought about telling him, *My plan is to fuck your brains out,* wondering if he would laugh or be shocked. Or pull her into bed with him. She looked away, feeling a little dizzy.

"There's a big dinner in the second hall for everyone in about an hour," she said instead. "It's like an informal social mixer, according to Malory. The real stuff starts tomorrow."

"And what's that?"

It was Ashley's turn to sigh. "For me, that's a morning of one-to-ones in the vendor's hall, then lunch, and then after that, I have one of my big audience readings, and another in the evening. Mal is keeping the vendor's hall open until 9:00 PM, so I might go back down and do a few more one-to-ones if there's demand for it."

"I think there will be," said Freddie. "I saw your name all over the signs downstairs. You're the guest of honor."

"Hmm." She wondered if any of the suits her father had brought to the show above the pub would have bothered to buy tickets. "I bet half of them are here to see if I have a breakdown."

"Because of 2004?"

"Because of 2004, because of Robbie Metcalfe." She pushed a strand of pale hair behind her ear; her ponytail had come loose. "I wish I didn't know that Dean Underwood is able to go where he pleases these days." She smiled to show she was joking, even though she wasn't, not really. "What if he comes here? Maybe he wants to finish the job he started." She hadn't told Freddie about the phone call she'd made to DCI Turner; she was afraid he'd think less of her somehow.

"Hey." He sat up, leaning in so that his face was very close to hers. Ashley's urge was to turn away and break eye contact, but she forced herself not to. "None of that shit's going to happen again, okay? That particular nightmare is long gone."

"I hope so."

"And I'm right here. Anything weird happens, we'll figure it out together. And as a big bonus, there's no well-meaning Mrs. Templeton here to mess things up."

Ashley felt her cheeks grow hot. So she hadn't imagined that moment in his room at the B and B. The wind crashed against the windows, making the panes rattle in their frames. They both laughed again, and Ashley put her hand on his shoulder, feeling the warmth of his skin through the material of his shirt.

"I'm glad you're here, Freddie."

He reached up with one hand, cupping the side of her face. His thumb brushed the edge of her lip. "Me too."

Looking back on it, Ashley was not quite able to say who kissed who first; she only knew that suddenly they were together, a soft kiss that quickly became hotter, faster. He put his arms around her and rolled her onto the bed with him, and then on top of him. It felt so wonderful to be pressed against him that, for a few moments, Ashley's head felt completely empty of everything else save for the warmth of his body, the long hard planes of it, and the taste of his mouth on hers.

There was a flurry of knocks on the door, followed by her brother's voice sounding somewhat terse.

"Ash, are you in there? You're not in your room so . . ." He cleared his throat. Ashley and Freddie broke apart and stared at each other, eyes wide. "Malory said you might be here. Ash? I want to go through some setup stuff with you before dinner."

Convinced her brother would hear the bed springs squeaking, Ashley slowly moved off the top of Freddie, who had plastered one hand over his own mouth to keep from laughing.

"Okay, Aidan!" Ashley called back. Her voice sounded ridiculous to her own ears. She took a quick breath, trying to force some normality into her tone. "I'll be there in a sec."

CHAPTER

46

THE DINNER ITSELF was surprisingly good, and given the weather rattling around outside, quite atmospheric. Ashley found herself imagining that she was in a murder mystery novel, sitting at a table with other suspects, waiting for the detective to arrive at the country manor to reveal all manner of terrible secrets; her character was having a secret tryst with the handsome American visitor, an outrageous scandal to her buttoned-down, uptight English family. And then she remembered that her life was embroiled in a real murder mystery; she remembered finding the body of Robbie Metcalfe in the woods, and she felt ashamed. She pushed the last course— sticky toffee pudding—away from her, barely touched. She found she was glad when the staff cleared the plates away and they could stand up again.

There was a bar in the corner of the hall, so she went there and bought a vodka and Coke. Looking around the room, there were several work colleagues she recognized. There was Cleo Bickerstaff, a stout woman in her fifties with a kindly face, who was continually draped in pastel-colored silk scarves; Desmond Morris, a preening man in his late sixties with a penchant for white suits and black cravats—he had a large gold ring on his pinky finger that was set with a fat opal; it caught the light and winked at her as he sipped at his martini. And there was Merlin Jones, who was closer to her own age, although he looked as though he'd stepped out of a time warp from the late sixties—he wore a crocheted waistcoat and beads in his hair. According to Malory, Alison Mantel and Donald St. Clair were arriving early the next morning. Despite herself, Ashley smiled. The business of psychic mediumship was a strange one, with strange colleagues, but she found that she was glad to see them all there. Freddie was chatting animatedly with an older woman, and she had lost sight of her brother, so she wandered over to Cleo to say hello.

"Darling! How are you?" Cleo pressed her powdery cheek to Ashley's, briefly enveloping her in silks and scent. She smelled faintly of lavender and lily of the valley. "You've been all over the news, of course. What an awful thing you have been dealing with. Are you eating enough? You look too thin for my liking."

"It's been a weird few weeks." Ashley smiled.

"And there's that ghastly business in the *Daily Mirror*. That old kook will just not leave you alone, will he?" Cleo tutted. "The likes of Wagner keep us from making an honest living. I assume your father has summoned the litigation hounds?"

Ashley felt her smile falter. "You know what my dad is like. He says it's verging on harassment now, but I . . ." She cleared her throat, thinking of all the bile she'd poured into her journal about Wagner. "I just wish he'd leave me alone."

"It's all dreadfully unfair on you," Cleo cooed. "My mother used to say that some people are magnets to dark events, drawing terrible things to them against their will, but then she was out of her box on brandy half the time."

Ash laughed uneasily. "I hope for my sake she's wrong." She cast about for a way to change the subject. "Are you here every year?"

"I *cannot* miss the Moon Market—it's such a boost to my income, darling. And I'm thrilled to see you here for the first time, I'm sure you've brought half the audience in all by yourself." Cleo took Ashley's free hand and squeezed it. "What changed your mind?"

"I guess it was just time." The wind rattled the windows again, and Ashley spotted a Heedful One in the far corner, half-hidden in shadows. It wasn't moving. "It's the biggest event up here for us, isn't it? And I need to . . . put all that behind me." She said the words confidently enough, but the sight of the Heedful One—in this place, of all places—had set her skin crawling. Desmond, having refreshed his martini at the bar, came slinking up. His white hair shone like the moon, even under the subdued lights.

"Graced us with your presence, have you?"

"It's nice to see you too, Desmond."

"Desmond," snapped Cleo, "do you have to be such a little shit? Be nice to Ashley. She's having a *terrible* time."

"Oh, yes, all over the news, TV appearances, bookings through the roof, no doubt." Desmond sipped his drink and glared at her over the rim of his glass. "Tell me, *spirit oracle*, what are the moral implications of making money off the back of that little boy's corpse?"

Ashley nearly choked on her drink. Her heart fluttered in her chest, and a sickly wave of heat traveled up from her shoes to the top of her head. "I beg your fucking pardon, Desmond?" She lowered her voice. "We're all in the same business here, or have you forgotten?"

He narrowed his eyes at her. "I'm sure I don't know what you mean."

"Oh fuck off. Feeding off of bereaved relatives is your bread and butter."

Even Cleo looked a little shocked at that. "Ashley, darling, there's no need for that. He's jealous of course. Desmond hasn't been on the television since they were invented."

"All I'm saying"—Desmond raised his voice a little—"is that it's very base, isn't it, traipsing around in the muck looking for dead bodies. What we do, contacting the spirit world and filtering their voices through us, is an *art*. Not a publicity stunt."

Ashley felt sick. It infuriated her to hear Desmond rattling on about how worthy and special their talents were, when she knew that the next day she would stand in the hall in front of a hundred desperate, grieving people and feed them lie after slippery lie, fed to her in turn by her brother in the broom closet. It didn't matter if she did see strange things, if the Heedful Ones followed her wherever she went, because the majority of what she did was still snake oil, it was still a con, and she was just as culpable as any of them. Could she really argue with Desmond when she was just as steeped in lies? It didn't mean she had to listen to him, though.

She downed the rest of her vodka and Coke, crunching an ice cube between her teeth; it was like an ice pick to the head, deliciously, agonizingly cold, and she felt some of her own boiling heat retreat.

"It was lovely to see you, Cleo," she said, smiling tightly. "I'm sure I'll catch up with you more at the market tomorrow."

She stalked off, leaving Desmond to glare at her retreating back. Very quickly, she spotted Malory in the crowd, wearing an off-the-shoulder green velvet dress. Absently, she wondered where Freddie was now.

"There you are." Malory slid her arm through Ashley's; her skin was hot, almost feverish. "It's a bloody nightmare, Ashie."

"What's happened?"

"The weather," Malory said darkly. She nodded at the windows. Outside, it was as black as pitch, and the rain seemed to be crashing in waves against the glass. For one odd, sickening moment Ashley imagined they were on a ship at sea, caught in a typhoon. "It's going to get very bad overnight. They're even talking about snow. Can you believe it? Hottest summer on record, and it snows in autumn. We've already had around twenty canceled tickets, and Alison Mantel has said she won't make it."

"Shit. I'm sorry, Mal. I know you've been planning this for ages."

"You don't know the half of it." Malory sighed. "I'm going to see if I can arrange cars for Alison and Donald—perhaps if they don't have to use public transport, we might be able to get them up here. It'll cost a fortune."

Ashley felt a twinge of the vertigo she often experienced when talking to Malory. It was odd to hear someone who lived in a house like Red Rigg complaining about spending money.

"At least we have the people who've already arrived. A captive audience! Could you do me a huge favor, Ashie?" Malory squeezed her arm, then pointed to a space over by the doors. Ashley could see Penny standing there, alone. "Go and entertain the brat for a bit, will you? I need to go and shout at some taxi firms."

The feeling of discomfort she'd been experiencing since the spat with Desmond felt stronger than ever. Why was Penny even here? There were no other children around. There was a burst of raucous laughter from the other side of the hall, and Ashley winced.

"All right," she said. "Go and do what you have to do."

47

W HEN ASHLEY REACHED her, Penny was leaning against the wall, watching the party grow louder with her hands in her pockets. She looked up when Ashley appeared and stood up straight, as though she'd been caught doing something she shouldn't.

"Hey, Penny, remember me? Malory's friend."

Penny nodded. "Ashley. You're the special guest." The girl had a strong Manchester accent.

"Yeah, I suppose so." Inwardly, Ashley winced. She had never been particularly good with children. After the fire, her time at school had been miserable and fraught. The other children had either kept their distance, as though she were an unexploded bomb, or mercilessly bullied her. And when her family moved to Cumbria, the few friends she did have had been lost to her. "Listen. Do you want to go and get some ice cream? It's getting too loud in here for me."

"Sure."

"Brilliant. You'll have to show me where the kitchens are. It's been, uh, a while since I've been here."

Penny nodded, and they left. Beyond the noisy hall, Red Rigg House felt empty and too quiet. The wind and rain were a constant, distant howl in the center of the building, and as they passed through the main hall, with many of the stalls already set up ready for the morning, the place felt abandoned. Ashley thought again about it being like a ship at sea; specifically, the *Mary Celeste*.

"So, are you enjoying your time with Malory?"

Penny nodded seriously. "She's letting me see how stuff is run, how the charities she's in charge of actually work. It's really interesting."

"Really?" Ashley smiled. "Wouldn't you rather be, I don't know, at a pop concert? At the cinema?"

"No, not really." They had made their way down the main staircase and were turning back on themselves; there was another staircase hidden behind the first, leading down to the floor where the servants of the house had once lived and worked—now, it contained a sprawling kitchen area. "I want to be able to run my own business one day."

"That's very grown-up of you," said Ashley, thinking that the kid needed to lighten up. "What sort of thing do you want to do?"

"Anything, really, that makes money," the girl said straightaway. She glanced up at Ashley, almost guiltily. "My dad can't work and Mum does her best, but I have three little sisters and . . ." She shrugged. "I just want things to be better."

A pang of guilt moved through Ashley's chest. She half wanted to tell the kid to let them get on with it; that if you became the prime breadwinner for your family you would never escape them, never live your own, independent life. *God, I'm such a dickhead.*

"I met Malory when she did a visit at our school," Penny continued. "She was asking everyone what they wanted to do when they grew up, and she was giving out advice. Some kids got to go on courses that she sponsored. We all got book vouchers."

The good saint Malory strikes again, thought Ashley.

"When I told her that I wanted to run my own business one day, she seemed really, I don't know, happy. She said she liked that there was someone like her, and that she'd be glad to show me how this stuff worked."

Ashley thought of Malory calling Penny "the brat."

"So she brought you to the Moon Market."

Penny nodded. "She said it was the busiest week of the year for her, and it was the quickest way for me to learn."

"Huh. And what do your parents think about you being away from home?"

"They're glad," said Penny. "It's an opportunity." Ashley thought of her own mother saying something similar just before she went away to Red Rigg House, and she felt her throat grow tight. "My dad believes in real-world experience, so he thinks this is great. More useful than school, anyway."

They had reached the kitchens. There was a handful of staff still there, loading plates and dishes and cutlery into the row of dishwashers. One of them gave Ashley a nod as she headed to the freezer; there was a terse discussion going on between a few of them, and they paid Ashley no mind as she pulled out a huge tub of ice cream and began spooning it into bowls.

"Chocolate all right?"

Penny nodded, and Ashley was struck again by what a serious kid she was. Behind them, the kitchen staff were arguing about leaving early, about whether they were coming in tomorrow at all. One of them was insisting that roads would be closed; apparently, places were already flooding. *And here we are*, thought Ashley, *at the bottom of a mountain.*

They took their bowls of ice cream out of the kitchen and back up the stairs, and Penny suggested they eat in the western conservatory. This was a room of glass that stuck out from the rear outside edge of the west wing. There were low glass tables there, and big wicker armchairs with soft floral cushions. There were a few lights on in the gardens outside, so through the windows it was possible to see the trees and grass waving frantically. The rain on the glass was very loud, but it was warm in the conservatory. They found seats and looked out at the wild dark.

"Can I ask you a question?"

Ashley ate a spoonful of ice cream and nodded.

"Is what you do . . . is it a real job?"

Ashley put her bowl of ice cream down on the glass table, her heart sinking. This was one of the reasons she didn't get on with kids—they had no fear of awkward questions.

"Yeah," she said, working to keep her voice light. "I provide a service and I get paid for it. Pretty much the definition of a job."

"That's not really what I mean," said Penny. "I mean, like, can you really talk to dead people? My mum always said that ghosts aren't real. And I don't think I've ever met any adults who really believed in them. But you do. I asked Malory about it, and she said that you were 'special,' but I'm not really sure what she meant by that."

Outside, the wind began to rise, higher and higher. The rain on the glass sounded louder, harder, like it might be turning to hail. The shadows of the trees and plants raced and teemed, and above them, Red Rigg Fell loomed, a ragged shape of utter blackness.

"Malory is kind. I . . ." Ashley stopped. For a second, she had thought she had seen a figure out there, moving across the lawn, but then it was gone, lost in the chaos of the storm. From somewhere far off, there was a rumble of thunder. Another Heedful One, maybe. An ancestor of hers, if her grandmother was to be believed. "It's difficult to explain, Penny. I try to help people. Sometimes, when someone passes away, it leaves their loved ones broken in a way that is very hard to repair. And it's my job to try and make things easier for them. To give them the tools to heal themselves." Ashley paused. This was how she justified it to herself, but she had never said it out loud before. Each word spoken seemed to make it flimsier. "Sometimes people just need to hear that their family members loved them, and that they would want them to go on with their lives. Or—"

"Or they are burdened with too much money, which Ashley here is happy to take off their hands."

Ashley spun in her chair to see Richard standing behind them. Penny frowned and cast a worried glance at Ashley.

"What do you want, Richard?" Ashley smiled tightly. He had startled her badly, and her heart was racing. "Me and Penny were having a private conversation."

Richard laughed. "Sounded like you were trying to soothe your own conscience to me. I'm here because Malory was wondering where Penny got to. It's past her bedtime, and I'm to show her to her room, if I find her." He looked at the girl and smiled, and some half-hidden memory made Ashley stand up. She took a step so that she was blocking Penny from view.

"What were you talking to Melva about the other day?" she asked in a low voice. "You really upset her."

Richard scowled. Once, she had found his icy good looks deeply appealing, but today she noticed that he had dark circles under his eyes, and his skin was too pale. There were clusters of crow's feet at the corners of his eyes, and they were a little bloodshot. He wet his lips and glanced at the girl.

"You should leave," said Richard. Ashley blinked in surprise. "By morning, none of us will be able to get out, so go now. Leave well enough alone."

"What are you talking about?" Ashley hissed. "I've only just got here. Obviously, I am not leaving. Your sister has been campaigning to get me here for months."

At the mention of Malory, something in his face that had been open and raw shut down. He leaned past Ashley and held out one hand.

"Come on, Penny," he said in a falsely cheerful voice. "Time for you to get some sleep, okay?"

Ashley pushed his arm away. Everything about Richard felt wrong, and she realized she was frightened of him, just as she had been as a kid.

"I'll take her," she said firmly. She made herself look him in the eyes as she spoke, trying not to remember the tussle outside Melva's cottage. "I can take her, okay? Now piss off."

Richard hung there for a second longer, a spasm of fury passing over his handsome features.

"You should never have come back here, Ashley."

He turned and stalked back out of the conservatory.

CHAPTER

48

I T WAS DARKER than she liked in Penny's corridor, the ceiling lights flickering as they approached.

"Are the lights going to go out?"

"It'll be the storm messing with the electrics," said Ashley. "Here. Do you have a phone? Of course you have a phone—you're a teenager."

Penny smiled lopsidedly and pulled a small cell phone from her pocket—it looked a little battered, as though someone had owned it before her.

"Okay, let me give you my number." Penny unlocked it and passed the phone over. Ashley typed in her numbers and added herself as a contact. "If the power goes out and you're worried for any reason . . ." *Shut up, Ashley, you'll freak her out.* "Give me a ring."

Penny nodded. Ashley tried not to think about how the messages from Freddie had failed to get through. When they approached the door to Penny's room, she took out an old-fashioned key and unlocked it. Inside, a couple of lights were on, making the place look cozy and inviting, yet the noise of the storm was even louder, and through the windows, it was only possible to see a teeming, chaotic darkness.

Ashley smiled at the girl in what she hoped was a reassuring way.

"If I were you, I'd put the little TV on to drown out the noise a bit. And make sure to lock the door behind me, okay?" She tried to make her voice sound as breezy as possible, but she still noticed a small frown crease Penny's forehead. "And remember, call me if there's a blackout. These old houses are used to them, but you might not be."

She took a step into the room, half meaning to check that Richard wasn't lurking there, when she realized that there was a Heedful One in the corner behind the door. Its blurred face turned to look at her, and whatever she was about to say died in the back of her throat.

"Are you all right?" Penny had gone to turn the TV on and now stood looking at Ashley. Behind her, the news was playing on the television set; a very sober man sat at a desk, looking into the camera, and then he froze, the screen filled with crackling digital static.

"I'm fine. I'll leave you to it."

She stepped back out into the corridor—reminding herself that the Heedful Ones had never harmed anyone that she knew of—when the darkness of the corridor seemed to ripple, and the Heedful One billowed into the hallway right next to her. She had a moment to see that Penny was coming to the door, still with that concerned expression on her face. Then, the Heedful One was on the girl, moving through her—the image Ashley had of Penny flickered, as though she were caught in a pall of smoke, and the girl changed. She saw Penny in a dark, enclosed space, shivering and crying. There was dirt on her face, which was as white as paper, and blood, so much blood. Ashley knew that as she stood in front of the girl, there was something terrible standing behind her; it was precisely the feeling of a nightmare, the sense that the monster was with you even when they couldn't be seen.

If I turn and look at it, she thought wildly, *I will go mad. I will drop dead here, my heart turned to stone in my chest.*

In her vision, Penny looked up, her eyes filled with tears, and she began to scream. Ashley had a moment to notice a handful of other details—that Penny was wearing a white shift dress, that the ceiling was low and uneven, and her feet were bare. Then it was gone. The Heedful One, who had brought this appalling sequence of images, was gone, and Penny was back to herself, standing in the doorway of her room with an expression of confusion that was edging toward fright. Ashley had backed away across the corridor until she had bumped into the wall opposite; she could feel a picture frame digging into her shoulder.

"Are you all right?" Penny said again. "Are you having a stroke or something?"

Despite everything, Ashley laughed. "I'm not that bloody old, you know." She bent her head for a moment, taking in a deep breath, then forced herself to stand up straight with a sensible expression on her face. "Sorry, Penny, I just had a woozy moment there. Do you ever do that? I've not had enough to eat, I suspect, and everything went a bit gray."

"We've not long had dinner," Penny pointed out, reasonably enough. "And ice cream."

"Anyway, you go and chill out." Ashley shooed her back into her room, then pulled the door to. "Good night, Penny. I'll see you in the morning."

When the door was shut and Ashley had heard Penny turn the key in the lock, she stood for a long minute, looking down at her feet. Eighteen years ago, in this very building, the Heedful Ones had swarmed on her and given her a dream of fire. It had turned out to be true.

What did this one mean? And could she stop it?

49

Now, MANY OF the interludes I have shared with you about Red Rigg Fell have been stories firmly rooted in history—they happened long ago, so it's easy to dismiss them. But today on *Murder on the Mind* I have a very curious story about something that happened in living memory. It was the late 1960s, a time when the film industry was beginning to throw off the influence of producers and film studios and move into the era of the auteur: the radical director with a powerful vision of what films could be; how they could be more than sword-and-sandal epics or vehicles for aging cowboys. There was one, who for the purposes of this podcast, we will call Rudolph Piotrowicz.

Rudolph came to Green Beck and Red Rigg Fell with the idea of filming location shots for his latest project, a film called *In the Mirror Darkly, Darling*. The film focused on a young couple looking to make a new start after their infant child dies in a terrible accident. Inevitably, when they move to their remote country home, the wife begins to see and hear strange things on the edge of their property and within the home: shadowy figures on the shore of the lake, small footsteps pattering overhead in their run-down yet still very beautiful sprawling manse. Eventually, it turns out that the husband is responsible for the child's death, and all the supernatural goings-on are manifestations of the wife's subconscious knowledge of this fact. The film starred two up-and-coming actors of the time, a young Mia Farrow

and Shakespearean stage actor Charles Reedus, and the pair flew out
to the Lake District to film with Piotrowicz in the autumn of 1967.

The climax of the film included a set piece on the flanks of a
bleak mountain. The wife, finally driven to the depths of insanity,
flees across the fells in search of their lost child, convinced she can
hear her daughter calling her—while her husband pursues, sure that
she intends to inform the authorities about his involvement in their
daughter's demise. He intends to murder her.

The two young actors spent hours on the sides of Red Rigg Fell,
sometimes simply waiting for shots to be set up—filming on location
was a much more uncomfortable and inconvenient process than it is
these days—and over the weeks, the mood of the place sunk into them,
like damp or black mold. Farrow would write, years later, about how
she would retire to her tiny, cold hotel room in the evenings and cry
herself to sleep for no reason she could put her finger on, although she
would try to blame it on homesickness, on the gloomy surroundings,
or on her costar's changeable moods. Reedus was like a weather vane
in a hurricane, turning abruptly one way and then the other. He would
be full of energy, eager to clamber up the hill, throwing every part of
himself into the role, and then he would be pensive and irritable, stalk-
ing off at odd moments so that they would have to send runners to
chase after him. It was a fraught and even explosive set. The weather
was relentlessly unkind, with storms, pelting rain, and even one freak
snowstorm that made the fell impassable for days. When inspecting the
dailies, again and again Piotrowicz would find that the film stock itself
had warped or discolored, ruining hours and hours of work. Lights
would shatter. Cameras would stop working. It was a nightmare shoot.

One night, Piotrowicz intended to lay down some simple shots
of the couple having their final confrontation on the summit of Red
Rigg, but Reedus was missing from his trailer, nowhere to be seen.
The runners were sent to retrieve him, but concerns were raised about
the safety of that, given the darkness, the weather, and the terrain, so
they were brought back. Piotrowicz, deciding to cut his losses, shut the
shoot down and went back to his own hotel room.

The next morning, with frost icing the tips of every blade of grass,
Charles Reedus was found wandering the edge of the frozen tarn, still

dressed in his costume—certainly not appropriate attire for a night on the fell. For a good hour, no one could get a word out of him, and when he did begin to talk, his words were scattered and strange, so much so that people began to worry that he had suffered a stroke or a head injury of some sort. A doctor was brought up to Red Rigg to look him over.

And with that, the bottom seemed to fall out of the whole project. This is how stories end sometimes, not with a shock or an explosion, but with a cold wet day in early November, where no one has the energy to fight the inevitable.

There are interesting things to note about those people who spent months on the side of Red Rigg Fell, however. Mia Farrow, of course, went on to become a lauded and respected actor, although not without a great deal of personal anguish and pain. Rudolph Piotrowicz's wife and unborn child were tragic casualties in one of the most infamous massacres of the twentieth century, and Piotrowicz himself became a rightly reviled character, a man of despicable appetites, tolerated and even feted by an easily corrupt Hollywood. But I digress.

Charles Reedus returned to his home in Los Angeles a broken man. With the loss of his starring role in *In the Mirror Darkly, Darling*, he seemed to lose all appetite for show business. He married, had three children, and moved to the East Coast. Then, one day, he woke up early, retrieved his gun from the case within the bedroom closet, and shot his wife, two daughters, and son to death before turning the gun upon himself.

CHAPTER

50

ASHLEY LAY IN bed for a good half an hour before she remembered the blue tablets Aidan had given her. She took a couple and managed to sleep, drifting off to the uneasy sounds of the storm crashing against the house. When she woke again, she sat up in bed, her heart racing. Something had woken her up—a noise, a movement, something she couldn't quite put her finger on. Blinking against the drowsiness of her tablets, she checked her phone: 1:34 AM. She'd only been asleep for an hour or so. Outside, the storm had quieted, the rain falling in an unrelenting rush.

The wardrobe opposite the bed was standing wide open, the darkness inside like a black monolith. Ashley stared at it.

I did not leave that open.

She held herself very still. She told herself she was being ridiculous. *You were very tired. You threw your jumper in there and forgot to close the door, that's all. Or the floor is uneven; the wardrobe door probably opens by itself all the time.*

All the same, she knew she wouldn't be able to sleep again with the dark empty eye of the wardrobe watching her, so she scrambled to the end of the bed—it was much bigger than the one she had at home—and swung her legs down. There was a confused moment when she saw some sort of dark mass crouched there—*Is that where I left my bags?*—and then the mass was moving, jumping up, reaching out for her. Cold, wet hands grabbed her by the shoulders and threw her roughly to the floor. Ashley gasped with pain and fright as she hit the wooden boards with force.

"What did you do?"

A man's voice. Ashley kicked her legs, trying to move out from under him, but the figure fell on her, one hand mashed into her face. He rose up, leaning his weight on her, and in the hectic lamplight from outside, she saw him clearly for a handful of seconds—his weathered face looked like some nightmare carved into the side of a mountain. Dean Underwood. A mixture of revulsion and panic coursed through Ashley like a bolt of electricity. *He's here to burn the place down again!*

"What did you have to do that for, aye?" His hand slipped from her face to her throat, cinching there like a rope pulled tight. "Calling the fucking police on me?"

"Get off of me!" To her horror, Ashley's voice was little more than a squeak; with the fall and the panic, the wind had been knocked right out of her. "Fucking get off!"

The grip around her neck tightened.

"Eighteen years I ain't done nothing to no one, and now I've got the police sniffing around me again. Do you know what that's like, you bitch?"

Pushing with everything she had, Ashley arched her back, trying to throw him off, but as diminished and wiry as Underwood was, she was still smaller and slighter, and he was filled with a rigid kind of rage, one she recognized from her glimpse of him in the corridor all those years ago.

"All that work I've done, and they're going to take it away from me because of you!" Underwood leaned down over her. Spittle landed on her face in a foul-smelling rain; the stench of stale beer was on his breath. "Why can't you leave me alone?"

At that moment, Ashley got one of her arms free and grabbed his face, jabbing her thumb into his eye. Underwood hollered and fell back; the instant his weight was off her, Ashley scrambled away.

"Help!" Her lungs felt like they were full of concrete. She gasped for breath and tried again. *"Help!"*

Underwood was between her and the door. He was a bedraggled figure, his clothes clinging to him, his hair hanging in wet rattails.

"It's too loud," he said. "The storm. They won't hear you."

Belatedly, Ashley realized her phone was on the bed.

"What do you fucking want from me?"

"I could ask you that!" He gave a strangled laugh. "You went to the police about me, didn't you? They wouldn't tell me who, but I'm not stupid, girl. I know it was you. They'll put me back in that box! Because of you. You fucking meddling bitch."

She was cold and wet and terrified, but despite all this, Ashley felt a sick kind of fury flood her chest. Robbie Metcalfe's mutilated body rose up in her mind's eye along with the shattered forms of the parents they'd met: Magda Nowak, Ben Cornell, Mrs. Sutton.

"I went to the police because you are a *child murderer*." Ashley screamed the last two words, hearing her own voice break as she did so. "Or have you forgotten that?" She gasped, half laughing. Now it felt like her chest was full of too much air. "Thirty-nine kids you burned to death in this fucking building, so yeah, I went to the police about you. You should have been locked up for *life*."

The chaotic light from outside glinted off Underwood's teeth. He was grinning at her. "And I wish you'd burned to death with the rest of them. I should have burned this whole evil house down—I should have done a proper job, and then at least this place would be gone." He took a breath, and with a jolt of shock, Ashley realized he was crying. "This fucking place and its secrets. It's ruined my whole life. It took my brother from me."

Ashley took a step toward him. Even with her throat still throbbing from his grip, she realized she was no longer scared of him. She was scared of what he might tell her.

"Was it you?" she said, her voice little more than a whisper. "Did you kill Robbie Metcalfe?"

She realized as she said it that she didn't believe it. Not anymore.

Underwood pulled his hands through his hair, tugging at the roots.

"I didn't mean to kill any of 'em. I didn't mean to kill no one but this house."

"What is it about this place, Dean?" As she asked it, she felt a cold hand close around her heart. Asking these questions was coming too close to a truth she didn't want to face. "What is going on here?"

"There are secret places," he said in a dull, monotone voice. "Secret ways. Some places are just bad. I—"

At that moment, the door crashed open and Aidan half fell into the room. The hallway lights were on, and Ashley could see other people out there too—Malory, Richard, one of the burlier members of staff from downstairs. In the stark yellow light of the hall, Dean Underwood looked like a fragile, broken thing. He cowered back from them even as Aidan and the burly staff member grabbed him and wrestled him out of the room. Malory pushed past them and threw her arms around Ashley.

"We've called the police," she said into her ear. "Oh my God, Ashie, are you all right?"

"I'm fine," she said, watching Underwood's back as they dragged him out, taking any answers he had with him. "No harm done."

51

"MAYBE DEAN UNDERWOOD was right about this place."
Ashley and Freddie sat on the bed together, his notes on
the Gingerbread House Murders spread between them. The police had
arrived and taken Underwood away, and the commotion had woken
half the guests—much to Malory's ire. Ashley had given a statement
to the police and had watched while they put him in the car, but
even so, returning to her own room had felt impossible. Aidan had
offered to try and take her home, but the thought just exhausted her.
Instead, she had gone back to Freddie's room to talk over the case. It
was three o'clock in the morning, and outside the icy rain had turned
to snow. Despite the radiators making a racket, it was cold in the
room. Ashley was wearing one of Freddie's jumpers, which was so big
on her it almost made her look like she was sitting in a woolen tent.

"That man is out of his mind." Freddie sighed. "I told you, didn't
I, that I would keep you safe from this stuff? And a lunatic sneaks
right into your room in the middle of the night. Jesus H. Christ."

Ashley shook her head, half smiling. "And I've told you, it's not
your job to keep me safe. And in a way, maybe this was exactly what
I needed to happen."

"What do you mean?"

"I've been terrified of this place for years, right? Because I thought,
I don't know, that it was cursed. That Dean Underwood would come

back and finish the job. Well"—she shrugged—"the very worst thing that could have happened, happened. He turned up. He targeted me. And I'm still here, while he's back behind bars. Probably for the rest of his life. The worst happened, and I survived it."

"I still feel awful."

"Don't be daft." She swatted him on the arm. "Listen, can I tell you something?"

"Sure."

"The day job. It's maybe ninety percent a scam. But it's not just me—everyone down there in that hall, doing readings, contacting the dead, they're all in on the same con." She took a deep breath. The urge to tell Freddie about the Heedful Ones was powerful, but would he look at her the way Penny had in the corridor? "But I do see things. I see what you might call ghosts. I don't know."

She risked a glance at him. Freddie was simply listening, no sign of judgment on his face that she could see.

"I saw them all the time when I was a kid, and then after the fire in 2004, they went away. And I didn't see them again until I was in that police car, looking for Robbie. Then, they were back. They've been back since." She paused. Her head felt light, either with panic or relief; she couldn't tell which. "So, do you think I'm crazy?"

"I think you're one of the most levelheaded people I've met," Freddie said.

"Are you taking the piss?"

"Love that phrase. And no, I'm not. History is full of people who appear to be able to see things others can't."

"That's the other thing. My grandmother could see these things too." Ashley laughed, a little nervously. "They put her in the madhouse for it. When I tried to tell Mum and Dad about the things I can see, when I was a kid, they freaked out immediately and banned me from ever mentioning it again. They don't seem to see the irony in asking me to contact spirits for a living."

"Do they speak to you, these ghosts? Who are they exactly? Are they even people?"

Ashley smiled lopsidedly. "I wish I had good answers to those questions. They don't speak. They don't really communicate at all."

She thought of the things she had seen when the Heedful Ones touched her—Dean Underwood's brother eviscerated on the grass, Penny screaming in the dark—but telling Freddie about that seemed a step too far. "My grandmother thought they were family members. Ancestors. People related to her who had died years ago."

"Are they here now?"

Ashley glanced around the room, feeling incredibly self-conscious, her cheeks burning.

"No. But they're certainly around the house."

Freddie nodded. "All right, let's put aside the question of psychic abilities for the moment. There can be no doubt that you have a strong emotional connection to Red Rigg House—emotional connections don't always have to be positive. You almost died here, Ashley. You were here when dozens of other children died."

"Except that I probably wasn't," Ashley said quietly. "No one really knows where I was when the fire happened, other than not in the dormitory."

"My point is, it's hardly surprising that you're having a tough time here, is it? And the weather isn't helping." He gestured to the window, where a hectic snow flurry was barreling against the glass. "Take it a bit easier on yourself, is all I'm saying."

"That's easier said than done," she said, smirking.

"Here"—Freddie pulled his phone out and started recording—"tell me precisely what it is that you feel when you see Red Rigg House, when you walk around the building. Maybe getting it all out will help."

Ashley looked dubiously at the phone where it lay on top of the pages of notes. "Do you really think so?"

He shrugged. "Hey, if nothing else, it'll make a great bit of atmosphere for the podcast."

"Oh, I'm so glad my trauma makes for good listening material." Ashley laughed and shook her head. "What do I feel here? What do I feel? There is a weight of history to this place. All the stones and all the wood have soaked up the years, making it heavier—I thought something similar the first time I came, when I was fourteen. We lived in a council flat built in the late seventies, so the idea of a house that had been around for hundreds of years was fantastical to me. This place is old, and the ground it was built on is ancient."

She paused, and Freddie nodded.

"This is brilliant, Ash. Keep going."

She leaned back against the bedpost, resting her head on the wood.

"Maybe some places are like sponges, soaking up all the time and history around them. And maybe sometimes that can go bad. A place can be corrupted, or tainted." She thought of what Underwood had said before her brother had burst into the room: some places are just bad. "When we got here today, I was surprised by how little it affected me. I was apprehensive, worried that I would freak out and ruin everything for Malory, but I passed over the threshold and didn't die on the spot or burst into flames. So I thought everything was all right. It doesn't feel so safe now though." Penny trapped in the dark, blood on her hands, her dress. "Not with the storm rolling down off the hill, not with the lights flickering and the temperature dropping. Right now it feels as though we're miles and miles away from light and safety—or perhaps there is no light and safety after all. Perhaps there is nothing out there but monsters in the dark."

She closed her eyes. As though they'd been waiting for her, images of the last few weeks clamored to be seen: David Wagner's angry gray face in the audience, full of hate and loathing; little Robbie Metcalfe in the undergrowth, moss eating the soft pale skin of his cheek; Katherine Sturges lying under the oak tree, discarded like a broken doll; the blood and sweet stink of the meat, with its little passenger hidden beneath, cold wax hands clawing at nothing; a hand grabbing her in the dark; and Dean Underwood, his hands around her throat.

"Or maybe the thing that is wrong here is me. Perhaps I bring all this terrible grief with me everywhere I go. I came here in 2004, and almost everyone who came here with me died in the most terrible way, burning and screaming and suffocating, and now that I live here, in this beautiful northern place, children are dying again. Maybe it's me that's cursed. Maybe it's me who has soaked up all the terrible things." A hot tear slid from the corner of one eye and rolled down her cheek. She didn't move. "Perhaps I brought the storm with me and allowed the monsters to follow."

"Ashley."

She opened her eyes and came back to herself. She was surprised to still be in the room with Freddie; somehow she had expected to open her eyes to a place that was deep underground, although she couldn't have said why. At some point while she had been talking, he had moved the notes away and was sitting next to her. He looked very serious as he reached up to wipe away her tears.

"I'm sorry," he said. "I should not have made you do that. And I know you were joking, but I never want to use your trauma as filler for a stupid podcast. Okay?"

"Ah, this is embarrassing." Ashley put her hands to her face and rubbed her eyes. "What a state I'm in."

"You look beautiful."

This time when they kissed, there were no knocks on the door to interrupt them.

*　*　*

Later, Ashley woke up when it was still dark outside. Freddie was asleep beside her, his big arms wrapped around her as though she might float off without something holding her down. For a few minutes, she luxuriated in the feeling of being wrapped in that warmth, being held so tightly and securely. Here, she almost believed, nothing could possibly harm her. It was as cozy and safe as she had felt in years.

But inevitably, his body heat was too much, and after a little while, she extricated herself from him and wriggled to the far side of the bed. He made a small noise in the back of his throat and turned over, still fast asleep. Ashley slipped out of the bed and tiptoed naked over to the window.

Beyond the glass was a frozen world. For the moment, the storm appeared to have stopped, but the snow had covered a lot of ground in a handful of hours. Everywhere she looked, there was a thick blanket of white snow, crisp and otherworldly under the moonlight. Even the trees beyond the gardens were suffocated with it, and Red Rigg Fell stood like a jagged tooth against the night sky, more vital and more present than she had ever seen it. She had the persuasive idea that this was its true form, a hill so pale that it could have been made of bones, and perhaps she was the only one who had ever seen it so. *The rest of the time it's hidden,* she thought, shivering in the dark. *But it can see me. It can always see me, because I know what it is.*

Outside on the lawn, a flock of Heedful Ones rose from the icy slopes and gathered, their smudged, distorted faces lifted up toward her.

52

THE NEXT MORNING, breakfast was chaotic, and later Ashley would think that she should have spotted it as an omen of what was to come that afternoon. Half of the kitchen staff had indeed left in the night, leaving the place perilously short-staffed.

In the dining room, the other guests sat and waited anxiously for their food, eyeing the tall windows thick with frost. A great number of them, Ashley couldn't help overhearing, were talking about the visit from the police in the middle of the night. Beyond the glass, they could see the deep snowdrifts in front of the house; the groundskeeping staff were out there already, trying to keep the road clear while the snow gave them a break. Ashley stood by one of the windows with a hot cup of tea clutched in one hand. There was a small patch of blue sky, but the clouds surrounding it were a queasy combination of gray and yellow, promising more snow to come.

"I hope they have plenty of food down in that kitchen." Cleo Bickerstaff appeared at her elbow. Even at breakfast she was wearing a peach head wrap secured with a glass emerald clip. She took a sip from a large cup of black coffee. "Because we could be stuck here for bloody weeks, darling. What was that film where they were stuck in the hotel? And that dreadful man froze to death in the maze?"

Ashley smiled a little. "*The Shining*?"

"That's the bugger." Cleo did a huge theatrical shudder. "I know the heating is on in here, but I'm bloody freezing. Especially looking at that." She nodded at the snow. "Do you not feel the cold, dear?"

"I quite like it, actually."

She had put a cream silk scarf around her neck to hide the faint bruises Dean Underwood had left, but she felt Cleo looking at her closely. Malory had been keen to downplay last night's events, but it would be just like Cleo to know what was going on anyway.

"Did you hear that they had to get the police out last night?" Cleo tutted. "Are we even safe in our beds, I ask you. Do you know what happened?"

"They had an intruder on the grounds, I think."

"Up here?" Cleo was incredulous. "What was it, a polar bear?"

"I don't know what happened, really. Nothing serious, anyway." Ashley rushed on before Cleo could ask more. If it got out that the man who had once tried to burn down the building had paid a visit, Malory would have no guests left. "Where's Desmond this morning? Breakfast not good enough for him?"

"Well." Cleo took a conspiratorial step closer. "He had a bit of a funny turn last night. You can imagine my face when he turned up, knocking on my door at five in the morning! I told him, I said, 'Desmond, I never would have taken you for the sort to be sidling up to a woman's door in the middle of the night,' if you take my meaning. He said he could smell burning, that he was hearing things, shouting, elsewhere in the house. I thought for a second he was putting me on, but his face was very gray; he didn't look at all well. I told him he had to shield himself from the energies of the house. *Anyone* knows that you have to do that, coming to a place like this."

"What happened?" Ashley felt a stab of genuine dislike for Desmond. It was just like him to try and create a sensation from a real tragedy. But why wouldn't he save his histrionics for the market itself? He wasn't selling any tickets in a corridor in the middle of the night.

Cleo nodded to the window again. "He's off. That's why they're clearing the path to the road, but I told him, you're not going any-where in this, darling. He'll be back in an hour." Cleo took another sip from her coffee and narrowed her eyes. "That, or he'll be one big bitchy popsicle by the side of the road."

"Bloody hell, Malory's going to do her nut if he's not there for the one-to-ones."

"Mmm. Speaking of which, I want to go and get my crystals charged and ready." Cleo clinked her coffee cup to Ashley's mug of tea. "I shall see you there, my sweetheart."

* * *

Ashley approached her own table with only the mildest nerves. One-to-ones were mostly psychology and cold reading, no Aidan to whisper secrets in her ears, and because of that, she usually enjoyed them—as much as she could, anyway. She did palm reading and rune throwing, but the tarot was the most popular, and as she sat and made herself comfortable, it was these she reached for first. There was still a couple of minutes before the doors were opened for the punters, so she shuffled the cards—hands moving in a familiar dance across their slippery faces—and then drew three for herself.

The first card was the Lovers, which made her smile. She had seen Freddie briefly before breakfast; somehow, they had both known not to come down to the dining room together. Outside his room, he'd pushed a strand of her hair behind her ear and kissed her softly on the corner of her mouth. He had plans to record short pieces all over Red Rigg House, either taking in the atmosphere of the market or narrating the building's history himself. He had promised to be there for the big show in the afternoon. But the Lovers card meant choices too, the giving up of one thing to pursue another. For a brief, fragile second, Ashley imagined going back to the States with Freddie, leaving behind her family and their demands, leaving behind Green Beck and Red Rigg and the Gingerbread House Murders. Alarmed by how the very idea of it made her heart turn over in her chest, she moved on to the next card.

The Seven of Swords. The card of liars, Melva called it—deception, betrayal, manipulation, and dishonesty. *Someone is lying,* thought Ashley. Then, on the heels of that, *No, it's me, I'm the liar. I'm always the liar. My whole life is built on a foundation of lies.*

Frowning, she turned over the next card. The High Priestess, symbolizing secret knowledge and hidden mysteries. Traditionally, the High Priestess was encouraging you to embrace your intuition, to develop your own psychic talents. It was usually a popular card to draw in a reading, since the clients Ashley read for were always keen to hear about their own mystical abilities. Here, though, drawing it for herself . . . *There are certainly plenty of bloody mysteries about.* She thought of the twisted wooden dolls sent to the parents of the missing children, the repulsive baby made from glistening flesh that had turned up on her doorstep, and her strong sense that these two things were connected. *What is this telling me? That I need to trust my own instincts? Should I be watching the Heedful Ones?* She shook her head, angry with herself. *It's not telling me anything; they're just bloody cards.*

Lost in these thoughts, Ashley jumped a little as a shadow passed over her. It was the first of her customers, a slightly wild-looking woman with a shaved head and an orange corduroy cardigan. Ashley plastered on her game face and prepared to delve into the mysteries of the occult for twenty quid a pop.

* * *

It was a disaster.

Every reading was stilted and awkward. Normally, Ashley was at home with the tarot, able to draw out what the customer was hoping to hear, somehow finding it in the faces of the Major Arcana, but that morning they could have been blank for all the meaning she could glean from them. The customers themselves were twitchy, agitated, and quick to lose their rag. Most of them glanced repeatedly at the tall windows, where it was possible to see the snow falling heavily again, to the point where Ashley actually snapped at one woman, asking if she would rather go and ask the weather for advice. To make matters worse, the Heedful Ones were seeping into the edges of the hall, their tall flickering shapes gathering in corners, lurking next to velvet curtains, or crowding at the doors. Despite the early hour, the hall was gloomy. Pan pipe music floated tinnily from the speakers.

Ashley was glad when the session was over, and she had a chance to grab some lunch before the first of her big shows. She found Cleo and Desmond together in the drawing room that had been set up as a green room for the "talent." Cleo was scoffing a sandwich, but Desmond looked unwell, the gray skin of his cheeks greasy.

"I told you, didn't I?" Cleo nodded at him. "Didn't even make it down to the lane."

"Are you all right, Desmond?" Ashley's earlier dislike of him had dissipated. Cleo was right; he looked grim, as though he might be on the verge of a heart attack. The thought was alarming. How would they ever get him to hospital in all of this?

"I don't like this place," he said in a small voice that was quite unlike him. "The energy is all wrong."

"But you've been before, haven't you? Malory said you're one of her regulars for the Moon Market."

Desmond sniffed, some of the acidity returning to his voice.

"I don't know what to tell you, Miss Whitelam. Something about this *place*, this *year*, is off. If the roads clear, I will be leaving."

For the first time that morning, Ashley thought of Penny. She hadn't seen the girl, or Malory, since the night before. The vision she'd had when the Heedful One had passed through her felt tattered and faded by daylight; it was almost possible to put it down to nerves and to her proximity to the place where so many people had died. She thought of Richard offering to take the girl up to her room and grimaced.

"Have either of you seen that kid? The girl who was hanging around with Malory?"

Both of them looked at her blankly.

"Her name is Penny? Lots of hair, glasses?"

"I don't know, darling, but she'd hardly be in the green room with the talent, would she?" Cleo popped the last crust of her sandwich in her mouth and spoke around it. "I imagine Malory has her squirreled away somewhere."

"If she has any sense," Desmond said darkly, "she'll have got far away from here."

53

"How are you holding up?"

Aidan was setting up in the hidden room, but he had leaned out through the door to direct a skeptical eye at Ashley.

"Fine. Or at least, as well as can be expected." Ashley was sitting on the edge of the stage, her head down, her long pale hair loose now and falling on either side of her face.

"You look tired," said Aidan. "Did you get enough sleep last night? I mean, after the police came and got that lunatic."

Ashley thought of Freddie and smiled underneath her curtain of hair. There were some things you did not talk to your brother about.

"I never sleep well in hotels."

"At least we know that particular weirdo won't be back. I imagine they've chucked him back in Ashford by now. No nightmares?" He added the last in a deliberately casual tone.

"Honestly, I'm fine." When she had been very small, around five or six years old, Ashley decided to tell her big brother about the Heedful Ones. She had idolized him as a kid, and she wanted to impress him. But when she'd begun chattering away about the dark figures she often saw hanging around in doorways or following her home from school, Aidan had given her such a look of disgust; it had been like being punched in the stomach. She had read his thoughts so clearly, it was like they were written on his face: *Stupid baby sister and her stupid made-up stories*. He had said, *"You're such a loser,"* and that was it. She never mentioned it again. She wondered what he would say if she told him she was seeing those figures again. He probably didn't even remember the first time she'd mentioned it. "I'll be glad to get home, though. I'm willing to admit that."

"I bet Mum's going spare, with you out of the house for a full twenty-four hours."

Ashley's stomach dropped. "She doesn't know about it, does she? Underwood turning up here?"

"No," Aidan said grimly. "Malory is doing her utmost to make sure no one knows about it, especially not Mum." He poked his head around the door again. "All set in here. Your earpiece all right?"

Ashley pressed one finger to the tiny bud in her ear. "All good."

"Great." He came out of the room and stood fiddling with the cuffs of his shirt. He looked more nervous than she felt. When he spoke, he didn't quite meet her eyes. "I know you're going to do great, sis."

* * *

To begin with, the show seemed almost disappointingly ordinary. It was a packed room, every chair taken despite the weather keeping visitor numbers down. The light reflected from the snow outside made the room seem clean and bright and cheerful. Freddie had taken a seat at the back, his large frame sticking out like a sore thumb amongst the English pensioners.

Ashley introduced herself and the show, explained how the whole thing would work, and cracked a couple of small jokes about the storm and the likelihood of them all being stuck there together, which got some warm chuckles from the audience. Aidan's voice in her ear was clear and quiet, and even he seemed to be having a good time, enjoying the novelty of the secret room. He had given Ashley her initial targets, and she breezed through the first two or three. Then, to break things up a little, Ashley opened the floor to questions. It was a mistake.

A woman in the front row was the first to have her hand up. She leaned forward eagerly, her eyes hungry. She looked to be a few years younger than Ashley, her blond hair hanging loose across her shoulders in soft waves, and she had a piercing in her eyebrow.

"I want to know if you've felt anything since you've been here. You know, in the house. About the fire."

Ashley swallowed. She heard Aidan swear softly.

"Just tell her you haven't sensed anything yet and move on," he said. "If you deal with it quickly, you—"

Her brother's voice was lost in a sudden roar of static that stopped as quickly as it started. Ashley did her best not to wince.

Fucking hell, Aidan, what was that?

Meanwhile, the girl was watching her closely. Everyone was, she realized.

"This is a place with a long history. The fire in 2004 was only a small fraction of it, as terrible as it was." Ashley glanced out the window. It was just possible to see, beyond the maelstrom of snow, the ragged peak of Red Rigg Fell. "I can sense a great many spirits here, but I haven't felt anything that suggests that the . . . that those who lost their lives in 2004 are specifically trying to make contact." She waited for Aidan to tell her off for giving too much detail, but there was silence from the earpiece.

"They would be here, though, wouldn't they, those dead kids?" There was a small murmur from the audience at that, but the woman plunged on regardless. "What do you think they would feel about the fact that you escaped the fire? Has being back here brought back any memories?"

Ashley nodded slowly, as though it were a good question, trying to give herself time.

"It was a long time ago," Ashley said eventually. "And there are big parts of the incident that I don't remember. Just blank spaces really." There was a strange noise in her ear, a kind of electronic cough. *Bloody things must be on the blink,* thought Ashley. "It's not something I really like to talk about."

She looked over the audience and saw that they were rapt, listening in a sharp attentive way that they hadn't while she had been reading other audience members. With a sinking sensation in the pit of her stomach, she realized that this was what they really wanted—the gory details of the Red Rigg tragedy. In the back row, Freddie was sitting up straight, as though he could sense her discomfort. There was another murmur from the earpiece, something almost like a voice.

"Tell us about the vision you had, where you saw the house burn down," the woman in the front row asked, undeterred. "What was that like?"

Ashley took a long, slow breath and looked at the ceiling. She should never have come back. There was never any escaping it.

"There was a darkness in the room," she said in a quiet, normal voice, not the one she used for the stage. She was vaguely aware of the audience leaning forward in their seats, eager not to miss a word. "A deep, terrible black like the bottom of the ocean, or a place deep, deep underground. I was afraid to get out of bed because I knew that if I touched that darkness, I would be lost. I . . ."

A voice spoke in her ear. It wasn't Aidan's. *The dark is waiting for you.*

Ashley froze. In the front row, people were glancing at each other, eyebrows raised.

And the dark is hungry, the voice continued. Ashley opened her mouth, about to break the cast-iron rule of the earpiece—never answer back—when the woman with the blond hair spoke again.

"Are you all right?"

Ashley smiled and nodded. Someone was playing silly buggers with their equipment, that was all. She tried not to think about the cold voice, so quiet and clear it was like the snow itself was speaking. She had to keep going.

"It was like a waking nightmare." Ashley deliberately made her voice stronger, louder, more confident. "That feeling when you're in a dream and something terrible is going to happen, but you can't wake up. I could smell smoke, and I could feel a terrible heat growing all around. The air itself felt hot."

We're waiting for you, Ashley. In the dark.

The voice again. Ashley ignored it. She wondered what Aidan was doing in the secret room and if he was trying to figure out who was disrupting them.

It's time for it to feed again.

"And then, I saw them, the other children. They were trying to get out. The door wouldn't open." She thought of the girl whose hair had caught on fire, the boys who had tried desperately to break the windows. Some things could not be spoken aloud. "The ceiling was on fire. It was around then that I came back to myself, and I was making quite a racket." She cleared her throat. "I was taken into a side office to calm down."

"You knew they were going to die," said the blond woman in the front row, her voice full of wonder.

"I had been given a vision," Ashley said softly. She hated this part, but it was this that her whole career had been based on, after all. "A glimpse of what was about to happen, in this very house."

"It's so hungry now, Ashley, down here in the dark."

The use of her name made her twitch, but she kept her eyes forward.

"What was the point of it?" A hard-faced woman in the middle of the audience was frowning as though she'd bitten into something sour. "What's the point of having a vision like that if you can't do anything about it? If I had been given a warning like that, I would have screamed the bloody house down . . ."

"I did," said Ashley sharply. "They practically had to sedate me."

". . . screamed the bloody house down until they evacuated everyone," the woman continued regardless. "You wouldn't have got me back in that dorm. Oh no, not until everyone was safe."

"I was a child." Ashley raised her voice a little; other audience members were chipping in with their own versions of what they would have done. "A *child*. They just took me to be a homesick kid, which is entirely fair. I can't be blamed for that night, and neither can the people who were looking after us. The only person to blame for that fire is Dean Underwood."

"But you weren't there when the fire happened in the end, were you?" This was from a man in an expensive-looking Superdry jumper, a plaid green shirt underneath it. He didn't look like a punter, and immediately Ashley was wary. He leaned forward, and she saw that he had a notebook open on his knee. "You left the dormitory before the fire happened and didn't return to Red Rigg House until three days later, when you'd been assumed dead. You didn't manage to save the rest of those children, but you saved yourself, didn't you?"

The voice in her ear had stopped. Instead, there was a rhythmic rushing sound, like the sea pounding the shore, or a heartbeat deep underground. She desperately wanted to rip out the earpiece, but she couldn't.

"I don't remember any of that," said Ashley tersely. Where was Malory? Why was no one supervising this audience? "This is what I mean when I say that large portions of that night are lost to me."

"Convenient," said the man with the notebook. To Ashley's shock, he stood and looked around at the audience with a smug expression on his face. "I think there's a lot you're not telling people about your so-called abilities, Ashley Whitelam."

"Who are you?"

"My name is Geoff Cousins, and I make it my job to expose people like you. I run a podcast called *Skepticpod* . . ."

"Are you fucking kidding me?" There was a ripple of nervous laughter from the audience. Ashley wished her dad was there—Logan Whitelam would already be dragging this toerag out the room by his hair. As it was, Malory was nowhere to be seen and Aidan was stuck in the hidden room behind her. Freddie in the back row had half-risen out of his seat, clearly uncertain what to do.

"I'm not the kidder here, Miss Whitelam," said Geoff Cousins.

"Get out," Ashley said. A suffocating heat was curling around her throat, making her voice tight, unpredictable. "These people have paid good money to be here today, and you're ruining it for them."

She knew from the way he smiled that this had been the wrong thing to say.

"Money is the key factor here, isn't it? Don't worry, I only have one real question for you. I wanted to ask if you knew what this is." He fished something out of his pocket and held it up in the air. It was too small to see clearly from the stage, but it didn't matter; Ashley knew what it was. She recognized the tiny flash of pale seafoam color. It was an earpiece, the same make as the one she had in her ear. When she didn't answer him, he turned to show the rest of the audience. Ashley saw their faces, the confusion and the suspicions.

"This is an earpiece," said Cousins, his voice oily with satisfaction. "Miss Whitelam wears one just like it in her ear—she has one in there now, in fact. And in a hidden room behind the stage, someone sits and feeds her information through it. That's how she knows all about you, all of your bereavements and your troubles, scalped off your Facebook page and other social media accounts so that you can come here and give her your hard-earned money. What do you think about that?"

"That's enough. You will get out now, or I'll have you taken out." Even as she said it, Ashley wasn't sure how she was supposed to achieve such a thing. There was no one here to help.

Geoff Cousins laughed. "Pull your hair back for me, love, and show us those ears. If you've got nothing in them, I'll leave right now. How about it?"

"I'm not doing anything for you." Ashley curled her hands into fists. "Get out."

"All right, how about this then." Geoff Cousins put the earpiece away and took out his phone. He turned and held its screen outward to the rest of the audience. "Apologies, you probably can't see this very well, but I happen to have images of Ashley Whitelam's secret journal. I bet you'd all be interested to read it."

Ashley froze.

"Here, let me read a bit of it out for you." Cousins narrowed his eyes at the screen. "This is from a month or so ago, by the looks of it." He cleared his throat. "'Plenty of sad stories tonight, but when aren't there? A woman who lost her child, a wife who lost her husband, and—a rancid cherry on top of the cake—David Wagner turned up to cause trouble again.'" Cousins paused to turn to the audience again. "David Wagner, for those of you who don't know, is the poor man whose son committed suicide after talking to the *spirit oracle*. It goes on: 'Dad likes to say that without sad stories, we wouldn't be able to make a living, and I suppose he's right. If they didn't come to me, they'd go to someone else—and as far as I can tell, we're all crooks.'"

"Where the fuck did you get that?" spat Ashley. She had walked to the very edge of the stage. "That's my personal . . . it's my personal property."

The audience's murmuring had died down to a stunned silence.

"Ah, but there's so much stuff in here your audience would love to hear, Miss Whitelam. How about this bit, which I think refers to various news outlets taking an interest in your recovery of Robert Metcalfe's remains: 'Bloody journalists causing havoc. Dad is over the moon about the "free publicity," but if we have this much scrutiny every time we put on a show, it'll go tits up sooner or later. No psychic needs someone looking too closely at their methods.'" He paused, looking enormously pleased with himself. "Would those methods include the earpiece currently in your ear, Miss Whitelam?"

Ashley stood where she was, unable to move. Her stomach felt as though it had melted, as though it had turned molten with shame, and she wondered if she might just be sick right there, in front of everyone.

"Leave me . . . Leave me alone . . ." Even to her own ears, her voice sounded weak and duplicitous. "I've got nothing . . . I can't . . ." Her journal was in her bedside table at home; it never left the room, let alone the house. How had he gotten access to it?

"Oh, this is my favorite bit." Cousins continued as if she hadn't spoken. "This is after David Wagner took his story to the papers and revealed some of Miss Whitelam's murkier history." He raised his voice. "'David Wagner needs to get over it, the miserable old bastard has done nothing but ruin my—'"

Freddie stood up. She remembered how he had saved her at the pub gig when the presence of the Heedful Ones had freaked her out, how he had put his arm round her and escorted her from the room. She felt a burst of warmth and pleasure behind her breastbone. *Freddie will get me out of this.*

And then Freddie turned to the back of the room and left, shutting the door firmly behind him.

54

MALORY SAVED THEM.

Or at least, Malory arrived and canceled the session, her cut-glass accent giving her words an unmistakable tone of command. The audience filed out, muttering and shooting glances at Ashley as she stayed on the stage. It looked as though Geoff Cousins intended to stay—his face was bright with triumph, and he clearly wanted to ask more of his pointed little questions—but Malory took him sharply by the elbow to the back of the room, then shut the door on him.

"Bloody hell, Ashie, what was that all about?"

Ashley stood where she was, shaking slightly. From behind her, the door to the secret room popped open and Aidan came out. His face was white.

"I . . ." She rubbed her hands over her face. "Fuck. He knew about the earpiece. I think he might even have arranged to jam it somehow. And the fucker had my journal!"

Her brother held out his hand, and she took it, leaning on him slightly as she came down the steps from the stage. She popped the earpiece out and looked at it.

"Aidan, what happened?"

"I don't know." He pushed his hair out of his eyes, not looking at her or Malory. "It all looked like it should have been working, and I could hear you, but you weren't hearing me. But, Ash, there's something else. That bloke, Cousins? I recognized his voice. He was in the bar at the pub in Ambleside, and I saw him here too, yesterday. Talking to . . ." He trailed off and shot a look at Malory, who frowned.

"What?" demanded Ashley. "Who was he talking to?"

Aidan sighed. "Your bloody American friend. It looked like they knew each other well too."

Ashley's stomach did a somersault.

"That can't be right." But she was thinking how Freddie had left the hall just when she needed him the most.

"I'm sure there's a reasonable explanation." Malory held up her hands. "I'm so sorry I missed it all, Ashie, I've just had an *utter* dog's dinner of a morning and lost track of time. For tomorrow's session, I will stand at the doors myself and keep an eye out for this Cousins bastard, I promise."

Ashley shook her head. Tomorrow's show was the least of her concerns.

"I'm sorry, sis, but how much do you actually know about him? I hope you didn't get too close."

"What?"

Ashley looked at her brother. He looked sad, he looked sympathetic, he looked every way a brother should look when his sister has been betrayed, yet behind it all she was sure there was something else. Triumph. She walked away from both of them and opened the door to the hall. In the hallway beyond, a number of the punters were still standing in groups; every single head turned to gawp at her as she came out. Ashley strode past them, feeling their eyes on her like hot coals, until she found herself back in the lobby. There, standing off to the side of the big doors were Freddie and Geoff Cousins, deep in conversation. Cousins was laughing, looking well pleased with himself, while Freddie was talking in a low, terse voice. His face was as serious as Ashley had ever seen it.

"You utter dickhead."

They both turned to look at her. Behind his wire-rimmed glasses, Freddie's eyes grew wide.

"Ash, listen—"

"So what is it? Like a crossover episode, where you get the dirt from me directly while this arsehole plans to show me up in public and record the meltdown?" She laughed, a bitter pain flooding her throat. "Christ, I'm an idiot. All that stuff about not wanting to use my trauma, what a load of bullshit."

"I know Geoff from the podcast community, Ash. We've been to a few of the same conferences together, and I didn't mean—"

"Oh bollocks to you." Ashley was aware that a fair crowd of people were watching. With difficulty, she lowered her voice and leaned in closer to Freddie. "I shared personal stuff with you, Freddie, because I thought you were my friend." She felt like she might cry, a final humiliation, so she pulled herself away from him and jabbed a finger at Cousins. "You'll be hearing from our solicitors, mate. And if I even get a sniff of you anywhere near me again, you'll get to meet my dad. And I promise you won't like it."

*　*　*

Ashley prowled the corridors, too angry and too hurt to stay in one place for long. She knew it was likely that Aidan and Malory were looking for her, probably Freddie too, but the idea of having to look at their faces—embarrassed for her, or sorrowful—made her feel even worse. She paused by a pair of tall windows in one of the corridors. Outside, the weather had, incredibly, gotten even worse. The snow was a whirling blizzard, the shape of Red Rigg Fell entirely lost. The bright, almost eerie light that had been in the hall earlier was gone, replaced with a stormy gloom that made it feel a lot later than it was. As if the sight of the weather had drained away her energy, Ashley felt exhausted and grimy. She wanted a shower, maybe even a nap.

When she opened the door to her own room, the first thing that hit her was the cold. The window sash was up, and a sizable amount of snow had gotten in, covering the narrow table under the window in a miniature drift. The curtains were stiff with ice. Swearing freely, Ashley stormed into the room and pulled the window shut with a bang. It was only then that she spotted the thing on the bed, lying in the middle of crisp white sheets. Her heart thudded against her chest in a sudden gallop.

"Jesus Christ!"

It was a shape made of branches and twigs, dark and somehow dirty against the clean bedspread. It was a changeling doll, and as far as she could tell, it was almost identical to the ones the parents of the missing children had received. Ashley went to touch it, then drew back. All at once, she felt utterly exposed—she looked at the dark space under the bed, the wardrobe, the ensuite bathroom. Had she closed that door before she left? She couldn't remember. Moving before she could think twice, she yanked the wardrobe door open— empty apart from her clothes and her small suitcase—then dipped onto her knees to glance under the bed. Nothing. Next, she went to the bathroom, but it was also empty.

I'm alone here, she told herself. *Whoever left it is gone.*

Hands shaking, she pulled out her phone and dialed 9-9-9, but the line was dead. Her phone had no bars at all, and even the internet was down.

"Fuck, fuck, fuck."

It couldn't be Dean Underwood; he was with the police. It had to be a prank of some sort. That was it. Freddie had had access to her room. Freddie knew what the changeling dolls looked like. He and Cousins had planted it there and probably bugged her room to record her ridiculous reaction to it. How fun that would be for them, to have a live reaction to one of these sinister dolls. She took a few deep breaths, calming her racing heart. She went over to the bed and looked at the shriveled form. The twigs and branches used were dark, some of them riddled with vicious-looking thorns. Hands made of splayed splinters of wood lay against the sheets, as though grasping them in a fit of rage. A strong woody scent rose up from it, like pine trees, like a walk in a winter wood. It had been tied together with white butcher's twine, bunched at the joints like ribbons of sinew—a cleverly made thing. If Geoff Cousins and Freddie had made this together, then they had put a great deal of effort into it.

Ashley frowned. The changeling made her think of bones. The blackened bones of a child, burned in some terrible heat.

When she looked up, a Heedful One was there, pressed to the other side of the bed. She watched its smudged nubbin of a face, its dusty, incomplete body. It did not move. It waited for her to know.

"It's not a prank," she said aloud, her voice a scratchy whisper. And then on the heels of that, she asked, "Where's Penny?"

55

Ashley found Malory back down in the main hall, where the guests were milling around the tables, perusing the selection of crystals, incense, wind chimes, and other esoteric bric-a-brac. All through her search, she had kept her eyes open for the young girl but had seen no sign of her. Ashley grabbed Malory's arm, and the older woman jumped.

"Ashie, you gave me a fright!" Malory had a box full of coupons in her arms. "How are you feeling now?"

"Where's Penny?"

A crease appeared between Malory's exquisitely plucked eyebrows. "She's around here somewhere, I expect. Listen, is this all right with you?" She took a coupon from the box and held it up. "I'm offering these to anyone who was in your, uh, curtailed session today. It gives them fifteen percent off at the bar and a free set of volcanic rock beads."

"Malory." Ashley shook her slightly. "The girl. When did you last see her?"

"Oh. Well." Malory blinked slowly. "Last night, I suppose. I was busy, so I told Richard to send her off to bed."

"Richard." Bile pressed at the back of Ashley's throat. A memory from years ago rose in her mind, clear as day: the teenage Richard, sneaking into the dormitory in the middle of the night, his shape bent over one of the beds. "He didn't take her to her room. I did. Where is he now?"

"Richard?"

"Yes, *Richard*, for fuck's sake, Malory!"

"I don't know. He hates these kinds of things, so he's probably sulking somewhere. Somewhere in the house at least—it's not like he can drive off at the moment, is it?"

"Can you put out an announcement or something about Penny?" Ashley waved a hand vaguely at the ceiling. "On the Tannoy, or something?"

Malory's eyebrows vanished under her fringe. "A Tannoy? This isn't a supermarket, Ashie."

"Malory, please." She squeezed her friend's arm hard. "I'm really worried something has happened to her. We have to find her, okay?"

Finally, a trickle of unease seemed to cross Malory's expression. She bit her lip.

"All right. I'll ask around. She must be somewhere. In fact, some of the kitchen staff will be free until dinner—I'll ask them to look around for her."

"Good. Thank you." Ashley took a breath. "Do you have phone signal?"

Malory smiled ruefully. "We rarely get it on a good day, let alone in the middle of all this. Honestly, I'm surprised the lights are still on. Listen"—Malory took Ashley's hand; her fingers were hot—"if I find her, I'll leave a message with Carol in reception."

"Okay. I'll go and have another look around."

"And try not to worry," said Malory. "She can't have gone far."

You were supposed to be looking after her, Ashley thought, but she forced herself to smile.

"I know."

* * *

Ashley tried to approach her search systematically. She started on the lower floors, where the sprawling kitchens were, as well as the old servant's quarters that were largely used for storage since Malory's parents had passed away. Ashley scooted around the main hall, deliberately avoiding eye contact with Cleo and Desmond as well as the punters. She could see that Cleo was bursting to talk to her, but she kept her head up, scanning the room.

Ashley moved to the smaller rooms, where the other psychics had been doing their own shows. No sign of Penny. From there, she went to the first floor of the west wing, which was where the guests were sleeping. Here, she stood for a moment, frustrated. Of course, if the rooms were locked, how could she check for Penny? She settled for knocking on each of the doors in turn. Unsurprisingly, she received no answer to most of them, and those that did blinked at her with confusion while she asked about Penny—no one had seen her.

The second floor was private, the part where Malory and Richard still lived. Ashley knew from chats with Malory over the years that they had converted it into a long, meandering apartment, with its own kitchen, bathrooms, living rooms and bedrooms, almost entirely separate from the rest of the house; she had always said that they were both tired of living with décor more suitable to their distant ancestors. Ashley hesitated at the bottom of the stairs. Penny would have no reason to be there that Ashley could think of, but it was also the place she was most likely to find Richard. She followed the stairs up, past the sign that politely advised that the second floor was off-limits, and let herself into Malory and Richard's apartment.

It was clean and fresh and normal. In comparison to the rest of the house, it was filled with light; the walls were painted soft, pale greens and blues; rather than fusty oil paintings, the walls were hung with blown-up photographs and the odd piece of modern art; the furniture was sleek and dripping with design, upholstered in white leather or neutral fabrics. She couldn't hear anyone moving or talking; there were no sounds at all, apart from some music playing very faintly somewhere down the corridor ahead of her.

"Penny? Are you up here, love?"

Nothing, and then the tiniest noise, a foot moving over a polished floorboard perhaps. Ashley headed toward the sound. She thought how wonderful it would be to find Penny now; how she would feel stupid for overreacting; and how she would be embarrassed and mortified, but how much better that would be than the alternative.

"Penny?"

She paused by one of the modern paintings, frowning. It showed a barren red landscape, a single blackened tree twisting its way out of the dry earth, and she had the sudden awful thought that this was where the Heedful Ones came from. No wonder they would rather be here, haunting the living. As if she'd summoned it, she caught a shadowy shape out of the corner of her eye. A Heedful One hung just outside a closed door, and then, a second later, she heard a dry scraping noise, as though something was being dragged along the floor. Ignoring the Heedful One, she yanked open the door and stopped.

The room was clearly Richard's. His collection of guitars were mounted on the wall, bookended by framed film posters: *Rosemary's Baby*, *Manhunter*, *Eyes Wide Shut*. But it wasn't these that drew her eye. On the floor were six changeling dolls lying in a neat row, as though waiting for someone to take them away. Ashley stumbled back into the corridor, her heart in her throat, only to back straight into Richard.

"Ashley."

"Get away from me!"

"Ashley, wait!" His arms closed around her, holding her firmly in place. "Don't go getting the wrong idea, all right?"

"Get off!" Ashley tried to pull away from him, but she had always been slight, and his arms only pinned her all the tighter. The hair of his beard scratched at the back of her neck. "Fucking let me go, Richard, or I will scream this whole bloody house down. Where's Penny?"

"Look, you have to understand," he spoke just behind her ear, his hot breath hideously intimate. "There's only so much I could do. I told you to go, didn't I? I told you both to *go*."

"Fuck you."

Ashley threw herself to the side, and in the second before he reacted, she struck behind her wildly, hitting him in the groin. He gasped with pain, and then she was free. Richard leaned forward, his hands on his thighs.

"You fucking *bitch*."

"Where's Penny?"

He straightened up slowly, shaking his head. To her surprise, he started laughing, and then, when he looked at her, she saw that his eyes were wet.

"It's time to learn to keep that mouth of yours shut, Ash. Or you'll never leave Red Rigg."

Ashley turned her back on him and ran back down the corridor. She didn't slow down when she came to the stairs, but flew down them two at a time, a high giddy feeling in her chest, as though her heart had come unmoored and was floating separately from her. When she made it to the ground floor, she skidded to a halt and checked her phone. Still no signal. She went to the big front doors and, with some effort, managed to open them.

Outside, the grounds staff had shoveled a path to the driveway, but it was already vanishing under a new flurry of fresh snow. Dressed in the thin white jumper she had worn for the afternoon show, she plowed out through the snow. Her jeans were instantly soaked to her knees, and fat, wet snowflakes stung her face and hands. Within a few feet, she lost sight of the house and every other landmark; there was just the snow, the wind, and a blank unknowable sky. Covering the screen with her shaking hand, she checked her phone again, but there was still nothing. Her eyes and nose were streaming with the cold, but she forced herself to move farther away from the house. *The closer I get to Green Beck,* she thought, *the better chance I have to call the police.*

It was hard going. In a very short time, even Ashley's tolerance for the cold was exhausted, and every part of her felt frozen to the core. Already uncertain if she was even heading in the right direction, she kept moving, stopping every ten steps or so to see if she had enough phone signal.

"Come *on.*"

She stopped again, her whole body shaking. For a brief second, she saw it; one tiny bar, a flicker of white against her phone wallpaper. Then it was gone, and the phone slipped through her numb fingers, dropping neatly into a bank of crisp white snow. Ashley fell to her knees, pawing through the snow to try and find it. The cold was a physical pain now, stinging and pinching at every part of her, and the dark was growing thicker and thicker.

Her fingers touched something slick, but they were so numb she couldn't get a purchase on it, or even tell whether it was her phone or just a rock. At that moment, part of the darkness came forward, and she almost dismissed it as a Heedful One until she saw that it was wearing bright green wellies. The figure stopped, standing over her, a furred hood pulled low over a shadowed face.

"Aye, Ashley lass, it's a bit nippy to be out for a walk." Melva took her arm and pulled her to her feet. "You'll catch your death."

56

"YOU'VE JUST HAD a fright, love. Here, have a biscuit."

Ashley looked at the plate of Jammie Dodgers Melva was offering and shook her head. Melva and Ashley were in a small office room off the main foyer, full of filing cabinets and partly taken up with a large cherrywood desk covered with paper. Ashley sat in the big leather swivel chair, and Malory stood close by, looking concerned. There were no windows in the small room, just the light from a desk lamp, and in it Malory looked too much like her mother Biddy. *I could almost be back there,* thought Ashley. *In a minute, Malory will give me a hot cup of tea with whiskey in it, and then they'll make me go back to the dorm, and the whole thing will start over again.*

"Have you found Penny yet?"

Malory looked away and pushed a strand of black hair behind her ear. "No."

"*Christ*, Malory, that child is in your care! How can you not know where she is? Have you checked her room?"

"I don't know if you've noticed, Ashie, but this"—Malory gestured sharply to the room, taking in Red Rigg House and the Moon Market as a whole—"this has all been a total shit show. Half the guests haven't arrived, half the talent want to leave, and my guest of honor had a meltdown in the middle of her big comeback."

"I beg your fucking pardon?"

"Ladies, please." Melva held up her hands. "Tearing each other to bits won't help."

"My point," Malory continued, losing some of her sarcasm, "is that I've been rushed off my feet, and Penny is practically an adult, not some snot-nosed toddler. She's probably hiding out somewhere with her phone, like all teenagers."

"You don't understand." Ashley shivered. All her life, she had sought out the cold, but the cold she had experienced outside Red Rigg House was something else. It was cruel, and it had teeth. It meant her harm. The bone-white shape of Red Rigg Fell rose for a moment in her mind's eye. "There was a doll on my bed, and I found more of them in Richard's room. Malory, I think your brother—"

"Dolls? What on earth are you talking about?" Malory turned to Melva. "Perhaps we should find her something stronger to drink."

"The dolls, the changeling dolls. Melva, remember I asked you about them? And I told you that whoever was killing those children was sending these twisted wooden replicas of babies to the parents?"

Melva sighed. "Aye, I remember that piece of nonsense, yes."

"Richard has several in his room! And now Penny has gone missing." Ashley lurched to her feet. "If you're not going to do anything, I will bloody find her myself."

She took a teetering step forward, her legs wobbling. Melva grabbed her arm with her big butcher's hands.

"Take it easy, Ashley. You're not quite up to scratch yet."

"Are you accusing my brother of something?"

Ashley turned to look at her friend, caught by the tone of her voice. She wasn't angry, nor surprised; instead there was a thick coating of dread there, as though she'd been waiting to say the words for a long time.

"Mal, Richard isn't a good guy. I think you know that."

Malory smiled lopsidedly. She looked pale, with an almost greenish cast to her skin.

"I know it better than anyone," she said. "But this? *Killing* children? That's something else. He wouldn't have the stomach for it."

The shadows next to Malory deepened, and a smeared dusty face appeared, like a smudge of white paint left by a thumb. The Heedful One came forward until it was almost resting its chin on Malory's shoulder. Ashley suppressed another shiver.

"Can you be sure of that?" she said instead. At that moment, there was a knock at the door, and without waiting to be asked, Aidan stepped inside.

"There you are!" He glared at Ashley. "I've been looking all over. You know you have more one-to-ones booked in before dinner?"

"Fuck the one-to-ones," said Ashley, with feeling.

"What?"

"Aidan, love, I think you'll have to tell them she'll do them tomorrow," said Melva. "Or I'll do them, if they'll take me. Your sister is in no fit state."

"Do they even still want to have their palms read?" Ashley wasn't quite able to keep the acid from her voice. "Now that they know what a fraud I am."

"What are you even doing here?" Aidan directed this at Melva, frowning slightly.

"I thought you might all be in a spot of trouble up here, what with the weather, so I came to lend a hand." Melva stepped past Ashley and scooted Aidan back toward the door. "Now. Malory and Ashley are going to go and look for Richard, or Penny, whoever turns up first, and you and I, Aidan, are going to see what we can do about these customers needing the veils pierced for them and so on."

"Hold on." Ashley grabbed her brother's sleeve. "Do you have a phone signal?"

"Nope. Nothing since the snow really started to kick off."

"Shit."

*   *   *

When they were gone, Ashley and Malory headed up to the first floor, a painful silence hovering between them. They reached Richard's room, and Malory threw open the door; inside, the floor was clear, with no sign of the changeling dolls. Ashley stared at the blank space, mortified.

"He must have moved them."

When Malory didn't reply, Ashley raised her voice. "I'm not making this up, Malory."

Her friend turned to her. "We always knew there was a chance that coming back here would bring things up for you, Ashie. You've been so brave, and so resilient, but I think maybe it's time you had a rest. Investigating those awful murders, hanging around with that *American*, coming back here, and then Dean bloody Underwood turning up in the middle of the night. It's all been too much."

The hallway lights flickered. Outside, the wind was barreling against the walls like it wanted to get in.

"Fine. If you won't believe me, come to my room then. The changeling doll should still be there. We *have* to call the police, Malory—if nothing else, they need to know that there are more of these things around. It's evidence."

"Certainly." Malory closed the door to Richard's room. "If the house is still standing by the time we get there."

* * *

Ashley half expected the doll to be gone—it would probably be easier if she were imagining everything after all. But when she flicked the light switch, it was still there, dark and obscene in the middle of her sheets. It occurred to her that she did not want to sleep there tonight.

"Oh my God," said Malory. Her hands flew up to her face, fluttering like wings. "What is that thing?"

"I told you." Ashley pushed her hair behind her ears. She realized that she hadn't told Freddie about the changeling doll left on her bed, and that was like an extra kick in the gut; they had been partners in crime detection, and now they were nothing. Worse than nothing. She was an idiot, and he was a jerk. "Listen, does Richard have any places around the house that he considers particularly his own? Apart from his room?"

"All right. Okay." Malory pushed her fingers through her hair, pulling it back from her face. Her eyes were glittering, filled with tears. "Oh God, okay. Look, this place has the most ridiculous cellar you've ever seen. Honestly, it's like another house down there, and he was always very partial to it. Part of it is used for storage now, but there's also a big section that I have barely looked at in years, not since Mummy passed away. It wouldn't be a bad idea to look there."

"Great, good." Ashley took a step forward and took her friend's hand. Despite the snowstorm, her hands were feverishly hot. "It could well be nothing, Mal, and honestly, I really hope it is. Your brother is a dickhead, but I really don't want to find out he's a murderer or anything. I just want to find Penny."

At that moment, the lights went out.

CHAPTER

57

THERE WAS A chorus of distant shouts from around the building, faint and mostly tinged with amusement. Ashley and Malory backed out into the corridor, clutching at each other.

"I knew this would happen eventually, as soon as it started to snow like that. Total white out," said Malory. "I always said to Richard that we needed to do something about the wiring in this place, but you know what he's like." There was a brittle edge to her voice, as though her casual words were costing her a great deal of effort. "Here, there will be some torches in this side cabinet."

The corridor was lined with windows that looked out across the gardens, and now that Ashley's eyes had adjusted to the lack of electric light, she realized that they were bathed in the eerie half-light of the snow. *Owl light*, she thought, although she couldn't have said why. While Malory was rummaging around in the low wooden cabinet, Ashley looked down the corridor to see Heedful Ones, so crowded they were standing shoulder to shoulder, and every one of them was looking at her and Malory, their snub faces somehow filled with something she hadn't seen before—anger. She took an involuntary step backward.

"Fucking hell."

Malory glanced up. "What?"

"I . . . nothing. It's just that this place is spooky enough already without all the lights going out."

"Ha."

Ashley hadn't seen this many Heedful Ones since they led her to Robbie Metcalfe's body or since the night the east wing burned down. She had the sudden awful idea that there were always this many. It was simply that in the dark, with only the uncanny glow of the frozen world outside, she could finally see all of them.

What do you want from me?

"Here you go." Malory stood and gave her a bulky plastic torch, the casing slightly cracked. Ashley switched it on, a beam of yellow light piercing the corridor. The Heedful Ones vanished. Malory turned her own torch on, and they made their way carefully back downstairs.

A number of people had gathered in the foyer, and a member of staff was handing out pen-sized torches from a big box.

"If you'd just bear with us," he was saying, "these blackouts don't usually last very long. We have a backup generator, which should get us back on track shortly."

"What about the heating?" someone asked. "When's that coming back on? This old house is bloody freezing."

Ashley looked around for Freddie or Aidan, but couldn't see either of them. Geoff Cousins wasn't in sight either, thankfully. Malory led her through the throng and downstairs, past the kitchens, and then down another corridor that looked very bare in comparison to the rest of the house—no paintings on the walls, cold gray flagstones underfoot. From there, they went down another set of stairs, and the dark and the cold seemed to become a solid thing. When they had brought her in from outside, Melva had given her an oversized jumper to wear, cornflower blue; Ashley pulled the sleeves over her hands. In the torchlight, she could see her own breath as a white vapor.

At the bottom of the stairs, they came to another door, and beyond that was a wide room with a low ceiling. It was filled with freestanding shelves, which contained a variety of cardboard boxes, some labeled *paperwork*, others sealed with thick brown parcel tape. There was an old bicycle down there, and some large Tupperware boxes that were labeled *M*, *R*, and *B*.

"Storage," said Malory, flicking her torchlight over them. "When Mummy died, I brought her clothes and paintings down here. I just wasn't sure what to do with them."

The far side of the room contained furniture covered with huge white sheets, almost silvery with dust. Malory led them right up to the wall.

"Well, I guess he's not down here," said Ashley, swinging her torchlight around. "And Penny isn't either."

"Wait."

Malory went to a portion of the wall, pressed her hand to it, and a door popped open, just like the one in the hall where Ashley had had her show.

"There are loads of the bloody things," said Malory. Ashley couldn't make out her face in the shadows, but she could sense the bitter smile she was wearing. "Whoever built the house had a thing for hidden rooms."

"Don't you know? Who built it?"

"Not the Lyndon-Smiths, at least," said Malory. "It's likely Mummy knew—one of those boxes is probably full of the history of the place."

"You never looked it up yourself?"

"I've had more than enough of the history of this place, believe me."

Beyond the door was a wide corridor with an even lower ceiling. As they walked down it, they came to more of the tall storage shelves, with more boxes of various sizes. Ashley paused by one of them and shone her torch over it. The boxes here were different, less uniform, more colorful.

"This is a box of drumstick lollies," said Ashley. "And here's a box of Snickers bars."

"Left over from last Halloween," said Malory. "We had a charity ball for underprivileged kids. You *were* invited but didn't attend, of course."

"Yes, what an idiot I was, as I'm having a lovely time now that I'm here."

Malory gave her a sharp look, and Ashley winced.

"Sorry, but, you know. Exposed as a fraud by my boyfriend, missing child, worst storm in decades, power out, nearly froze to death outside . . ."

"He's your boyfriend, is he? Were you two sleeping together?"

In the dark, Ashley felt her cheeks grow hot.

"'Boyfriend' is probably too strong a word." Saying it out loud, she realized how much she had been hoping for it though. Clever, funny, handsome, tall, from a world very far from the rainy Lakes and her clingy family—Freddie had been pretty much perfect. Until he had helped Cousins humiliate her. "We were having fun. I thought it meant something."

"Were you in love with him, Ashie?"

"Piss off."

Some of Malory's natural cheer had returned, and if they had been sitting in Green Beck's single pub drinking white wine, they would have had a rueful giggle over it all. As it was, standing in a cold, dark corridor, the whole thing felt wrong, like lines of cocaine at a children's birthday party.

The wide corridor ended in another row of freestanding storage shelves. These contained boxes of fruit: bananas, apples, oranges, peaches. Ashley put her hand in one wooden crate and pulled out a nectarine. She frowned.

"These are fresh," she said.

"We always need fruit."

"But why keep fruit all the way down here? Why wouldn't it be in the kitchens?"

Malory shrugged. "Like I said, this is where Richard creeps around. I've never understood half of what he does. Like when he dumped you."

Ashley snorted. "He didn't dump me, Malory. We had a blazing row because he's an insufferable prick. Besides, I was a teenager. He was a mistake from start to finish." She sighed. "Let's go back up. I want to check in with Melva and Aidan, see if they've seen Penny."

"No, wait. Look." Malory slid her boot across the floor, then pushed a box out of the way. Underneath it was a wooden portion of floor.

"Is that . . . is that a trapdoor, Malory?"

"Yep."

"This place is ridiculous."

"Yep."

There was a simple loop of rope on one side of the wooden square. Malory pulled it up, and it swung away to reveal a square of deeper darkness and a ladder leading away, out of sight.

"I don't like this," said Ashley. She wanted to be out of there; she wanted to be at home in her parent's garish cottage, being fed tea by her mother with all the lights on in the living room and the TV blaring away in the background. The hole in the ground was old, and there was nothing good beyond it. Ashley knew this. "We really need to call the police."

"We can't," Malory said simply. "We'll get the light and heat back way before we get the phones and internet, believe me. If Richard is down here, if Penny is down here . . . We need to find them, don't we?"

Malory's face was lit from beneath, her dark eyes very wide. *She knows that Richard is bad,* thought Ashley. *She's only just beginning to admit it to herself.*

"Fine. You go first, and I'll hold the torches."

Malory lowered the bottom half of her body into the hole, her heeled boots clicking against the metal ladder, and then she began to make her way down. Ashley had the uneasy impression that her friend was being eaten inch by inch by some stone monster. Eventually, she vanished inside, and Ashley kept the beam of the torch trained on the top of her glossy head.

"How deep is it?"

"About ten feet or so. Not so deep. I'm at the bottom now."

"I'll drop your torch down to you."

When that was done, Ashley put her own torch into one of the big sagging pockets on Melva's jumper and began to climb down herself. The bars of the ladder were cold but clean; someone clearly used this passage regularly. When she got to the bottom, she found herself in a tunnel with rough stone walls.

"Fucking hell. I had no idea this was all down here."

"It's like the mines of Moria, isn't it?" said Malory.

"The what?"

"You know. From *The Lord of the Rings*."

Despite herself, Ashley smiled.

"I forgot you love those old movies."

"Old?" Malory tutted. "If you're not careful, I'll leave you down here."

The tunnel led one way, so they followed it. Ashley cleared her throat and shouted for Penny, only to be rewarded with a warped, uncertain echo of her own voice. The farther they walked, the older the place felt. There was the sound of water trickling somewhere, and Ashley felt afraid; she felt closed in, trapped. The weight of all the stone and earth above them felt like an actively dangerous thing, as though it might decide to collapse on them at any moment. And over all of it, she kept thinking about Penny, about the vision of Penny she had seen through the Heedful One. Blood. Darkness. Terror.

"Shit. Look at that."

Malory had stopped. Ahead of them, the darkness of the tunnel had become diffused and full of movement. There was a tall white candle sitting in a sconce screwed into the wall, and it was alight. Wax dripped and ran down the sides, a spatter of drips on the uneven floor.

"Someone lit that recently," said Ashley. Her fingers tightened on the torch. "Fucking hell, Mal, they are down here. I know it. Penny! Penny, are you there?"

Malory grabbed her arm. "Ashie, we probably shouldn't let him know we're coming. What if we set him off or something?"

They continued along the corridor in silence. Every twenty feet or so, there was another candle, and after a while, they came across another tunnel intersecting their own, but this one appeared to be in total darkness.

"I think we should stay with the candles," said Ashley, and Malory nodded her agreement.

They walked for longer than Ashley thought possible, and after a while, it seemed difficult to gauge how long they had been gone, or how far they had traveled. The tunnel felt as though it existed outside of time, just beyond their normal reality.

"We can't be under the house anymore," she whispered. "We must be under the gardens."

"Farther than that," Malory said quietly.

Eventually, they came to a set of shallow steps, and beyond that, a round room with three tunnels leading off into the dark. None of them appeared to be lit.

"Now what? We could go on moving around these tunnels for weeks and not find them. We could get lost ourselves."

Ashley rubbed a hand over her forehead. Despite everything, she wished that Freddie was with them.

"I'm not going back," she said. "Not until I've found Penny."

There was the tiniest noise, the scrape of a shoe against stone. Ashley spun around to find Richard behind them. With a sinking feeling, Ashley thought of the corridors of stone that had led off the one they had followed; he had simply hidden down one of those and waited for them to pass. His hair had come loose from its top knot and fell in dark straggling tails to either side of his face, and there were deep red scratches on his cheek. At the sight of them, Ashley felt a great boiling anger flow into her chest.

"Richard, you fucker, where is she? Where's Penny?"

There was a shout from somewhere behind him, undoubtedly a teenage girl's voice. Ashley stepped forward, preparing to shove past Richard and go to her. That was when he brought his fist up and showed them the knife.

"I'm ending it." His voice was ragged and his eyes were red, as though he'd been drinking heavily, or crying. "God damn it, I'm ending it all, Malory. It can't go on. It can't!"

"It's all right, Richard." Malory sounded older than Ashley had ever heard her. She sounded tired. "You can let Penny go."

"All of it!" Richard brandished the knife, and Ashley watched the yellow candlelight move along it like heated butter. It looked very sharp. "All of it has to end, do you understand me, Mal? All these years, all this blood." He bit down on a sob, and Ashley saw that tears were streaming from his eyes. "I won't have it."

"Penny can go, Richard."

Ashley heard Malory take a step forward behind her, and she wondered if she was going to try and wrestle the knife from her brother. It seemed like a terrifyingly risky move, and she felt a great wave of love for her friend. Malory the saint, Malory the kind, Malory the brave.

"I had to get her away," Richard said. "I couldn't think what to do, but she wouldn't come with me." He reached up and touched the scratches on his face with his free hand.

"Let the girl go," Malory said again. "I finally have everything I need."

Ashley turned toward her friend, not understanding what she had said, and caught a glimpse of the heavy black torch just before it connected with her temple. There was a flash of brilliant pain, like a firework going off in her face, and the strength dropped out of her legs. She fell, the cold ground coming up to meet her.

58

FOR AN UNKNOWABLE time, Ashley moved around the edges of consciousness, the great throbbing pain in her head anchoring her to the dark. Gradually, she became aware of things again; she could feel the freezing-cold stone underneath her, its uneven surface digging into her back; there was an uneven guttering light that shifted and flickered; there was a child crying.

This last thing tugged at Ashley, pulling her away from the shadows where the pain in her head wanted her to stay, and when she eventually opened her eyes, she finally saw Penny, sitting some feet away, her knees drawn up to her chest and her back leaning against the wall. It was dark where they were, a single candle burning in a sconce above them. Ashley tried to sit up, but doing so made lights swell and pop behind her eyes.

"Don't," whispered Penny. "Don't move. It'll see us."

Ashley opened her mouth to ask her what she meant, but her tongue was stuck to the roof of her mouth. *How long have I been out?* They appeared to be in a round room, or at least, the wall behind them curved toward itself; the dimensions of the place were lost in the dark beyond the candlelight. Penny looked unharmed as far as Ashley could tell, although her hair was untidy and covered in dust, and her eyes and nose were a livid pink from crying. Queasily, Ashley reached up to touch her own head; there was a sizable lump, and her skin was sticky with blood, but it had at least stopped bleeding.

"Are you okay?" she asked eventually. "Penny, what happened?"

But at the sound of her voice, Penny put her head down and hugged herself all the tighter.

"No." Penny hissed. "No, no, no. You have to be *quiet*."

"We've got to get out of here. It'll be all right, Penny."

And yet, there was something wrong, Ashley realized, something wrong beyond the darkness and the cold and blood that had soaked into the collar of Melva's jumper. She and Penny were not alone in the room; she could feel it in the way she sometimes knew when she came home that her mother was in the house even if she couldn't hear her, or the way she knew when walking home from Green Beck at night that there was someone on the lightless road ahead of her. As her eyes adjusted to the gloom, she could see a shape, something slouched on the ground some feet beyond the uneven circle of candlelight. It was hard to make out where the dark ended and it began, but there was no doubt that the thing was watching them, listening to their whispered conversation. Goose flesh broke out across her arms. All her years of seeing the Heedful Ones when no one else could, and this thing, whatever it was, terrified her in a way they never had, not even when they'd shown her visions of the other children burning to death. *It wants to eat us*, she thought, although she couldn't have said why. *It's so hungry, down here in the dark. It's been here forever, and its appetite is eternity.*

There was a noise, and the shape moved slightly. Penny whimpered. As it stood up and came toward them, Ashley saw the curve of a familiar cheekbone, a lock of inky black hair. It was Malory. She was carrying, of all things, a wooden baseball bat in one hand. The end of it was smeared with blood and hair.

"What did you do, Malory?" Ashley sat up as straight as she could, her head pounding. "Where's Richard?"

Malory looked down at the bat in her hands as though she'd never seen it before.

"Oh, I hit him. I broke the torch on your head, sorry. This is his bat, actually. From when he was a kid. He won't be back. I told him Penny could go, but I guess that's not a good idea, not really. You've seen our real faces, haven't you, Penny dear?"

The girl shrank against the wall, her head still hidden against her knees.

"What the fuck are you talking about, Malory?" Ashley began to get to her feet, and Malory raised the bat, pointing it at her.

"Don't move, Ashie, or I'll have to bashie your brains in." She grinned, looking completely unhinged.

"Aye, what a mess you've made of all this, Malory Lyndon-Smith. What a bloody mess." Melva came out of the shadows. She was wearing thick rubber gloves, green like the ones Ashley's mother used in the garden, and they looked wet.

"Melva!" Ashley got fully to her feet, leaning against the wall to help keep her upright. "What is going on? You have to help me get Penny out of here. Malory isn't in her right mind."

Melva shot a sideways look at Malory. "Aye, you're likely right there—I just found her brother back aways up the tunnel, a big dent in his stupid head. But you'll want to sit down anyway, Ashley. None of us are going anywhere until we've got this whole sorry business out in the open. And I suppose I will tell it, since that has always been my place, God help me."

"What are you talking about? What do you know?" Standing up was making her head pound, so reluctantly she sat again.

"Just be quiet, Ashley. And listen.

"Red Rigg Fell is old. Unspeakably old, my granny used to say, and she would know, as it was her who passed the learning of it down to me. And there is a curse on it, something furious and hungry that has existed there since the time humans were just beginning to walk upright. It is the hungry kind of evil, and it has to be fed."

Melva had lit another candle on the far side of the room, and now Ashley could see that there were a few sticks of furniture there; a battered-looking table, mismatched chairs. There was a lozenge-shaped hole in the wall at about waist height and a dark stain that spread below it, as though something periodically leaked through it. Melva sat on one of the chairs. Malory still stood with the baseball bat, a dreamy look on her face that Ashley did not like at all.

"Do you hear yourself?" Ashley said from her place on the floor. "I'm not some sort of crystal-wearing, aura-chanting imbecile, Melva."

The old woman nodded, as though accepting that, and carried on. "Before Red Rigg Fell even had its name, a child was brought here by a group of frightened, easily led men, and they beat her to death. And as she was dying, she laid a curse on the mountain and everyone who lived below it. She made the mountain hungry. She made it *ravenous*. We've always known it, the people of Green Beck, and the people of whatever Green Beck was before it had that name. We made sure to know, passing down the knowledge through an unbroken line. I hope you can appreciate that, Ashley—the work that's gone into it, down the centuries. Rome rose and fell, and we kept right on whispering our secrets."

Ashley just shook her head.

"It has to be fed, the hill, because if it isn't, whatever there is inside will come out and start looking for ways to feed itself. And by then, its hunger will be huge, Ashley, and it'll be us that it feeds on first. Do you see? So, every few years, we feed it. I handled the feeding in my youth, and when I got too old, it was Malory who took it up. I told her how it had to be only a year or so before she first met you, Ashley."

"Are you . . ." Ashley glanced at Penny. It was impossible to know how much of this the girl was taking in. "Are you really saying what I think you're saying? The children who've gone missing around the Lakes . . . Robbie Metcalfe, Eva Nowak, Harry Cornell, Eleanor Sutton. All those kids."

"I wanted my first to be special, Ashie," Malory broke in. She sounded cheerful now, as though she were finally getting to tell a good friend a delicious secret. "I wanted it to be perfect. And *you were*. When you came to us in 2004, I knew it the second I saw you, with your handed-down jumper and your scuffed shoes. You were already so separate from the rest of the children that I knew it would be easy to isolate you and take you away from them. With your blond hair and your sad eyes, you were practically angelic."

Ashley swallowed.

"You can't be serious."

"Why do you think I singled you out? Gave you special treatment, gave you my old clothes and protected you from Richard?" Malory shook her head slightly. "It was all ready to go, so close, and then bloody Dean Underwood set his stupid fire, and I lost my chance."

"He set that fire because he thought someone at Red Rigg House had killed his brother." Ashley felt sick. "Was he right?"

"His brother was one of mine," said Melva. "The poor wee sod."

"I can't believe this. I can't. I've known you both nearly all my life." Ashley looked up at her old friends, willing them to take it all back. The urge to cry was sitting at the back of her throat like vomit. "Is this some sort of awful joke you're having with me? Is that it?"

Malory held up the end of her baseball bat and peered at it critically. "I don't think Richard found it very funny."

"You have to understand, Ashley—it's not because we want to do it. It's not even us that does it, not in the end." Melva glanced at the hole in the wall, with its dark and ancient-looking stains. "It's a tithe that has to be paid to avoid more suffering. We treat them well, while we can, and then we give them up to the dark."

"Every few years, you said." Ashley spoke quickly, aware that they were heading toward some awful conclusion that she desperately needed to avoid. "It's not been every few years lately, has it? How many this year already?"

At this, Melva glanced again at Malory, a sharp little sideways movement.

"Aye, well. Things have gotten out of hand."

"Because it's always hungry, Ashie," said Malory. "And I think that's because I didn't feed it right the first time. I promised, and I didn't deliver. And you see what happened. But I think we can fix all that today."

"You can let Penny go then." Ashley saw the girl flinch out of the corner of her eye. "Right? Leave her be."

"Aye. I think so," said Melva. But Ashley didn't like the way the older woman wouldn't meet her eyes.

"And I want something to eat," Ashley carried on. She wasn't sure how to get out of this, but she sensed that keeping them distracted was a good start. Perhaps Aidan would come looking for her, or even Freddie. "I know you feed all the kids before . . . I know that you give them food, right? Well, I'm starving. I've not had anything to eat in hours. Malory . . ." She forced herself to look at her old friend. There were tiny specks of blood on her white shirt. "You can do that for me, right? We've been friends forever. You're my . . ." A sob rose up in her chest, but she swallowed it down. "You're my best friend, Malory."

Something in the other woman's eyes softened. She smiled fondly. "I always kept you close, Ashie, because I knew you were special. And when you found Robbie, I knew it. You're linked to this place. You were always meant to come here." She laid the bat down on the floor. "I'll go and get you something. I'll bring you a little of all the best stuff."

"And could I have a drink too?" Ashley said quickly. "A glass of wine or something?" She wanted Malory out of the room for as long as possible.

"Why not? It's a special day."

When Malory had gone and the sound of her footsteps faded, Ashley struggled to her feet. The pain in her head was less sharp, and she felt full of a painful, furious energy. She reached down and put a hand on Penny's shoulder.

"Come on, love, we're getting out of here."

Behind her, she heard the scrape of wood against stone as Melva picked up the baseball bat. Ashley rounded on her old friend.

"I feel like I'm losing my mind, Melva. Are you really going to stand there and stop us from leaving?"

"It's all a big mess, you see," Melva said apologetically. "It's my fault. I saw something in Malory when she was a girl. She was so clever, so curious. Everything I told her about the fell—about the curse, and how we needed to feed it—seemed to fit with the way she saw the world. There were the people that lived, she said, who contributed to society, and there were the people who got used up; little people of no real worth. When I showed her the real face of the curse, she didn't even flinch. Malory understood the sacrifice in ways even I couldn't. I didn't spot how broken she was until it was far, far too late."

"All the more reason to get out of my way."

Melva shook her head. "You don't understand, lass. Malory has been fixated on how she lost her chance with you for years, and when you got involved with the police and actually found one of her bodies, that sealed it for her. She is convinced you must go to the fell. And I think if she could just move on from that, it might heal her."

"This is madness, Melva. You know that, right?"

"I tried to warn you off!" Melva's thick fingers tightened on the bat. "So did Richard. But you just kept on coming, didn't you? Poking your nose in, along with that Yank. And you've got to understand, Ashley, that I've known Malory all her life. I promised Biddy that I would look after her, before she passed on."

"Did she know? Did her mother know what she was?"

Melva smiled, and somehow it was the worst thing that Ashley had seen that day. "Oh, lass. They all know. We all serve the fell in our ways."

59

OR SOME MINUTES, there was silence. Ashley pictured Malory back down the tunnel, back in the cellar of Red Rigg House, picking out wine for the friend she intended to kill. The idea was fantastical, yet deep in her heart, Ashley found that she wasn't as surprised as she ought to be. There was perhaps some part of her that had always found Malory's interest in her unfathomable, even sinister; after all, what use did rich people have for poor people, except to consume them? Melva was looking away from them, a pained expression on her old, lined face. Ashley went back to Penny and crouched by the girl.

"Penny, love, can you look at me?"

The girl lifted her head. There was a defiance to her expression that hadn't been there before, and Ashley was glad to see it. Ashley leaned so that her head was next to Penny's.

"Listen," she murmured. "Keep your eyes on me, okay? At some point, I'm going to make a move—don't ask me what yet—and I'll need you to be ready. Can you do that for me?"

Penny nodded. "Who are these people? Why are they like this?"

"I wish I knew." Ashley put her hand on top of the girl's hand and gave it a quick squeeze. "Don't think about them. Be ready."

When Ashley stood up again, she saw that a Heedful One had joined them in the chamber. It drifted toward the candle on the far side of the room, and as it passed through the flame it guttered and flickered, making the shadows dance and jump wildly. Melva sniffed, taking a step away from it.

"Shouldn't be any drafts down here," she said gruffly. "But we're under the fell now. There are parts of this place even I don't know."

"Who built it?" asked Ashley. The Heedful One had left the candle and was skirting around the edge of the room toward the second sconce. "These aren't natural tunnels."

"More knowledge we've lost, that. For all that I know and have passed on to Malory, there is much more that never made it to me. But I believe the tunnels were built as extensions of older, natural forms in the fell. There were copper mines here once. It was always an unlucky place to dig, though, and they didn't last long."

The Heedful One had made it to the second candle, and this time, when it passed through it, the flame winked out, leaving a thin trail of black smoke behind. Melva swore under her breath. Without the second candle, the room was drowned in shadows.

"I'd best relight that," she said, eyeing Ashley warily. The sconce was a few feet away from where she stood. "You just stay where you are, lass."

Melva went to the candle, taking a lighter from her pocket, and at that moment, a figure appeared in the doorway. For a second, Ashley took it to be Malory, but then the newcomer staggered, and she saw the blood-streaked face; it was Richard, a portion of the left side of his head crumpled and bending inward—it hurt her to look at it. He rolled his eyes toward them. Blood poured steadily from his nose.

"Found you," he said, his voice slurred. "Followed shadows. They led me. To you."

Melva turned her attention fully on Richard, and Ashley leaped forward and grabbed the baseball bat, yanking it out of the older woman's hands. Melva yelped.

"Ashley, wait!"

Ashley did not wait. All too aware that she was slighter and shorter than Melva, she brought the bat down with all her strength, striking the older woman on the collarbone. There was a distinct and terrible snapping noise, and Melva staggered backward, colliding with the wall. She held herself up against it for a moment, then slid down partway, her big butcher's hands clutching at her chest and throat. Penny had sprung up from her place on the floor, her limbs stiff and her hair a mess, like a scalded cat.

"Ashley, don't." Melva was panting, her cheeks bright pink. "You can't judge us for this. If we don't feed it, it will come out!"

"Oh shut up, you old weirdo."

Ashley brought the bat down a second time. Melva had her hands up to shield her face. Ashley struck once, twice, three times, Melva's fingers breaking with small pops, like firecrackers. Eventually, Melva dropped her hands, and Ashley took one hard crack at her head. The old woman slumped, her eyelids flickering. A great wave of nausea rose up inside Ashley, and she began to shake. She dropped the bat, and it clattered on the floor.

"I think he's dying," Penny said, pointing at Richard, who had also fallen onto the floor. "Should we do something?"

"Shit."

Ashley approached Richard where he lay, and he rolled his eyes up to meet hers; they were full of blood.

"I should have . . . stopped them . . . years ago," he said. His voice was slurred. "But we . . . we kept each other's . . . secrets."

"Yeah, you should have." Ashley held out her hand for Penny. "There's nothing we can do for him except call an ambulance when we get out and hope they can make it through the snow. Come on. We have to go before Malory gets back."

CHAPTER

60

I T WASN'T LONG before they were lost.

Ashley couldn't understand it. The journey from the cellar had been relatively straightforward, but clearly Malory had dragged Ashley some distance while she was unconscious. When she asked Penny if she knew the way back, the girl shook her head.

"We came here in the dark," she said quietly. "He used the light on his phone. He said it was too dangerous to light the candles."

"Bloody hell."

What was worse was that it felt like they were already going the wrong way. The tunnels were less even, the walls formed of bare rock. In one or two places, water trickled in icy rivulets across the stone, and the ground was so uneven that every now and then they would have to stop and climb up a short drop. Ashley couldn't shake the feeling that they were heading deeper into Red Rigg Fell. Yet there was nothing they could do but keep heading forward.

"There will be a way out eventually," said Ashley, trying to sound like she believed it. "We just have to stick together."

After they'd been walking for some time, a terrible howl broke the silence. It started off low, a sound of misery and anguish, and then became a high-pitched screech, a banshee yell. The tunnels took the sound and rolled it around the jagged walls, but Ashley knew what it was without a doubt: Malory had realized they were gone. And she would be coming after them.

"Keep moving." Ashley put her arm around the girl's shoulders and steered her ahead. "Just keep in front of me, all right? Watch the floor."

They moved as quickly as they could, trotting over the treacherous ground, only lit now by the occasional candle rammed into a sconce, but Ashley knew—could feel, almost —that Malory was coming along behind them much faster. She knew these tunnels, these caves; she had walked in them since she was a child, apparently. Ashley pictured Melva leading Malory underground, whispering poisoned secrets into her ear. She shivered.

"Where are you?"

The voice echoed along the passage, eerie and almost inhuman.

"Where are you, Ashie? We're so hungry."

Ashley swallowed. Was she sure it was Malory? Did it really sound like her? Or was it something else entirely? She remembered coming to in the round chamber, how she'd known that something was watching them, and that it meant them harm.

"Don't listen to it," she said brusquely to Penny, who was looking extremely pale. "Just keep moving."

"So hungrrryyyyy."

Eventually, they came to a place where the candlelight ended, and all that was ahead of them was a deep and velvety darkness, so complete it almost felt like a solid thing. They both stopped. The voice behind them was getting closer, and Ashley thought she could hear footsteps now too, or something very like them. A thudding and a scraping, as though something large were dragging itself along. *It's just Malory. It's just Malory.*

"We have to keep going."

"But how?" Penny's voice wobbled dangerously. She sounded like a little girl of nine or ten, up far too late and terrified out of her wits. "We can't see."

"It's okay. Look, take hold of my hand. All right? Don't let go of me. We'll go slowly, and I'll go in the lead."

It took everything she had to sound calm, but in truth, Ashley's heart was trying to burst through her chest; her head throbbed relentlessly. What if there was a hole in the ground somewhere ahead, and they fell in it and broke their legs? What if the ceiling fell and suffocated them? Or what if, in the dark, they missed the turning they needed to get out? But there was nowhere else to go.

They stepped into the dark. Very quickly, the watery light of the last candle was lost to them, and they had to feel their way ahead, clinging to the left-hand wall. It was an agonizingly slow process, and all the while, the sounds of pursuit were growing closer.

"We're going to die down here," Penny whispered. "I want my mum."

"Shhh, sweetheart. Just hold on to me and keep moving. It'll soon be over."

"You won't let it take me, will you?" Now Penny sounded even younger, like a child of six, afraid of the monsters under her bed. "You won't let them eat me?"

"Absolutely not. They have to get through me first."

And then, a glimmer of something moved in the darkness ahead. At first, Ashley thought it could be daylight, but then it shifted and turned its snub face toward them. It was a Heedful One. It looked at them as though it wanted to be sure it had their attention, and then it headed forward. A moment later, another one appeared, and another, all moving in the same direction. There was a flurry of movement, and several passed them by, surging like salmon in a mountain stream. Following them, Ashley felt more confident.

They're showing us the way, she thought in wonder. *All we have to do is follow them.*

The noises behind them continued, but now that she had a clear path, Ashley moved much more quickly, and the more she walked with the Heedful Ones, the more clearly she saw them. They flowed together, a shoal of fish or a murmuration of birds at dusk, moving and turning and thinking as one. There was something glorious to it, or almost joyous. When they brushed against her, Ashley didn't feel disgust or terror, only a kind of fond familiarity. *They don't mean me harm*, she thought. *They never have. They've only ever tried to warn me, to show me the way.*

Ashley and Penny made their way through the secret interior of Red Rigg Fell in this fashion for an unknowable period of time. They came to rough-hewn steps, worn in the center as though they had been used for millennia, and they climbed them. In the dark, out of sight of sun and stars, with the damp cave air on their faces, it was as though they had fallen out of the natural world into some sort of in-between place, an underland. Time was broken. They had been there hours, minutes, years; all of them seemed possible to Ashley.

Finally, the steps ended, and ahead of them Ashley saw something that wasn't a Heedful One. A glimmer of bluish light, soft and uncertain.

"Do you see that?" Ashley croaked. They hadn't spoken aloud for some time. "I think it's snow."

"Snow?" asked Penny.

They hurried toward it. Down a slope of scree they came to a natural cave. Halfway up the other side, there was a chink in the stone; through it Ashley could see a band of shining white, and the air was fresher and cleaner.

Behind them, much closer than ever before, a voice called out. "Don't leave me, Ashie. You don't want me to starve, do you?"

"Quickly!" Ashley threw herself down the slope, Penny's hand still grasped in hers. The Heedful Ones scattered. When they got to the far side, Ashley felt her stomach turn over; the rent in the rock was very narrow indeed. She shoved Penny toward it. "Get through it, now. Go!"

When she turned back to look, she saw Malory. Her friend's hair was hanging in her face, and her usually immaculate clothes were wet and streaked with dirt. She had Richard's knife in one hand.

"The kid can go," Malory said, gesturing with the knife. "But you have to stay. It was always supposed to be you, Ashie. It's what you were meant for, don't you see?"

"Fuck off." Behind Ashley, Penny was squeezing herself through the hole, blocking out most of the light.

"Don't you want to do something good though, Ashie?" Malory continued. She began to pick her way down the slope, stones scattering before each step. "All your life conning people in the worst way, playing with their grief and their sorrow to line your own pockets. What if letting the fell have you meant that no more children had to die?"

"Except that's not what it would mean, because you're a fucking lunatic." Ashley raised her voice. She felt angrier than she'd ever felt in her life. "You're a parasite, feeding off people less fortunate than yourself and calling it charity! Richard thought you were a monster, and he was more than halfway there himself. Melva thinks you're cracked." She laughed, a sharp, bitter sound that echoed strangely in the cave. "Imagine being so worthless that a fellow child killer thinks you've gone too far."

The snow light grew stronger again. Penny was through the hole. Ashley backed up toward it, but Malory was running now, across the cave floor and up the slope. With a kind of hysterical desperation, Ashley turned sideways and began to squeeze herself through, but as she had suspected, even her slim frame was just slightly too big. She got her right-hand side through, her right arm and leg, and then the rock seemed to catch at her and squeeze her, pinning her by the chest.

"Fuck."

From outside, Penny took Ashley's hand and began to pull. Although she couldn't see the girl, Ashley could hear her grunting with the effort of it.

"Stop, stop it!" Malory reached the top of the slope. "You have to stay here. This is where you're meant to be!"

Malory grabbed her other arm, and with a surprising amount of strength, pulled it toward her. She took the knife and sunk the blade in sideways, digging deep into the fleshiest part of Ashley's forearm. Ashley screamed.

"If I have to feed you to it piece by piece, that's what I'll do!" Malory pulled the knife toward her, as though she were paring the flesh from a fishbone. Agony shot through Ashley's body. She saw her own arm turn crimson, and then the rock seemed to give slightly. She looked up, past Malory's contorted, blood-flecked face, and saw a great dark shape on the far side of the cave. She had a sense of bulk, of incredible age and unending patience, and it shifted, as though it, too, were about to creep down the slope toward them.

Penny gave another tremendous yank, and Ashley fell backward onto a bed of hardened snow.

61

Later, Ashley would think of her time on the side of Red Rigg Fell with Penny and remember only pieces, snapshots that almost seemed disconnected from each other. There was her arm, which had been bleeding merrily, a good chunk of flesh missing and steam rising up from it like something being cooked on the hob. The storm had lost its fury, and although the night sky was still black with clouds, only a light snow was falling. Below them was Red Rigg House, crouched at the edge of its own woods, lights burning in the windows.

They got the power back on, Ashley thought.

She and Penny began to make their way down, awkward and slow, picking carefully through snowdrifts, around boulders. Ashley left a trail of blood behind her, which turned into icy scarlet crystals almost instantly. Thankfully, they were not high up, but the going was hard nonetheless.

"We're going to make it," Ashley said, trying to make her voice firm, confident, believable. "Not much farther now."

Penny nodded. She did seem to believe it, and Ashley was glad.

* * *

Before they left the flanks of the fell, Ashley looked up and saw another figure half-shrouded in the thickening snow. She was small and frail, a child of ten or eleven perhaps, her shoulders covered in a thin, deerskin cloak. The Heedful Ones crowded around this figure as though they were hiding her, or protecting her. The girl watched them closely with mismatched eyes, and there was an expression on her face that Ashley couldn't read.

"It's you," Ashley whispered. "The one who placed the curse."

The girl's eyes widened, and despite the dark and the snow, Ashley saw that one was blue and one was brown. Just like her own.

"Who am I to you?" Ashley asked. She pointed at the Heedful Ones with her bleeding arm. "Who are they?"

The girl's lips moved, her voice carried away by the wind and a vast gulf of time.

You are my blood, the girl said. *And they are the shadows of everyone who came between—between me and you, a line of blood through time. A chain that connects us. They have been waiting for someone who could end the curse.*

"Is it over?" Ashley bit down on a sob. "Please, is it done?"

My family gave me to the men that would kill me. But you . . . You brought a child out of the mountain, unharmed, said the girl in the deerskin cloak. *She will live when I didn't. The hunger can end.*

The snow and wind picked up, and with that, the girl was gone.

"What did you say?" asked Penny. "Did you say something?"

"Nothing," said Ashley. "Just keep walking."

Not long after, Ashley and Penny made it past the tree line, where the trunks were lit with skittering beams of yellow torchlight. Aidan's voice came through the night, hoarse with worry.

"Ashley? Are you there? Ashley!"

CHAPTER

62

ASHLEY WAS IN hospital for a few days after that. She had a mild concussion, and the wound on her head needed stitches—she looked at herself in the mirror of the tiny hospital toilet and noted that the blood had stained her almost-white hair a cheery pink in some places. Her arm was a mess, and the surgeon had advised her that she would have quite an impressive scar, as well as the potential for some nerve damage. All in all, Ashley thought she had come out of Red Rigg Fell largely unscathed, all things considered. Penny was treated for shock and mild hyperthermia, and then quickly shipped back to her family in Manchester. Ashley's father came immediately, blustering his way around the hospital, bothering the nurses and being too loud, but he refused to answer her questions.

On the third day, Aidan came in to visit her.

He looked pale and gaunt, and he shifted in the chair constantly like he was waiting for a job interview.

"You know something," she said eventually. "So spill it."

He gave a bitter little bark of laughter. "Where to start?"

"What happened to Malory and Melva?"

"Melva. After that whack you gave her—"

"Several whacks."

"She went back to Red Rigg House and found a hunting gun in one of the old sheds. Unregistered firearm is how the police put it. She shot herself in the head, and she must have been bloody determined to do it too, with all those broken fingers. I'm sorry, Ash."

"Don't be." Ashley rested her head against the bed board and sighed. "It turns out I didn't know her at all. What about Malory?"

"They didn't find her."

"What?" Ashley sat up straight, wincing at the immediate throb of pain from her head and arm.

"They're still looking. That place, Ash, under the ground . . . it's like a warren. DI Platt said they could be trawling through it all for years. Piles and piles of evidence to gather and sort."

But Ashley had stopped listening. She was thinking about the word "warren" and how it sounded like a place where something lived, where something dug down into the earth and waited.

"Ash?"

"Okay. So Malory has vanished."

"Not completely. They found . . . well, they found a large amount of her blood but no body."

"She wasn't injured when I saw her last," said Ashley.

"The police are speculating that she could have fallen and hit her head, but it's a lot of blood for that, apparently." Aidan shrugged.

"What about Richard?"

Aidan grimaced and shook his head. For a few moments, they sat together in silence. Nurses were talking quietly just beyond the door. A beeping noise from down the hall started and then stopped.

"The weirdest thing about it all though, and Platt told me this in strictest confidence, was the remains they did find. There are heaps of them apparently, human bones dating back hundreds of years—never whole skeletons, just pieces. Arms, legs, ribs, the odd skull. It's going to take them forever just to date them all, let alone identify people. There's a special archaeological police unit coming up from York to look them all over."

"Christ, what a mess."

"Your rescue of Penny is all over the news, by the way." He looked at her slyly, from underneath his eyelashes. "Dad has arranged a number of interviews."

Ashley laughed, then winced at the sharp pain in her head. "He can get stuffed. I'm done with all that. Done with all of it. You can tell him if you like. Soon as I'm out of here, I'm moving away from Green Beck. It's poison."

"You'd really leave it all behind? What will Mum say?"

"I really don't care, Aidan." She looked down at the bandages on her arm. She was scarred and battered, but she was still here. That felt like a sign. "It's time I started living my own life."

Aidan nodded and looked down at his feet. Ashley assumed he was simply as exhausted as she was, but when she met his eyes, she saw something else there.

"What is it?"

He sighed and looked around the room, as though what he needed to say was written on the walls somewhere.

"Your American chap. Freddie Miller."

"He wasn't *my* chap."

"Look, Ash, I can't think of a good way of putting this, so I'm just going to say it. Miller wasn't the one who told Geoff Cousins about the earpiece, or how the show works. It was me."

He had the grace to look away from her.

"I beg your fucking pardon?"

"It was me, all right? It was me."

Ashley felt like her stomach had turned to ice. She was too surprised to be angry.

"*Why?*"

"I don't know! I guess I was just at the end of my tolerance for it all. Do you know what it's like to hide away in little rooms, to sneak around on people's Facebook profiles and delve into their innermost lives? And then it's you who gets all the glory, who gets Dad's attention. It's a grotty, filthy way to make a living, and it's not something I ever wanted. But what chance did I have? Any dreams I had fizzled away the night you went missing at Red Rigg House."

"Unbelievable." Ashley shook her head. "You decided you didn't like what we did anymore, so you had me publicly humiliated?" She shifted in the bed. She wanted to get up and throttle him. "Helping the police find Robbie Metcalfe was your idea in the first place!"

Aidan rubbed the back of his neck. There were hectic spots of red on the tops of his cheeks. "I lived under your shadow for so long. You can understand that, surely?"

"You gave them pictures of my journal." It wasn't a question.

"I knew you had one." He shrugged. "I snuck into your room at night, took a few pictures. I think I thought it could be leverage at some future point, I don't know. And then we had that argument . . ."

Ashley shook her head again, remembering the drugs that helped her sleep and made her too drowsy to react when it felt as though someone was moving around her bedroom.

"Yeah, well, now you know," Aidan continued. His mouth was turned down at the corners, as though he were trying not to be sick. "When you went missing from the house, I was frantic. I thought it had happened again—whatever it was that happened when you went missing from Red Rigg House when it burned down."

Ashley thought of the tiny slither of memory that surfaced when she thought of that night in the dormitory, after they had put her back to bed. A small hand in hers, so thin and so cold. She thought of the girl in the deerskin cloak.

Aidan was still speaking. "And when I found you, covered in blood . . . Look, I'm sorry, sis. It was a shit thing to do, and I'm sorry."

"I think you'd better leave me alone for a bit," Ashley said stiffly. "I don't even want to look at your face."

Aidan nodded and stood up to go. He paused by the door, looking back at her, but Ashley kept staring straight ahead. She knew that if she looked at her brother in that moment, she would have said something stupid, or even worse, forgiven him.

*   *   *

Despite what she had told her brother, when she was released from hospital, Ashley did return to Red Rigg. The house itself was closed up, the entire thing deemed a crime scene, but there was a small memorial service on the north side of the mountain, amongst the gorse and the grass. Magda Nowak was there, and Ben Cornell and Elspeth Sutton;

they had laid flowers on the ground. Mrs. Sutton had one of Eleanor's stuffed animals in her arms; she kissed it once and placed it with the flowers. A priest, brought by Mrs. Nowak, said some soothing words, most of which Ashley missed as the wind rose and fell. It was a bright, crisp day, the sky above them the blue of a robin's egg.

When the priest had finished his piece, Ashley walked away from the parents, moving carefully with her arm in a sling. There would be more memorials, she supposed, as the police gradually identified the remains found within the mountain, and perhaps that was the ultimate fate of Red Rigg: it would become a graveyard, a sacred place. As it always should have been.

As she made her way back down the path toward the road, Ashley realized she wasn't afraid of the mountain anymore.

63

Six months later

F REDDIE PULLED OVER by the side of the road, and they both got out of the car. It was a fine hot day, with a peerless blue sky hanging like painted paper over fields full of wild yellow sunflowers. Ashley leaned against the bonnet and took a sip from the huge cup of iced Coke she'd bought at the last gas station. She liked Kansas, she realized, because it was flat. The sky kissed the horizon wherever she looked, and there were no glowering fells to break it up. Freddie joined her, putting the bag of burgers between them.

"You're right," he said, "this is a great picnic spot. Lunch here, and then on to Wichita? I've got a promising lead, several interviews we could chase up."

"Sounds like a plan." Ashley took a bite of her burger, dripping a healthy blob of tomato ketchup down her shirt. The shirt itself was bright blue and printed with a big picture of Foghorn Leghorn, the slogan "Genuine American Crypid" in cheerful pink and green letters underneath. Before flying out to the States, she had merrily thrown all of her white and cream cardigans and shirts into a bin bag and dropped them off at a nearby Oxfam.

When they'd eaten their burgers and fries, they got back into the car. Ashley paused with the door open, reluctant, just for a moment, to put anything between her and that view. No hills, no thunderous English clouds, and no Heedful Ones—she hadn't seen a single one since she'd climbed down Red Rigg Fell, and she was surprised to realize she almost missed them. Not enough to go back to England, however.

Ashley grinned and slammed the door.

ACKNOWLEDGMENTS

LIKE UNSEEN GHOSTS crowding on a haunted hill, there are always more people behind the writing of a book than you might realize, and *The Hungry Dark* was no exception.

As ever, huge thanks to my brilliant agent and friend, Juliet Mushens, who has always gone above and beyond for me, and to the wider team at Mushens Entertainment—superstars, every one. Big thanks also to the editorial team on both sides of the Atlantic: Lizz Burrell, Natasha Bardon, Faith Black Ross, Thaisheemarie Fantauzzi Perez, and Yezanira E. Venecia.

A writer doesn't get very far without a group of friends to bounce ideas off of/wail about plots holes with/cling to in times of misery. Heartfelt thanks to Andrew Reid, Den Patrick, Adam Christopher, and Michaela Gray, as well as the Penge Thelemites (also known as the Onesies; also known as the brilliant people I play DnD with). Extra special thanks to Peter Newman for making the latter half of 2023 extremely interesting indeed.

At the risk of sounding like a pretentious arse, I'd also like to use this space to thank Dame Hilary Mantel, who very sadly passed away while I was writing *The Hungry Dark*. Her loss is devastating to anyone who loves literature, and I'm pretty sure that without her brilliant *Beyond Black*—a book that has haunted me for years—I never would have met Ashley and her own troubled ghosts. It's a small tribute to one of the greatest writers who ever lived, but it's all I have, and it is heartfelt.